several times a year for 'research purposes', an arduous task that involves sampling cream teas, swimming in wild Cornish coves and following actors around film shoots in a camper van. Her hobbies include watching *Poldark*, Earl Grey tea, Prosecco-tasting and falling off surf boards in front of RNLI lifeguards.

: @PhillipaAshley

Also by Phillipa Ashley

The Cornish Cafe Series
Summer at the Cornish Cafe
Christmas at the Cornish Cafe
Confetti at the Cornish Cafe

The Little Cornish Isles series
Christmas on the Little Cornish Isles: The Driftwood Inn
Spring on the Little Cornish Isles: The Flower Farm
Summer on the Little Cornish Isles: The Starfish Studio

Phillipa Ashley

A Perfect Cornish Summer

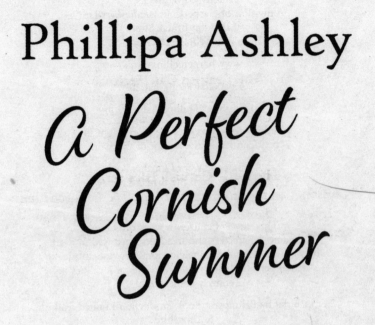

avon.

Published by AVON,
A division of HarperCollins*Publishers* Ltd
1 London Bridge Street
London SE1 9GF

www.harpercollins.co.uk

A paperback original 2019

A catalogue record for this book
is available from the British Library

ISBN: 978-0-00-831612-9

Set in Birka by Palimpsest Book Production Limited, Falkirk,
Stirlingshire

Printed and bound in Great Britain by
CPI Group (UK) Ltd, Croydon CR0 4YY

MIX
Paper from
responsible sources
FSC™ C007454

In memory of Mike Fosbrook,
my inspirational English teacher

Prologue

September 2008

Porthmellow.co.uk Town Blog Forum

MoaningOldMinnie: *Another shop closed? That's three in the past six months. This town's going to the dogs! Why doesn't somebody from the council or chamber of trade do something before we have tumbleweeds rolling round the harbour?*

'I swear someone's going to drown one of these days,' the old man said in his thick Cornish burr. 'And guess who'll be the one to have to fish the little buggers out.'

It was all Sam Lovell could do to hide a smile at her neighbour Troy Carman's expression as he watched the teenagers in wetsuits opposite the Smuggler's Tavern. They were laughing and jeering as they egged each other on to leap off

1

the harbour wall into the inky waters. Every Sunday evening in Porthmellow, from spring through to autumn, it was the same: the town band playing outside the pub and teenagers tombstoning into the harbour. A last hurrah of the weekend before everyone had to go back to work and school the next morning.

Sam rested her half of lager on the peeling table. Like a lot of things in Porthmellow, the tavern was in dire need of a spruce up. 'Didn't you do a bit of tombstoning when you were a lad?' she asked.

Troy shook his head at the kids shrieking as they climbed onto the top wall above the harbour. 'Back in the day I might have, and we didn't have these fancy wetsuits, then. I used to do it in my cotton underpants. Our mum went mad. I only had three pairs. One to wash, one to wear and one for Sunday best. Full of holes, they were too, by the time they'd been through her mangle a hundred times.'

'Troy. I love you to bits, but that is way too much information,' said Sam, trying to purge from her mind the image of her elderly neighbour leaping into the harbour in a pair of pants as murky as the water.

Although the sun was shining on the terrace of the Smuggler's Tavern this September evening, it was too little too late. The summer had been grey and gloomy far too often, keeping visitors away from their remote part of Cornwall. Times were hard and many families had had to miss out on a holiday altogether. It was exactly what the little harbour town didn't need – not to mention Sam herself, who had left her job to start her own catering business the previous year.

Who could have foreseen a global crash? Certainly not Sam, who'd been too busy keeping her family together after losing three of the people she loved most within the space of a couple of years.

But on evenings like this, Sam almost found herself able to put that to the back of her mind.

Troy finished his pint of Proper Job and wiped foam from his lips. At seventy, he was still working part-time as a deputy harbourmaster and no one knew the waters around Porthmellow better than he did. Although, Sam thought with a smile, the man approaching her table came pretty close. Drew Yelland was a few years older than her, tanned as tea, his fair hair burnished by the sun, a gold earring glinting in the evening light.

'Hello. Sorry I'm late.' Drew kissed her on the cheek and nodded cheerfully at Troy. 'We were late sailing back into the harbour. Bunch of bankers on the boat today. Didn't know their arses from their elbows. Didn't seem too bothered about the recession either. Don't think it's going to dent their consumption of Bolly. Talking of which . . . your glasses look empty. I'm dying for a pint. Can I get anyone a drink?'

Troy flashed a mouth full of teeth, which, oddly, made Sam think of tombstones. He rubbed his hands together.

'Don't mind if I do.'

'I'll help,' said Sam and gathered their empty glasses onto a tray. She always did this, wanting to help the landlady who'd had to let some staff go because trade had dropped off. She also wanted to talk to Drew.

'How's business on the *Marisco*?' she asked as they waited

for the landlady to pull their pints. Drew ran a small sailing charity that took groups out for trips on a vintage trawler.

'Could be better.' Drew handed over some cash for the beers. 'To be honest, bookings have fallen off a cliff since the crash and things aren't going to get better over the winter. We rely on the corporate and private money to subsidise the educational trips. The business customers are cutting back on teambuilding days and Joe Public can't afford luxuries like learning to sail. Which basically means we can't afford to take out the kids who really need a treat and a chance to build their skills and confidence.'

'I'm so sorry, Drew . . . I know where you're coming from. It's tough at Stargazey Pie too – people still need to eat, luckily, but it's still hard,' said Sam, grimacing. 'I'm not sure I'd have set up the business if I'd known what was coming. I had a good job already at the craft bakery and it felt mad to leave it last spring, let alone now.'

'Would any of us do anything if we could see into the future?' Drew picked up the tray of drinks from the bar.

Sam shook her head. 'I'm glad I couldn't see what was coming with Mum and Ryan.' And Gabe, of course, she almost added, but she didn't want to mention his name. The pain was still too raw. When the love of your life shopped your own brother to the police and then left town while your brother went to prison – well, it tended to leave its mark on you.

'You've had a rough few years, but keep the faith. Keep at it. Stargazey will be a success. We'll just have to ride out the storm somehow. We can't stop it from coming.' Drew grinned. 'And anyone who's Porthmellow born and bred will tell you that.'

4

Nodding, Sam held open the door for Drew. A burst of brass band music hit her ears and she blinked at the contrast of the gloomy interior with the bright sunlight glinting on the water. Sam zoned in on the 'To Let' sign on the fish and chip shop at the end of the harbour. Gabe and his family had worked there and lived in the flat above it until he and Sam had split up; his parents had retired a few months previously and no one had taken it over yet.

The ice-cream parlour next door was shuttered up and wouldn't re-open until spring. Bryony Cronk's new dog grooming business had set up in the old greengrocer's shop, but both units either side had blanked-out windows. Despite its shabbiness, Porthmellow was in Sam's blood, she loved its harbour and its quirky clock tower, every sunny day and each wild winter storm. Drew was right: no one could predict the climate, economic or otherwise. Just as there was nothing she could do about tourists choosing to go elsewhere.

While Sam and Drew had been inside, Troy's wife Evie had joined their table. Sam saw her wincing a little, knowing she'd started to suffer from arthritis in her knees. It was a steep hike down to the harbour from Stippy Stappy Lane where the Carmans' terrace stood a few doors down from Wavecrest Cottage, the home Sam shared with her sister, Zennor. Until a year ago, their brother, Ryan, had lived there too.

Drew fetched Evie a G&T and they returned to watching the kids jumping in the water.

'Is that your Zennor?' asked Evie, pointing to a tall, slender girl with long black hair, poised ten feet up on the wall above the harbour. 'Haven't got my driving glasses so I can't really tell.'

Sam shook her head. 'Yes. It is,' she said, wincing as Zennor threw herself off the wall and landed with a splash. She bobbed up immediately, squealing in triumph, and Sam heaved a sigh of relief.

Zennor was just one more kid who thought they were invincible . . . same as their brother, Ryan, had. Same as Sam's ex Gabe used to do when they were kids. She could picture Gabe now, in his board shorts, lean and slender, his smooth olive skin glistening with water as he climbed again to the top of the wall around the pub.

People would jeer or urge him on, but Gabe never cared what anyone else in Porthmellow thought – except perhaps for Sam.

She'd stand by, trying to act cool while all the time her heart would be in her mouth. What if he hit his head on the rocks or some piece of rubbish under the water? She remembered the time he'd vanished underneath and not come up as quickly as usual; he'd been under just long enough to make her squeal out in horror and cause everyone to stare at her. Then he'd popped up yards away by a boat. She'd been ready to jump in after him . . . ready to risk it all to save him.

Not anymore.

At twenty-one, her days of risking life and limb for a bit of a laugh were long gone, She had too many responsibilities these days.

A loud scream startled her out of her reverie, but it was followed by gales of laughter from the teenagers.

Troy clicked his tongue against his teeth. 'Bloody dangerous.

Harbourmaster would like to stop it but there's no point. Kids'll do it anyway.'

'Zennor's no kid,' Sam said, 'but I can't stop her. I thought she'd have grown out of it by now.'

'She's just having a bit of fun. I'd have a go myself if my knees would let me. How old is she? Fifteen?' said Evie.

'Just,' said Sam.

'She'll soon stop when boys get on the scene,' said Drew.

'They already are. Ben Blazey's up there too,' said Sam, spotting a skinny young lad in a shortie.

Evie laughed. 'Young Zennor will eat him for breakfast. He never says boo to a goose, that boy.'

'He creates enough racket on that scooter of his,' Troy grumbled. 'How he makes it over from Mousehole to here without killing himself I don't know.'

Drew smirked at Sam and she bit back a giggle.

Evie held up a finger. 'Ah, thanks for reminding me, Troy.' She delved in a large shopping bag. 'Have you seen this?'

'What's that?'

She spread a crumpled flyer on the table. 'Picked it up in town the other day when I went to my computer class. Thought you might fancy coming?'

Sam peered at the leaflet. 'Autumn Festival on Mousehole quayside. Folk Bands. Hog roast. Food fair. Cookery demos. Cider tent. Sounds good.'

'I saw that too. How do you fancy coming with me and Katya? Thought we'd take Connor along too,' Drew asked Sam. Katya was Drew's wife; they had a baby son together, Connor.

Sam wanted to go, but she was sure Drew was only being kind, inviting her along with his family. Drew had been one of the townspeople who'd looked out for the Lovell family after her mum had died. He was part friend, part surrogate older brother since Ryan had been sent away.

'I don't know. Saturday is it? I should be working . . .' Sam made her pies in a small unit tucked in a back alley and sold them direct from the kitchen or from a stall at events. She'd have loved a mobile unit herself but the business was still in its early days. She baked every morning for six days a week and did a few outdoor events as well as Friday nights on the Porthmellow harbourside. She'd managed to scrape up the cash for a second-hand stall and small oven to heat the pies. Her dream was to have a proper van like some of the bigger street food businesses but she couldn't afford that yet. For now, she had to take every opportunity to get some revenue in to pay the rent and loans on her catering kitchen. There wasn't much time or money for extras or treats.

'We can go along later in the day,' said Drew. 'Don't you shut at lunchtime on Saturdays?'

'You have to have some time off,' said Evie.

Before Sam could make an excuse, Zennor jogged up. She was barefoot, dripping, and pink in the cheeks from cold and excitement. 'Hello! Fancy coming in, anyone? Troy? I hear you were champion tombstoner back in the day.'

Troy slapped his palm over his glass. 'Eh. Don't drip in my pint, maid. Watered down enough as it is without you adding to it.'

'We were talking about going to the Mousehole Autumn

8

Festival,' said Sam, still unsure whether to accept Drew's offer. She was sure that Katya might not enjoy another woman taking up family time.

'I saw the flyer. The bands sound shit,' declared Zennor, shaking her head. Water corkscrewed off her locks and spattered the flyer, making the print run.

'Eh!' Troy groaned.

Sam shot her sister a glance. 'Zen. Do you mind?'

'About the water or saying sh—?'

'Both, as a matter of fact. Why don't you go and get changed? It's getting cold out here.'

Zennor shrugged. 'I'm fine.'

Sam bit back any further remark. She had to remind herself she was Zennor's sister, not her mum – even if she had had to take on that role at just twenty.

'So, does anyone fancy going?' said Drew. 'The invitation's there.'

Evie clapped her hands together. 'Why don't we make it a party? We could fork out for a taxi so we can all enjoy ourselves properly. It says the festival's sponsored by the Cyder Farm.'

Sam could have hugged Evie. She'd probably guessed that Sam would be happier in a gang, even if it did include two pensioners.

'That sounds like a much better idea,' said Zennor. 'I'm up for it if cider's involved.'

'You're not eighteen yet, maid,' said Troy.

'One small one won't hurt her,' said Evie. 'And we can all keep an eye on her.'

Zennor giggled. 'Can I ask Ben? He's having a shitty – sorry

9

crappy – time at home at the moment.' She shot a look at Sam.

'The more the merrier,' said Drew. 'Shall I go ahead and book a minibus?'

As her companions buzzed with excitement, Sam peeled the flyer from the table and held it up. The evening rays shone through the soggy paper and the words had merged: bands, festival, food . . .

Their mother had loved a sing and a dance. She always enjoyed hearing the fishermen's choir and the town band and liked nothing better than when everyone joined in at the end of the evening with a rousing chorus of 'Trelawney'. And she loved seeing the streets packed on a sizzling summer day or taking the girls and Ryan to the Flora Dance at Helston or the Obby Oss on May Day in Padstow. Their father walked out on the family when Sam was very young and her mum, Roz, had brought them up on her own. She pictured her mum dancing on the beach at Newquay as the sun set, a flower garland in her hair, holding hands with Sam and Zennor . . . At the memory of those carefree times, and the reminder of what she'd lost, her heart physically ached. Sam longed to experience that again, to see Porthmellow's streets alive with music and laughter, a buzz in the town . . . joy and fun . . .

'Sam?' Evie's hand was on her arm. 'Are you all right? Will you come?'

Sam forced a smile to her lips. 'Yes . . . yes. Why not? Let's go . . . but actually, I've got another idea.'

'What's that, my love?' said Evie softly.

All eyes turned to Sam and before she could chicken out, she spoke her thoughts as they tumbled through her brain.

'This might be mad but . . . why don't we kill two birds with one stone? Go to the event, but treat it as a research trip too? I mean, look around us. The town's going downhill fast right at a time when local people need help. We need to attract more visitors and really put this place on the map. Make it famous for something.'

'Yeah, but for *what*? We're just another Cornish harbour town with vicious seagulls, weird locals and crap weather,' said Zennor.

Sam had to smile. 'We're not just another town. We're unique. We have character – and *characters* – and dramatic weather that makes the headlines. We could be as famous as Padstow or Mousehole or St Ives. Why shouldn't we be?'

Drew put his pint down. 'I like your way of thinking, but famous for what?'

'For *our* festival. I think we should have our own.'

Eyes widened. Zennor snorted. Troy blew out a long breath. 'But who's going to organise it? Sounds like a lot of work and disruption to me, maid.'

Troy was right, of course, but it was too late. The idea had taken root in Sam's mind and was gathering energy and power like a great wave bearing down on the harbour. She couldn't shake off the thought that her mum would have been at the centre of a festival if she'd been here. As the town band reached a crescendo of 'Trelawney', Sam imagined her dancing on the quayside, smiling and laughing.

Evie was right too, and her mum would have agreed. Sam

11

was working *too* hard. She was only twenty-one and she had the weight of the world on her shoulders, a business, young sibling to support through college, another who'd come out of jail and she never saw. Organising a festival would be hard work but it would be fun too, and be a fitting way to honour her mum's memory and maybe bring a bit of sparkle back to the town and her life.

'We're going to organise it,' she declared, buoyed by bravado. 'Us lot. We're going to get it off the ground and we're going to make a big success of it.' She threw a glance at Drew. 'Because storms or not, we have to do something to help Porthmellow.'

Chapter One

Early May, Eleven Years Later

The 10th Porthmellow Food Festival

June 29-30 – Porthmellow Harbour
Don't miss our biggest and best ever festival!
Over 100 food, drink & craft stalls – live music all day
Chef's Theatre with cooking demonstrations including
Star Chef Kris Zachary of BBC *Weekend Kitchen Show*
'Cornwall's coolest food event' – *The Sunday Times*

Sam brushed rainwater from the laminated poster in her hand. *Ten* years. That was a third of her life. How could they have flown by so fast?

She still had to pinch herself at how the festival had grown since that first mad idea outside the Smuggler's Tavern.

Blinking raindrops from her eyes, she tried not to look down. She was only six feet up on the stepladder, but it was more than enough for someone who hated heights at the best of times. This was most definitely *not* the best of times. The rain and wind had been torrential since she'd set out from the cottage at six a.m., hoping to get the posters up before she had to get things going at Stargazey Pie. It was hard to believe it was the start of May.

Gritting her teeth, she tried to clip the cable tie around a council sign warning people not to drive off the quay. One false move and she could topple onto the cobbles or plunge through the deck of the *Marisco*. Now, that would go down really well with Drew: a great big Sam-shaped hole in his precious boat. Her fingers were slippery and numb with cold, but she wanted to have the posters up now spring was – allegedly – well underway. Hordes of people would start to flock to the town and hopefully flock back again at the end of June for the festival.

'*Woof!* Woof! Woooffffff!'

Sam gripped the ladder as deafening barks rang out across the harbour. Her foot slipped and she had to let go of the poster to hang on. It fell onto the wet cobbles and into a large oily puddle. Still holding on for dear life, Sam twisted round to see a Rottweiler jumping up and drooling as it tried to sniff – or possibly taste – her feet.

A woman in a long leather coat and a Megadeth T-shirt glared up at Sam as she struggled to hold the beast back. Sam steeled herself. 'Morning, Bryony. Mizzly out here today, isn't it?'

Bryony prodded the laminated poster with the toe of her

14

Doc Martens. 'I'd hoped you'd decided to give the festival a rest for a year.' The dog barked again so Bryony ramped up her own volume. 'My Sacha hates all the noise and smells.'

Bryony stroked Sacha's head while Sam tried to let the words wash over her. It didn't do to argue with Bryony, Cornwall's self-declared canine expert and the most unlikely metal fan on the planet. Woe betide anyone who dared question her views on dogs, music . . . or the festival, or tourists, or the weather, or anything else. Sam had often thought that if Professor Stephen Hawking had ever visited Porthmellow, Bryony would have been sure to take issue with his theories on black holes. She lived in a small house not far from Wavecrest Cottage. Sam often heard Sacha barking from fifty metres away.

Spotting a rare gap in Bryony's tirade, Sam dived in while she could. 'Well, the festival does bring lots of people into the town who might not otherwise come. Local people and tourists and it's put Porthmellow on the map as a foodie and arty haven.'

Bryony huffed. 'Arty? The crowds are horrible and the music is trash. Sometimes I think I should close up altogether and leave town for a week.'

'Is that a threat or a promise?' muttered Sam, then instantly regretted taking the bait. She couldn't afford to deliberately rile people in her position as festival chairman so she kept her tone firm but polite. 'You know that the people spend loads of money in the galleries and other businesses while they're at the festival,' she said. Including yours, Sam wanted to add, knowing full well that Bryony's Grooming Parlour did a roaring trade at festival time. Funnily enough, despite her objections to the festival, she hadn't yet made good on her yearly threat to clear out while it was on.

'Sacha almost choked on a wooden chip fork after the last one,' said Bryony. 'Probably left behind by some idiot watching that crappy folk band.'

'I'm sorry Sacha was ill but the chip fork might have been from anywhere and we do our best to clear everything up. You know we're all volunteers . . .' Bryony curled a lip, and Sam gave up. 'Would you mind passing me that poster?' she asked.

'I've got to open up. Some of us have proper jobs.' Bryony rubbed her dog's head. 'Come on, Sacha, sweetheart. We've got a standard poodle and two cocker spaniels to lick into shape this morning.'

Bryony marched off with Sacha, leaving Sam still two feet off the ground. She'd known Bryony since her schooldays and so she ought to be used to her grumpiness by now. While there were people who didn't like the festival, Bryony was probably one of the most vocal. By and large, the villagers had been very supportive, but as her mum used to say, 'you can't please all of the people all of the time'. Over the years, Sam had seen plenty of snide comments on the festival Facebook page, and more recently, Instagram and Twitter. When it had happened the first time, she'd been annoyed and upset but she'd toughened up since. Anyway, she didn't care. Getting the festival up and running had been a lifesaver at a time when she desperately needed something to throw herself into and, just as important, it really had helped to revive the town.

The rain crackled on her waterproof and ran down the

gutters, threatening to wash her poster down a drain. She scrambled off the ladder to retrieve it, but another figure, this time in a scarlet waterproof, white jeans and flowery wellies, darted forward and fished it from the gutter before Sam reached it. Sam smiled. A friendly face was just what she needed after her encounter with the prophet of doom.

'Here you go. I saw Bryony barking at you. Has she been a pain?' Sam's friend Chloe handed over the poster. Chloe was a newcomer to Porthmellow, having moved from Surrey the previous autumn after her divorce. Chloe had been an events organiser and still did some freelance work for her former company. Despite her tiny stature, she was a bundle of energy, endlessly brimming with ideas. Sam was convinced she was powered by some kind of nuclear reactor.

'She had another go at me about the festival and wouldn't even pass me a poster. She's obviously in the wrong job. She should be running Alcatraz.'

Chloe's dark brown eyes shone with amusement. Her black hair was caught in a chic updo that complemented her delicate features. Chloe's mother had been born in Hong Kong, while her father was Welsh, and her combination of Han Chinese and Celtic genes had literally given her the best of both worlds in terms of looks. Even early in the morning in a Cornish downpour, her make-up was subtle and she looked elegant and unruffled. Sam's own crinkly russet hair was plastered to her head. She'd dragged on the first thing she'd spotted; her jeans from the bedroom chair, a long-sleeved T-shirt straight from the tumble dryer and her ancient waterproof off the peg in the cottage porch.

17

In contrast, Chloe was a living, breathing advertisement for the designer boutiques that clustered around the trendier end of Porthmellow harbour. Three had moved in since the food festival had started, along with a prestigious gallery, a stylish homeware shop and a deli. There were only a few units to let now, and even the chip shop had gone more upmarket, offering salads and wraps alongside the cod and saveloys.

It *might* be a coincidence, but Sam was convinced that the new businesses had been encouraged by all the visitors who flocked to the festival and the town in the summer months. Stargazey Pie had done well too. A couple of years previously, she'd been able to move from her back-street kitchen to a smart catering unit on the edge of town and buy a mobile van that was now a popular fixture for events all over Cornwall with its artisan pies. It was hard work and she might never be rich from it, but she adored being her own boss and making a living from doing something she loved.

'I delivered most of my posters and leaflets to local businesses yesterday,' Chloe was saying. 'You got the short straw, I'm afraid, being out of doors. I was just about to pop back to HQ for another batch. I think I can get around the whole of Porthmellow by coffee time. Can I help you first? I feel so guilty being in and out of the shops while you're braving the full force of the Atlantic.'

'This isn't the full force. Not by a long way.' Sam smiled. 'It's when the waves crash over the top of the clock tower that you have to worry.'

'Ah yes. I've been on holiday here in some bad weather and seen the photos of the huge storm from a few years ago, but never experienced anything like it myself, fortunately.' Chloe paused. 'Dear God, we wouldn't get conditions like that during the festival, would we?'

Chloe peered at the white crests beyond the breakwater that protected the harbour from the sea. Sam had seen waves a hundred feet high crashing against it a few times, and yes, sending spray higher than the clock tower. During the worst storms, the village frequently featured on the TV news, but its occupants were well prepared. It was generally only fool-hardy emmets who fell foul of the rough weather, hence the sign at the end of the harbour warning visitors of 'danger of death' if they ventured out onto the quayside in a storm. Which they often did, despite the cautions.

'This is Porthmellow and you never know what the ocean might throw at us,' she said, amused at Chloe's horrified expression. 'But I doubt it in June, so don't worry about it. Even if it rains, people will still turn up. We're hardy types down here.'

Chloe let out a sigh of relief but before she could reply, her mobile buzzed. She fished it out and a smile spread across her face.

'It's a message from Kris Zachary's PA asking me to phone her asap. She said she'd call to finalise the arrangements. Probably wants to make sure the kitchen theatre is up to scratch. Booking Kris was *such* a coup though, even if he was pricey. He's already attracted a lot of press interest, especially with his um . . . private life being all over the telly lately. Those twinkly blue eyes . . . and the way he handles that dough. It'll be worth it.'

19

'Hmm. He's certainly high profile at the moment, even if it is for the wrong reasons,' said Sam, thinking of the headlines about the chef's break-ups with his wife, *and* his new girlfriend. Kris was an on-screen charmer with a reputation as a tough business character.

'Him accepting at all is a sign that Porthmellow's on the foodie map on a national scale. Though I know you want to keep it community focused, we have to make money and bring people and sponsors in,' said Chloe.

'I just hope Porthmellow will be good enough for him. If not, it's tough,' said Sam. A raindrop ran down her nose. Time was racing by and she had to finish the posters and get to work in Stargazey Pie. 'There's no rest for the wicked, eh?'

Chloe nodded. 'Then I must have been very wicked indeed.' She tugged her hood forward as the rain came down harder. 'I must admit the festival is a much greater demand than I expected. No one has any idea of how much work is involved. I've run events but none as big as this. Even though we're all volunteers, it's still serious stuff.'

'I don't think I've really thanked you for joining the committee, by the way,' Sam said. 'I don't know what we'd do without you and the other volunteers.'

'Oh, I wanted to get involved. I can't bear to sit around doing nothing and it's been a great way to meet new people.' Chloe's eyes lit up at the praise.

Sam agreed. The festival had helped Sam make new friends too and cement relationships with people of all ages and backgrounds. Chloe had said she'd chosen Porthmellow because of the happy holidays she, her daughter, Hannah, and her ex had spent in the area, and the fact that Porthmellow was still a real community where people lived and worked year-round, not simply full of holiday homes or deserted in the off-season. Even so, Sam thought it must have been hard for Chloe to move so far from home, especially as Hannah was in her first year at uni in Bristol. Chloe clearly adored her daughter, but Sam had yet to meet her. Sam thought, not for the first time, that Chloe must have been quite a young mother to have a daughter at uni. She didn't look a day over thirty-five.

'Thanks, Chloe. Will Hannah be coming to the festival?'

Chloe hesitated. 'I don't know. I doubt it. She'll have exams, I expect, and she said something about wanting to go travelling afterwards. I'd be way too busy to see much of her anyway.'

'I guess so,' said Sam, detecting an edge of disappointment in Chloe's voice. Perhaps she shouldn't have asked. Hannah had shown no signs of making an appearance in Porthmellow since Chloe had arrived eight months ago, so perhaps it was a source of family tension. Sam certainly knew all about that.

'I'd better call Kris's PA back then carry on with the posters,' said Chloe. 'See you on Wednesday at the committee meeting?'

After Chloe had left, Sam carried on fixing posters. As she worked, she couldn't help reflecting on the last ten years – and even further back. A decade on and the festival was growing year on year, with well over a hundred stalls, plus live cookery demos in the Chef's Theatre and music and fringe events in the festival marquee. Funding was as much of a headache as ever and sponsorship from the council, grants and business was vital. Even with that support, the committee still had to beg favours and borrow so many of the things they needed, not to mention giving masses of time for free.

Not everything had gone well. Sam's own love life had suffered while she'd been trying to make a living. At thirty-two, there was still no Mr Right on the horizon – not even so much as Mr Right Now. Sam had thrown almost all her energy into work, the festival and looking out for Zennor. She'd had plenty of interest and offers – a bit like one of Porthmellow's sought-after harbourside cottages – but once any guy had seen the work required to maintain the place, they'd given up.

And being honest with herself, Sam had never truly wanted to put in any work on a relationship herself. No matter how much she hated to admit it, she'd never really got over Gabe. She certainly still hadn't forgiven him for turning Ryan in to the police.

As Sam climbed the ladder to pin up her last poster, she found herself replaying what had happened eleven years before on the night Ryan had been arrested. She'd been alone in Wavecrest when Gabe had arrived. Zennor and Ryan were out and she'd been looking forward to them having some time together in the cottage. The moment she'd opened the door, a smile on her face, she'd leapt on him.

'You're late. I've been going mad with lust,' she'd whispered.

Before he could reply, she'd kissed him but he had pushed away gently – so gently – and said: 'Sam. Sam, I need to tell you something. It's not good news.'

And her heart had stopped, her chest had tightened. Was Gabe going to tell her it was over between them? That he'd met someone else?

Instead he'd sat her down and said, 'It's about Ryan.'

The fear had taken her breath away. 'Oh my God. What's happened to him?'

'He's OK. He's not hurt,' Gabe had said. 'Not yet.'

And so, it had started.

Although it had *really* started the year after their mum had died.

Ryan had been in trouble ever since he'd hit his twenties and quit working on Troy's mate's fishing boat, and gone to 'manage' the amusement arcade. Manage was a joke word as he'd spent as much on machines as the youngsters who came in. He'd run up debts and borrowed money. Sam was very worried about the people he hung around with, a bunch of wasters from Porthmellow and roundabout. She was convinced he was going to end up in trouble, but he seemed to get by; breezing along as usual, pretending everything was fine.

What Sam didn't know – until Gabe found out and told her – was that to pay off his debts, Ryan was planning to take part in a robbery of the arcade where he worked. Even worse, the same gang were also planning to rob various premises in Porthmellow. They were people who Ryan knew well, and drank with in the pub; friends of the Lovells who'd helped them after their mother had died. Sam's stomach clenched at the memory, even now.

Gabe had come to the cottage and told her that he'd discovered Ryan had been involved and that he was going to have to call the police. Sam loved Gabe, but Ryan was family. She'd known he was no saint but had no idea exactly how much trouble he was in.

She'd pleaded with Gabe not to shop Ryan, convinced that if he could only have another chance, he'd turn over a new leaf. But Gabe had gone ahead anyway.

Ryan and the gang were arrested while the robbery was in progress but that was only the start of even more turmoil. While he was awaiting trial, Ryan had refused to come home and stayed with some 'mate'. He said he felt guilty for letting down his sisters and was too ashamed of the village's reaction. He told Sam he never wanted to come back, even though he loved her and Zennor.

Even though Sam knew he deserved his punishment, he was her flesh and blood. She was shocked when he'd been given a custodial sentence of eighteen months, but thought that with her support he'd get through it. After the first time she'd visited him in prison, he'd refused to see her again, telling her he didn't want his sister in such a place. Even after he'd finished his sentence, he told Sam he was too ashamed to come back to Porthmellow and wanted a fresh start, away from his past.

Sam recalled his words: 'I'm toxic for this family. Don't forget me, but accept that I can't go back to the bad days and that means staying away.'

After that, Ryan vanished from her life for a few months without a trace. It was one of the most agonising times of Sam's life when she didn't even know if he was alive or not. She'd spent ages on the Internet looking for any trace of him. She'd called him every day until he'd changed his number. Once or twice she'd hear a rumour he'd moved to an area of Plymouth, then drive round the local pubs, looking for him.

It had been hopeless, of course, and only led to disappointment and heartbreak.

Throughout this time, her relationship with Gabe had also imploded. Before, during and after Ryan's trial, Gabe had tried to explain his reasons to her, insisting he had to go to the police for Ryan's sake as much as because it was the right thing to do. He said he wanted to prevent anyone else from getting hurt in the village and to save Ryan from himself.

Everything Gabe said made perfect sense to Sam. He was right, of course, but that didn't matter. She could never forgive him for turning in her own brother. Sam was forced to choose – and Ryan won. She'd brought him up, acted like a mother to him even though he was older, and Gabe had let her down so badly. She dumped him.

Gabe tried to make her change her mind but, in the end, he gave up. He found a job as a trainee chef in London, left Porthmellow and she'd never heard from him since. In the space of a few years, Sam had lost her mum, her brother and the love of her life.

After a few months, Ryan finally got in touch and Sam thought she might be able to persuade him to come home. But his call was only to say he was 'OK' but was never coming back to Porthmellow. Since then, she'd had very little contact with him.

All she heard of him these days was the odd card on her birthday and Christmas. In fact, she hadn't seen him face to face since that first jail visit, and didn't even know exactly where he was living or what he was doing for a job.

The scandal also took its toll on Zennor and Porthmellow

itself. Some people blamed Ryan while others saw Gabe as the villain of the piece for turning on one of their own. It had cast a long shadow over Sam's life too. Despite a few short-lived relationships and dates, there had been no one serious since Gabe. Sam's heart had never really been in it when it came to meeting someone new, even if she kidded herself that she'd tried. Over the past year or so her growing festival and work commitments had given her the perfect excuse to put her personal life on the back burner, but she couldn't help thinking her youth was slipping by. She wanted her own family and to find love again, but at the moment, she couldn't see how it was going to happen.

She couldn't blame Gabe for *that*. She had to change her own mindset and perhaps this tenth festival ought to be a turning point. She should get out there again, go on some dates, really try to make it work this time . . .

Sam shivered and realised that she was now soaked to the skin. Even her waterproof had started to leak and her jeans were literally dripping wet.

She slapped up her final leaflet and hurried off towards Stargazey's business unit. She'd almost reached it when Chloe thudded up behind her. She was breathing hard and waving her hands. It wasn't like Chloe to look so worried so Sam was instantly on the alert.

'Sam! So glad I've tracked you down.'

'Why? What's up?'

'That phone call earlier from Kris Zachary's PA. It wasn't great news. He's had to pull out of the festival.'

Chapter Two

Sam groaned. That was all she needed. 'What?'

Chloe scrunched up her face. 'Sorry to be the bearer of bad news, but he's been declared bankrupt and his whole organisation's gone into administration. He might even face tax evasion charges.'

'Wow. I had no idea.'

'No one did, but it's true. His PA said he's had to cancel all his future engagements for the next few months at least. It could be next year before his case comes up, if it gets that far.'

'Crap.' Sam pushed her hands through her damp hair in frustration. 'Where are we going to get a new star chef at short notice?'

'I'm sorry . . . it is a shock . . .' Chloe brightened. 'But the good news is that at least we've only paid part of his fee.'

Sam let out a groan. 'Part of it is still a couple of grand. That's money we can't afford to lose. Plus we need to find the money for a new chef.'

'Hmm . . .' Chloe considered. 'That's not so good.' She looked deflated, and if Chloe seemed beaten, they really were in trouble. The festival had grown from its early days and made a small profit but it was run on a very tight budget. There was no way they could afford to lose thousands of pounds.

'I suppose there's no chance of us recovering the money we've already paid him?' Sam asked, clutching at straws.

Chloe wrinkled her nose. 'Well, I did broach the subject with his PA and she said she'd try to see what she could do, but wasn't hopeful. From experience, I think we'll just join a long list of creditors and be right at the bottom of the pile. I doubt if there's any point trying to sue.'

'We can put it to the committee tomorrow evening,' said Sam, giving herself a mental shake. They couldn't let this setback, big though it was, ruin the festival, although she had no idea what she was going to do.

'In the meantime, I'll have a think about what we might be able to do. Perhaps we can get one of the local chefs to step in, although Kris was going to be a big draw and get lots of publicity. Thanks for trying, though . . .' She slapped her hand on her forehead. 'Arghh. We'll have to change all the posters we just hung. They have Kris's name splashed across them.'

'Yes, we will.' Chloe grimaced. 'Although I suppose that's the least of our worries now. I'll phone around some of my contacts in the events world and see if anyone has any bright ideas. Give me a couple of hours?'

'Anything you can suggest would be brilliant. Thanks,

28

Chloe. I don't know what the committee – or I – would do without you.'

Chloe beamed. 'Ditto. It's given me something to do since I moved to Porthmellow but you must let me know if you think I'm taking over?'

'Don't worry, I will but you're not,' said Sam, revising her opinion of Chloe being a little over-enthusiastic. She was very grateful for her help.

'I'll keep you posted.'

'I'll WhatsApp the rest of the committee and have a think while I get on with work. I'm late opening as it is and Stefan will be fuming.'

Sam and Chloe hurried off in opposite directions. In two minutes, Sam had reached the small unit on the mini trading estate on the outskirts of Porthmellow. The food festival was important, but she also had a business to run.

Stargazey was her bread and butter, or rather, her pie and mash. It had also helped to feed and clothe Zennor, until she'd finished studying and established her own successful graphics design company with Ben. The two of them had set up ZenBen Graphics in an old garage premises in the back streets behind the harbour and were doing well, in a modest way, designing websites, ads, publicity material and signs.

Sam pushed open the door of Stargazey, unhooked her apron from the staffroom door and started to wash her hands.

'What time of day do you call this?' Stefan stood in the doorway to the kitchen area, holding out blue latex-gloved hands dusted in flour. Stargazey made all its own crimped pie cases, using a traditional all-butter pastry that Sam had perfected over the years.

'I've had a few problems, sorry I'm running late.'

'You're drenched.' Stefan tutted and rolled his eyes. He was part right-hand man, part surrogate father to Sam and had been a friend of her mother's. He acted as if he were the boss, could be snarky and sarcastic but he had a heart of solid twenty-two-carat gold, and Sam would have hated to lose him from her business or her life.

'I know.'

'Were these festival problems, by any chance?'

'As a matter of fact, yes. I was putting up posters—'

'In this weather? Have I ever told you that you're mad as a box of frogs?'

'Many times.' She smiled, thinking of Bryony's barks almost toppling her off the ladder. 'Sadly, the rain's the least of my worries. Our headline chef's pulled out.' Sam tugged an attractive blue hair net over her mop of russet curls. She reached for a pristine white overall from the staff cupboard.

'Kris Zachary?' Stefan pulled a face. 'Can't say I'm devastated about that. He has far too high an opinion of himself, that man. Thinks he's God's gift to focaccia, though Kieran fancies him . . . says he has "twinkly eyes" and was hoping you'd introduce him. Personally, I'm always worried one of the hairs from his goatee will end up in one of his dishes.'

Sam burst out laughing, despite her worries about the festival. Kieran was Stefan's husband. They'd been together for the past eight years. Kieran did the accounts for Stargazey and audited the festival finances free of charge.

'I'm afraid Kieran isn't going to be able to get a selfie with Kris any time soon. He's facing a possible trial for fraud, apparently, and I guess that'll be all over the web soon, as if we didn't have enough to do.'

Stefan tutted. 'You know I think you're mad running the festival and this place at the same time. This town doesn't know how lucky they are to have you.'

Sam allowed herself a smile. There had been a time when she'd felt she was on the verge of being her community's worst enemy. Her brother had caused so much trouble and heartache in the village, and she'd always – and still did – felt partly responsible for that. She'd asked herself a few times if that was another reason why she'd started the festival.

'Better get back to work. We're behind.'

'And whose fault is that?' said Stefan, shaking his head.

'OK. I get the message.' Sam tied a plastic apron over her white overall, washed her hands again and pulled on a fresh pair of gloves. In the kitchen area, Stefan resumed preparation of the pie cases, while Sam focused on the fillings. She was serving the spring menu at the moment and offering a choice of four flavours including two vegetarian and two meat. They used nothing artificial and she insisted on high-quality ingredients such as locally milled flour, local meat and fish, and the fresh vegetables grown in abundance in the mild Cornish climate. Even the quality pie tins were an investment. Sam knew her pies might cost a bit more than a mass-produced chain version, but she was adamant they were worth it and so far, her customers had agreed.

Competition in the artisan and street food industry had

31

grown massively since Sam had started the business but she was proud of her product and loved coming up with new recipes to tempt hungry customers. So what if she had to work all the hours to survive? She was quietly proud of having grown the business.

She thought back on the weeks she'd spent helping to convert the horsebox into an eye-catching van that was a fixture on local market days, events and festivals throughout the year. She changed the menu to suit the seasons, and in summer, offered cold quiches, pies and savouries alongside pre-prepared salads. She even had some bookings for quirky weddings and evening parties and she loved devising a special pie to the couple or birthday person's own requirements.

There was no event that evening so Sam and Stefan spent the day filling, lidding and egg washing pies, all by hand ready for their next event the following day. The time flew by and while Stefan took a lunch break, Sam called Zennor to talk about the news and the removal and redesign of the posters. She wished they hadn't added Kris's name in the first place, but every cloud had a silver lining because the bad weather earlier in the day meant that the other committee members hadn't managed to post even half the leaflets. Ben and Zennor offered to remove as many as they could in their lunch break and after work, Drew had promised to join them.

Sam had tried her hardest to think of how they could get another headline name at short notice but was too busy with work to do anything more than mull it over in her head. By the end of the day, she'd resigned herself to running the festival without a big name and using local chefs – it would certainly

32

be a lot cheaper, but not the ten-year anniversary celebration they'd been hoping for. She was cleaning down the kitchen with Stefan when Chloe rapped on the back door. Through the glass, Sam could see her waving her hands in the air and grinning like the Cheshire cat. Sam threw a used piece of paper towel in the bin and opened the door.

Her friend burst into the lobby like an excited spaniel. 'You will not believe what I've come to tell you. It's amazing.'

'What's amazing?'

Chloe held up a finger. 'Now wait, you have to guess.'

Sam was weary after a day of climbing ladders, making pies and crushing disappointment but she couldn't help but be infected by Chloe's enthusiasm.

'The festival has been given a lottery grant to fund it for the next zillion years?'

'No . . . but it's almost as good.' Chloe smiled. 'Go on, guess.'

'Aidan Turner has agreed to open it by emerging from the harbour wearing only a mermaid's tail?'

'In your dreams. And he would have to be a mer*man*, but, sadly, no. Try again.'

'I can't. I'm too knackered so please, please put me out of my misery.'

'I've got another chef for the festival! And he's massive – and cheap!' Chloe did a jazz hands pose. 'Ta da!'

'Wow. That is amazing. It's a bloody miracle. It's fantastic! You're a star . . .' Sam rocketed from the depths of despair to sunny skies in the course of ten seconds. 'How did you manage that?'

33

'I thought you'd be pleased! I phoned a colleague in my events company for help and she'd worked with him at a big TV food show and said he might help. I couldn't believe he was available, but it turns out he has links to the local area that go way back—'

'Who is it?' Sam demanded and a micro second later, icy little fingers plucked at her skin. No. It couldn't be . . . it wasn't . . .

Chloe burst into a grin, and actually jigged around on the spot with delight.

'It's Gabe Mathias!' she trilled. 'Can you actually *believe* that? Much better than Kris Zachary. More famous, and he's Cornish!'

Sam's stomach turned over. Every hair on her stood on end. With a massive effort she forced a smile to her face. 'Gabe Mathias? Wow. Wow . . . wow . . .' she kept saying like a toy dog whose batteries were running down.

She was just so shocked . . . so horrified; the penny had started to drop the moment that Chloe had mentioned local connections. God, why hadn't Chloe found someone else? Sam would have welcomed anyone, *anyone* else with open arms. In fact, if they'd asked SpongeBob SquarePants to head-line the food festival, rather than Gabe, she'd have snapped him up in a trice.

Chapter Three

Chloe seethed with doubts as she trudged up the steep road that led to her apartment. Oh dear. Had she done the right thing in asking Gabe to take over from Kris?

She'd assumed Sam had enough on her plate, and had been thrilled when her contacts had led to the actual Gabriel Mathias stepping in as star chef at such short notice. In fact, she hadn't been able to believe her luck. He was well-known, well-respected – solvent – and let's face it, extremely easy on the eye. His Mediterranean recipes, Greek heritage and Cornish background seemed like a dream combination for the festival. In fact, hadn't he even been *born* in Porthmellow?

She couldn't understand why the festival had never booked him before. Perhaps he'd been too expensive – although his agent had said he was willing to do them a 'good deal' that wouldn't be as pricey as Kris Zachary. It had all sounded almost too good to be true – and judging by the look on Sam's face, perhaps it was. There was definitely an air of panic behind Sam's expression of surprise. Oh . . . bugger.

Too late now. Chloe dropped her keys in a ceramic jar on the kitchen counter top. It was pale blond wood, free of clutter, just like the rest of the apartment. Whitewashed walls with a few well-chosen pieces of art from local galleries. The Crow's Nest was perched high above Porthmellow at the top of a captain's house that had been converted into three smaller flats.

It was quite a climb up from the harbour, but it kept her in good shape and its nooks and crannies were the total opposite of the neo-Georgian pile she'd shared in a leafy Surrey suburb with Fraser, her ex-husband.

Chloe had bought the Crow's Nest after she and Fraser had split and had it completely renovated before she'd moved in. The plastic turf on the terrace had been ditched in favour of wooden decking, and the stone wall replaced by glass so she could see over the rooftops of Porthmellow towards the harbour and open sea. She did feel as if she was sitting on the bridge of a ship, gazing down on the comings and goings of the harbour and with a grandstand view of the waves.

She'd kept the cheesy Crow's Nest name: it was rather fun after all, and she definitely needed a bit of fun. Besides, she knew her Hannah would love the name . . . at least she *hoped* she would. Chloe wasn't sure about anything as far as her daughter was concerned and with the way things were between them, it was unlikely that Hannah would ever see the flat anyway.

Chloe liked her kitchen and her home to be immaculate, with nothing out of place. She hadn't always been like that. Before Hannah had gone to uni she'd been more than happy to live amidst the chaos of daily family life. Shoes discarded in the hall, school books and magazines littering the sitting room, a hamster's cage on the dining table, and Hannah's room resembling a junk shop.

Since she'd moved to the Crow's Nest, it made her anxious to have a thing out of place in the apartment, or a hair out of place on her head. She knew a shrink would say it was her way of bringing order to the chaos in her personal life and she didn't care. It was her way of coping with the loss. She missed her ex still, and even though he'd had an affair with the barista at the office coffee shop, she still harboured an idea that he might come crawling back to her, apologetic and reformed. She knew that was unlikely and she should forget about him but she was only *human*. She missed Fraser's company, before his affair, they'd been happy enough. For all his faults he was a good if over-protective father, funny and for most of their marriage, a loving husband.

Most of all, she missed Hannah like an organ that had been torn out of her body.

Chloe sank onto one of the kitchen stools as a fresh pang of guilt seized her.

Sam had asked her again about Hannah that morning and once again Chloe hadn't been quite honest in her reply. In fact, she hadn't been honest with any of her friends in

Porthmellow. She hadn't exactly *lied* to them, but she certainly hadn't told the truth either.

Because the truth was too painful to admit. Hannah wasn't a Fresher. She'd actually left university the previous year and was now living in Bristol with her boyfriend, Jordan, and their baby – Chloe's granddaughter – Ruby. Neither Sam, nor any of the committee members knew she was a granny. She couldn't face talking about the situation. It was too raw and bizarrely, Chloe also felt ashamed of it. Everyone around her seemed to have close bonds, especially Zennor and Sam. Even though she'd heard on the grapevine that they were estranged from their older brother and that Sam might empathise, she still couldn't bring herself to talk about her own family problems. She might break down or act unprofessionally. It felt like something she had to deal with herself so she buttoned it up and put on a front.

She poured a glass of iced water from the chiller and took it out onto the balcony. The drizzle hadn't quite stopped, though she didn't much care. On the horizon, a shaft of light had pierced the pewter clouds and lit up the angry waves.

Although it didn't make her feel any better to see the sun, she couldn't help thinking of how much Hannah would enjoy the view. Her daughter always loved Cornwall, and they'd spent many happy holidays in Porthmellow right up until Hannah had gone to university.

Ruby would love the beach, she was just getting to the age when the sand would be fascinating. Chloe allowed herself a moment to picture her granddaughter – just over ten months now – clutching her granny's hand while paddling in the sea.

She would sit on the beach rug she'd bought in the hope that Ruby would visit, Ruby letting sand trail through her chubby fingers . . . Ruby giggling and Hannah wiping ice cream from her daughter's mouth. Later, while Ruby slept in the cot that Chloe had bought for the spare bedroom, she and Hannah would make *jiaozi* dumplings together and share a glass of wine on the terrace while the sun set over the headland.

However, her fantasy seemed more ridiculous than ever. Hannah knew that Chloe had moved to Cornwall, but it had made no difference. Hannah had responded briefly that she didn't want to have any contact with either her mother or father and they were to leave her alone. Only that morning, Chloe's latest email had come back with a terse line saying; 'Don't try to contact me, Mum.'

So Chloe had thrown herself into organising the festival not only for the good of the town, or to make new friends, but to blot out the agony of being estranged from Hannah and Ruby, who she'd never met. People thought she was privileged and had a perfect life. If they knew the truth, they might say she hid her inner self and the pain behind her veneer of clothes and make-up and designer interiors.

That would have been far too simplistic. What had happened between Chloe, Fraser, and Hannah was more complicated. It was like a gold chain that had rusted and knotted and tangled until it was now impossible to undo.

However, helping with the festival was one aspect of her life she *could* control, and she was determined that the chaos of her own family life wouldn't ruin that.

Chapter Four

Gabe's PA strode into the office above his London restaurant, brandishing a tablet. 'Hey, Gabe. What's this in your online diary?'

Gabe braced himself. Suzy was on the warpath and Gabe couldn't blame her.

'Why have you blanked out a month in your diary with the words Porthmellow Festival?' she asked.

'I won't be away for the whole month, just the festival weekend. I just wanted to make sure you knew I might have to make a few re-adjustments to my schedule.'

'Gabe. I love you to bits but you might have run it by me first. You have a meeting with a publisher in Scotland the weekend of this festival.'

'I thought this was more important.'

'Really? A little Cornish knees-up?'

He smiled. 'A, it's not little. B, it's in my hometown. And C, they'd booked Kris Zachary as star chef.'

Suzy opened her mouth then shut it and opened it again. 'Ahhh. I see. So, you wanted to go riding to the rescue on your white charger?'

He grinned. 'Something like that. The call came from a friend of a friend too. I could hardly turn it down.'

'You find it easy to turn most things down. I thought you'd cut your ties with Porthmellow. I always had the impression you felt you owed the place nothing. You told me you never go to the place now, even when you visit your parents.'

Suzy was correct. Gabe hadn't set foot in Porthmellow since his parents had sold the chip shop. They lived in the countryside ten miles away now and on his regular visits to them he had no reason to go back to the town itself. No matter how much his heartstrings had tugged, or how strong his curiosity to see Sam Lovell again, any sentimental or romantic feelings had been blown apart after Sam had thrown him out of the house the night that Ryan had been arrested. In the months afterwards, he'd not exactly had a warm reception from some of the villagers. He'd been spat on and called a 'grass' and much worse. They had no idea of the impossible decision he'd had to make and he couldn't tell them.

After over eleven years, he'd thought he no longer cared . . . then the call had come from Sam's deputy, Chloe, via a mutual friend. While Chloe hadn't explicitly mentioned that Sam had asked him to step in, Gabe had wondered if she might – just might – have suggested his name. Perhaps Sam was holding out an olive branch.

'What's so special about this festival, then?' Suzy asked, cutting into his thoughts. 'It must mean a lot to you.'

'Like I said, I didn't want to let down a friend,' he said, being deliberately vague about who that friend was. 'Besides, anything I can do to get one over on Kris bloody Zachary is fine by me. Rumour has it that two of his suppliers will go bust because he's been cooking the books and I've already had calls from some of his staff who are out of a job. Most of us in the business knew he was on the fiddle so it was only a matter of time before he was caught. I don't want the people at this festival to suffer too, so this is my small way of helping out.'

Suzy raised a perfect eyebrow. 'So, you *do* have a heart. You're not the ruthless super chef that everyone thinks.'

'I'm just a regular Cornish bloke who loves his food. Haven't you read my PR, Suzy?'

Suzy laughed. 'I wrote some of it, Gabe.' She sighed. 'I'll get on the phone and grovel to the publisher and rearrange your stay in Edinburgh.'

Suzy left, leaving Gabe pacing his office. When the call had come from Chloe Farrow, via a hotelier friend, he'd been ready to refuse . . . Porthmellow Festival. He'd seen it grow year on year to become the well-regarded event it was now. He'd heard good reports of it, although he'd never been. Once or twice, he'd wondered why no one had ever asked him to take part. Then he'd answered his own question. He was hardly one of Porthmellow's favourite sons and most of all, there was no way he would ever be invited to any event run by Samphire Lovell.

This Chloe, who'd said she was deputy chairman of the committee, hadn't sounded local which meant she might not know the history between him and Sam. She'd been so charming and breezily unaware of what had gone on that Gabe had been swept along. He shook his head, recognising that Sam would never have asked him for anything ever again. It was wishful thinking on his part to think she was behind the invitation.

This realisation brought the powerful emotions of the past flooding back: anger, bitterness, determination to show that he'd moved on, was a new person now. This festival would be the perfect way of demonstrating that.

Gabe opened the browser on his computer. He clicked on a page he'd bookmarked after Chloe had called.

Gabe picked up his phone. 'Suzy?'

'Yes, Gabe.'

'Um . . . Can you do me another favour?'

'That's what you pay me for,' she said.

He smiled to himself. 'What's my schedule looking like over the next four or five weeks?'

'Four or five? Er . . . hang on.'

He waited while she hummed and ahhed then she said, 'There are a few meetings here in London. An after-dinner speech you agreed to do in Birmingham.'

'Besides that. Anything *really* vital?'

'Not really vital . . . apart from running the restaurants, of course. Can I ask where this is going?'

Gabe ignored her sarcasm. 'You know that new offshoot I was thinking of buying in the south west.'

'The one in Brixham or Salcombe? Actually, I've had the agents on asking for a decision on the Brixham restaurant. They have another offer on the table.'

'Tell them to accept the rival bid. I've got another idea.'

'Wow. That's two in one day.'

Gabe laughed. 'I'm on a roll. I'll send you the details of the restaurant later. After you've phoned the agents, would you mind finding me a place to stay in Porthmellow for a couple of months? Not a hotel. I need my own space. A short-term rental if there is one. Holiday cottage or something like that. Make sure it has a great kitchen.'

Suzy let out a squeak of horror. 'A couple of months! You want to disappear off to Cornwall for *months*.'

He smiled to himself. Suzy was a great PA, but one of those types who thought civilisation ended at the M25. 'I can do most of my work things online and drive or fly back here for anything else. Porthmellow's not the moon, you know.'

'I don't know. I've never been.' She sighed. 'I'll get onto it but it won't be easy. Finding a place for that long in prime holiday season . . . I'll do my best, but you might end up in a caravan.'

'I don't really mind what it is as long as it's close to the village. Pay what you have to.'

Gabe put down the phone. A mix of fear and exhilaration coursed through his veins, but he couldn't deny the truth. Despite all the ill feeling and bad memories, when it came to the crunch, he didn't have the heart to let down Porthmellow in its hour of need – and certainly not Sam.

Chapter Five

@**Pastyking:** This festivul is crap. More feckin' grockels. #summerfestival #wasstoftime

Sam rolled her eyes as she scrolled through her Twitter feed. There were always going to be some folk who weren't into the festival spirit. It did take over the town for days, after all. Parking could be a nightmare and the streets were packed with visitors from all over the country. However, if people were going to troll the festival, she thought, she at least wished they could spell.

She shoved her phone in her bag, determined not to read any more social media posts for the rest of the day and closed the cottage door behind her with a sigh of relief. It had been a long day, starting at dawn in the rain, working hard at Stargazey topped off with Chloe's bombshell about Gabe headlining the festival.

She walked into the sitting room where Zennor was cleaning out the guinea pig palace. The pigs themselves were snuffling around the floor, wheeking in delight while Zennor scraped their dirty hay into a bag. Sam had to smile at the contrast of the yellow Marigolds with her sister's outfit: DMs, leather leggings, a tutu and their mum's floppy felt hat.

Colt-like and slender, Zennor affected an eclectic, 'trolley dash round the charity shop' look. She could throw on a bin bag and still look cool, thought Sam.

Sam tossed her bag on the floor and collapsed onto the sofa with a huge sigh.

'How are Harry and Gareth this evening?' she said as she placed a cushion on her lap and scooped Gareth onto it, feeling his soft black and white fur under her fingers. He was a shy and delicate soul, but he let her stroke him and uttered little yips of pleasure

Zennor smiled. 'OK. Harry's lively enough, but Gareth seems down in the dumps.'

Sam stroked his head with her fingertip. 'Aww, Gareth. What's up?'

'Harry suddenly decided he didn't hate cauliflower leaves anymore and that he *had* to have Gareth's leaf so he nicked it from right under his nose. Gareth just stared at Harry as if he'd been mugged. Which he had. Harry didn't even eat the leaf. Naughty Harry,' Zennor raised her voice. 'That was *so* rude. I don't know if Gareth will ever get over it.'

'Poor Gareth. He's too nice to mug Harry back, aren't you, sweetheart?' Sam lifted Gareth up and blew him a kiss and caught Zennor smiling smugly at her. Sam sometimes joked about the pigs being a nuisance and smelly, but Zennor knew she adored them. It was strange how soothing it could be to watch them zooming round the living room or chewing a carrot at the end of a tough day. If only her own life was that simple . . . she was still reeling from the news that Gabe was to star in her festival and wondering how to tell Zennor.

'Anyway, let me chuck out their crap and wash my hands and I'll fix the mojitos. I bloody need one after the day I've had,' said Zennor.

Not as much as me, thought Sam, while Gareth squeaked contentedly in her lap and his brother, Harry, a peach-blond stunner of a pig, whizzed through his play tube on the carpet. The two pigs lived in harmony most of the time and no wonder as their home and toys were palatial compared to the rest of the cottage. They were actually the fifth and sixth pigs since Zennor and Sam's mum had passed away.

Sam remembered Brad and Angelina – two gorgeous long-haired creatures who'd had to be kept separate in the end because they were always either trying it on with each other or fighting. They were followed by Dr Jekyll and Mr Hyde who'd got on surprisingly well. Sadly, for the Lovell sisters – but probably happily for the pigs – they'd expired within two days of each other.

Zennor had wept for ages after every demise while Sam fetched the trowel and prepared another plot in the guinea garden of remembrance at the rear of the cottage. Each little grave was marked with a different shell arrangement, designed by Zennor, to suit the departed pig's personality. Zennor had threatened to dig up the skeletons if they had to move, not that Sam could ever see a day when they'd leave Wavecrest Cottage. Too many memories, happy and heart-breaking, were woven into the fabric of that house. Wavecrest was as much a part of them as a bone or vital organ.

Zennor's re-entry into the room was marked by Mexican-style whoops from Sam as she weaved her way between Harry and the guinea pig toys with a glass in each hand.

'Right. Mojito time! With actual mint from Mum's herb patch. I thought we'd have fajitas for dinner. I've prepared the veg and salad. I thought you wouldn't want to cook after a day at Stargazey.' She glanced at Sam. 'Everything OK?'

Sam prevented Gareth from escaping down her legs and under Zennor's feet. 'Yeah. How about you?'

Zennor put the glasses on the coffee table. She flopped down onto the sofa beside Sam, sipped her mojito and let out a deep sigh.

'*What* a day I've had. Our biggest client keeps changing their mind over their new corporate logo. Fifteen times we've reworked the bloody thing and the MD has finally deigned to look at the designs and wants us to revisit the original one.' She sipped again as Sam listened, trying to focus on Zennor's brain dump. 'Then the wifi packed up for three hours – three whole sodding hours – just when we needed to test out the garden centre website we've been working on like for *evah*. And when I called the bank to sort out the charges on our account, the fuckwit at the call centre asked me to spell my name four times and asked me if I was named after a laxative? I have *no* idea what he meant but personally, I thought it was as funny as stepping in dog poo.'

'*So* rude,' said Sam, echoing one of Zennor's favourite phrases while putting off the news about Gabe's return as festival headliner. Gareth was squirming on the pillow, clearly ready to join Harry for a bit of a kickabout on the carpet, so she gently returned him to the field of play where the pigs started nudging a ball around.

Zennor sipped her drink again and leaned back against the couch. '*Why* can't I be called something simple and normal like Emma or Kelly? It would be so much easier.'

'At least you were named after a beautiful mermaid,' said Sam. 'Mum called me after a plant. I mean – have you ever met another Samphire?'

'No, but you do go so beautifully with a nice piece of fish.'

Sam laughed. 'I suppose we should be grateful that Mum had a good imagination. She was never conventional. She said Dad wasn't either, which might be why he ran off with that exotic dancer.' Sam couldn't remember much about her father although looking back on her mum's old photos of him, she supposed he was handsome in a nineteen-eighties big hair and moustache kind of way. None of the Lovells had any contact with him whatsoever and Sam was content to leave things that way.

In contrast, she saw her mum as clear as day, as if she were standing in front of the girls now. Roz Lovell had been slim and pretty even in her late forties, always stylishly if Bohemianly dressed in clothes she'd 're-purposed' from charity shops and festivals. With only one parent working as an art lecturer at the local college, there had never been a lot of money around at Wavecrest, but there had been plenty of creativity and laughter.

Zennor looked a lot like her mother, apart from the green hair. Sam's own light brown curls were her mum's too, but her mother, always honest, had said her oldest daughter had her father's features. Barry Lovell had left them when she was only eight. From the few photos of him, Sam found it hard to judge. Ryan had looked like their mum, in Sam's opinion, but maybe that was because she didn't want to think her brother took after their father in any way.

'I'm not even sure we all have the same dad. How do we know?' Zennor had once said.

'Because Mum said so. Her word was good enough for me,' Sam had replied with a fierceness that surprised even herself.

Plus, the two girls looked just like each other. Or they would, if Zennor didn't have mojito-coloured hair. She lifted a tendril.

'Do you like it?' Zennor swished her locks. 'It is very mermaidy. Ben said it was "cool" and I didn't even need to ask him first.'

'Wow. That's progress.' Sam pictured Ben, six feet five of gawky awkwardness who took the idea of 'strong but silent' to the extreme, in Sam's opinion. Half the time, you could hardly get a word out of him he was so shy. Sam had been amazed that he'd volunteered for the festival committee. On the other hand, Zennor had enough to say for the pair of them. 'I'm still sure he's completely smitten with you.'

Zennor sighed. 'I thought so too, once, but he's keeping it

very well hidden if he does fancy me. We've known each other since school so I've given up waiting for him to say anything. He's a brilliant designer and I trust him as a business partner one hundred per cent and he is gorgeous in a geeky has-no-idea-of-his-own-attractiveness way.'

'Isn't that the best way?' Sam said, remembering how Gabe's lack of ego and lack of respect for appearances had attracted her when she was younger. He'd brushed off all the abuse while he was serving at the fish and chip shop – some of it bordering on racist – but it must have stung.

'Sam?'

'Ow!'

Zennor had touched her arm with the cold glass, making Sam squeak like the pigs.

'You were miles away.'

'Yeah . . .' Sam looked down at her hands. 'Gabe's coming back to Porthmellow.'

Zennor almost dropped the glass and mojito splashed onto to the couch. 'What? I don't understand – why? When?'

'I found out earlier today. Kris Zachary had to pull out because his business has gone bust. Gabe's taken his place.'

Zennor's remaining mojito splashed out of the glass in her excitement. 'Now, hold on. Slow down. Why does *Gabe* had to be involved?'

'Because Chloe asked him to.'

'What? Doesn't she know about you and him – about Ryan and the trouble he caused?'

'No. Why would she? She's had no cause to even think of Gabe until today but when she heard Kris had pulled out, she phoned round some of her London events contacts. One of them knew Gabe and you can guess the rest.'

'Fuccckkk. You must have almost fainted.'

'Not quite. I was gobsmacked, but what could I say? Chloe had no idea of the connection and she still doesn't. I had to pretend I was pleased, but I'll have to tell her something at least before she hears it on the village gossip mill.'

'My God. I'm amazed. I mean – Gabe must know you run the festival. How can he even think of showing his face again?'

'I suppose he knows I'm involved but Chloe did ask him directly so perhaps he felt obliged.'

Zennor whistled loudly and the guinea pigs ran up to her feet. 'Well, boys,' she said. 'Whoddathought Gabe Mathias would be back in town. He was the love of your auntie Sam's life. She was always saying "oh, he's so insecure underneath the bravado. He has no idea how gorgeous he is—"'

'That was years ago!' Sam protested. 'When I was young and naïve. I know better now and anyway, I could never have stayed involved with a guy who'd turned my own brother in to the police.'

Zennor stroked the pigs. 'No way. It's a deal breaker.' She sat next to Sam. 'I really wish he wasn't coming back. I know how hurt you were when he told the police about Ryan. I hated him too, so God knows what you must have gone through. Even though I was young, and probably not much help, I understood a lot more than you thought. I just didn't know how to say it, or help you.'

Sam looked at her and a lump formed in her throat. 'No one could help. There was no answer to a situation like that.

I suppose Gabe did what he had to do. I had no right to ask him not to report Ryan. I wished I hadn't even tried.' Sam swallowed the lump, thinking back to the night that Gabe had told her he was going to the police. He'd turned up on her doorstep with a face as white as uncooked pastry. He'd started the conversation with some shit about being sorry and that he'd had to make the most difficult decision of his life. Then he'd dropped the bombshell that he'd found out Ryan had been part of the gang planning a robbery of the amusement arcade, and was planning others, and that he was going to tell the police.

Sam shuddered when she remembered that night. She'd totally lost it. She'd cried and shouted and *begged* Gabe not to do it. She'd even grabbed at him and flung the ultimate piece of emotional blackmail at him: 'If you loved me, you wouldn't do this to my family . . .' She'd clung to him to stop him from leaving, but he'd prised her off him and walked out of the door.

She'd tried to call Ryan as soon as Gabe had left, but it was too late. It turned out that there had been no point begging Gabe. He'd already made the call before he turned up at the cottage, probably in case Sam warned her brother. Which was exactly what she had tried to do. Ryan was caught red-handed with two accomplices while the theft was in progress. Gabe hadn't even trusted Sam . . .

He'd been right not to.

'Sam?' Zennor was at her side, her arm around Sam's back. 'Even though I'm angry with Gabe, it's you I'm really worried about. This has really rattled you, hasn't it?'

Sam's body tensed. That night she'd not only lost Gabe and Ryan, but her self-respect and pride, not that she'd ever admit as much to a soul, not even to Zennor. 'A bit, but it's gone now. Gabe and me – we're history. The festival is way bigger than me and if he can help it be a success then I suppose I'll have to live with it.' She forced a smile. 'Let's not waste any more time and energy on the past. Why don't I put the pigs away while you dish up dinner?'

Once the pigs were tucked up, Zennor served the fajitas and the girls sat around the little kitchen table so they could help themselves to the peppers, onions, beans and accompaniments. Despite her long and busy day, Sam had no appetite though she did her best with the meal for Zennor's sake.

No matter what she thought, Gabe *was* going to be part of the festival and she'd inevitably have to have some contact with him, even if Chloe did most of the liaising. How would she react when she saw him again? She'd thought she'd put him to the back of her mind but that was while he was hundreds of miles away. How would he have changed in eleven years? She knew he was knockout gorgeous from his TV shows, and his dry sense of humour and easy air of self-confidence came over well on screen, but was it only a persona? It was one thing watching him through the safety of a screen. How the hell would she handle seeing him in the flesh?

Chapter Six

'Mizzle's coming in.' Troy brushed water from his cap as he walked into the Fisherman's Institute for the committee meeting. Sam had rarely seen him out in public without it. It was a classic fisherman's cap with a soft top and a peak, and must once been black but was now faded by the sun and creased by saltwater. Beneath it, she knew Troy still had a decent growth of hair, having glimpsed it when he'd removed the cap briefly to attend the funeral of a local sailor.

'It is,' said Sam, laying out her notebook and tablet on the table in the upstairs meeting room. 'How's Evie?'

'All right enough. Knee's playing her up. Always does when mizzle comes in.'

'I'm sorry to hear that.' Sam liked Evie a lot. In fact, everyone liked Evie and Troy was devoted to her, but over the past few years, painful osteoarthritis had reduced Evie's mobility massively. She was waiting for a knee op in the hope that would help.

'She doesn't complain, my Evie. Is there a brew on?' Troy asked hopefully.

'Not yet. I've only just got here myself.'

Troy grunted. 'I'll put one on. If you want a job doing, you know what they say.'

'I do,' Sam said, smiling to herself. Troy rarely required an answer to his questions. Irascible and grumpy, with a very dodgy sense of humour, he drove a few people up the wall. He also knew every inch of the town and everyone in it. Small and lithe, he still worked part-time for the harbour commission even though he was now eighty. His official title was 'Festival Facilitator', which really meant 'Fixer'. Troy liaised with the harbour commission and numerous other local issues and people, who could otherwise have been very tricky to deal with.

She heard him whistling 'Trelawney' in the kitchenette off the smaller upstairs meeting room. The granite building had ceased to be a refuge for the fishermen many years previously and was now a community venue that anyone could use. Downstairs, the larger function space played host to always-sozzled parties, sometimes-sozzled wakes, the 'Knit and Knatterers' and many other local groups. The festival committee met there at least once a week in the run-up to the festival. During the event itself, the Institute acted as Festival HQ, providing a hub to deal with any problems or emergencies and a place where all the volunteers could refuel and refresh.

In addition to Troy and the other six main committee members, there were dozens of people who helped to manage all the different aspects of the event. There were countless issues to think about: she'd been astonished when she'd realised quite how much. Without all her helpers, it would never even have got off the ground. With scores of stalls, thousands of visitors over the festival weekend and a budget of tens of thousands, it had evolved into a proper big deal.

Word had travelled that Gabe would replace Kris, as she'd known it would. It had to. Chloe, Sam and their helpers had spent the past day taking down the posters. Fortunately, Kris's name had only gone on around a hundred flyers and his name wasn't on the festival banners, thank God, so that had saved money and work.

Zennor had also taken charge of altering all the online website literature, while Chloe had drafted a press release about the change and sent it out to her contacts. It had generated a few stories in the regional media, Kris's bad fortune had a silver lining for Porthmellow, attracting some extra and much-needed publicity. But as for dealing with the return of the man himself, Sam was still dreading it. Many of the locals would still remember that she'd split with Gabe and why. She'd gone to the meeting at the Fisherman's Institute, bracing herself for comments about their past relationship. She'd already begged Zennor not to make any sarcastic remarks about Gabe, which would make the situation even more awkward than it already was.

A few minutes after Troy, Zennor arrived, chattering nineteen-to-the-dozen with Ben and Drew. Ben said very little in reply and slouched by the table, as if he was trying to melt into the background. Sam was amused because if Ben had wanted to be inconspicuous, he'd have been better off not wearing black motorcycle leathers and eyeliner that made him look like a character in the steampunk novels that Zennor loved so much. He'd ridden into Porthmellow from his place, a wooden chalet on a site near Mousehole. He really had turned into a stunning young guy, but was still painfully shy.

Sam did hear him say a few words to Drew about his new bike; some exchange about engine capacities that temporarily silenced Zennor. Ben had known Drew since childhood, and besides, Drew was the type of guy who was so unobtrusively approachable, you felt you could tell him your deepest darkest secrets.

Zennor flitted over to Troy who was carrying a tray out of the kitchen. 'Want any help with the drinks?' she asked.

Troy chuckled. 'Thanks, my maid. We'd better put the kettle on again now the rabble have arrived.'

Zennor whipped a teabag out of her messenger bag. 'Will do. I've brought my own tea.'

Troy did his best gargoyle impression. 'Not that scented muck?'

'If you mean Earl Grey, no. It's Moroccan mint. I got it from the deli in Newlyn.'

'Why d'you waste your money on that? I'd have dug you up a few plants from my garden. Bloody garden's overrun with mint. It's only a posh nettle, you know.'

'I like it,' said Zennor firmly. 'And it's very good for your gut health.'

Troy chuckled. 'Mebbe I will try some then. You know I have a few problems in that direction.'

Zennor paled. 'I'd better put the kettle on!' she said, zipping into the kitchen, leaving Sam trying to hold in her laughter. Troy wasn't shy in discussing his digestive problems, in front of anyone, friend or stranger. None of them seemed too serious, but they often surfaced – apparently – when he'd had too many pickled eggs in the pub.

Soon everyone had a steaming mug in front of them, and Sam steeled herself for a brew that was bound to be strong enough to strip paint off a trawler's hull.

'So, the local hero is finally coming back to Porthmellow, eh?' Troy sipped his tea and smacked his lips. 'Mind you, he probably wants to get in our good books himself on account of how we're going to be seeing a lot more of him from now on.'

'What do you mean?' Sam asked, disquiet rippling her stomach.

Troy's bushy eyebrows waggled in surprise, like a couple of excited caterpillars. 'Haven't you heard? I'd have thought you'd have been up to date with all his movements. He's taken a lease on Clifftop House *and* I reckon he might be interested in expanding his empire down here. You know the old Net Loft is empty? The one that was a Thai restaurant . . . or was it Malaysian? Or Spanish? I dunno, I don't eat much foreign food.' He wrinkled his nose in disgust.

'No, you're only on the committee of one of the south west's most successful food festivals, aren't you, Troy?' Drew said, shaking his head, and Troy chuckled at the joke.

Sam was less amused. Her stomach swirled again as the implication of Troy's comment sank in. Gabe was renting Clifftop House? That was moments from her own front door ... *and* he was possibly looking at buying a restaurant in Porthmellow? This got worse and worse ...

'I'm strictly here to advise on matters relating to the harbour. Ask me about moorings or vessel wash, and I'll give you chapter and verse, but I'm no gourmet. Unless it's out of the sea. I know my dab from my whiting,' Troy said proudly.

'Sorry to interrupt the culinary discussion but where did you hear all this?' Sam asked.

'And moving into the big house? That's almost next door to us!' Zennor shot Sam a none-too-subtle glance.

'Where did you hear about Gabe being interested in the Net Loft, Troy?' Drew asked, his interest obviously piqued. Even though he'd been older than Gabe, Sam knew they'd got on well.

'Maddie Mylor's auntie told me,' Troy said. 'Mind, she *did* say it was confidential and Maddie had asked her not to pass it on but she won't mind you knowing. Half the town does anyway or will soon enough. Maddie said that some London type called her about empty premises and about a house for rent. That's probably why he could step in at short notice, because he's moving down here ... Didn't you and Gabe have

60

a thing a while back?' Troy said, turning to Sam. 'You were sweet on him until that business with young Ryan, weren't you?'

Even though she could have cheerfully throttled Troy, Sam managed to keep her tone light. 'We went out briefly, a *very* long time ago. We were only kids.'

'You were twenty. Gabe was twenty-one,' said Drew. 'From what I can recall.'

'Sometimes, Drew, I wonder why we're friends,' said Sam, with a smile in her eyes.

'So do I.' Drew's cornflower eyes twinkled in his face as they exchanged glances. He was in his late thirties now, with caramel hair naturally highlighted from his life outdoors brushing his shoulders. He was rugged, fit and gave off an air of easy capability that was very appealing, especially tonight, dressed in a pair of faded jeans and a dark blue shirt that suited his colouring really well. Sam was slightly surprised to see him out of his usual T-shirt and work trousers and wondered if he had a date. Sadly, his marriage to Katya had only lasted a few years, and Connor, now eleven, lived with his mum. As far as Sam was aware, there hadn't been anyone 'significant' since. They had that much in common. A thought suddenly struck her . . . Gabe . . . what if he brought a partner with him? A girlfriend. Oh God.

Sam's mind churned at the prospect of Gabe's love life.

'Sam?' Troy's eyes bored into her. 'You were miles away, maid.'

'Sorry.' Sam forced herself to focus on the festival. 'Well, if Gabe does intend to move to Porthmellow, it can only make our job easier,' she said briskly. 'If he's around, it will be simpler for the committee to deal with him, not that I expect he'll want to get his hands dirty by talking to us direct until the day itself. He'll have a team of people for that. I'll put Chloe in charge of liaising with them, since she dealt with them in the first place and has contacts.'

She was aware she sounded a bit stuffy and pompous but she didn't care. It was inevitable she'd have to speak to and see Gabe at some point, but she intended to have as little to do with him as possible. After what had happened between them the last time they'd seen each other, she was absolutely sure he felt the same.

She checked her watch. They should have started the actual meeting almost fifteen minutes ago, but one of their party was missing. 'More importantly, where's Chloe got to? It's not like her to be late. I hope there's nothing wrong.'

Chapter Seven

Chloe perched on a stool at the breakfast bar and punched Hannah's number into her phone before she could chicken out. This was a bad idea. Her daughter would see it was 'Mum' calling and probably not pick up. The most likely scenario was that the call would go to voicemail again.

Her thumb hovered over the off button.

'Mum?'

She gripped the phone. 'Hannah?'

'Who else would it be?'

'No one, but . . . it's good to hear you.'

Silence. A pause. Would her daughter ring off? 'Is everything OK?'

'Yes. Fine . . . We're fine. I'm fine and Dad was, the last time I spoke to him. I only wanted to see if you and Ruby are OK.'

Another pause. 'Yes. We're OK.'

Chloe couldn't stand the tension. She heard noises: doors opening; doors *slamming*?

'I should go,' Hannah said.

'Not yet, please. I . . . Are you . . .' Is *he* there? Chloe ached to ask the question but it was too incendiary. 'Are you on your own?'

'I was. But not now.'

'Oh. I see.'

'Why do you ask, Mum?'

Hannah wasn't stupid. 'No reason. I only wanted to see how you were. To see if there's any way we can . . . come together. I hate – I mean I'm really sad about – the way things have gone between us.'

Chloe heard a man's voice clearly saying '*Hannah? Who is it?*' That had to be Jordan. Was he controlling Hannah? Threatening her? Chloe wanted to be sick.

'I have to go, Mum. Ruby's crying.'

'Is she OK?'

'Of course she's OK. Why wouldn't she be? I can look after her.'

Suddenly, the conversation had taken a turn for the worse. 'Hannah. Wait. I wasn't implying that you couldn't . . .'

'I have to *go*.' There was a note of desperation in Hannah's tone. Chloe couldn't hear Jordan anymore, but could sense his presence from two hundred miles away.

'OK. Hannah, I want you to know that you can call me any time or text or email me. Or your father. If you need us.'

'Mum. I'm fine. Please, why won't you understand that I'm *fine* . . .' There was a child's wail and then the male voice again. Chloe couldn't hear what was said but Hannah muttered, 'Yes, I'm *coming*!' Then, 'Sorry.'

The phone clicked off. Chloe stared at it in her hand before tossing it onto the sofa. She hugged herself and paced around the flat. *Fine. I'm fine.* For God's sake, that phrase had to be the biggest lie on the planet. Hannah and Chloe had both said it to each other more than once when the opposite was clearly true.

Yet Hannah had at least taken the call. That had to be something and all Chloe's instincts as a mum told her that Hannah *wanted* to take a step towards reconciliation . . . but the call had also left her no further forward. Jordan was in the house, and possibly listening in to Hannah's side of the conversation. Maybe when her daughter had some time alone, she might call back . . . Plus those final comments . . . what did they mean?

'Yes, I'm *coming*!' That was obviously meant for Jordan. Or possibly little Ruby. And the 'Sorry' – that could have been directed at either of them, or at Chloe herself. Or maybe she was overthinking things. She was at a loss for what to do next, if anything at all. Instinct made her want to rush over to Bristol that minute, but common sense told her to leave things as they were, and hope Hannah reached out to her.

Chloe caught sight of herself in the mirror. Her mascara had smudged, leaving her with two spidery imprints under her eyes. She'd better go and wipe it off in the bathroom. She picked up the phone again on the off-chance Hannah had texted her. There was no message, of course, but she did notice one thing.

The time.

'Oh shit!'

She was late for the festival meeting. In fact, it had probably already started.

Chapter Eight

S am glanced at her watch again. Almost half an hour late. That was nothing for some people, but it was unusual for Chloe whose punctuality and organisational skills were terrifyingly good. It didn't matter too much because Sam and the others had passed the time by looking through the new publicity material that Zennor and Ben had created. Her fingers had itched to google 'Gabe Mathias girlfriend', but she hadn't dared in case someone caught her.

Ben chipped in a few times during the discussion, explaining that he'd taken the opportunity to revamp the poster design and fix a few things he wasn't happy with in the first place. A hundred posters had been scrapped and obviously it had created extra work but he and Zennor seemed cool with that, so Sam counted her blessings.

However, time had now run out and they needed Chloe's input so Sam began writing a text to see if she was OK. She hadn't even finished the message when the door was flung open and the woman herself breezed in on a cloud of citrussy perfume and enthusiasm.

'Evening. So sorry I'm late! I got a call from a client and I couldn't get rid of him, no matter how hard I tried. Doesn't he know I have far more important things to deal with than his international conference? I had to fly down the steps from the Crow's Nest so apologies if I look a bit dishevelled.'

'Hi Chloe, it's fine,' said Sam, relieved that her right-hand woman had turned up safe and sound.

'You look all right to me,' said Troy. 'Couldn't you tell this bloke to bog off because you were late for us?'

Chloe laughed. 'I should have done. Thought he'd never get off the phone.' She blew out a breath. 'Anyway, I'm here now. What have I missed?'

'Nothing much,' Troy said.

Sam cringed.

'Ben and Zennor's new posters,' Drew said. 'They're brilliant.'

'Great.' Chloe beamed at them.

'They're not bad, not that I'm an expert,' Troy said. 'Cuppa?'

'Yes, please. I'm gagging for one,' Chloe replied.

Troy got up. 'Builder's brew all right for you?'

Chloe's smile slipped momentarily before reappearing. 'Um. Yes. Fine. Thank you, Troy.'

Sam exchanged a glance with her. Chloe liked her herbal teas, but Sam knew she didn't want to offend Troy. While he went to make the drink, Chloe dumped a box file on the table and whipped out a pale lime MacBook.

Despite her comments about being dishevelled, Sam

67

thought her friend looked as camera-ready as ever, in printed wide-leg trousers, a vest-top and buttery leather biker jacket all of which looked like it'd been tailored to fit her petite frame. It felt like an exuberant pedigree Shi-Tzu had entered the Scrufts section of a dog show.

Sam instinctively shoved her short and unvarnished nails under the table.

'I hear you've saved the day with our star chef,' said Drew.

'Oh, no. I had a lucky break, that's all. You know I still can't believe the actual Gabriel Mathias is going to headline *our* festival.'

'There you go,' said Troy, placing a steaming mug in front of her. 'That'll put hairs on your chest.'

'Sounds gross,' said Zennor, but everyone else was smiling, and even Ben had a smirk on his lips as he tapped away.

Chloe took it in good part. 'Perhaps not *too* many hairs . . . but it's the thought that counts. Thanks, Troy.'

'So, how much does Gabe want?' Troy asked. 'Stepping in at the last minute to bail us out is sure to cost.'

Chloe brightened. 'Ah but there's the thing and it's another reason why I'm so late. Before my client called, Gabe's PA phoned me with some great news. Gabe knows we lost money because of Kris going bust, so he's offered to do it for . . .' Chloe did a jazz hands gesture. 'Free!'

Zennor snapped to attention at this news and mouthed 'WTF?' at Sam.

'Wow,' Sam said it again. It seemed her go-to reaction for any announcement regarding Gabe. It covered so much: surprise, amazement and horror.

'That's very generous of him,' said Drew, sliding a questioning glance at Sam, which she couldn't fail to notice. Zennor pressed her lips together, as if she wasn't as impressed by Gabe's generosity as the rest of the committee.

'It's bloody gobsmacking. I'd have thought he'd have been keen to make as much money as he could from his poor relations,' said Troy.

'Actually, he said it would be a pleasure to put something back into the community,' said Chloe. 'And it could be me, but I think he seemed rather surprised that he hadn't been asked before.'

'We haven't been able to afford him before,' said Sam quietly. 'I mean his fees are way out of our price range. I heard it from one of the organisers of the Devon Grub Festival,' she added quickly.

'Well, he must still feel he has a connection to Porthmellow, even if he hasn't been back much since.'

'I haven't seen him round here at all,' said Troy.

Drew joined in. 'I think he comes down to visit his parents. I saw him at the market in Truro a few years back when I was taking my mum out for the day. In fact, it was my mum who spotted him buying something at a posh bread stall. She's always had a soft spot for him.'

'Unlike some,' Troy muttered. 'He left here under a bit of a cloud. But Sam'd be able to tell you more about that than me.'

Sam found her voice. 'That was years ago, Troy, as you well know. We were kids and we've all moved on a very long way since then. The important thing is that he's agreed to bail us out now, which as you say is very generous of him. Chloe – what's the next step? Are his team coming down to talk about the details?'

Chloe exchanged a glance with Sam. She obviously suspected that Sam and Gabe had 'history'.

'Erm . . .' she said, uncharacteristically flustered. 'No. Actually, Gabe said he'd come and discuss things himself.'

'What? When?' Sam shrieked, she couldn't help herself.

'Next week,' Chloe said. 'I hope it was OK . . . I told him you'd speak to him direct to make arrangements, but I think he wants to meet everyone on the committee. You're the chair. I don't want to take over.'

Sam spotted Drew hiding a smile. She needed to change the subject.

'So. There's a lot to get on with, even without our unscheduled change of chef. Zennor and Ben are amending the marketing and publicity. Drew wants to update us on how he got on with the insurance and health and safety people, and Troy was going to tell us if the harbour authority is happy with the plans to put a temporary bridge over the harbour entrance. We can charge an extra fee for crossing it and it would be a real novelty.'

Troy gave a sharp intake of breath. 'You'll be lucky.'

Sam braced herself. 'OK. We'd better have Drew's report first and then Troy can give us the bad news, if there is any, so we can come up with a solution. Then I'll update everyone with the latest on the stallholders and sponsors.'

Sam hid a smile as Chloe laid out a lacquered pen next to a Moleskine notepad. She might be a newcomer and a little over zealous, but she'd become popular among the committee because she was willing to get involved. Some of the die-hard locals didn't like her 'taking over' the festival, but as they weren't prepared to take on the responsibility themselves, the rest of the committee thought it was tough. Sam had had to grow a thick skin as festival chairman. Not all the decisions she and the committee made were popular. Admittedly, it meant disruption, road closures and crowds for a few days, but on balance, the whole community benefited from the increased trade.

They came to the end of the agenda and while they were packing away their stuff, Chloe spoke up.

'I have an announcement,' she said and everyone's ears pricked up. 'It's not official committee business but it does involve you all.'

'Sounds serious,' said Sam.

'Only for me.' Chloe smiled. 'Actually, it's pleasure, for all of us I hope. Some of you know I have a special birthday coming up next month.'

'Are you twenty-one again?' Troy quipped, and everyone tittered politely.

She rolled her eyes. 'In my dreams.'

'But you're only a maid.'

Chloe laughed. 'Thank you, Troy, but not anymore. I'm not having a big party but I couldn't possibly let the occasion pass without celebrating with the people who've made this incomer so welcome in Porthmellow. So, if you can make it, I thought we'd have a bring-your-own-supper evening on Saturday the fifteenth. It'll do us good to have a bit of R&R before the preparations turn completely manic. I'll provide all the booze, of course, and cook something, but if anyone wants to bring along a favourite dish, that'd be fantastic. Evie's invited too, of course,' she said to Troy.

'She'll like that. She's a good cook, my Evie, one of the best.'

'That sounds brilliant,' said Sam, delighted to have a distraction from anything Gabe-related.

'Thanks. Don't think you have to make anything, Sam,' Chloe said. 'I know it's your day job.'

'I'd love to bring something.'

'OK.'

'Are vegans included?' Ben piped up, reminding Sam of a baby bird worrying if he was going to get his share of the worms.

Chloe smiled at him. 'Absolutely.'

Troy huffed. 'As long as it's not rabbit food.'

'We can both rustle up delicious vegan meals,' Zennor cut in, much to Sam's amusement. She was like a big sister, defending her little brother.

'Well . . . some of them are really nice . . .' he mumbled.

'Your veggie chilli is *amazing*,' Zennor declared.

Troy looked as if he'd swallowed a wasp but stayed silent, much to Sam's relief.

'Sounds good to me, Ben,' said Drew. 'I love chilli and it's a great idea to have different types of food. I'll do my best. It won't be gourmet cuisine and it'll probably involve fish.'

'I love fish,' said Chloe. 'And um . . . I was going to say that partners are invited too, of course, if you – if anyone – wants to bring someone. Unless you think they'd be bored with us all talking shop about the festival.'

Chloe had directed this last remark at the whole committee,

72

but Sam suspected she meant it for Drew mostly, and she supposed herself. After all, Evie and Troy were obviously going to come along together, as were Zennor and Ben even if they weren't officially a couple.

'I think we'd drive any outsiders mad,' she said lightly. 'So, it'll just be me.'

Troy tutted. 'You'll have the floor of that flat down on top of your neighbours if you ask any more and that old balcony can't be rated for more than half a dozen folk.'

'Troy's right about the health and safety,' said Drew with uncharacteristic seriousness before breaking into a smile. 'I'm joking, Chloe, but Sam's right. I don't know how anyone else would put up with us, so I'll be on my own too.'

'OK. I only wanted you to know that friends would be welcome,' said Chloe but Sam thought she'd visibly relaxed now she knew 'plus ones' weren't coming along. 'Thanks, guys. I hoped you wouldn't think it was cheeky to ask you to bring some grub, but it sounds like it's going to be a lot of fun and I promise to keep the fizz flowing. There may even be some nice champagne.'

'Champagne,' Drew whistled. 'Well, I guess you're only forty once.'

Chloe started to reply, but she was cut off by Troy's snort. 'Pah. Forty's nothing. I've done it twice over, but we'll be there. My Evie likes a drop of French fizz. Don't see the attraction myself. Makes me gassy. You might like to keep the windows open.'

Zennor gasped in horror. 'Troy! That's way too much information!'

Everyone else burst out laughing and Chloe smiled politely. 'In that case, I'll get the air freshener ready, Troy,' she said, to more sniggers.

Sam wasn't quite sure Chloe was so amused by the banter as she pretended. She didn't know them that well, and perhaps Drew's bringing up her age hadn't gone down too well. Maybe she was sensitive about it after her divorce. Forty was a big milestone in anyone's life, but not one Sam had to worry about for a good while yet . . . even so, the years could fly by and she'd once thought – hoped – she might have settled down and possibly be thinking of a family by now. The trouble was she'd never been able to see herself with anyone but Gabe. Once again, the idea that he might be – probably *was* – in a relationship with a partner he might bring to Porthmellow churned away in her mind.

The meeting broke up as twilight descended over the harbour. Usually the committee rewarded themselves for their hard work with a trip to one of the local pubs, meeting up with others who helped with the organisation.

Chloe slotted her tablet and files into a leather case. 'I'll join you later at the pub if it's OK. I need to make a call first. It's work again.' Her grimace was apologetic.

'OK,' said Sam. 'We'll keep your seat warm.'

'Thanks.'

After Chloe had left, Zennor and Ben scooted off to the pub to get a round in and Troy decided to head home to Evie so only Sam and Drew were left behind to pack up.

'Want a hand with your stuff?' he asked as Sam put her iPad in her bag and picked up a box of files.

'Thanks. I'll have to cart it to the pub with me so I could do with some help.'

'It should be quiet at the Tinners' tonight. The Smuggler's has a folk band on and it'll be noisy and packed.'

'Oh. I wondered why Zen and Ben were so keen on the Tinners'. Mind you I wouldn't have minded a bit of a sing along. And a very large glass of wine.'

'I can do the wine . . . but I can't stay too long this evening.' He took the box from her while Sam locked the room. She followed him down the stairs and returned the key to a hook on the wall.

'Plans?'

He smiled. 'Maybe . . .'

'Oh. Sounds intriguing.'

Drew answered with a cryptic smile and Sam walked out of the Institute and skirted the harbour. There was no point taking the boxes back to the house, as the Tinners' was conveniently half the way home in one of the back streets behind the harbour.

Drew carried the box in his arms, while Sam had her laptop and bag. They passed by the Harbour Café where the closed sign was turned over. Faint music drifted over the water from the Smuggler's on the opposite side of the water. Now the meeting had ended, Gabe had been on her mind again. She knew she'd be googling him as soon as she got home.

'Tell me to mind my own business but are you OK?' Drew asked, breaking into Sam's thoughts

Sam had a sinking feeling. 'Yeah, why wouldn't I be?'

'Because I know you too well and we've been friends for

too long. I know how you felt about Gabe and how he felt about you. We were all mates, after all, even if I was a few years older than you both. How do you feel about him coming back to take part in the festival?'

'Not thrilled, but you've worked that one out.' She threw a smile at her friend. He deserved her honesty, or something like it. 'There's nothing I can do about it and the simple fact is that we need a headline chef, and one that's going to appear for free – well, I'd be nuts to turn it down. Think how it would look, if I refused his offer because of a family dispute that half the town will have forgotten by now?'

'I can see you're in an impossible position. I just wanted you to know that I'm aware it'll be tough for you.'

Sam laid her hand on his arm. 'You're a lovely guy. Has anyone ever told you that?'

'Not as often as you might think.' His eyes twinkled.

'Is that going to change?'

'I can't possibly answer that.'

Sam narrowed her eyes. Drew did seem jaunty this evening and his mysterious comments led her to put two and two together.

'Yes! I *thought* you were seeing someone new.' She stopped in her tracks. 'There's a new woman, isn't there? Don't try to deny it.'

He appeared to be considering then smirked. 'OK. She's very new. She's called Caitlin.'

Sam gave a little whoop of triumph that her guess had been right. 'Caitlin? Do I know her?'

'Don't think so. As a matter of fact, I'm seeing her later this evening only I didn't want to say so earlier. This is only our third date.'

She let out a mock gasp. '*Third* date? My God, should I buy a hat?'

'Not just yet, but I don't mind admitting I'm pretty smitten.'

'Wow.' She planted a kiss on his cheek, delighted to have been trusted with the news about his new girlfriend. 'But you're not bringing her to Chloe's party?'

'Oh, I'm not sure she'd fit in. After all, would *you* bring a new bloke to one of our committee booze-ups?'

'On careful reflection, no. Not unless I wanted to split up with them. And besides, there is no one in my life at the moment.'

'At the *moment*, eh? I heard you were seeing Hunky Carl Trenow.'

She gasped, shocked that Drew knew about her most recent 'relationship' with the handsome helm of the Marazion lifeboat. 'What? I only went out with him three times and we were meant to be keeping it quiet.'

'Not quiet enough. It was all around Porthmellow.'

'In that case, you'll know we called it a day,' she said curtly, still taken aback at how fast the gossip had spread.

'Word has it you wouldn't let him wear his yellow wellies in bed. Most women beg him to wear them, apparently.'

'What? That's outrageous!' She huffed loudly. 'I hope Carl didn't say that or I'll sort him out. Things never even got that far . . .' She paused, realising she'd shared too much information with Drew. 'Who told you about the wellies?'

'Oh, it was a bit of banter at the station and on the quayside.

We all knew it was rubbish. Most people thought it was more likely that Carl bored you to death.'

She made a mock strangling gesture. 'This bloody place. The gossip is terrible. Carl – and I *never* called him Hunky Carl – and I decided not to see each other again because we didn't click, and that's all. He was obsessed with playing with his Xbox and he thought gourmet food was having HP sauce on his chips rather than tomato ketchup. To be honest, I was *sooo* relieved when he was called on a shout before our final date, and when he asked me to go to a lifeboat barbecue, I told him I couldn't make it because I had a meeting about the Portaloos. He didn't call me again and that suited me fine.' Sam's cheeks turned warm, thinking of people discussing her sex life – or lack of – with Hunky Carl, the most boring 'hero' on the planet.

Drew laughed. 'What are we like, eh? Both as bad as each other at romantic stuff.'

'Yes, but you have the mysterious Caitlin now . . . Where's she from? When do we get to meet her?' Sam asked.

Drew grinned. 'She comes from Falmouth way. Penryn as a matter of fact.' Drew pushed open the pub door. 'You'll see her soon, I promise. I don't want to introduce her to you until we're both ready.'

'Fair enough. I'm very happy for you,' she said, burning with curiosity yet trying to respect his privacy.

'Thanks.' Drew left Sam's stuff by their table in the pub and delivered the news that he couldn't stay to a wide-eyed Zennor before heading off out of the door, whistling a sea shanty.

Sam smiled to herself. He loved to play up to the rugged man of the sea thing, but was a sensitive soul really. He was part of the local fishermen's choir and played the guitar and wrote his own songs, which he occasionally performed with a couple of mates in the local pubs. In fact, Drew's band were booked to play at the festival on the Saturday evening and Sunday afternoon.

Since his marriage had broken up he'd had a couple of girlfriends, one who he'd lived with for a while, but he was the first to admit his job took him away from home a lot, which didn't fit in with a conventional family life. Not all the sailing trips were based around the local coast. Most were to Scilly or south Devon, but odd times he sailed as far as the Channel Islands or the western isles of Scotland. Sam wished him well, but something less than pleasure stirred amid her professed happiness for him. Drew sounded serious about this Caitlin in a way she hadn't heard before. Why did she feel slightly *torn* about that fact? Was it the idea that everyone seemed to be coupling up? No, that was silly.

Chloe arrived and found Sam queuing at the bar to get in another round. 'Hi there. Zennor just told me that Drew has a date tonight. He's so lovely. I often wondered if you and he were a thing when I first moved here,' she said, then paled. 'Sorry, that's a bit cheeky of me.'

'No, it's not and yes, some people have been waiting for us to get together but we're just good friends, as they say. If anything had been going to happen, it would have by now but we're very happy as mates. And anyway, as you say, Drew's seeing someone called Caitlin.' Sam hoped that by stating the situation between her and Drew out loud, she might remind herself of how she *ought* to feel about it.

'Oh. That's a shame. I mean, whoops, not a shame for him and the lucky Caitlin, obviously but I thought . . . well, he is very easy on the eye.' Chloe smiled again. 'Not as gorgeous as Gabriel Mathias, of course. I mean . . . I'm sorry, I hadn't realised that you'd known him so well when he lived here.'

Sam realised that she'd have to tell Chloe the truth about her and Gabe before she heard the full details elsewhere.

'I ought to tell you something before half the town does. I didn't just know Gabe, we once went out. It was years ago before he was famous when his mum and dad still ran the chip shop next to the post office.'

It was fair to say that Chloe's jaw dropped.

'We'd been to the same school and we'd always fancied each other but we started going out properly after we left. I was nineteen and Gabe was just a year older than me.'

'Wow. You went out with Gabriel Mathias?'

'Yes. Hard to believe, eh?'

'Yes. No, not at all, you're so lovely, Sam, and I can see why but it's so . . . so surreal.'

Sam smiled to herself at being called 'lovely'. Not everyone in Porthmellow would agree, but it was nice of Chloe to be kind. 'Gabe wasn't quite as gorgeous then. I mean, he was gorgeous to *me*. By far the sexiest boy in the village, but he was skinny and bolshie and he worked in the chip shop so he was always covered up in an overall and a hair net and some of the other kids used to tease him and call him Vinegar Face and Grease Ball.'

'How awful for him.'

'I liked him. I used to go in late or early to the shop and chat to him. I'd hang around and order stuff I didn't want so I could talk to him. I can't tell you how many pickled eggs and saveloys I fed to the seagulls.'

Chloe laughed.

'Joking apart, I knew he was a nice guy. Thoughtful, ambitious and he loved his parents. We both loved cooking, even then. Mum had taught me to cook and Gabe had big dreams of becoming a chef, but he told me he didn't feel he could leave his mum and dad to run the business. His grandparents had built it up from nothing after they'd escaped from Cyprus during the war with Turkey. The family had made a new life here and Gabe didn't know how to tell them he didn't want to carry it on. He was training to be a chef at catering college by the time we started seeing each other, as well as doing shifts at his parents' chip shop. He was doing well and ambitious even all those years ago.'

Wow. Sam paused for breath, suddenly aware of how much she'd been gabbling. Why she felt the need to explain, she had no idea. Then she realised that actually, her shoulders felt slightly less tense. It was almost a relief to tell Chloe about her relationship – *past* relationship – with Gabe, and as Chloe was new to the town, and had no preconceptions, Sam felt she could be honest and open.

'I had no idea. I knew he'd lived here but his PA never mentioned he knew you . . . damn. I'm sorry. That sounds dreadful,' said Chloe.

'No, not at all. Why would his staff even be aware he knew me?'

'I thought that Gabe might have mentioned the connection . . . sorry.'

Sam shrugged. 'Don't be, but I'm not the slightest bit bothered that Gabe hasn't told anyone he knows me. In fact, I'm relieved, because the reasons we split up are . . . a bit personal, although there are a few people around here who have their own idea. It was complicated and—'

'Sam. Please don't think you have to tell me any of the details. It's your business.'

'Thanks, but, well, let's say that Gabe and I grew apart. We split up at the same time as my brother, Ryan, was having some problems. You've probably heard about those.'

'A little. I do know he spent some time in prison. I'm sorry. It must have been very difficult for you.'

'It was and it came not long after my mum had passed away.' Sam sighed.

While Zennor and Ben took their drinks over to the pool table, Sam told Chloe just enough about what had happened between her, Gabe and Ryan to explain why seeing him again might be awkward for her, but no more. No one but Gabe and herself knew everything that had passed that night and Sam had no intention of ever sharing it.

Chapter Nine

@**Porthmellowchick:** @Cornishmaid Just spotted #Gabe-Mathias in the harbour car park!!! He is lush!!!! Would of got pic but have to go to work. Keep an eye out. #summer-festival

That Monday morning, Gabe found a space in the car park behind the post office, locked the Range Rover and headed for the ticket machine. He'd had trouble finding the keys among the unfamiliar surroundings of Clifftop House where he'd arrived late the previous evening.

He'd brought with him only what he could cram into his 4X4. The house was partly furnished but he'd arranged for a few pieces of furniture and equipment to be shipped by a removals firm. He'd be glad when they arrived later in the day because after a night in the rented pile, he still had a sense of disorientation. All his childhood insecurities and fears had flooded back the moment he'd driven down the steep hill into the harbour and through the narrow streets to Stippy Stappy Lane, which eventually petered out in a track at the gates of Clifftop House.

Wavecrest Cottage was one of three in a terrace a hundred yards down the track towards the village. He knew that Sam and Zennor still lived there. Exactly the same as they always had . . . whereas he was now the tenant of the biggest house in Porthmellow.

When he'd told his PA to get a house with a great kitchen and he didn't mind the bill, he hadn't meant rent a great big Victorian pad that looked down on the village, which is exactly what Clifftop House did. How many times had he dreamed of living in the grand Victorian 'gentleman's residence' in its lofty position above the waves? Christ, the place even had a turret, which had always reminded him of Dracula's castle. In fact, the turret had been his favourite feature of the house, back when he was a young boy and addicted to Gothic horror films and Manga comics.

Gabe groaned. He wasn't a lad now. He was a grown-up and he'd only spent one night in the house and was already regretting it.

Suzy had insisted that Clifftop was the only place available at such short notice on a three-month rental. Gabe had agreed reluctantly, but now wished he hadn't. He should have gone for something more discreet, tucked away inland rather than making a statement like this. It looked as if he wanted to lord it over the village . . . which he didn't.

And yet. Why *shouldn't* he rent Clifftop House? Why should

he be afraid to return and ashamed of his success? He'd worked bloody hard to get where he was. All the long shifts in baking hot kitchens, the abuse from top chefs, the low pay, the burns, the cuts, the worry of starting out on his own . . . and it wasn't as if he owed anyone in Porthmellow anything, was it? They'd hardly begged him to return. And as for Sam . . .

He cursed under his breath and as soon as he did, he realised he was cursing himself. He couldn't blame her for what had happened. He couldn't even blame Ryan entirely, and it was his decision to come back.

The festival call had been the catalyst, but maybe, subconsciously, he'd already wanted to come back to Porthmellow, possibly build a few bridges. The Net Loft restaurant premises coming up for lease at the same time had cemented that idea. Since Chloe's call, he'd had all sorts of ideas.

He'd never intended to become a 'personality' when he first started cooking but a couple of appearances at festivals and on regional news programmes had led to an offer to guest on a national weekend cooking show. Gabe had found that the exposure helped keep his own restaurant in business and so he'd accepted more and more offers until he'd been offered his own series. He'd only recently finished filming the second run but wasn't sure he wanted to do any more. They were a major commitment that took him away from 'hands-on' cheffing.

If he decided to re-open the Net Loft and spend more time in Cornwall, away from the madness of London, it would mean ramping down his TV commitments at a time when he could have been accepting more offers. But he didn't want to end up one of those people who viewers can't get enough of to start with, until the day they started to find him bloody annoying. He hated the word 'celebrity' even now and refused to have it uttered in his presence, even though tolerating it publicly was a necessary part of his business brand.

His agent wouldn't agree. She'd wag her ring-encrusted finger and warn him, '*Carpe diem*, Gabe. Grab every opportunity while you can, my love, or people will forget you. You'll be old hat before you can blink.'

Trouble was, Gabe felt old hat already. He'd worked since he was fourteen, clawing his way from chip shop assistant to successful chef and he was tired . . . not so much physically as in his soul.

So, how in the name of Christ would returning to Porthmellow with all its unhappy memories help? And how would moving a few doors up from Samphire Lovell make his spirit any less ragged than it was now? It was more than likely to tear it to shreds.

Gabe baulked at the parking charges as he reached the ticket machine. *What*? That was steep, wasn't it? Four quid for two hours? It was nothing compared to London but for Porthmellow he was surprised. He hadn't been back for five years, but it used to be free. He didn't begrudge a penny to the council, but he was surprised that they thought people would pay that much for an amble around the harbour and shops.

His parents had retired from their fish and chip shop shortly after he'd left and he'd recently bought them a bungalow in the countryside. They rarely went back to the village now, but had told him it was on the way up, especially since the food festival had become established. His team had done their own research, of course, because Gabe was thinking of buying the restaurant premises, but now he was here, he could see with his own eyes. The old library, where he'd borrowed lots of books about food, had been divided into flats above a bookies and vaping shop. On the upside, new cafés and galleries, a bike hire centre, bakery and beauty spa had sprouted up in the back streets, he'd spotted them as he'd driven down the hill.

Porthmellow really was on the way up . . . unless you wanted to borrow a book.

He fumbled in his pockets for some extra change then scrutinised the sign again. There was no option to pay by mobile: the council hadn't got that far yet, and he was fifty pence short of the required fee. He would have paid with notes but it only took change, which meant he'd have to run to the nearest shop – the newsagents – and get some coins.

'Shit,' he muttered. He'd better get a move on because if a warden spotted his fancy 4X4, he'd be sure to slap a ticket on it faster than Gabe could fillet a Dover sole.

'Gabe? Gabe Mathias? I'd recognise that mane of hair anywhere.'

Gabe turned to find a gnarled old guy stood behind him, showing a set of yellowing teeth, one of which was gold. He recognised him immediately as Troy Carman, who worked for the harbour, or certainly used to. He must be over eighty now but he still looked fit. His forearms were corded and his face was as brown as a hazelnut and weathered like a prune. Gabe braced himself.

'Hello, Troy. How's things?' he said.

'I'm doing fine. I needn't ask about you. Nice motor.' Troy cackled and nodded at the Range Rover.

'Thanks. Sorry, I was just on my way to the newsagents for some coins. Hadn't realised I'd need a mortgage to park in the village now.'

Troy cackled. 'Bet you could buy the whole bloody car park. It's a sign of the times, lad. Mind you, I've got a pass, as an official of the harbour.'

'I thought you'd have retired?'

'Retire? Not me. No, I still work as part-time for them. They can't get rid of me, see, on account of these anti-ageing laws.' He smirked again. 'How much are you short?'

'Fifty pence. Better get my cash before I get a fine.'

'Oh, you're all right today. Foxy Seddon is on maternity leave and the council haven't found a replacement for her yet. I wouldn't bother if I were you. They send round a temporary warden every now and then, but he was here on Saturday so I doubt he'll be back.'

'You're probably right but I'd better pay my dues,' said Gabe, thinking of how the villagers and possibly local press would have a field day if it got out that he was too mean to pay for a car park ticket. So Foxy Seddon was a traffic warden, thought Gabe, remembering a fierce girl who'd reminded him of a mini version of Miss Trunchbull when they were at school. Now she was having mini Trunchbulls of her own. He really had been away a long time.

Troy chuckled. 'Well, I suppose you've got to set an example, being a celebrity.' He dug in the pocket of his baggy blue overalls. 'Here. I've got some change. Hang on.'

'No. It's fine. You don't have to give me money.' Gabe was dismayed to be given a handout by a pensioner.

'Save you a trip to the paper shop.' He held out two twenty-pence pieces and a ten pence on his grubby palm.

'Thanks. I owe you,' said Gabe. 'I'll pay you back as soon as I get some change.'

'Oh, no need to do that. I'll have my reward telling everyone at the Smuggler's how I gave the millionaire Gabe Mathias a loan.'

Gabe swore silently, but managed a smile. 'I appreciate it,' he lied.

Troy smirked. 'I'll be looking forward to you buying me a pint while you're down here. And a nice plate of that fried whitebait you cooked on the breakfast telly the other day. Not that I watch much telly, but my Evie saw you and told me.'

'Really? How is she?'

'Arthritis is bad, poor maid, but she still gets about and she loves TV cookery shows. She said she thought you put too much flour in that batter for those seafood pancakes you made the other week. Bet they were lumpy.'

'Really?' Gabe said, slipping into the polite and good-humoured tone he'd learned to adopt after years of comments on his cooking. He had always liked Evie Carman, though. She'd been kind to him, and had once stepped in when he was being bullied about his greasy hair and 'creosote tan' by some local lads who'd been referring to his Greek heritage.

He must have been around twelve and about to tackle the pair of them himself when Evie had told the 'moronic little sods' to 'bugger off'. Although Evie was fifty years older than Gabe, she'd had plenty of experience of abusive comments in her lifetime.

Her Cornish mother, long dead now, had taken the unheard-of step of marrying a black American GI who'd been stationed near Porthmellow in the war. Evie's parents had settled locally and her heritage meant she stood out in the community 'like a sore thumb' – Evie's words, not Gabe's. Thank God the world and Porthmellow had moved on since then, thought Gabe. Not far or fast enough by a long way, but sufficiently for Evie to have stayed in the town where she was now a stalwart.

Evie had trained as a teacher and retired a dozen years previously, while Gabe still worked in the chip shop. Her warmth, good humour and firm but compassionate manner had endeared her to the whole community, and to Troy, who was besotted by her, above all else.

And, Gabe reflected, maybe Evie did have a point about his batter . . . it didn't show on screen but there were a few tiny lumps. 'I'll try to pop in and ask for her tips,' he said, trying to hide his amusement. 'Sorry to hear about her arthritis.'

'Evie would love that. Always had a soft spot for you. Mind you, she'd hardly recognise you. You were a lanky streak of piss when she last saw you, always ready to pick a fight with the world. Now look at you – a regular George Clooney,' Troy said, chortling at his own joke.

Gabe hadn't heard anyone chortle in a long time and strangely, Troy's backhanded compliment raised a smile on his own lips. George Clooney was a great actor and a good-looking bloke, but he was old enough to be Gabe's dad. Unexpectedly, Troy slapped him on the back. For an eighty year old it was some whack and Gabe lurched forward, which made Troy chuckle even more.

'Well, I can't stand here rattling on with you. I've a meeting with the harbourmaster about this festival to go to. I'm on the committee, you know,' he added proudly.

Gabe resisted the urge to rub his back where Troy had slapped him. 'I didn't know that. You're obviously in great demand.'

He showed Gabe his remaining teeth. 'I am. Oh, and by the way, you'll doubtless be crossing paths with Samphire Lovell while you're here. She runs the whole thing with a rod of iron, but you must know that.' Troy smirked. 'Can hardly avoid her, can you, lad? Even if you wanted to.'

Still cackling, Troy ambled off over the car park towards the harbourmaster's office, leaving Gabe staring after him.

It wasn't often Gabe heard such 'plain speaking' from the people around him these days. He was used to criticism in the press and online, but Troy's direct manner was a breath of fresh air compared to some of the sycophantic hangers-on he had to deal with in London, most of whom wanted to make money out of him. But how refreshing that directness would be when he'd been in Porthmellow for a few days, he wasn't sure.

He paid for his ticket, stuck it on his windscreen and

hurried towards the harbour for his meeting with the estate agent, but Troy's parting words drummed on his brain.

'You'll doubtless be crossing paths with Samphire Lovell while you're here. Can hardly avoid her, can you, lad? Even if you wanted to.'

He shook his head in disbelief. Troy Carman had managed to imply in one sentence, that he knew Gabe had been sweet on Sam and that he was eager to see her and dreading it too. The cheeky old sod . . .

Yet Gabe had to admit, the old codger was absolutely right.

Chapter Ten

@**CornishMaid:** Anyone know what bands are playing at the festival? @Porthmellowchick #Cornishfestival
@**Metallicafan:** Who cares. They're always shit anyway. My dog sounds better. #crapmusic #metalrules

Sam was on her way home to Wavecrest Cottage en route from the village salon. After work, she'd gone to the hairdresser's and while she was waiting to be shampooed, she'd finally given in and googled *Gabe Mathias: girlfriend*. She'd looked in the past, of course, but not for a few years, knowing that it wasn't healthy or helpful.

She wasn't sure whether she liked what she discovered or not. Gossip blogs and past news stories unearthed the fact that he'd been 'seen with' several women since he'd opened up his own restaurant, one of whom – a glamorous cookery writer – he'd lived with for a couple of years until last year according to Wikipedia. Sam had already known about that relationship from an old snippet on an Internet site. However, there was no one listed on his Wiki page as a spouse or partner now and the personal life section was surprisingly short. Plus, the Porthmellow gossip mill hadn't mentioned a partner, or Troy would have said something at the meeting.

So far, no further on . . .

She'd closed her phone and as usual ended up rattling on about the festival with the stylist. By the time she'd remembered to say: 'Just a trim, please,' the floor looked like Bryony's dog grooming parlour. After she'd left, she caught sight of the smart but scarily short bob in the window of the fudge shop, and let out a squeak of panic.

The hour in the salon had been a brief moment of pamper time in a mega busy day baking for a stint at a paranormal festival in Tehiddy the following evening. Now, walking home, she was enjoying the spring sunshine, which had real warmth in it as summer approached. The chinking of glass and bursts of laughter followed her as she turned in to an alley that led to steep steps that would take her to the streets above the harbour. Despite being used to the climb, she was breathing harder by the time she reached the lane of pastel-coloured fishermen's cottages that included Wavecrest. Not that Sam could *see* her cottage, because the street was completely blocked by a large removals van. Its tyres rested on the thin strip of pavement and there was only the thinnest sliver of daylight visible on either side of the van.

A man in maroon overalls was standing at the rear with his hands on his hips, staring at his van.

She jogged up to him. 'What's happened?' she said, although she could have supplied the answer herself. Delivery drivers got stuck on this corner several times a year.

The driver scratched his head. 'Bloody sat nav led me up here. Now I'm wedged in.'

'Someone should have said you wouldn't get through with a vehicle this big. You can't go forward, there's an overhanging bay window on one of the cottages around this corner. Your van will damage the building if you try to squeeze through here, and I wouldn't recommend trying.'

'I've seen the window. I've been trying to reverse, but it's a bloody nightmare with that bend behind. That corner's so sharp with that road sign right behind and I'm worried I'll take a chunk out of the white cottage I drove past. That one with the funny stone porch. I can't risk doing any damage. My boss'll skin me.' He peered hopefully at Sam. 'I was hoping someone could watch out for me, but I haven't seen anyone over thirteen or under ninety yet. And even with help, I'm not sure I can make the turn.'

She looked at the van and the driver. He was totally nonplussed. 'So, what are you going to do?' she asked.

'Have to wait for another driver to come out and see if they can do it.'

'I'm guessing that could take a while, even if he or she can move it . . .' She paused as a thought formed in her mind. 'Where are you going by the way?'

'Big place at the end of this road, I hope, though the lane seems to peter out into a path. Apparently, there's a house called Clifftop House along there? You heard of it?'

She gawped. My God, if someone was moving into Clifftop House, it had to be Gabe. Which meant his stuff was in this van. She could leave it here, stuck like a cork in a bottle and let Gabe's driver sort it out. He might be waiting a very long time, she thought with grim pleasure, but that soon evaporated. Gabe was moving in a few doors up from her for God knows how long. This was far worse than she'd imagined.

'It is up here, isn't it?' the driver said anxiously, taking Sam's shock for ignorance.

'Yeah. It's there, but it's a little way along the track at the end of this lane. You can't see the house because it's on the edge of the cliff behind some gates. The owners should have told you to bring a smaller van. Here, hand over the keys.'

He snorted. 'What? You must be joking.'

'Why? Because I'm a woman?'

'No, because you're not qualified or insured.'

'One: I drive a pick-up and a converted horsebox with a full kitchen in it down lanes much narrower and twistier than this pretty much every day of my life. And two: I live up here and my sister will be home soon – or she would if she could get past in her car. You're stopping us from sitting down together for a very large gin and tonic.' She held out her palm. 'Keys, please.'

He folded his arms. 'I can't do that.'

Ignoring him, she climbed into the driver's seat.

He stood in the doorway. 'You . . . I . . . shouldn't really be doing this. You're not insured,' he repeated.

'And what will your boss say when they have to send someone who is qualified to get your van out? And meanwhile,

96

no one can get from the properties above here to the village. There are elderly people in some of the cottages and a lady who's expecting a baby in a week's time. What if the emergency services can't reach a house? Give me the keys, please.'

The man handed them over. 'I must be mad.'

'Keep an eye out for traffic from behind, please,' said Sam.

Still grumbling, the driver went behind the truck. Sam saw him in the wing mirror and started to back up. The van was big and space was very tight, but she knew the lane like the back of her hand, and the exact micro second of when to turn to miss the white cottage with its stone porch. She reversed steadily down the hill and opened the door.

'Hop in,' she said. 'I'm going to take you via the scenic route.'

His eyebrows scrunched together. 'What? You said this was the only road.'

'The only *road* to Clifftop House, yes, but not the only *way*.'

Shaking his head, he got into the passenger seat.

'Buckle up,' said Sam wickedly, before reversing a few yards more and turning the van into a gravel driveway between two cottages. The driveway was a tight squeeze but not as tight as the lane. It led to a concrete track that ran behind some garages at the back of the cottages.

The man had one hand on the window to brace himself as the truck bumped along. 'Jesus. Is this a road?'

'Not strictly speaking. It's unadopted but if you want to get to Clifftop House it's your only chance.'

'I'm not supposed to go off road . . .'

'Off road?' she laughed. 'This isn't off road. You've obviously never been to Cornwall before.'

Carefully watching out for people coming out of their back gates, Sam drove the truck with inches to spare on either side and turned sharp right again at the end onto a dirt track overhung by trees.

The driver swore. ''kin hell. This isn't a track, it's a footpath.'

'This section is a green route technically,' she said as branches snapped and crackled against the van. 'But look, there's Clifftop House.'

She slowed down as they emerged from the hedges into a sandy area on the heathland. The sea suddenly came into view. Sam drove slowly along the rutted track and stopped the vehicle alongside the coastal path outside Clifftop House. She daren't get too close in case she saw Gabe. Hmm. Maybe she should have considered that before she made the offer to move the van.

'This is as far as I go. You'll have to buzz the gates to be let in or call the owner, but be careful how you drive over the coastal path. There might be people or dogs about and it's illegal anyway.'

'Bloody hell.' The man blew out a breath as Sam opened the van door.

'How will I get out of here?' the man asked, looking in the wing mirror in horror.

'Sorry, I can't help you there. I expect your client can help. Ask him to drive you out.' She rolled her eyes. 'If he can still remember his way.'

Sam jumped down from the cab. But as her boots hit the earth, she heard a voice behind the van.

'Hey there! How have you managed to get that huge thing down here?'

Sam slid to the ground and came face to face with Gabe.

Momentarily stunned, he regarded her as if she was alien, but eventually found his voice. 'Sam? What the hell are you doing?'

The driver called from the passenger seat. 'I told her she shouldn't be driving it! I knew it was illegal, but she wouldn't listen.'

Gabe's eyes glittered. 'I bet she wouldn't.'

Sam exploded. 'Now hold on. "*She*" is actually here, you know, and I didn't force this guy to let me drive. It's his fault he got wedged on Stippy Stappy Corner in the first place. He was about to take a chunk out of Old Man Garner's cottage *and* he'd blocked the road. I was doing my civic duty to move this thing. I mean, who needs a van this big, anyway? Clearly someone with far too much stuff!'

Gabe stared open-mouthed at her while the driver cowered in the passenger seat. Her heart thumped. Obviously, she'd seen him on screen; she'd watched enough reruns of his cheffy appearances, but in the flesh, he was shockingly gorgeous.

'I was only trying to help,' said Sam. 'Anyway, I'll be on my way now. I was on my way home. I've got work to do.'

'I thought you said you were desperate for a large gin and tonic?' the driver muttered.

'That too. Bye.' She moved away.

Gabe caught up with her. 'Wait. I was hoping to talk to you.'

She kept on going, striding along the track downhill towards Wavecrest Cottage. 'I've nothing to say to you.'

'Great. That's perfect. So, you're going to ignore me and freeze me out?'

'I'm the chair of the festival and I'll behave with total professionalism when it comes to that,' Sam said coldly. 'Even if it wasn't my idea to ask you. Chloe, the deputy chair, had no idea of our . . . connection, or she would never have suggested it.'

'I must admit I was a bit surprised to be approached. Especially after all this time.'

'All what time? Seems like yesterday to me.'

Gabe shook his head and held up his hands in despair. 'So, it's going to be like that, is it?'

She swallowed hard. She knew she ought to count to ten, or twenty or even a hundred, but right now it seemed as if no period of time would cool her down. She'd known this moment would come and she'd rehearsed how it would be, armed herself with a long list of polite platitudes. None of them were helpful now. Seeing Gabe again had flooded her with memories that drowned out all her social armoury.

'Like what?'

'Daggers drawn. Naked hostility. Sam, I should never have agreed to come. I had hoped that you'd agreed to Chloe asking me. I should have checked with her, but I see she had no idea of our history.'

'No. I had to tell her that we were . . . that we were close once, a very long time ago, but she doesn't know the exact details of why we split up – although she probably has half a dozen different theories by now, helped by the village grapevine.'

'Hmm. I bumped into Troy Carman earlier.'

'Great,' Sam said. 'He's on the committee, by the way. Evie too.'

'He told me.'

'I have to go. I'll see you at the next committee meeting.'

Gabe touched her arm. The lightest most fleeting touch. Then he drew back and folded his arms as if he was ashamed of making physical contact with her My God, she thought, this was going to be excruciating.

Gabe's expression was so serious, goosebumps popped out on her arms. 'I would pull out but I can't let people down now,' he said.

'That would make a change,' she muttered, desperate to get away.

Before he could stop her, Sam turned on her heel and headed towards the cottage. She heard Gabe calling to the driver, but didn't dare look round. Soon his voice was lost in the dull roar of the waves dragging at the shingle on the beach below the cottages and the cries of gulls high above her. Only when she was outside her garden gate, did she risk a glance behind her. There was no sign of Gabe, only the rear of the van disappearing between the gates of Clifftop House before they slid shut.

Chapter Eleven

'Are you all right, Sam?' Zennor asked. She was already home, putting fresh fleece in the pig palace when Sam walked into the sitting room.

She collapsed down on the sofa. 'Why wouldn't I be?' she replied, more sharply than she'd meant, so she tempered it with a smile. Gabe was back, like a spectre – only a living, breathing, vibrant spectre who'd turned her life upside down again and brought so many memories tumbling back.

She had tried to calm down before walking inside. The shock after so long had rattled her far more than she'd expected, but she didn't want to bring her raging emotions into the house. She really wanted to put things into perspective for Zennor's sake as much as her own, but it was harder than she'd anticipated.

'You're all red in the face and you look as if you're ready to murder someone. Even your hair means business.' Zennor pulled off the Marigolds.

'What?' One hand instinctively went to her new haircut. 'Oh. My hair . . . yes . . .'

'Makes you look professional. Scarily professional.'

'Thanks,' said Sam. Trust Zennor to make her smile even after an encounter like the one she'd just had. She decided to come clean. 'I . . . um . . . I saw Gabe on my way up here.'

Zennor dropped the gloves onto the bag of bedding. 'Oh my God. Not at Clifftop House? He really is moving in, then?'

'Yes. I drove his removal van up to the gates.' She finally allowed herself a grim smile at the memory of the driver's face before bracing herself for her sister's reaction.

Zennor squealed in horror. 'What the actual fuck? I didn't see you come past?'

'That's because we didn't. The driver got stuck on Stippy Stappy Corner, so I took the scenic route behind the garages. I expect he and Gabe are wondering how they're going to get back out right now.'

Zennor gasped. 'You're wicked,' she said, but her eyes were gleaming. 'Bet the van is stuck forever.' She sighed. 'Oh God, I can't stand the idea of Gabe living *next door* to us.'

Sam affected a shrug. 'I really don't care.'

'You *do* care, Sam. No matter what you say about Gabe.' Zennor sat next to Sam and Gareth ran into her lap and let out a series of high-pitched squeaks. 'Oh my God, Gareth is chirping! That means he's excited and happy.' She nuzzled Gareth's fur.

'I'm glad someone is . . . and you're right. I care very much about Gabe coming back here. I thought I'd prepared myself for seeing him again, but I obviously haven't.'

Zennor stroked the pig as she searched Sam's face. 'How did he look? Like he does on the telly?'

Sam stopped. How had Gabe looked? Gorgeous, sexy. That dark black hair, his olive skin. He was carrying a little more weight than when she'd last seen him, but so was she. He'd been lean to the point of skinny even in his early twenties, probably because he'd shot up to over six feet in his late teens. His shoulders and chest had broadened and the grey T-shirt he'd been wearing had showed off his upper arms perfectly. Cooking could be hard physical work, as she well knew, and Gabe clearly hadn't let himself over indulge despite being surrounded by gourmet food.

She shrugged. 'I didn't take too much notice. I was driving the van.'

Zennor frowned. She probably didn't believe a word. She started to interrogate Sam: 'So, you didn't notice him or *speak* to him?'

'Not much. I had no reason to once I'd parked the van outside the gates.'

'So, you just said "hi" and "bye" and left?'

'I said I'd see him at the next committee meeting. What else could I say?'

'Oh, I dunno. How about "why did you shop our brother to the police and ruin his life?" That would have been a start.'

'I could have said that, I guess, but the van driver was there. Zen, I . . . have so much I could say to him that actually I'm not going to say *any* of it. I'm going to be professional and polite and have the absolute minimum possible to do with him. Chloe knows we were a thing once and you know how helpful she is: she's already offered to deal with him on a day-to-day basis. She fancies him anyway.'

'Urgh.' Zennor wrinkled her nose. 'She obviously doesn't know him!'

'Now, come on. He hasn't done anything to her family, has he? As far as I know, he's never done the same to anyone else. It's a personal thing between him and us.'

'I expect everyone thinks he's a hero for coming back to "save" the festival,' Zennor said, then stuck her tongue out like she used to when presented with a plate containing the tiniest hint of a green vegetable. Ironic, now she was a vegetarian, thought Sam, and had to smile.

'Why are you smiling?' Zennor asked.

'Nothing. You being so protective. I thought that was my role as big sister.'

'It was once. Not now, I'm all grown up.' Zennor hugged her. 'Shall I make the drinks? I've got a lentil curry out of the freezer ready for the oven. We can have some couscous salad with it. Won't take five minutes to rustle up.'

Sam stretched out and sighed. It was true that food was comforting. Like their mother, she and Zennor had always enjoyed cooking and nurturing the rest of the family. And, however cheesy, it didn't really matter what was put on the table when it was served with love. 'Sounds delicious. Thanks, Zen,' she said, adding a smile to show how much she appreciated coming home after a long day at work to a meal that had been provided by someone else.

With Zennor rustling around the kitchen, Sam tried to zone out, intent on practising the mindfulness that Zennor herself was into. However, today's encounter with Gabe had been too momentous to banish from her mind, no matter how often she tried to 're-centre'.

Gabe's appearance had been like a flood tide, bringing the flotsam and jetsam of her past life with it.

She closed her eyes, listening to the sound of Zennor gently humming against the occasional chink of pots and cupboard doors opening. She thought back to the days when Zennor used to refuse anything even resembling a plant.

That was back in the day when their mother had been alive. Their mum had brought the three children up on her own after their father had decided to leave the lot of them and go live in Brazil with a dancer he'd met in a dodgy club. At least that was where he said he was going. He simply vanished off the face of the earth as far as his family were concerned. However, Roz made the best of it.

It had been a devastating blow when Roz had been killed in a road accident when Sam was nineteen, Zennor was fourteen and Ryan twenty-one. It wasn't easy to get social services to agree that Zennor could stay with Sam and Ryan. Sam was a trainee baker at the time while Ryan had got his first job on the trawler. Not that he kept it for long. He decided that a life at sea wasn't for him and left to work in a bookies in Penzance before moving to his 'management position' in the arcade.

That's really when all the trouble started; Sam was now convinced that Ryan had never really come to terms with their mum's sudden death. It was only after she died that Ryan's 'issues' came to a head and it all blew up.

Sam had started going out with Gabe six months before

Roz died, though she'd had her eye on him for far longer, of course. She'd noticed him when it seemed other girls didn't know he existed. The serious, intense boy in the chip shop, who served up the meals with barely a smile. Like he was there as a penance. She now knew why. Gabe adored his parents, but felt under pressure to take over the business, when his dreams lay in going to university.

The irony was that in the end, he'd set aside his academic studies to train as a chef. It had obviously worked out, judging by the fact he'd rented Clifftop House, and by the customised Range Rover Sam had glimpsed through the gates – not to mention the two restaurants he owned in London. Now it appeared he was launching his takeover of Porthmellow. What if his rental of Clifftop House wasn't only temporary and he intended to move in permanently? Surely not? Sam shuddered inwardly. Well, she'd find out soon enough and she'd just have to deal with it.

'Here you go.'

Sam opened her eyes to find Zennor standing over her with a large pink gin with strawberries in it. 'Dinner's in the oven. You weren't asleep, were you?'

'No. I am a bit knackered though. I went into Stargazey early this morning as we had a big order for a festival.'

'You work too hard.'

'I've no choice. Who's going to pay the bills? Not that you don't contribute your fair share. I didn't mean that,' Sam added hastily, accepting the drink from Zennor. It was a huge relief that she, Zennor and Ryan all jointly inherited the cottage after their mum's death, so there was no rent, but there were still all the other usual bills to pay, not to mention food – and gin, which right now, felt like an essential.

She couldn't deny she was tired though. The festival was a major commitment on top of the business and she had to admit that Gabe's reappearance had been on her mind at night, and she'd lost sleep over it.

She decided to actively switch focus onto Zennor's problems, both work-related and Ben-related, since Sam knew that the two were intertwined.

'Thanks for sorting out the new festival marketing stuff so fast. Was Ben OK with making all the changes?'

'Oh, he was fine. You know Ben.' Zennor sipped her cocktail. 'He doesn't say much. He prefers to get on with things in his own way.'

Sam did know, but she also worried about Ben. He was helpful and hardworking and never moaned or blew his own trumpet. Sam thought he was too quiet and that it would be far too easy to take him for granted. Zennor was a chatterbox and not afraid to say how she felt but they were both quirky souls so perhaps that's how they'd ended up in business together and it seemed to work. She and Ben even dressed a little like each other with their his and hers Doc Martens. They might have been twins and perhaps that was the key: they were too content with being surrogate brother and sister to be boyfriend and girlfriend. Sam knew Zennor had harboured hopes of something more but perhaps she'd decided their friendship was too precious to risk.

'Are you both . . . OK?'

'OK?' Zennor scrunched up her nose. 'Is this going to turn

108

into a birds and the bees talk, because if it is, you're a bit too late and Mum got there first a long time ago.'

Sam laughed, but cringed inwardly. 'Not the birds and bees. It's only that . . . well, I've been so wrapped up in the festival and now this Gabe thing, that I've probably not been the best big sister lately.'

'You've always been wrapped up in the Gabe thing.'

Sam opened her mouth to protest, but Zennor cut in. 'Only joking. Partly. I do like Ben. A lot, but as you know he's shown no sign of wanting to be anything but mates.'

'Is he gay?'

Zennor sprayed pink gin everywhere. 'No. I mean. Oh God, I have asked myself that many many times, because we've known each other so long, but I don't think so. He's had a few girlfriends over the years.' She wrinkled her nose. 'His sister told me he'd been out with a couple of women, but no one lately. I sometimes wonder if he's asexual.'

'Wow. Is anyone asexual?'

'Apparently. I googled it. You can be.'

'Life would be less complicated,' said Sam.

'I'm not sure,' said Zennor. 'I wonder if he's just terrified of me. I think he might see me as sexual predator . . . I think we'll just go on being friends until we're as old as Troy and Evie. We'll probably be riding to the bingo together in our buggies one day.'

Sam laughed but couldn't think of a single reply that revealed that yes, actually, Zennor might well be right. Maybe Ben was terrified of Zennor in a sexual way, but if so, there was absolutely nothing she could do about it.

They tucked into their meal. Sam found herself having to force down each morsel even though it was delicious. Despite all her resolutions, she couldn't stop thinking about her earlier encounter with Gabe. Zennor had asked the wrong question. It hadn't been the way that Gabe had *looked* that had disturbed Sam so much. It had been the way he'd made her *feel*.

Chapter Twelve

'So, what do you think, Mr Mathias?'

The estate agent's voice lifted hopefully as Gabe studied the deserted interior of the Net Loft. He'd arranged a viewing of the restaurant. It was a sad sight, with dated pine tables and chairs stacked at one end and fading menus scattered on the cracked tiles. He'd arranged to view the place one afternoon with the same agent who'd rented Clifftop House to him. The agent was younger than him and her accent wasn't Cornish. She probably had no idea of his history in the town, which was refreshing.

'It could be an incredible venue,' she said brightly. 'And a very lucrative one with your name behind it. You must have already studied the books but, of course, it could be so much more. Porthmellow really is on the way up as a foodie destination, especially since the festival has become nationally known.'

Gabe contented himself with a polite smile and a noncommittal 'mmm' before returning his attention to the surroundings, trying to see beyond the abandoned fixtures of a failed business. The high-beamed ceiling had a mezzanine at one end. The building had had a variety of purposes over the years and really had once been an old Net Loft. In those days it would have been used for boat building, storing sails and pilchard nets. The stone walls and high-beamed ceiling had immense character and the mezzanine could be a wonderful place for private dining and parties.

The canny agent must have detected a glint in his eye.

'Any time you want another viewing, just let me know,' she said. 'How's Clifftop House, by the way? Have you settled in? Do you know how long you might be staying? Your PA said you wanted it for three months.'

'I like to keep my options open,' said Gabe. 'I'm not sure.'

The agent looked crestfallen. Maybe she'd hoped he would buy Clifftop House when the lease was up.

Her phone rang out and she gave an apologetic smile. 'Oh, excuse me. I'm so sorry but I must take this urgent call. I won't be a moment.'

She went outside to have her conversation, leaving Gabe alone in the restaurant and giving him a chance to have a look around on his own. He climbed the open staircase to the mezzanine, which had a small bar at one end and doors onto a small balcony at the other. Gabe unbolted the doors and stepped onto the balcony, the fresh breeze and sharp sea scent immediately refreshing him after the stuffiness of the interior. From here, he could see the busy life of the harbour, watching the boats coming and going, listening to the shouts of the fishermen landing their catches and the gulls squabbling for scraps. He spotted a few familiar faces from his past. A man with a pot belly hauling nets who'd taunted him when he was younger . . . and an older lady with a wheeled trolley chatting to two other pensioners. Gabe smiled. Evie Carman. Some people were always a pleasure to see.

Gabe went back inside and locked the balcony doors, turning his attention to the mezzanine area and the floor space below. Yes. He could really make something of this place. With some TLC, he could refurbish the dining areas and balcony so people could enjoy cocktails overlooking the harbour on sunny evenings. In his imagination, chatter and laughter filled the space and delicious aromas wafted from the kitchens.

Ideas for the menu invaded his mind. Seafood dishes, of course, and local meats and produce. He could take on young chefs from the area and give them a chance just as he had been given in his first chef job in Cornwall.

On a fine evening such as this, it was all too easy to imagine putting down fresh roots in Porthmellow.

Was that why he'd asked Suzy to rent a place for way longer than he actually needed?

He hadn't done anything so impulsive for a long time and he still didn't quite know why he'd leased the place way beyond the time of the festival. He didn't need to be in Porthmellow for all that time. His curiosity to see the town again – and most of all, to see Sam – had got the better of all rational sensible thinking. After their first encounter he was beginning to regret his decision. It was far too big and, yes, far too close to Sam for comfort.

And yet . . . when he lay awake in the ornate four-poster in the turret bedroom, he could not help feeling a thrill that she was so close to him, just a minute away, lying in her own room at Wavecrest Cottage. Memories of holding her close, of summer evenings in the dunes, in his old car flooded back to him when he heard the waves crashing on the rocks below the house and the gulls crying as they wheeled around the tower. He'd missed those sounds, the tang of ozone on the air. He'd missed Porthmellow, missed Sam.

Now she was so near and yet so far away . . .

'Mr Mathias?'

'Yes?' He turned, with an energy coursing through him that must have shown on his face because the agent was beaming. 'I see you've been having a better look around. Wonderful space, isn't it? Especially for someone with your vision.'

'It has potential, yes,' he said politely.

'So, you're definitely interested in taking up the lease or putting in an offer on the premises?'

Gabe smiled. 'I need to think about it. I'm seeing a couple of other places while I'm down here.' That was a lie, but he didn't feel guilty. The agent was good at her job and probably guessed he was bluffing.

'That's no more than we'd expect. I'll give you some time to think it over and be in touch soon, if that's OK?'

'Fine,' Gabe said.

After she'd answered a couple of his questions, she left him outside the restaurant. Gabe lingered on the quayside for a moment, and out of the corner of his eye he spotted a couple of young women nudging each other and holding up their phones. The podgy trawlerman had also clocked him and nudged his fisherman mate.

Ignoring them, Gabe decided to head back to the house, half hoping and half dreading to bump into Sam on the way. He hadn't got more than a few steps when Evie Carman called out to him. She wheeled her roller towards him so Gabe hurried over himself. It was clear she now struggled with her mobility and he was saddened by that. She'd always been such a bundle of energy.

'Oh, my word. It's you. You're so big!' She threw her arms around him.

He couldn't help but laugh as he returned the hug, momentarily transported back to the days when he was a teenager. Despite her arthritis, her smile and the glint in her eye were undimmed.

'You're handsome too,' she said, her Cornish accent as strong as ever.

'You'll embarrass me,' said Gabe, noting faces watching them.

'Oh, go on. You can live with it. How're you doing?'

'Good. How about you?'

She waved a hand. 'Up and down. I'm waiting for a new knee. In fact, I saw your parents when I went for one of my hospital appointments last month.'

'My great-uncle's had his knee done a few months ago,' said Gabe. 'He's back in his garden again now.' He chatted to Evie about his family for a few more minutes before she changed tack.

'Have you seen Sam yet?' she asked.

Gabe couldn't lie to Evie. Like many of the older residents of the village, she knew that he'd reported Ryan to the police, though not the full story. She hadn't openly judged him or blamed him for it at the time. They hadn't talked of it beyond Evie telling him she was sad when he and Sam split and he told her he planned to leave town. Gabe thought he owed her an honest answer now.

'I bumped into Sam a couple of days ago.'

Evie winced. 'I'm guessing it was awkward for you both?'

Again, he couldn't lie but he was growing uncomfortable with the line of questioning. 'It wasn't all sweetness and light, no.'

Evie patted his arm. 'I'll admit I was surprised to see you back at all after you and Sam broke up. That was a great shame, if you don't mind me saying, although I could understand why. You and Sam seemed made for each other until that business with Ryan. Can't have been easy, making a decision like you did.'

'You can say that again.' Gabe was now eager to get away, much as he liked Evie.

'I'm sure there's some folk who might be funny with you but you ignore them. The only people whose business it is, is you and Sam and Zennor.'

Gabe felt twitchy with discomfort. Evie was spot-on in her assessment but he still didn't enjoy hearing it.

She sighed. 'Well, you'll have to learn to rub along together, if you're going to be involved in the festival and spend any time here. You've rented Clifftop House, so I hear, so you must be staying a while?'

Gabe rolled his eyes. 'Is it all over the town already?'

'What do you think?' Evie shook her head. 'This is Porthmellow, Gabriel. Nothing stays a secret for long. Anyway, I must be getting on, I've got a doctor's appointment. I'll see you around town again soon, I hope?'

'Definitely,' said Gabe.

With a quick peck on his cheek, Evie walked off, the roller rattling on the cobbles. Gabe was left with mixed feelings. Evie had treated him no differently than she ever had and he found that strangely comforting, but she'd also reminded him that helping out with the festival would be far from plain sailing.

Chapter Thirteen

@**Porthmellowchick:** @CornishMaid OMG. I saw #Gabe outside the old Net Loft. You will not believe what I found out about him. Will DM u. #summerfestival #gossip

At the Wednesday committee meeting, Chloe took some teabags from the cupboard in the Institute kitchenette and popped a carton of milk next to the coffee pot, along with a packet of local shortbread from the small supermarket in town. They didn't normally have biscuits at the meeting, but it seemed like a special occasion, so why not? It had given her a small moment of pleasure to choose them, in the absence of anyone else to treat.

She'd been determined to be first after turning up late to the previous one because of her phone call with Hannah. Chloe hadn't tried to contact Hannah again, no matter how tempting it had been. Even though she'd been sure that

Hannah had only broken off the call because Jordan had come into the room. Hannah had plenty of opportunities to get in contact if she really wanted to and for now, Chloe had to sit on her hands and wait for her to make the move.

And now she had another thing to worry about: her birthday party.

She'd been delighted when everyone had seemed so enthusiastic. Right up until the moment Drew had made the joke about the Big Four O.

Chloe had a sense of humour, she didn't mind the banter. That wasn't the problem.

The thing was that she wasn't going to be forty. She'd passed that milestone a long time ago.

No, her party was to celebrate being fifty.

So why, oh, why hadn't she just come out and said it?

She didn't want to entertain the possibility it had something to do with Drew. For a start, he was *so* not her type. So not Fraser . . . yet she'd found Drew stealing into her mind more often lately. She'd even dreamed about him; something involving being alone with him at sea, and having to take the helm while he climbed up the rigging. Goodness knows what *that* was supposed to signify. Chloe wasn't going to share that. Maybe she liked him because he was so different to Fraser, and not only in looks. Fraser was driven and ambitious, totally at home in the boardroom cut and thrust. Drew was quiet, passionate about the sailing, but ambitious only in as far as it might help the trust. Other than that, he was focused on his family, his music and the festival.

Fraser would say he was a loser. He'd already told her that

all the drop-outs and people who didn't want to handle 'real life' had buggered off to Cornwall. He'd implied that Chloe was running away too . . . which was partly true. Porthmellow had drawn her because of its happy memories, whereas everywhere she went in Surrey only reminded her of the life she'd lost. People tried to be kind, but the house she'd shared with Fraser, the places they'd been and people they'd known had too much association with their old lives as a couple. She'd preferred to make a clean break.

It sounded good, a clean break: faster to heal, easier to recover from, less pain . . .

But it hadn't been like that, and while she was making new friends and had thrown herself into community life, she still missed the 'old days' and found herself sometimes asking 'what if?'

What if Fraser hadn't left and the divorce hadn't affected Hannah so badly? Or if even now, he decided they should give their marriage another try. What if her daughter hadn't met Jordan Rees? What if Chloe could bring herself to be honest with her new friends about her family problems? And now, by not being honest about her age, she'd added another little white lie to the mix.

As for her new friends in Porthmellow, did she know them well enough to share the truth about Hannah and Fraser? After all, they had their own problems and busy lives, from Evie's arthritis to Sam's hectic life, and Drew . . . he seemed like a good listener but Chloe didn't feel she really knew him.

No, she wouldn't burden anyone else with her worries.

She opened the shortbread and found a chipped plate on which to lay out the biscuits.

Drew was first into the meeting room where Chloe had already put out her files on the table.

'You're keen,' he said cheerfully.

'I pushed the boat out and got a packet of shortbread from the deli in the village. My treat,' she added hastily. 'I wonder when we'll get to meet Gabe Mathias. Someone saw him in the post office yesterday. He's moved into Clifftop House.'

Troy tutted from the doorway. 'Big draughty place that. Too grand for one man, especially Gabe. Time was, he was a skinny little bugger. I once told him off for tombstoning in the harbour.'

'Really?' Chloe asked.

'Yeah. You know what the local kids are like. They all do it, but Gabe had to go one better and try and jump off the top wall outside the Smuggler's.'

'Oh God, you're joking! That has to be thirty feet above the harbour.'

'No joke. There's a fence to stop people now, but if I remember correctly, Gabe was dared to by a bunch of lads. I tried to stop him and they called me an old fart and jumped anyway. Cut his chin and hurt his guts with the impact. Stupid little devil.'

'He looks like he might have been a daredevil,' Chloe said.

'He was at times,' Drew chipped in. 'He took a lot of stick from the local lads, for working in the fish shop, I suppose, and, sadly, his background – not all the kids, only a few morons.'

'You and Sam must have stuck up for him.'

'Oh, we did.'

'Hello!' Sam walked in, laden down with her laptop and a box. 'Who stuck up for who?'

Chloe wondered how long Sam had been listening and felt guilty.

'We were telling Chloe about Gabe jumping from the pub into the harbour,' said Drew.

Sam frowned. 'Did he? I don't remember that.'

'You were one of the people screaming at him not to,' said Drew.

'Was I? Oh – oh, maybe I do now. He stayed under a while, and he'd cut his face. It looked far worse than it was.'

'He was badly bruised too.'

'Really? I can remember the blood, but not the bruises.' Sam put her box on the table. 'You'd have to ask him about it yourself. By the way, Ben and Zennor can't make it tonight. They have a big rush job on to design some leaflets for a theme park near Looe. They send their apologies.'

'No need. They give up so much of their spare time anyway, real work has to come first.' Chloe bracketed her fingers around the 'real'.

'I'll fill them in on anything important and obviously share the minutes. Are you OK to take them this evening?'

'Fine,' Chloe said breezily, relieved that Sam didn't seem to have taken offence that she'd been talked about. 'Absolutely fine.'

'I'll start making the drinks. What are you having?' Drew said.

'I don't mind making them,' Chloe said.

'Let's both do it,' Drew said with a firmness that surprised Chloe, then he laughed. 'You can supervise me.'

So Chloe joined him. Neither of them needed help making three hot drinks, but she knew Drew wanted to be helpful. He started to tell her about his latest charter; a group of insurance executives from Berkshire, who were cocky as hell until they realised what hard work it was crewing a traditional sailing vessel, and that it was slightly different to taking out a mate's motor cruiser for a jaunt on the Thames. Sam seemed intent on checking through the agenda and laying out copies around the table. Chloe thought she looked a bit tired, not surprising with all the work and stress of the festival, but then, Sam probably thought the same about her.

Once the tea was made and as it was only the four of them this evening, Sam kicked things off. Troy folded his arms and subsided back into his seat with an eye roll. Drew exchanged a glance with him, and a small smile before Sam started to talk about road closures, an issue that Troy had plenty to say about, as he was liaising with the harbour authority and local council. It seemed an odd choice, given that Troy's methods of diplomacy made Donald Trump look like a model of tact, however, Troy *did* know everyone. No one was offended by his plain speaking because he was rude to everyone. And anyway, no one else wanted to do it or had the time. The upshot was that the roads would be closed for the required period and the harbour authorities were reasonably happy with the arrangements. Chloe had rapidly learnt that 'reasonably happy' was a major victory as far as volunteer committees were concerned, so that was another problem that could be ticked off the list.

Sam ran quickly through a list of points, including car parking, first aid, liability insurance and the final tally of food stalls and exhibitors. Hearing the roll call made Chloe proud. As the festival had grown, more and more food and related businesses had clamoured to have a pitch and the stalls had now spread around all three sides of the harbour to the small recreation field and several side streets. Over fifty were booked, offering something to tempt all taste buds including a champagne oyster bar, locally distilled gins, ice creams, cupcakes, pulled pork, Cornish sushi, vegan treats, Thai curries, Spanish paella, cream teas, craft beers tent . . . Even reading the list of stallholders and exhibitors was enough to make Chloe's mouth water.

By nine o'clock, the sun had set and a blue twilight had crept over Porthmellow. Chloe glimpsed the lights of streetlamps and cafés shimmering on the harbour. The meeting had lasted two hours and she sensed people twitching in their chairs.

Troy tapped his watch and said in a mock polite voice: 'I hate to mention it, folks, as we're all having such a lovely time, but are we ever going to get to the pub?'

Soon after, they had packed up and headed for the bar of the Smuggler's. Their route took them past the Net Loft and as they passed by, a man and a woman walked out. The woman – a local estate agent – locked the door and shook hands with the man who Chloe instantly recognised as Gabe Mathias.

Drew broke into a smile and as for Sam . . . Chloe might have been imagining it or did her face blanch?

Troy wasn't so shy. 'Well, well,' he called to Gabe. 'Hello there, again.'

Chapter Fourteen

S am could have sworn her heart stopped momentarily as
Gabe walked over to them.

'Looking at expanding your empire?' Troy said.

Sam cringed but Gabe had a good-humoured smile on his
face. 'As a matter of fact, I was taking another look at the Net
Loft.' He glanced at Sam. 'But nothing's decided yet.'

Another look. The word struck Sam immediately as had
the handshake between the agent and Gabe. So, the rumours
that he was interested in buying a restaurant in Porthmellow
were absolutely true, thought Sam.

'Are you on your way to the pub?' Gabe asked.

'Why? Are you thinking of buying us all a round? I haven't
forgotten you owe me money.' Troy chortled.

Sam winced again, dismayed at Troy's invitation. 'I expect
Gabe's too busy,' she said.

'Not that busy, and I'm happy to pay my dues. If you don't

mind me joining you, I'll get the first round in.' Gabe flung a smile at Sam.

'That would be lovely. We can get to know each other better,' Chloe chirped up.

'Come on then,' Gabe added amiably. 'Good to see you again, mate. Looking forward to catching up.'

Drew shook hands with Gabe warmly. 'Good to see you back, Gabe.'

'How are you, mate?' said Gabe.

Drew laughed. 'Good. I don't need to ask you how you're doing.'

Gabe smiled. 'Looks can be deceiving.' He nodded to Sam. 'Hi, Sam.'

Sam tried to speak, eventually she had to cough then managed a 'Hi' before introducing Chloe: 'This is Chloe Farrow who you've been dealing with.'

'Chloe, hi. Good to meet you, finally,' Gabe said, stepping forward to shake her hand.

Sam had to bite her lip as they walked the short distance to the Smuggler's and into the beamed bar. It wasn't super busy, but Sam was sure that heads turned in their direction. Some people nudged each other, others, Sam could tell, were straining to listen. One bloke curled his lip and turned his back flagrantly. Sam wanted to sink through the pub bench.

'I think we should buy Gabe a drink, as he's volunteered to help us out for free,' Chloe said with a giggle.

'No need to do that,' said Gabe good-naturedly.

'No *need*, but we'd like to,' Sam said, feeling she should be taking the lead and at least acting as if she was unperturbed by Gabe's reappearance. After all he was helping out the festival for free and she ought to be friendly to him, in public at least. 'I'm sure we can all club together to buy you a pint.' She managed to smile as she said it, but she probably held Gabe's gaze a nanosecond too long.

Troy pulled a face. 'Speak for yourselves. I'm an old age pensioner.'

'I'll get this lot. Your turn next,' Gabe said to Sam.

Sam cursed herself. She already felt that every word she said, every look, betrayed her feelings about Gabe. She felt like she was walking around naked – emotionally speaking – and that Gabe, her mates, even the other customers in the pub could see her disbelief and anger – not to mention the physical attraction that made her shivery with lust.

As Gabe waited at the bar with Drew, she couldn't help but admire the breadth of his shoulders under his soft check shirt and – God help her – his firm bum in his faded jeans. The years hadn't only added a few pounds of muscle to his physique, but also a self-assurance and quiet charisma that held her spellbound. He was still very much Gabe, winding up Troy gently and sharing a joke with Drew. Judging by the giddy look on Chloe's face, he'd certainly succeeded in winning her over.

They returned with the drinks and Gabe slotted into the end of the booth next to Chloe. While pretending to be interested in Drew and Troy's conversation about fishing quotas, Sam couldn't help listening in on the conversation between Chloe and Gabe. After some initial chat about how the festival plans were progressing, Gabe started telling Chloe about some

127

of the chefs he'd had to put up with when he was working as a junior in the kitchen of a very expensive hotel. One head chef had thrown a heavy pan at him that had missed and knocked the brand-new extractor system off the wall, costing the restaurant thousands.

'The hotelier wasn't very happy. Not long afterwards, the guy got the sack for telling one of the guests he had the brain of a gnat and the manners of a warthog. The guest was a restaurant critic for one of the big papers.'

'Ouch!' said Chloe. 'Do chefs still behave like that? I know they can be divas and to be honest some of our events customers can be pretty rude, though no one's resorted to actual violence yet. Not on my watch, anyway.'

'A few still do get away with murder; it's such a high-pressure environment in a top kitchen – or any food service place – but word gets around. Most top chefs realise they've got to manage their staff properly. Anyway, there is karma in the world.'

'How?'

'I got his job.' Gabe became more serious. 'And I changed the whole culture of the workplace.'

'Wow. I'm very glad to hear it. What did you do?'

'I started throwing knives at people instead.'

'What?' Chloe exclaimed.

Sam burst out laughing before realising she wasn't meant to react as she wasn't listening to the conversation, and she definitely wasn't supposed to be taken in by Gabe's charm. It was difficult not to giggle because Chloe had realised a split second too late that Gabe was having her on. Sam noticed his Cornish accent had already thickened since being back in his hometown.

'You . . . you devil!' Chloe burst out, finally realising she'd been led up the garden path.

Gabe was all smiles. 'Seriously, I took three of the staff from that hotel with me when I started up my first restaurant. Two are now senior people in my own business and the other has opened her own restaurant in Ireland and is still a good mate. You don't have to be a bastard to gain respect and get on in this business. Tough and savvy, but not an absolute shit, excuse my language. Mind you, you also have to be prepared to rub people up the wrong way from time to time. As my grandad said: you're not a fifty-pound note, Gabe, not everyone's going to like you.' He grinned.

'Was that your grandad Chris?' Sam couldn't help asking, picturing a silver-haired old guy with a bristling moustache who occasionally used to turn up to the chip shop. She wasn't surprised that Gabe had stood up to the bullying chef or that he'd given his mates a job when he had the chance. Apart from that one act involving Ryan, he was a generous and compassionate man, there was no denying it, which was partly why he'd always stood out for her.

Gabe nodded.

'How is your grandad these days?' she asked him.

'OK. Ninety-three now. Still misses my gran. He's moved in with my auntie Leia in St Austell. Not too mobile, but he's enjoying life.'

'I liked him,' said Sam. 'I was very sorry to hear your gran had died.'

'Me too. She was a formidable woman. It was my nan who was the real energy behind the chip shop business. Grandad was at a loss when they all had to move here to live with my great uncle and auntie during the war in Cyprus . . . My nan always spoke well of you,' said Gabe.

'That's a real compliment from your nan,' Sam said, and she meant it.

'Yes, she was never afraid to be honest,' Gabe said. His voice was soft and there was genuine warmth in his rich brown eyes. Sam felt herself thaw a little. No matter what had passed between them, she had to admit that success didn't seem to have gone to his head. He still loved his family and was proud of his roots. She realised that obviously he must have been back in the area many times to visit his extended family and she'd never known it. A pang of regret struck her, surprising her with its sharp edge. She'd lost a lot of time . . . time they could have been together, maybe even had a family . . . if Gabe hadn't caused such pain to her own family, of course. That thought snapped her back to reality and she fell silent.

After a while, Sam went to get another round in and when she returned, Troy started up a conversation about hull maintenance with Drew. Chloe and Gabe were talking about food – a subject much closer to Sam's heart. They thanked her for the drinks.

'I was just telling Gabe how much I loved his recipe for Scotch Eggs. I hope that doesn't sound too fangirly,' she said. Sam hid a smile, as Gabe laughed. No wonder Chloe seemed smitten with him. He could have melted chocolate with one glance.

'You know, I have more messages and reaction to that recipe than any other. Ironic when it's a family staple, but I think it's easy to make and tasty. Family comfort food.'

'My mother's mother passed down some of her recipes and we— I still make them when I need some comfort food. Have you heard of Egg Foo Yung and *zong zi*?'

'The Egg Foo Yung yes, the *zong zi* I don't think so,' said Gabe.

'*Zong zi* is a traditional dish. A sort of glutinous rice wrapped in a bamboo leaf in the shape of a pyramid. I've made it sound awful but it's gorgeous. And *jiaozi* too.'

'Are those the little dumplings?'

'Yes. We always made them at home and ate them especially at Chinese New Year. The whole family would come together to make them. All of us.' She smiled at a memory. 'You could always tell the ones I made. They'd be super collapsed and messy unlike the ones my mum makes and my grandmother's. Theirs were like a pro's.'

'They sound delicious,' said Gabe. 'Especially the Egg Foo Yung.'

'Oh, it's still one of my mum's favourites,' said Chloe, clearly smitten with Gabe. Sam thought she could hardly take her eyes off him. Neither could Sam, although she was trying to listen politely to the conversation while sipping her drink.

'The *zong zi* sounds like a delicious combination, Chloe,' Sam said, finally deciding to enter the conversation.

'It's nothing unusual in London, but slightly rarer down here.' Chloe laughed. 'A bit like me . . . My mum's from Hong Kong and both my grandparents were born there. They all

131

moved here in the nineteen-fifties. Mum met my father when she was working for a law firm in Cardiff. Hence the Welsh-Chinese genes. I heard your grandparents came over to Porthmellow from Cyprus . . .'

'They took a big leap of faith in moving here,' Gabe said.

'Everyone's made me very welcome here so far. Especially the committee.' Chloe glanced at Sam.

'Who wouldn't?' Sam said. 'We're very happy to have you.'

'Sam's right. You deserve a warm welcome . . .' Gabe gave a small grimace.

'Your family didn't find that when they arrived?' asked Chloe.

'Times change. Ask Evie Carman. But any stick I took was less to do with my heritage and more to do with me wearing a hair net and having a chip on my shoulder. If you'll excuse the pun. Wearing an apron with The Cod Father on it wasn't the best way to look cool.'

Chloe laughed. 'I'm sure you scrubbed up. I've heard about the time you did a Tom Daley from the Smuggler's terrace.'

'Is it enshrined in local legend?' He winced. 'Yes, I did and I regretted it. Look, I still have the scar.' He pointed to a faint white line in the cleft in his chin.

'Every hero needs a scar,' Chloe teased, then seemed to regret it.

Sam caught his eye, intrigued at his response.

Gabe hesitated, as if he was choosing his words carefully. 'Believe me, I have *never* been a hero. Not in Porthmellow, anyway.'

Chloe laughed but Sam couldn't miss the faint tang of bitterness in his comment.

Chloe was still oblivious. 'At least you are a local. I don't think I'll ever be considered local if I live here until I'm a hundred and twenty.'

'That's true. Unless you can trace your roots back to St Piran, you'll always be an outsider in Porthmellow. Won't you, Sam?'

'I can't trace my roots back further than the war so I guess that makes me an outsider too. Chloe's definitely part of the community now, whether she likes it or not. It's like *Hotel California* down here. You know, that thing about never being able to leave,' Sam said.

'I'm not sure I ever want to leave.' Chloe exchanged a glance with Gabe before taking refuge in her G&T.

Sam was certain Gabe had been flirting with her friend, and who could blame him? Chloe was a gorgeous, lovely person. Sure she was a little older than him but seven or eight years was nothing in the scheme of things. She herself had no claim on him so why shouldn't Gabe and Chloe get together if that was what they wanted?

Sam's stomach clenched. No matter how many times she told herself that she wouldn't mind if they did start seeing each other, she did mind. Even thinking about it bothered her.

Hearing their laughter, Drew and Troy joined the conversation again. Drew joked about her new hair style again and she batted him playfully on the arm and he touched her arm in return. It was just the closeness of two old friends but for the first time ever, Sam was conscious of what Gabe might make of it, then annoyed at herself for even caring.

She slid a look at him to see if he'd noticed but he only had eyes for Chloe.

'If you're around,' she was saying, 'I'm having a get-together at the Crow's Nest a couple of weeks before the festival on Saturday the fifteenth. It's nothing big or fancy, just having the committee round for a few drinks and something to eat . . . erm, if it's not a busman's holiday.'

Interest sparked in his eyes then he frowned. 'I don't mind. Hmm. If that's June the fifteenth, I *should* be down here. I had planned to go back to London for a while in the meantime because I've got a lot on . . . I'd need to check my diary but as it's a special occasion, I'll try my hardest to be there.'

Chloe beamed. 'Oh. OK. Well, that would be great if you could make it.'

'Do you have my direct mobile number? You've been dealing with my office and my PA until now. It would probably be easier if I gave it to you?'

'Good plan,' said Chloe.

'In fact, maybe it's a good idea if all the committee members have my number, just in case it's needed,' he added.

'I can forward it to everyone to save time,' said Chloe. 'If that's OK?'

'Thanks.'

Moments later, everyone's phones beeped as Gabe's number reached the WhatsApp group. Like the rest of the committee, Sam took out her phone to check she'd received the message but resisted the urge to add it to her contacts there and then. Drew and Chloe helped a grumbling Troy add it to his address book. Sam might have been imagining it, but did Gabe try to catch her eye while the others were looking at their screens.

'Well, that's done,' said Chloe. 'Now, I need to warn you, Gabe, that everyone's bringing something to eat to the party. You don't have to, of course.'

'What? Not cook something? You try and stop me. What sort of thing?'

'Anything really, though we have some main courses and dessert covered . . .'

'How about some mezze slash tapas to go with the drinks beforehand?' he suggested.

'That sounds perfect. Around seven-ish? Hopefully if the weather's fine we can have drinks on the balcony.'

'I'll look forward to it. Is it a special occasion?'

Chloe pulled a face. 'In a way. Landmark birthday.'

'I'm not going to guess,' Gabe said.

Troy's bushy brows lifted. 'It's the big four-oh but you don't look it, Chloe, maid.'

Gabe's eyes widened. 'You look great. Must be all the healthy food.'

Chloe seemed flustered and looked down at her hands. Wow, thought Sam, she really *did* have a crush on Gabe.

Chloe laughed. 'It's very flattering of you to say so, but believe me I feel a lot older than forty sometimes.'

Eventually, Troy left to go home to Evie. Gabe and Chloe still had half-full glasses in front of them.

Sam yawned ostentatiously. 'Whoops. Sorry. It's been a long day and I need my beauty sleep.'

'Me too,' said Drew and drained the last of his glass. 'Walk you as far as the post office.'

'Go on then, you never know who's lurking in Porthmellow after dark.'

Drew smiled, but Gabe and Chloe were engrossed in something on Chloe's phone and talking about Chinese food.

Drew and Sam exchanged an eye roll.

'Come on. Let's leave them to it,' she whispered to Drew, her stomach swirling with unpleasant feelings that were suspiciously like jealousy.

They left the pub and Sam kept up the chirpy banter until she and Drew parted in the town. Only then did she allow herself to dwell on Chloe and Gabe, their shoulders almost touching, laughing over their phones.

It had only been her second meeting with him and it had been difficult but she'd coped. She had no choice because like it or not, he was now a key part of the festival and would be up and down to Porthmellow on a regular basis. He certainly seemed keen on Chloe.

Sam reminded herself she really couldn't have her cake – or her Gabe – and eat it. She'd made it very clear that she wasn't interested in reviving her relationship with him, so why shouldn't he enjoy a little light flirtation with Chloe – or even a whole lot more?

Chapter Fifteen

@**moaningoldminnie:** Absolutely dreading this festival. More tourists, noise and pollution not to mention parking issues. To think how peaceful Porthmellow used to be . . .
@**pastyman:** LOL. Shit innit?
@**moaningoldminnie:** There's no need for foul language but I do tend to agree with you.
@**Metallicafan:** My Sacha hates it.
@**Porthmellowchick:** @Cornishmaid #eyeroll #Hatersgonnahate #trolls

After their meeting in the pub, Sam heard from Chloe that Gabe had indeed returned to London as he'd hinted. Apparently, he'd said he'd be back 'soon' but given no precise date. Sam felt a mixture of relief and disappointment when he'd left, but at least it meant she had no distractions to pull her mind away from the myriad jobs on her list now the festival was only four weeks away.

Over the next fortnight, she noticed the pre-festival buzz building day by day throughout Porthmellow along with the committee's workload. There were performers to contact with schedules, there was information to send out to the stall-holders, endless paperwork about hygiene, insurance and safety, plus a string of minor glitches to iron out – and for Sam, this was all on top of running Stargazey Pie.

She and Stefan were setting up for a Friday evening shift on the quay while the town brass band was playing. It was a fine, clear late May evening: the hint of summer in the air, but still cool enough to lure hungry visitors and locals needing to warm up with a tasty pie while they listened to the band and walked around the harbour.

Sam loved the Friday night gig. The band drew locals and visitors from far and wide and the quayside was packed with people singing and clapping along to the medley of popular hits and Cornish folk songs. Some of the Porthmellow fishermen's choir had also turned up and an impromptu concert was taking place on the cobbles before the band came on. Pints in hand, they sang along to the band, attracting a delighted crowd.

Once the night kicked off in earnest, she was doing a roaring trade. With the pies made and chilled down the day before, all she and Stefan had to do was warm them up in the oven. With rich, herby aromas wafting out of the van, heads turned in their direction as people sniffed the air, tempted by the delicious smells, and the queues lengthened.

Woof! Woof! WOOOOOFFFFFF!

Barks cut through the air right in the middle of the band's rendition of the 'Flora Dance'.

People switched their attention away from the band towards a woman being dragged along the quayside by a large Rottweiler.

Stefan turned around from the chiller, which he was filling with cans. 'What's that racket?' he asked.

'Three guesses.'

Sacha's leash strained as Bryony trotted to keep up with him while he scrabbled along the cobbles, snorting in ecstasy. It wasn't only the punters who'd been lured by the scent of juicy chicken and rare breeds beef. To Sacha, the Stargazey Pie van must have seemed like oysters, Belgian truffles and the finest champagne all rolled into one and served off Aidan Turner's bare chest.

'He-eel, Sacha!' Bryony's bellow was now as loud as the music. 'Now, don't be such a silly boy!' Sacha strained in his studded harness and drool sprayed from his jowls. Customers backed away while Bryony tried to restrain Sacha from leaping on the van like the hound of the Baskervilles. Although Bryony's current ensemble of a T-shirt with a red hand with the middle finger extended saying '*You have a problem with me? Take it up with my dog*' might have had something to do with their reluctance to order a pie.

Sam kept a close eye on Sacha while handing over two Cornish beef and onion pies to a couple. She didn't blame the dog for fancying a pie. Sam smiled and said thanks to her customers, aware of Bryony lurking even closer, while Sacha snorted like Gnasher. She couldn't help thinking that Bryony was as much of a hazard as – but far less charismatic than – Dennis the Menace.

The couple left and there was a momentary lull for Sam while a group of young guys relayed their orders to Stefan.

'Your van drives my Sacha mad,' said Bryony as if it was Sam's fault.

'Sacha has good taste,' said Sam, wishing Bryony would at least lower her voice to foghorn levels.

'Why d'you have to create such a smell?'

'It's an aroma and that's normal because we're using *delicious and fresh local ingredients*,' said Sam, raising her own voice in the hope it would reach the wavering customers.

'Sacha, get down!' Sam flinched as Sacha broke free and almost got his gigantic paws on the counter top. He let out a snuffle that sounded like a herd of pigs. The customers pulled faces at each other and hurried off in the direction of the pub.

Sam loved animals and knew Sacha wasn't really a threat, just over enthusiastic, but some of her customers were wary of dogs. 'Bryony, can you keep Sacha away from the food service area, please?'

'Three chicken and bacon, two beef, and a Yarg and onion!' Stefan called, even louder than Bryony. Sam flinched but Stefan was grinning.

'I can't stand around here all day. I've got a training class to run. Come on, Sacha, darling.'

Bryony marched off, tugging a reluctant Sacha who peered back at the van before being brought to heel.

'Shall I start a fund for her moving expenses?' Stefan whispered while Sam unloaded the pies from the oven. Despite Sacha's appearance, they were doing a roaring trade, and she needed to restock as soon as she'd put the current batch into paper bags for the customers.

'I'll stump up the lot,' said Sam.

'What's wrong with her?'

'I don't know . . . She hates the festival, but she also seems to have a personal grudge against me.'

'I doubt it. That woman must have been born sucking on a bottle of vinegar.'

'Her mum and dad were both lovely people, but they moved out of Porthmellow when Bryony went to college. She stayed on and rented the flat over the dog grooming parlour. Anyway, I can't worry about her now.' Sam handed the pies to Stefan and spun round to face a group of teenagers in shorts and T-shirts. 'Hello, you look like you need warming up. What can I get you?'

The sun had sunk behind the top terraces by the time the band had finished and the temperature had dropped too. There were still a good number of people milling around or sitting at the pub tables with pints but custom had dropped off sharply.

'Shall we close up?' Stefan asked. 'It's been a good gig.'

Sam nodded happily. In the end, Bryony and Sacha hadn't dented trade too much. Sam loved it when they sent dozens of happy customers on their way. It made the hard work worthwhile. 'I think so. We're almost out of stock anyway, which is always a good thing.'

Stefan started to cash up and Sam was about to switch off the oven when a new customer jogged up to the counter.

'Not too late, am I?' Gabe grinned up at her.

He was the last person she expected to see because as far as she knew, he was still in London, and part of her had feared he might not come back at all until much closer to the festival. Her stomach did an annoying flip and a ripple of excitement ran through her. That shivery feeling was just as strong as it had been when she was nineteen. Sam swallowed. His temporary absence from Porthmellow had done nothing to damp down her fires, only stoked them higher.

'I thought you were still in London,' she said.

'My business finished earlier than I expected so I got a last-minute flight. Can't seem to stay away, I guess.'

Sam flashed him an apologetic smile. 'We were just about to close.'

He frowned. 'That's a shame. I was longing to try one of your delicious pies.'

'I would have thought you'd be into fine dining,' she said, trying to steady her racing heart. How did he still have the power to make her feel like this? Why couldn't she stop her reaction?

'Sometimes, but I like simple food too. Have you forgotten I was brought up in a fish and chip shop?' He smiled again. His black hair flopped over his eyes and he pushed it away. Was that a thread of grey at the temples? Wow . . . Sam thought, but she must look different too. Did she look older to him? His eyes were still the deep brown she'd always loved. Like a peaty pool on the moorland behind Porthmellow, she

142

used to think in her dreamier days, a pool with the sunlight glinting off it.

Or perhaps the colour was more like the glossy gravy in her beef pies. She stifled a giggle. How things had changed. Age and bitter experience had brought the Greek god that used to be Gabe crashing down to earth for her, no matter how he made her feel.

'What's up?' he said, a line appearing between his eyebrows. 'Do I have spinach on my teeth or something?'

'No.' Sam assumed her best customer-friendly voice. 'We do have a couple of pies left. There's a roast chicken in a scrumpy sauce or a Cornish beef with red wine and mushrooms.'

Gabe rubbed his chin. 'Both sound extremely tempting. What do you recommend, chef?'

Was he simply joking or seriously taking the mickey? Sam wasn't sure.

'We-ell . . . the chicken is free range, of course, from a supplier near Mullion. The scrumpy is a top-quality apple cider from the Tywardene farm, which I think you'll know, having drunk enough of it when you were younger.' She smirked and Gabe nodded.

'The beef is local too and farmed to the highest standards,' she went on. 'The mushrooms came from a market garden that recently opened on the north coast and the red wine – well, I have to confess – the wine was from the St Erth cash and carry, but it did win a gold medal in some sommelier awards.'

He considered for a moment. 'Hmm. What about the pastry cases themselves?'

'Hand crimped and baked in specially commissioned tins to my own secret recipe. I could divulge it to you, but then I'd have to kill you,' she said, and couldn't resist throwing him a beaming smile.

'That won't be necessary. Sorry to disappoint you.' His mouth turned down in mock horror.

Sam wanted to laugh but kept it to a smile. In the good old days, Gabe had made her laugh a lot and feel so good about herself, she could have taken on the world.

He sighed. 'They sound so delicious, I can't decide so I'll have both.'

'Great. That means I have no leftover stock. That'll be seven pounds ninety-eight, please.'

He pulled a note from his wallet. 'Here's a tenner. Keep the change.'

'Thanks. I'll add it to the festival fund,' Sam said pointedly.

Gabe shrugged. 'Whatever.'

After popping the pies in the trademark stiff paper bag and handing them over, Sam put Gabe's cash in the mini till. Instead of leaving to eat his pies at home as she'd expected, he hung around, blowing on the crust of the chicken one and taking tiny bites as it cooled. Stefan raised a significant eyebrow, but Sam refused to react to her colleague's knowing looks. She tried to busy herself by cleaning down the surfaces while Gabe tucked into the pie.

She'd convinced herself she didn't care what he thought of her – but she *did* care what he thought of her cooking. She was dying to know his opinion, but she would rather have run naked through the Festival Marquee than ask. So, she

144

took off her apron and climbed out of the van, ready to lock up. Gabe was eating the second of the pies while talking to the landlord of the Smuggler's Tavern.

Stefan shut the door and joined her. 'I'll finish up and take the van back to the unit,' he said.

'Thanks, but I can't leave you to pack and hitch up all on your own,' she said, with half an eye on Gabe still gassing to the publican. Sam couldn't hear him above the choir singing 'Lamorna'.

'Just take the offer for once. You look knackered anyway.'

Sam gasped. 'Wow. Thanks, Stef! I love you too.'

'Don't be distracted by any handsome strangers on your way home,' Stefan whispered in her ear, pointing his finger at Gabe.

Before the rude word was out of Sam's mouth, he'd jogged away towards the pick-up, jingling the keys in the air.

Sam lingered, tucking into a squashed rejected pie that she'd set aside for her own dinner. With their soaring, haunting voices, the choir made her hair stand on end. The accents and songs were so Cornish they captured what she loved about Porthmellow. She caught sight of Gabe, standing apart, a pint in his hand. She saw his mouth move. He was singing along with everyone else.

So now I'll sing to you, 'Tis about a maiden fair . . .

It was a famous folk song about a roving husband. Sam had heard it a hundred times before, but she imagined his deep voice as he sang, a little out of tune, but lusty and strong. You can take the man out of Porthmellow . . .

She and Gabe still had that connection, no matter how

145

hard she tried to deny it. They had Porthmellow in their veins, they had their love of food, the need to nurture and care for their family, friends and neighbours . . . Why had he ruined all that? Could the rift between them ever be healed?

Shaking her head at such fanciful notions, Sam left the van and walked down the quayside to take the coastal path route up to her cottage, finishing her supper.

She couldn't help thinking of Stefan's joke about Gabe . . . Except Gabe was no stranger, and that was part of the problem. At one time she'd known every inch of his tanned, toned body. He certainly knew every inch of hers.

She thought how Gabe had always supported her before and after they'd started dating. She'd lost count of the times he'd brought round supper for the three Lovells from the chip shop after their mum had died. Kebabs and salad, plaice and chips. Hardly gourmet cuisine and not that healthy, but devoured by three hungry young people. Without the Mathias family's help and that of their neighbours, the Lovells might have gone hungry because some nights in the early days, Sam had been too exhausted by grief and work to cook a proper meal.

Somehow, the days passed by and the family emerged from their grief. Zennor was showing a flair for art and design at school and even Ryan seemed to be settling into his job on a fishing trawler. Sam had thought the darkest times were behind her and brighter days might lie ahead, at least for her and Gabe.

How wrong she'd been.

She reached the cheery sign near the end of the outer

harbour that said 'danger of death in high waves' and turned left towards the coastal path that led up the cliff, when boot-steps rang out on the cobbles behind her.

'Sam. Hang on a mo.'

She stopped but didn't turn round because she recognised Gabe's voice. She waited for him to catch up.

'I'm going your way,' he said.

She hated the way her heart beat a little faster when she heard his voice. Surely, she should be over all that by now?

'Frank from the pub trapped me, but I wanted to tell you how much I enjoyed the pies,' he said.

'Oh, really?'

'Yes, really. They're very good.'

'I know,' said Sam. 'That's why Stargazey's doing so well. It might not be a multi-million-pound business, but I'm proud of it.' Even as she spoke, she felt bad. Gabe probably hadn't meant to be patronising, but she was tired and crabby – and most of all she was confused about the power he still had to make her feel as if she'd been lifted up and carried along on the air like thistledown.

'I can see you're proud of what you've achieved. You should be. It's not easy making a success of a food business, especially with what you had to deal with.'

'Don't patronise me, *please*.' The moment the words were out, she wished them unsaid. She wished everything unsaid, and Gabe gone. She'd spent so long getting over him and now he was back, he'd ripped open old wounds within days.

She walked off up the path, but Gabe followed her.

Within seconds, the path steepened into steps and both

of them were breathing heavily as they climbed. 'St-stop f-following me,' she said.

'Why sh-should I? I l-live up here.'

Sam spun round, gazing down at him a couple of steps below. '*Live* here? You count renting the biggest place in the village as living here?'

'The size of the house has nothing to do with how long I might stay.'

'Why did you have to rent *that* place?'

'A, because my PA assured me it was practically the only thing available on a short lease at short notice. And B, because I thought "why not?" Is that OK with you?'

'No, it's not OK.'

'Why not? Too grand for you, is it?'

'No, too close.'

She set off again, taking the steps on the twisty path two at a time. Soon she was gasping for breath, but at least she'd shaken Gabe off.

When she finally paused again, leaning on a handrail at the top of the hill, he was out of sight. She couldn't even hear him. However, she also couldn't afford to hang around too long so she forced herself onwards and reached the top of the cliff where the gradient levelled off. It was high tide and the waves crashed on the beach seventy feet below, buffeting the sea wall that had been built to protect the clifftop homes from tumbling into the sea.

'Sam!'

She gasped. Gabe was clambering over the edge of the cliff a few yards ahead. It wasn't possible . . . but yes, he'd actually climbed up a crumbling section of path that had been undercut by the sea in the previous year's storms. It was a quicker and more direct route but also happened to be incredibly risky as no one knew when parts of it might collapse. Her pulse rate ramped up even though he was safe now.

He hauled himself up onto the grass.

'What the hell are you doing?' Sam asked him.

'I took a short cut,' he said, getting to his feet.

'Around the cliff fall?'

'If you mean the old coast path. Yeah. Why not?'

'Didn't you see the signs? It's unstable and dangerous since the winter storms. Parts of it are liable to collapse and someone slipped last month down there and had to be rescued by the coastguard. They could have died, which is why it's been diverted further back from the cliff edge and up here.'

Gabe brushed mud off his jeans. 'I thought it was a risk worth taking.'

'You're barking mad.'

Gabe grinned. 'You already knew that.'

She shook her head. 'You could have fallen onto the beach . . . hurt yourself or worse.'

'Is that what you want to happen?'

She imagined him lying on the rocks at the base of the cliff, his body broken and suppressed a shudder. 'If you think that, you really are out of your mind.'

'Sometimes I wonder, the reception I'm getting from you.'

'Are you surprised?'

'Yes. No.' He raked his fingers through his hair, all trace of bravado gone. 'I don't know what to think, but I do know we need to talk and we need to do it now. I can't function around you, or in Porthmellow with the way things are between us.'

'Right. OK. So, you want us to be friends?' Sam asked.

'I want us to be on friendly terms, especially with the festival coming up, but first I want us to be honest with each other.'

She blurted out her response. 'Right I see. Honest . . . So, Gabe, is this you trying to use the festival to blackmail me into forgiving you?'

He shook his head in disbelief. 'Jesus, Sam. You've got me so wrong.'

Sam was fired up now, her emotions bubbling dangerously close to the surface. 'What exactly have I got wrong? Was I wrong or did you turn in my vulnerable brother to the police when he desperately needed help? I know he did wrong but surely you could have turned a blind eye, if not for Ryan then for me. I thought you loved me?'

'I did love you! How can you not understand that?' he said, his voice raised – which was a mistake. Her blue touchpaper was well and truly lit.

'Actually, I did get you wrong. I was wrong to trust you and to love you. Wrong to think you felt the same way about me. Wrong to even waste a moment of my time talking to you now. I'm very grateful you stepped in to help the festival. I would never have asked you, but you know that. For the sake of the town and all the people who've worked hard to make the place a success while you've been away, I'll be civil and polite and smile. But don't think for a moment I've forgotten that your – I don't know – misplaced sense of duty, of loyalty, of fuck knows what, made you report my brother

150

to the police and ruined his life. I haven't seen him since he left prison. That's been over eleven years. I know he's alive somewhere, but that's all I know. He won't speak to me, he doesn't want anything to do with the family and it's all your fault!'

She was trembling. She hadn't meant to unleash so much anger on him, but it had been bottled up for so many years.

'Have you finished?' His tone had plunged from warm to glacial.

'I . . . I . . . I've said more than I ever meant to,' Sam stuttered.

'I can see that.' His eyes blazed with annoyance.

She cursed herself. She'd really let him have it with both barrels and now she regretted it. 'Look. I'm sorry. I shouldn't have lashed out like I did, but it's been tough over the past few years and I never expected to see you again.'

'Me neither, but now we are here and you've raised the subject, I wish I could make you understand.' His voice brimmed with indignation. 'I thought I was doing the right thing for you, for the town and for Ryan. I haven't changed that view and if that upsets you, I'm not going to lie to you. You don't deserve it.'

'Gabe. This isn't a great idea. We're not going to get anywhere with this conversation and you know what? I'm knackered. I just want to go home.'

She hurried ahead, but she hadn't got far when something white flashed across her vision. She cried out and clutched her face.

'Sam!'

151

Gabe shouted, but Sam felt sick. The pain in her face was sharp and brought tears to her eyes briefly. When she took her hand away, her fingers were scarlet with fresh blood. She saw the white laminated poster a few feet away with a telltale red smear on it. A gust had whipped the plastic sheet up, it had frisbeed through the air and the sharp corner had caught her face.

It wasn't the only one that was loose. The tears cleared and she saw dozens of other posters tumbling around, flying over the cliff and out to sea. They'd been fastened with cable ties so someone must have deliberately cut or unclipped them from signs and lampposts and scattered them around.

Gabe caught up with her. 'What's happened? Jesus, there's blood all over your top.'

'It's nothing. A poster caught my cheek.' She bent down to pick up the bloodied poster.

'Hey, wait. Let me look at you.'

Sam wished him gone. There were tears as well as blood on her face and she didn't want him to see her like this. 'I need to get rid of this mess. There are posters all over the place. They could hurt someone else.'

'Let's sort your face out first.' He stepped closer, pulling a cotton hanky from his pocket. 'It's clean,' he said. 'Keep still.'

Sam bit back any further protest. Better let him get it over with and then she could leave. Besides, would it really hurt to let someone – even Gabe – show some concern, just for a few moments?

Sam closed her eyes and felt soft cotton against her cheek. The contact stung a little but she refused to flinch.

'It probably looks worse than it is, but it could have been very nasty if it had been any closer to your eye. Hold the hanky on it while I collect the rest of the posters up.'

She opened her eyelids, and held the cotton against her face. He'd backed off but his eyes were full of concern. Tears sprung afresh and she fought them away. All the old feelings swept over her: he'd always looked out for her and the family. Always been ready to support her, which is why his betrayal of Ryan had knocked her sideways. It still did. There had to be a better reason than simply that he felt it was his duty to the town. Gabe had never been self-righteous.

Realising she couldn't gather up posters while stemming the blood, Sam had to agree to let him do it. She managed a smile for him. 'Thanks.'

Gabe scooted around like a Wimbledon ball boy, gathering posters swirling in the low-level eddies. He collected around a dozen and brought them back. She smiled again and then stopped at the realisation her heart was softening – had already softened – towards him. Yet nothing had changed between them . . . had it?

He searched her eyes, still full of concern. 'How's the face?'

'As ugly as ever.'

'That makes two of us.' He held out the posters. Being laminated, they were almost impossible to rip up, but whoever had done it had a good go at destroying them.

'They've spent a lot of time on this. Look, they cut through the cable ties and judging by the muddy boot prints, they've stamped on them too. Do you know why anyone would do something like this?'

'Are there any paw prints on them?' said Sam.

'Paws? Not sure.' Gabe peered at the poster. 'Why?'

'I was joking, but only partly. Bryony Cronk hates the festival, even though she makes a packet from the extra custom.'

'Bryony?' He frowned then nodded. 'Oh yeah. The metal fan who lived over the dog grooming parlour . . . Hmm, she *was* pretty feisty if I remember but I wouldn't have thought this was her style.'

'Who knows? You think you know people and then . . .' Sam let the sentence hang but Gabe either didn't notice or ignored her barb.

'I'm sorry about this. Your face and the posters. There are some sick people around.'

'I'm used to glitches, though I'll admit, malicious vandalism isn't that common.' She pulled the hanky from her face and winced. 'Has it stopped bleeding?'

Gabe peered at her cheek. He was so close, she could smell him. Something vanilla-y, which could have been aftershave or actual vanilla. She tried not to breathe it in too deeply.

'Looks like it. It was only a small cut, but I bet it stings. You can keep the hanky.'

She had to smile, despite the bizarre situation. 'Thanks.'

He held out the posters. 'Do you want these?'

'Thanks,' she repeated numbly as she shoved them in her bag. 'I'll take them home. I'd better go.'

Leaving him behind, Sam made a beeline for the cottage determined not to look back. His hanky felt so soft against her skin and it smelled like him. Earthy and masculine yet sweet too. Would she ever get over fancying him? Would she ever stop caring what he thought – or caring about him? She couldn't help suspecting that despite his protests, he was thinking about moving here anyway, and the festival was a coincidence, that he'd done it for her. But why this year? What had really triggered his return after all this time?

Chapter Sixteen

S am considered washing and drying the hanky, but in the end, a few days later, she had thrown it away. She'd never be able to get it clean and it was sentimental to keep a reminder of Gabe.

She'd had a hectic time on top of her festival duties partly because her pick-up had been in for a service. Stefan had towed the mobile van to a music event with his old Jeep and done a run to the cash and carry for some basic supplies but Sam still missed her own transport.

Despite being so busy, her mind kept returning to her cliff-top encounter with Gabe. She was still regretting saying as much as she had to him and showing her emotions so clearly. She'd lashed out again – the opposite of the 'civil' relationship she'd claimed she wanted. But perhaps that had been a hopeless dream from the start. She and Gabe had once been passionately in love, so perhaps there could and never would be any middle ground for them. Perhaps it had to be either love or hate. As for her fleeting idea that Gabe might have an ulterior motive in coming back . . . well, why would he?

All these questions bubbled away in the cauldron at the back of her mind as she walked home after another busy day in the kitchen on a fine June evening. The nights were long and the days rapidly warming up. She'd been working in a tank top and shorts but even so, the heat of the ovens and the physical effort was enough to make her long for a nice cool bath and one of Zennor's strawberry daiquiris at the cottage. The whoops of teenagers leaping into the harbour carried on the still air as she walked up the lane home. Summer was well and truly on its way, and hopefully, with a bit of luck, they'd have a fine day for the festival. She was almost at the cottage when she saw Evie Carman pushing her roller down the hill towards her.

'Sam!'

Evie speeded up, scooting along at a pace Sam wouldn't have thought possible. She could see Evie was wincing with every step. Trying to rush down the hill on swollen knees must have been agony so Sam ran over to meet her.

'S-sam. S-so glad I've seen y-you.'

'What's up, Evie? Is everything all right?'

'No. Not really. It's him. Troy. The silly old fool's done something bad to his shoulder and now he's in agony. He won't thank me for telling you, but I'm desperate, to be honest. I think he needs to go to A&E.'

'Oh no. poor Troy . . .'

'He hurt it pulling down a box of books. I told him not to do it but he won't listen to me.'

Sam followed Evie into the Carmans' neat cottage. Her

heart sank as she glimpsed Troy through the doorway from the hall, slumped on the sofa. He was holding his elbow, his mouth set in a hard line.

'Argh. I'm so sorry, Evie, but my pick-up's in for a service. The garage had to keep it in because they're waiting for a new part.'

Evie's face fell. 'Oh dear. I wish I could drive but I don't trust my knees these days and our car's not insured for anyone else. Don't worry. I'll get one of the neighbours to help. Trouble is one side's on holiday and the other's got three kids she won't be able to leave. Our son's in the army and our daughter's not answering her phone. I don't know where she is.'

'Don't worry. I'll find someone,' Sam said.

'Oh, what about Gabe? I saw him drive into the big house not ten minutes ago.'

Sam nodded. The last thing she wanted was to approach Gabe, but the Carmans needed help and any ill feeling between her and Gabe came a definite second.

'I'll phone him and see if he can help.'

'You still have his number, then?' said Evie as Sam pulled out her phone.

'I have his *new* number. Because of the festival,' she added hastily.

Evie smiled. 'Oh, it's almost worth Troy doing his shoulder in to get a lift with him. Isn't it, Troy?'

Troy pulled a face. He did look very grey. 'It's only a sprain, I keep telling you, Evie! Owwww!'

'Oh Troy! Anyone can see you're in agony and you need to go to hospital.'

Troy didn't argue further and Sam was growing very worried about his ashen face. The pain and shock could be potentially serious at his age.

Evie huffed. 'I hope he hasn't dislocated it. Or broken it.'

'Shouldn't we call the paramedics in case he has?'

'No! I'm not having them here. It's not bad enough to get them out,' Troy yelled down the hall.

'Pipe down, Troy. Sam's trying to call Gabe.'

Sam found Gabe's number and dialled, and he answered within a couple of rings. As she'd expected, he said he was on his way, and minutes later, he was helping Troy into the back of his car. Sam unfolded Evie's little step stool and placed it by the rear door so Evie could get into the car more easily.

'Will you come with us, my bird?' Evie asked as she fastened her seat belt. 'It might be a long wait and Gabe will need the company.'

'I don't . . .' Sam handed over Evie's walking stick. She really didn't *need* to go, but Evie sounded desperate. The Carmans hadn't seen Gabe for a long time and probably wanted a more familiar face with them.

'I know it's a lot of trouble, but I'd like someone to talk to and I'm sure Gabe would. Wouldn't you?' Evie's expression was as pleading as Sacha's.

Troy groaned as Gabe fastened his seat belt for him. Evie reached around the head rest and patted his shoulder. 'Soon get you sorted, love.'

Looking up at Evie's worried face, she made her mind up. 'Of course, I'll come and wait with you until your daughter arrives. Then Gabe can bring me straight home,' she said, exchanging a glance with Gabe. She folded up the stool and jumped in beside Evie.

It took half an hour to reach the hospital in Penzance, then as long again for Troy to be booked in and sucked into the process.

At one point, Troy had to use the bathroom so Gabe waited outside to make sure he was OK and Evie took her chance to tell Sam how concerned she was.

'I worry about him, he's always on the go either for the harbour committee, or the festival or at home. I thought he was having a heart attack for a few seconds, the way he yelled out and held his arm, but then I realised he'd pulled the damn box on top of himself. I told him not to put it up so high or to get my little folding stool. At least we got to drive here in style and comfort. I feel like the queen in the back of Gabe's car.'

'Me too,' said Sam, 'but don't tell Gabe.'

'I won't.' Evie sighed. 'It really is a shame you two split up. I know the business with Ryan put an end to it but as I've said, I always thought you were perfect for each other. Must have been awkward for Gabe when he had to report him to the police. He had no choice, though, eventually most people in the village realised that, though I can understand how you must feel differently. It was a long time ago . . .'

Sam shifted in her seat. Even though she liked and respected Evie, she didn't want to hear these uncomfortable comments, especially as she disagreed with some of them so strongly.

But before Sam could frame a neutral reply, Evie saved her and patted her hand. 'I'll shut up before I really put my foot in it. I can see it's still raw. Oh, there's Troy.' Her face crumpled. 'I can't stand to see him in pain.'

'Nor me.' It was Sam's turn to squeeze Evie's hand. 'He'll soon be better; it can't be long now before he's seen.'

'I hope not. I know he's an awkward, crusty old sod but I do care for him.' She smiled. 'He'll kill me for saying this but do you know what he's named after?'

'No.' Sam leaned closer to Evie as Gabe helped Troy walk slowly back to the waiting area.

'He's named after Sergeant Troy from *Far From the Madding Crowd*. His mum read the book in school and fell for the character. Then, when the film came out, I had a crush on Terence Stamp – have you heard of him?'

'I think so. Wasn't he in *Priscilla, Queen of the Desert*?' Sam said, thinking of the outrageous elderly trans character in the movie. He was definitely a brilliant actor in that, but a sex symbol? She couldn't imagine it.

'Yes, but he was *beautiful* in *Far From the Madding Crowd*. Sex on legs. That scene where he gets his big sword out and charges at Julie Christie. Well . . .' Evie fanned herself. 'Then I met Troy at a dance and though he didn't really look like Terence much, the two sort of got fixed in my mind and that was it. Bang. We were married within the year . . . I don't know what I'd do without him.'

'Eh?' Troy said as he arrived back. He was breathing heavily and there were beads of perspiration on his forehead. For the first time, Sam thought he genuinely looked fragile, not the indefatigable committee member that she knew and loved.

'We were just saying, we hope you're called in soon because I can't stand any more of your moaning.'

Troy managed a cackle then groaned aloud. His face was grey.

'Oh Troy. Be careful.' Evie tutted good-humouredly, but she looked seriously worried.

'Mr Carman?'

'Thank God for that,' Evie said, picking up her stick as a nurse approached them.

The nurse led Troy and Evie to a treatment room, leaving Sam and Gabe alone together. She had noticed that all the time they were in the waiting room people stared at Gabe and sometimes the rest of them. Evie had loved it, whispering loudly that they were the centre of attention and 'hanging out with a celebrity chef'.

Sam hated being looked at, but Gabe smiled and joked with Evie at his own expense. Sam knew he was trying to cheer Evie up and distract her from Troy's pain, but she still didn't know how he coped with the fuss. Once the Carmans had left, a young guy with face tattoos like a Maori warrior asked for a selfie, but a nurse intervened and said it wasn't allowed and pointed out that 'patient and visitor privacy had to be respected'.

Sam popped outside briefly to answer a call about the festival and returned to find Gabe chatting to two delighted elderly ladies who said they were here because one of their friends had fallen off a garden trampoline at a ninetieth birthday party.

They left Gabe alone when Sam arrived back.

Gabe checked his emails while Sam flipped through a magazine. It was an NHS production about healthy living and advised people not to eat pastry or processed meat more than occasionally as a 'special' treat. She was finding it hard to concentrate. Another man, of around their own age, shuffled up the seats towards Gabe.

'Will you sign your autograph, mate? Me missus got your latest book. It's for her, really.'

Gabe smiled amiably. 'Sure, but I don't have any paper.'

'Here. This'll do.' The man plucked a leaflet from a rack and presented it to Gabe with a biro.

Sam saw Gabe trying not to laugh as he signed the flyer. The guy went off, grinning like Gabe had handed him a fifty-pound note.

When Sam could stand it no longer she whispered, 'What did you sign?'

'Your Guide to Sexual Health Services.'

Sam clamped her hand over her mouth. Gabe picked up a gossip magazine and started to leaf through it, but Sam could feel his body shaking next to her with the effort of trying not to laugh. It was funny, but it was also freaking her out sitting next to a 'celebrity'. She would have hated the mutterings, sly looks and open stares, though Gabe seemed to handle it well enough. She didn't think he enjoyed it, but it was something he'd learned to tolerate. It can't have come naturally to him as he'd never suffered fools when he was young and he must have to suffer a hell of a lot of them now.

'I need some air, but I don't want to go too far in case Troy and Evie need me,' she said.

'Go and get a coffee and stretch your legs,' said Gabe.

'Sure?'

'Would I have said so if I wasn't?' He shook his head and his eyes had that amused but kind look that had always driven her crazy. He knew her so well, even after all this time. She did need some air, but she was way too close to Gabe for comfort. She was finding herself smiling too often and enjoying being in his company way too much. She was on the verge of liking him. She was concerned about Troy and Evie, but still – how weird considering they were in a hospital – enjoying herself. She had to remind herself why it was dangerous to get too close to Gabe.

At the moment Sam stood up, Evie emerged, with Troy next to her. His arm was in a sling and he looked sheepish.

'Troy's dislocated his shoulder,' said Evie. 'They've given him some pain relief and put it back but it's very sore.'

'I had to have an X-ray,' said Troy. '*And* the nurse said it can be *extremely* painful.'

Evie rolled her eyes but patted his good arm. 'He has to rest it for a few days. The good news is that I got hold of our Gemma and she's on her way now. She'd been to a school play in Penzance and had her phone switched off.'

'That's a relief,' said Sam.

'Shall we wait with you until she gets here?' Gabe asked.

'Oh no. You've done more than enough. You two get off home to Porthmellow.'

'If you're sure?' said Sam, unwilling to leave Evie and Troy on their own.

Evie smiled warmly. 'More than sure. Go on. Gemma's only twenty minutes away and I'm sure you and Gabe have a lot to do.'

Reluctantly, Sam agreed and kissed Evie goodbye with a request that she keep her updated on Troy's condition.

'I'll be out in a minute,' said Gabe, handing over his keys to Sam.

'Oh. OK.' She assumed he was off to the gents' so she walked slowly to the car park. It was a big relief to know that Troy was OK. He'd clearly been in way more pain than he'd let on and Evie was worrying too. They might be an odd couple – Troy was odd, anyway, and Evie was lovely – but they were obviously devoted to each other and Evie's story about how Troy came by his name was priceless. Some stories did have happy endings, some people did stay together for – well as close to forever as humans were ever allowed.

She opened the Range Rover and climbed inside. Gabe's minute stretched to twenty and Sam checked her phone. Where had he got to?

Just as she was thinking of calling him, he jogged over the car park and opened the door. 'Sorry, I was longer than expected.'

'I thought you'd been admitted or something.'

'No. I was um . . . with the nurses.'

Sam raised an eyebrow.

'They wanted some selfies with me.'

'What? I thought they told that guy that he couldn't take pictures with patients?'

'There's one rule for the patients and one for staff. I agreed to donate some signed books and a meal at the new restaurant for the scanner appeal too.'

'Wow. You really are a hero,' Sam said sarcastically.

'In some quarters,' said Gabe, pushing the start button. The car purred into life. 'Let's go home.'

The irony of the word wasn't lost on Sam. *Home*. Gabe might have meant her home, or his former home, or the place he intended to settle in for however long. Whichever way, she knew she was going to have to get used to his continued presence and, more importantly, the way she *felt* about his presence. Neither of them said much as they drove towards Porthmellow along the road that skirted Mount's Bay. It was almost dark and St Michael's Mount was silhouetted against the indigo sky, with lights twinkling in the castle and in the tiny harbour at its base. Gabe pulled away gently as Sam peered out of the window.

He took the road through the centre of Marazion, it was late and there wasn't much traffic. The car moved slowly along the main street, with its shuttered cafés and shops, until it stopped at a pedestrian crossing to let half a dozen young guys across. They had obviously had a few, laughing and exchanging banter as they headed down a street on the near-side of the car towards a pub. One of them blew Sam a kiss and she rolled her eyes at him.

Once they were off the crossing, Gabe pulled away, but something caught Sam's eye and she twisted round. Her pulse rate shot up and her stomach knotted.

'Stop!' she shouted.

Gabe was driving past the central square now. 'Hey! What's the matter?'

She stabbed the window button and it slid down. She undid her seat belt and pushed her face through the open window. 'Wait!' The seat belt alarm started screeching.

166

'I can't stop here. There are people behind. Hang on.' Gabe pulled into a bus stop and she fumbled with the door. By now, the pub was a hundred yards behind them.

He put his hand on her arm, preventing her from getting out. 'For God's sake, wait. What's the matter?'

She tried to pull away. 'I just saw Ryan. Crossing the street. I'm sure it was him.'

His jaw dropped. 'Ryan? It can't be.'

'That guy who walked last over the crossing in the orange hoodie. It was the image of him.'

'I saw him, but his face didn't ring a bell. Mind you, I couldn't see that much of it.'

'The way he walked across in front of us. He had his hands shoved in his pockets, just like Ryan used to. He had red hair too. I'm sure it was him. I was sure . . .' Even as the words were out, doubts were creeping in that it really had been Ryan. It was just a fleeting glimpse under streetlights of a man in a hood, and yet there was *something*.

'My God.' He took his hand away. 'What are you going to do? I can't wait here. A bus could come along any time. Do you want me to park up and we'll go and look for him?'

Sam sank back in her seat. 'No. Yes. Arggh, I don't know. That guy was *so* much like him.'

'It has been ten years, Sam,' Gabe said softly.

'I'd know my own *brother*.' She closed her eyes and leaned back against the leather. Gabe's gentle tone had made her angry, but not at him. She hadn't meant to snap, but she was so shocked to see the guy, so sure in that split second that it had been her brother. 'I'm sorry. Maybe I was mistaken.'

'Maybe.'

'He had a beard, but he did look about the right age . . . and you know Ryan used to scrunch up his shoulders and shove his hands in his pockets when he was nervous or anxious?'

'Yeah, I remember. I'll turn around if you really want me to.'

Sam was torn. The man hadn't seemed part of the group even though he was with them. It was hard to explain, but she had a feeling he didn't know them that well. It *could* have been her brother, but it might also have been a random ginger bloke out for a drink with his mates. Besides, there was no reason whatsoever for Ryan to be back in Cornwall and *if* it had been him, surely Gabe would have recognised him too?

He laid his hand over hers again. 'Look. It's late. It's dark. I'm not saying it wasn't him, but why would he be here? If he was, why hasn't he been in contact?'

Everything he said made sense yet her skin still prickled with unease. 'Yes. You're right,' she said. She leaned back in her seat. 'I must be seeing things. I'm knackered.'

She closed her eyes, trying to shut out the sense of disappointment and the way she'd felt about Gabe touching her. She could still feel the warmth and weight of his hand over hers. It had been a long time since he'd touched her like that. It had felt good – right.

'I'm sorry,' he said.

She opened her eyes to find him staring ahead through the screen. His knuckles were white on the wheel.

'What for, exactly?' she said.

168

'Everything.'

'Everything?' What did that mean? Shopping Ryan or coming back to Porthmellow again and turning her life upside down? Or something else?

'I'll turn around and we'll look for him if you really want me to,' he said, his hand resting on the gear selector.

Sam shook her head. 'No. It probably wasn't him. You didn't recognise him, did you?'

'I had my eyes on the road so I couldn't say for sure.'

Sam let out a sigh. She was as tense as a wire. 'I'm tired and I just want to go home.'

'Good idea.' And with that, Gabe drove off. Sam sank back into the cocoon of the seat. It had been a hectic and emotional day, in a variety of ways. A day when she'd allowed herself to glimpse a time when she might forgive Gabe . . . or at least understand his reasons. If she scaled that hurdle, what might lie beyond for them? Happy years like Troy and Evie had enjoyed and still did?

She snuck a look at Gabe, intent on the road ahead, his fingers curved lightly around the leather wheel. He looked sexier than she'd ever seen him; no wonder he'd attracted so many admiring glances and attention in the hospital. And when he'd touched her, his skin had felt so good against her own. Deliciously warm . . . even such an innocent gesture had made sparks fly deep inside her body. Or was it only comfort she needed? Would any man do?

No. That was why she'd turned down offers of dates and why no relationship had lasted longer than a couple of months since Gabe had gone. She had to be honest with herself that her lack of a love life wasn't due to pressures of work or family duties or festival responsibilities, it was the shadow of Gabe, pure and simple.

Was that why she still hadn't forgiven him? Not because of what he'd done to Ryan but what he continued to do to her?

He caught her eye and smiled. Sam feigned a yawn and closed her eyes, resting her head against the head restraint again while her body told her it needed anything but sleep. She might be exhausted, but the thought of sharing her bed – any bed – with Gabe tonight, no matter what their differences, was more tempting than it had ever been. She had the feeling she only had to say a single word and he'd drive her straight through the gates of Clifftop House and there'd be no turning back.

'We're here,' he said.

She opened her eyes. Gabe was looking at her, his lips pressed firmly together. He'd stopped right outside Wavecrest Cottage.

'Oh. Right.' She unclipped her seat belt. 'I'll probably see you around.'

'Probably, although I've got some stuff to do in London so I might be away for a few days.'

'Oh, OK.' Sam tried to not sound disappointed even though she felt unaccountably dispirited by his answer. She opened the door and got out. 'Thanks for helping Troy and Evie.'

'It was no trouble.' His smile was fleeting and his eyes were quickly back on the road ahead as if he was eager to be gone.

Sam found herself torn between wanting to be out of his

sight and longing to stay, which was ridiculous. 'Bye, then.'

'Bye.'

She shut the door behind her and hurried straight into the cottage, listening to the sound of the Range Rover engine heading the short distance up the hill to Clifftop House.

Chapter Seventeen

Chloe loved Porthmellow in the evening sunlight, even if it did come with a 'breeze' that rattled your teeth. Walking along the quayside on her way back from her Zumba class to the Crow's Nest she passed the Tinners'. Locals and tourists mingled outside, sinking pints on the terrace.

The Zumba class had been fun and a relaxing break from work. It was a shame Sam hadn't been able to make it, but she'd had a shift in Stargazey. Thankfully, Chloe knew almost all of the other dancers by now and they always had a laugh, getting tangled up and bashing into each other. No one took the class that seriously, unlike some of the gym bunnies at her Surrey health club, which suited her because she had two left feet when it came to any kind of dancing.

In the weeks since, she'd thought about the after-meeting get-together in the pub many times. Sandwiched between two not unattractive younger guys, chatting with Sam and the other committee members, she'd really felt her spirits lifting.

Gabe had been funny and charming and while it *might* have been a professional persona, Chloe didn't think so. She could see exactly why Sam had fallen for him and thought it sad they'd split up.

Gabe was even taller than he looked on TV and it had to be said, way more good looking. He had thick dark hair and eyes the colour of burnt caramel. Yes, he was gorgeous, he made you want to look at him and listen to him . . . and yet, funnily enough even with a heart throb TV chef paying her attention, she was drawn just as much to Drew. She wondered what he'd think if he knew her real age . . . Argh. She was going to have to come clean, sooner or later. Either that or hide her birthday cards before the party.

'Hi there!'

Drew's shout came from somewhere nearby. Talk of the devil.

She glanced around her and he called again. With a smile, she peered over the quayside to find him looking up from the deck of the *Marisco*, a rope in his hand. Maybe he was lashing something down. He needed to, because the wind had risen very quickly while she'd been at Zumba.

'Hi!' she yelled, but her words were snatched away by the wind. He waved and she waved back, but left him to his work. The last thing she wanted was to get close to him while she was all hot and sweaty.

Chloe hurried home desperate for a shower, but some of the gusts were strong enough to take her breath away. A loud clatter made her jump. A few feet ahead, a metal pub table complete with parasol had been blown clean over. One of the fishermen picked it up, and was joined by a barman from the pub, who started to take down the other parasols. It wasn't easy, because the wind was flapping wildly as they wrestled with the canvas parasols.

Rattles and crashes rang out from all sides of the harbour as other loose items came rolling down the street: mostly cans and plastic coffee cups, but a wheelie bin had also crashed onto its side, spewing out rubbish that was immediately attacked by the gulls.

Overtopping the howls of the wind was the powerful roar of the surf breaking on the shingle to the right of the harbour. Waves slammed into the wall throwing up plumes of spray and foam and soaking the far quayside.

Chloe rescued a baby's blanket that had escaped from a buggy, which the mother wheeled towards her.

'Thanks!' said the mum, pulling her hair out of her eyes.

'Everything not nailed down is going to fly out of Porthmellow today,' said Chloe, her own eyes watering as she handed over the blanket. It felt soft between her fingers. The baby – no more than twelve months old – smiled and clutched it.

The mother peered over the handles and spoke to her child. 'Come on, Molly, we'd better get you home to bed before this wind gets any worse and blows us into the harbour.' She glanced up at Chloe and smiled.

'How old is she?' Chloe asked.

'She was one last weekend.'

'How lovely. My granddaughter will be a year in a few weeks' time.'

'They're such a handful, aren't they? This one has just found her feet.' The mother tickled her daughter under the chin. 'She can only do a few steps, but she's a demon at crawling and climbing the stairs. I swear my hair's grey already and I'm only twenty-six. You'll know that though, being a granny and a mum.' She looked happily at Chloe.

Chloe smiled back. 'Yes. They're tiring at this age . . .' She stopped. She wanted so much to talk about Ruby and share her experiences but she couldn't. Anything else she would say would be wishful thinking at best, and a total lie at worst.

The young mum sighed. 'Better get Molly home, then.'

'Bye,' Chloe muttered. Now the mother and baby were gone, Chloe resolved to hurry back to the Crow's Nest and steel herself to try again to contact Hannah. She was a few yards from the steps when a loud rip and a crash stopped her in her tracks. The noise was followed by shouts and the barman and fisherman running to the harbour. The large festival banner strung onto poles by the harbour had snapped clean out of its fastenings and was flapping wildly in the wind. One end dangled in the water but the other was still roped to the pole.

As the two men approached, there was a sharp snap and the other end broke free of the pole.

'Run!' The men dived for cover, and the banner just missed them. It sailed through the air, dragging a wheelie bin with it before dropping into the harbour. Chloe ran to the quayside to see it floating in the harbour and blocking the entrance a few feet from Drew's boat.

In seconds, Drew had climbed over the side of the *Marisco* and onto the small fishing boat berthed next to it. His feet were bare which meant – no, he *couldn't* be – but he was . . . slipping over the side of the boat into the water and swimming towards the banner. People started to gather around the harbour while Drew towed the huge plastic poster towards the slipway. Chloe jogged over to the crowd. There were shouts of 'be careful, mate' and two fishermen in wellies ran down to meet him. The banner must have been heavy, with its wet ropes and metal eyelets, but Drew managed to reach the slipway where the fishermen got hold of the end of it and dragged it onto the cobbles.

Drew emerged from the water, dripping wet but laughing.

Chloe heard the locals ask if he was OK. He grinned and one slapped him on the back.

'It's that there bloody Poldark,' said a grizzled fisherman.

Drew pushed his hair off his face and shook water off his arms.

Chloe was torn between worrying about what he might have swallowed in the mucky harbour water and admiring the way his shirt had stuck to his chest. OK. He was fit and strong and he compared very favourably with the 'helpers' on the ramp, one of whom still had a pint in his hand. What was wrong with her lately? Fangirling over Gabe and now ogling Drew? What would Fraser have thought? He'd have laughed and called Drew a 'yokel', probably. Fraser was suspicious of men who wore brown shoes with a suit, let alone anyone with a ponytail and an earring. Yes, Drew would have pushed every one of Fraser's 'drop-out' buttons . . . he pushed Chloe's buttons too, but in a very different way. Her wicked thoughts rapidly turned to concern as Drew was now shivering. Someone draped an old waterproof coat round his back and told him he was nuts. Chloe was inclined to agree.

She hurried over to him, careful of the slimy weed on the slipway. '*Are* you OK?' she asked. The wind was still gusting hard and Drew tugged the flapping mac around his T-shirt.

'A bit on the cool side but I'm fine.'

She shook her head. 'Why didn't you wait for someone to help fish out the banner?'

'I dunno. Impulse, I guess. I thought I'd dive in and get it before it could cause any more damage. It was blocking the entrance to the outer harbour and I wasn't totally sure it wouldn't sink, given the weight of the metal fastenings. Plus I couldn't be arsed to wait for all the fussing over 'ealth and safety and who was going to launch a boat etcetera, etcetera. Anyway, I used to jump into that harbour every night during the summer holidays. I know it like the back of my hand.'

'I suppose you are a grown-up. Allegedly.' She was amused by Drew's antics now he was safely on dry land. She brushed her fringe out of her eyes. The wind was still very strong and the halyards were clattering on the masts of the yachts. 'And we've got the banner back safely, but you must be freezing.'

'I wouldn't mind getting out of these clothes, to be honest. I'll pop into my house and get changed. It won't take a moment.'

'Me too. Can I get you a coffee afterwards? Or something stronger? You deserve it.'

He laughed. 'I'm not sure about that. Kenny, the lifeboat helm, called me a bloody idiot. I don't know what came over me, but an offer like that is too good to miss. I'll grab a hot shower and then shall I meet you in the Tinners' in five minutes?'

'Sounds good. I need a bit of a pick me up myself, to be honest.'

Drew frowned. 'Really? Why's that?'

Chloe regretted letting her guard down, but thought she could fudge an excuse. 'Oh, you know, one thing and another. Go on, get changed before you catch pneumonia.'

Moments later, she had dashed home, where she had a wash and threw on some jeans and a clean top. Drew still hadn't arrived in the pub when she got there, so she checked her emails, WhatsApp and Facebook while she waited, always harbouring the slim hope that there might be a message from Hannah. There had been no reply at all to her last message of a week before. Then Drew walked in.

Word about his impromptu swim had already spread and there was good-natured banter about mermaids while he waited at the bar with Chloe who insisted on ordering the drinks. She ordered a coffee and a brandy while Drew got a pint and they found a quiet corner in the lounge bar. The wind was still blowing outside and making the old windows rattle whenever anyone opened the door.

'Warming up?' she asked as he took a long drink of beer.

'Just about. Anything for the festival.'

Choe laughed. 'Even though I organise events for a living I'd no idea a local food festival was so much work or that there were so many things that could go wrong.'

Drew chuckled. 'You seem to be taking it in your stride. You did solve the problem of us losing the headline chef.'

'Yes . . . although sometimes I think that was a mixed blessing, given the history that there obviously is between

Gabe and Sam. I would have thought twice if I'd known, or at least asked her first.'

'Hmm. It's a bit awkward him being back, but Sam would want to put the festival's interest above her own problems.'

Chloe was by no means sure about that after the pub, and the glances and heavily loaded comments between Gabe and Sam. 'Maybe. I'd no idea of how close they were especially as . . . Look, Drew, tell me to shut up if it's none of my business, but I once thought that you and Sam might be . . . well, you know.'

She knew it was a bit cheeky of her to ask about his feelings, but she also hoped to draw him out a little more about the mysterious Caitlin who Sam had mentioned.

Luckily, Drew took the question in good part. 'Sam's a lovely person and a lot of fun to be around. We go back years, obviously. I like her a lot and I admire how she held the family together. She went through stuff no one should have to face at her age, but she's always been one for Gabe.'

'Even after he left the village?'

'Yes. I think the torch still burns bright on both sides, no matter what she's said about him.'

Drew was probably right. It was tempting to ask him even more about what happened but she didn't want to pry any further into Sam's private life.

'I thought the atmosphere was a little tense at the pub. It must be awkward for both of them . . . Anyway, how are you? Busy with the *Marisco*?'

'Now the season's here, I am. We're supposed to be out to-morrow night for a week's charter so I'll miss the next meeting.'

'Where are you going this time?'

'Back round the south coast to Brixham. Old stamping ground for me, I used to work out of there. Lived there for five years.'

'I didn't know that you'd crossed the Tamar,' Chloe teased.

'Now and again, I try to bear it.' Drew grinned. 'And besides my ex still lives there.'

'Your ex . . . you mean a girlfriend?' Chloe was genuinely surprised. Sam hadn't told her there was an ex-partner in Drew's life – maybe she wasn't so ex if Drew was making regular visits to Brixham.

'No, Katya's my ex-wife.'

'*Wife* . . . Oh, I see.' Wow. Even though she was reasonably new to the village, she thought she at least knew the basics about her fellow committee members, but this was a surprise. If Drew had a secret like this, what else didn't she know? Everyone was hiding something, she realised . . . or at least keeping it quiet.

'We're getting a divorce,' said Drew. 'We've been separated for years but we never got round to the legal stuff. I'm expecting it to come through in a few weeks.' He sighed. 'We grew apart years ago and as splits go, it's been pretty amicable, but it does feel like the end of an era.'

'I'm sorry. I had no idea you were married.'

'It's sad, even though it's for the best. Katya's Polish and she wants to take Connor back to Krakow to be closer to her family.' He sipped his pint.

'Connor . . .'

'My son.' Drew smiled. 'He's eleven. Starting big school next year . . .' His voice trailed off and his smile faded. 'Looks like that'll be in Poland now.'

'Oh, I hope not for your sake.'

He shrugged. 'Might never happen so what's the point of worrying about it?'

'I'd no idea.'

'Why would you? I tend to keep my private life quiet, but I go and see him whenever I can and it fits in with Katya's plans.'

Chloe could definitely empathise. 'That's very hard,' she said; she almost daren't say any more.

'I'm not happy about it, obviously.' He gazed down into his pint for a second before adopting a resigned look. 'Katya wants him to get to know her relatives better and I can't stop her. Connor seems OK with it – or he might be saying that because he doesn't want to upset his mum. We've always tried to be civilised in front of him, no matter what our differences are. She said I can visit him any time, but I know that won't be very often, with my work. I don't mind admitting the thought of losing him hurts.' He sank the rest of his pint. 'The thing is that I will be able to see Connor, but not as often. I don't have much family of my own and I know how close Katya is to hers. How can I deny Connor that support network?'

Chloe had never seen the usually laid-back Drew so passionate.

'I'm so sorry that you're in this horrible position, Drew. I do understand how it feels to be kept apart from your children. More than you think,' she said. 'I've got a daughter too.'

Drew smiled gently. 'I know. Hannah, isn't it? She's at uni.'

'Do I mention her a lot?' said Chloe.

He smiled. 'That's normal. You must miss her.'

'I do miss her. I miss her a hundred times a day. More than I can say . . .' Chloe felt her stomach tighten and her pulse quicken. She had the horrible feeling as if she'd turned on a tap, only a tiny fraction, but a droplet of pain had squeezed out, and now it was going to be impossible to stop the rest from gushing out.

'You see, I might have been a bit economical with the truth. Hannah's not at uni.'

'Oh.' Drew put his glass down. 'Come on, spit it out.'

Her hands were shaky but there was no going back. 'Hannah's twenty-two now. She actually left uni last year. She lives in Bristol with her baby daughter. Ruby's my grand-daughter.' She smiled. 'I'm a granny.'

'A granny. Wow. That's a surprise.' He frowned.

'No one knows. I haven't said anything about Ruby. I can't . . . it's too complicated. Too painful.' She flashed a smile. 'It's boring.'

'I'm not bored and I'm ready to listen if you want to tell me about it?'

'No.' She wrinkled her nose. 'I mean, yes, I *do*, but I don't want to embarrass myself in the pub. That really would set tongues wagging.'

He drained his pint and reached for his coat. 'Then come back to my house, I'll make us a proper drink and you can tell me all about it.'

Chapter Eighteen

Once inside his house, Drew started to take off his boots and Chloe reached down to unlace her trainers.

'There's no need for that,' he said firmly. 'These are my work boots and they probably have oil and tar on them.'

She straightened up, fascinated by this glimpse into Drew's home life. The small but smart modern semi was situated on a quiet street opposite the memorial hall. She'd always linked him with the romantic charm of the *Marisco* and it seemed odd to think he spent any time in such 'ordinary' surroundings.

She also couldn't help noticing a cherry-coloured coat hanging next to Drew's own waterproof. She was sure it wasn't Drew's colour and anyway, he wasn't a size ten. Maybe it belonged to 'Caitlin' although Drew hadn't taken her bait when she'd hinted about his current love life. The only woman he'd spoken about so far was Katya.

'I'll get us a drink,' he said warmly. 'Why don't you make yourself at home?'

He delved into a sideboard behind her while she took in the surroundings. The sitting room was neat but minimally furnished although there were some interesting contemporary paintings of Porthmellow and seascapes that enlivened the magnolia walls. She didn't think the place was minimal by design; she guessed Drew simply didn't need extraneous 'stuff', especially as he was away for a fair amount of the week.

There were a few framed photographs on the mantelpiece and side table. One was of Drew with the lifeboat crew he used to volunteer with, another showed him sitting outside the Smuggler's with his parents who Chloe had met at a festival fundraising event. The third photo must be of his son, Connor. Drew had his arm around the boy – almost a teenager – and he certainly had Drew's fair hair and smile.

Glassware chinked and Drew emerged from the rear of the sofa and held up a couple of bottles. 'I've got beer, gin – the bog-standard kind – some lemon liqueur that I don't recommend and some single malt, which I do.'

'The malt sounds great.'

He put it on the coffee table in front of her. 'My thoughts entirely. I'll fetch some glasses from the kitchen.'

He came back with two plain tumblers and a jug with some water. 'I've got some dry ginger if you'd prefer it.'

'A splash of water's fine,' Chloe said.

He smiled and poured her a generous measure, followed by a dash of water. He then poured his own drink and they chinked glasses. 'Here's to . . . whatever.'

'To whatever,' said Chloe. She sipped the whisky, and its warmth bled into her veins immediately. However, far from feeling relaxed, she was beginning to get cold feet about having a heart to heart with Drew.

Chloe took a larger sip of whisky. 'Is that Connor?' she said, pointing to the photograph. It felt far easier to focus on his life than her own.

He nodded and took it down from the mantelpiece for Chloe to see. Close up she saw he had finer features than his father. They both held fishing rods and had broad smiles on their faces.

'He looks like you and you both look very pleased with yourselves.'

'We'd been mackerel fishing. Got a good haul. He loves fishing. I take him out in the *Marisco* when I'm over Brixham way.' He laid the frame on the coffee table.

'Will Katya really move back to Poland?' Chloe asked.

'Maybe. She's an accountant,' he said. 'There's a job waiting for her back in Krakow with her brother's firm. Connor already has dual nationality and experience of a new country is something I'd never try to take away from him. Katya's made it clear I can visit whenever I like and it's only a couple of hours' flight from Bristol but it's not the same. I'm gutted, to be honest, but I want what's best for my son. My needs have to come second.'

Drew stopped and took a sip of his whisky. She could almost feel the anguish he was suppressing.

'I think – in fact, I do know what you mean . . . it was hard when Fraser and I went through the divorce. Hard for us and for Hannah. In fact, I got over it a lot faster than she has.'

He looked at her. 'A rift like that is never easy. It takes a long long time and the ripples go on and on, catching you unawares when you least expect it . . .'

'Yes. The split itself was painful and disruptive; I missed Fraser like mad. I still do miss him, but . . . I hadn't realised how unhappy I had been until the burden was lifted. Poor Fraser, fancy describing him as a burden. Makes him sound like an old sofa I needed to take to the tip.'

Drew laughed. 'Was he?'

'Oh no. He was – still is – tall, dark and handsome and charming. Surrey's most eligible bachelor in his youth. He ended up in our local county mag once. Even offered himself up for auction for charity. That was all before he met me, I hasten to add, but you know, I think he still likes the atten-tion.' She laughed, and surprised herself. She still fancied Fraser but for the first time, she genuinely thought she wouldn't take him back even if he offered.

Drew rolled his eyes. 'You'll forgive if I'm not impressed.'

'I forgive you but I have to be honest. I liked being married to this tall, dark, handsome bloke who only had eyes for me. Or so I thought.'

'Playing away, was he?'

'Not *all* the time.' Chloe smiled, but it was gallows humour. 'Sometimes he brought her round the house while I was away at events. Saved him money and he didn't have to worry about the bills appearing on the bank statements.'

Drew swore softly. 'What a louse. Didn't the neighbours notice?'

'Maybe, but they weren't the kind of neighbours to tell me.

We lived in a nice road in the semi countryside with big trees around the houses. One side never actually got round to moving in at all. The other side was a reclusive literary author who didn't like speaking to people. I did try to get her to join a book club when she first moved in but when she found out we'd chosen *Fifty Shades of Grey* as book of the month for a laugh, she made it quite clear she wanted to be left alone. So, you could have had Bacchanalian orgies every night and opened a crystal meth factory and one neighbour would never have known – and the other side wouldn't have cared.'

Drew laughed. 'Sorry for laughing. It's not funny.'

'Oh but it is, in a way. Now I have the benefit of some distance.' Chloe sipped her whisky. 'It's not Fraser that I miss now, though I did move partly to get away from the bad memories in the house. Also, of course, because I couldn't afford to stay there, but I don't care. I have far less money now, but I'm happier in other ways. I'm genuinely better off without him. I'm not always wondering if he's having an affair. I like my own company and I love Porthmellow. I like being able to chat to the neighbours every time I buy a book of stamps.'

'*But?*' Drew said over the top of his glass.

'I'm very very lucky.'

'I didn't ask if you feel lucky, punk.' He said it in a Clint Eastwood way that made Chloe giggle. He really was a lovely guy. And his choice of malts was top notch if this warm and peaty Laphroaig was anything to judge by. This stuff was as relaxing as a massage in a top health spa.

'I don't miss Fraser at all, but I do miss Hannah.' She tapped her chest. 'Right in here. It's a physical ache sometimes. So what you said earlier, about wanting to do what was best for Connor. I know how that feels, I wanted what was best for Hannah . . .' she began, clutching her glass tighter. 'And I'm afraid it split us apart.'

Drew let her breathe before he responded. Fraser had never let her breathe.

'I'm sorry to hear that,' he said softly. 'Do you mean that a problem with Hannah split up you and your husband?'

'No, Fraser and I were already well on the rocks when the issues with Hannah began. I mean that trying to do our best – or what we thought was our best – caused a rift with Hannah. In fact, we . . . don't have much contact at the moment.'

His eyebrows twitched in surprise. 'You talk about her all the time. I thought you spoke with her every day?'

'In my dreams. I'm afraid I've also been economical with the truth about my contact with Hannah.' She let out a sigh, wishing she hadn't lied or at least hadn't kept her friends in Porthmellow so much in the dark. 'We've been, I guess you call it estranged, for well over a year now.' She paused again, wondering how the months had flown by so fast. 'I can't believe it's been so long. She has a little girl called Ruby. I've never met her. Hannah lives in Bristol now with Ruby and his father – a guy called Jordan Rees. Hannah met him at uni. He was a mature student, though mature's the wrong word for him.'

'I'd no idea. I'm sorry to hear this, Chloe.'

'I haven't wanted to tell people. It's too much to deal with myself sometimes and mostly, I don't know how to explain it.

You're supposed to have a happy relationship with your kids, aren't you? There's Sam and Zennor who are so close, and they lost their mum. I don't want to moan to them. And Evie and Troy have such a loving relationship and family. I'm new here and I can't face all the explanations and questions, especially knowing that I – and Fraser – contributed to the rift. The committee need me to be capable and organised and professional. Not moping about.'

Drew was silent for a few seconds. Then he reached out and touched Chloe's arm. 'You don't have to pretend or put on a front with me, or anyone, but I can understand that it's too painful to talk about your personal life. I try to keep mine as private as I can, though God knows that's hard enough in a small place like Porthmellow. Come on, you've started now. Tell me about this Jordan bloke, though I have to say I don't like him already.'

Chloe allowed herself a smile. 'Jordan's not a monster . . . far from it. He's good looking, and he can be charming if he wants to, but even from the first moment Hannah brought him home, we took against him. He liked to put her down, make sarcastic remarks about her clothes and hair, and our "mega mansion" and "the middle classes". He picked a fight with everything we said, sneered at the décor, the sofa – even the cushions – and generally made Hannah feel guilty for being our daughter. I really tried to see his point of view for my daughter's sake. She seemed to worship him and think he was some kind of Che Guevara figure.' Chloe rolled her eyes. 'He even wore a Che beret once, not that it's a crime.'

Drew rolled his eyes. 'He sounds like a right tit to me.'

His grim humour made Chloe smile. 'Oh he's a tit, all right, but a very clever tit.'

'Hmm. I guess things went downhill from there?'

'Yes. At first Fraser took the head-in-the-sand approach. He couldn't stand Jordan but thought Hannah would see the light and leave him.' Chloe paused for breath.

'But she didn't.'

'Nope. She moved in with him. The irony is that Fraser found out Jordan's father is a multi-millionaire. Jordan has a trust fund. In fact, he isn't even called Jordan. He's actually called Gideon Jordan Rees-Carew.'

Drew snorted. 'Oh, for God's sake.'

'Not that pretending to be something you're not is a crime either. I wouldn't mind, but Jordan – Gideon – goes home and lives the life of luxury when he's not with Hannah. He leaves her in a scuzzy little bedsit with Ruby and has a whale of a time. Henley Regatta, Ascot, polo . . . and poker matches. He'd been gambling on horses and playing for big stakes in the card games. Hannah was never invited to the events and, in fact, I'm not sure she even knew. No matter what she claims.' Chloe paused. 'I'm sorry for unleashing this on you. I've never discussed it with anyone except Fraser before, not even Sam. Now I feel guilty for keeping her in the dark. She's a good friend and I should probably share it with her too, but she has her own problems and . . .' Chloe let out a very inelegant hiccup. 'Maybe I should shut up now.'

'No, you shouldn't. And I'm sure Sam would be sympathetic. But God, how do you know all this?' asked Drew.

'We heard that she was pregnant – again through a third

party – and we were so worried.' Chloe paused, having to take a moment before she confessed to an act she deeply regretted now. 'We . . . we actually hired a private detective to spy on him.'

Drew sucked in a breath. It wasn't the reaction Chloe had hoped for, but probably the one she'd expected. 'Oh.'

'We were desperate. She looked so terrible and so battered down mentally when she did come to visit. Fraser had been throwing himself into his work, staying later and later, and eventually, confessing he was having an affair with Coffee Girl. But even though we were in the throes of divorcing by then, we stuck together on this. We both love her so much, we had to try and do something. Fraser had a business contact who knew Jordan's father and he told Fraser the truth so we hired a PI to gather evidence. We had photos and videos of Jordan living the high life and even of the amount he'd been spending on poker and betting.'

'Did you show it to Hannah?'

She gulped down her whisky before replying. 'Yes.'

'And I'm guessing it didn't end well?'

Chloe cringed at the memory of the scene that had ensued when Hannah had found out what had been going on. 'She went berserk. She said she knew all about it and so what? She said we'd been spying on her and that we'd always stifled her and we didn't respect her choices. We were petty minded, obsessed with money – which was so unfair, I could hardly speak. She said we were boring and conventional and she was ashamed of us.'

As she lifted her drink to her lips, her hands weren't quite

191

steady around the glass. 'She said that she knew about Jordan's real life and he was ashamed of being born with a silver spoon in his mouth, but had to go home to keep his parents happy – as his mother was dying. She said he'd said she could go with him, but she'd hate it.' Chloe sighed. 'His poor mother *does* have a long-term illness, but she's certainly not terminally ill.'

Drew screwed up his face in disgust. 'Wow. Nice bloke. I loathe him already and I've never had the misfortune to meet him.'

'I tried not to, I really did and I tried to convince myself he had issues, but you know, some people are just vile. Fraser was less sympathetic and hit the roof and called him all the names under the sun and said Hannah was naïve and childish for staying with him.'

'Ouch.'

'I was furious with Fraser for that. It alienated Hannah even more and entrenched everyone's positions. She told us never to contact her again. I lost my cool and said I'd rather Jordan had been destitute and homeless rather than a feckless manipulative con merchant.' Chloe closed her eyes, recalling every word she'd slung at Jordan and the look of absolute devastation in her daughter's face.

'For a moment, I saw in her eyes that she believed me. She knew I was telling the truth about him. I'm convinced of it and that's why she reacted so strongly. The truth really *does* hurt. In fact, it can utterly destroy a person. Sometimes it hurts so much it's not worth even seeking it out. I genuinely wish I'd never known about Jordan, or at least never told Hannah about him. If I'd left things as they are, she might have come round in her own time but now I – and Fraser – have destroyed the thing we all love most in the world.'

Drew had been quiet for some time, letting Chloe go on but now he spoke:

'I don't know what the right thing to do was, or is. I can't help, but I know one thing. You shouldn't feel ashamed of loving your child or doing what you thought was best. Or of telling me – or Sam, or anyone you trust.'

'I don't know what to do now. Hannah has totally wiped me and her father from the face of the earth. Fraser's responded by being angry and he says it's up to her to contact us first but I'm not so sure. Someone has to hold out the olive branch, even if it keeps getting slapped down.'

'When did you last try?' he asked.

'A few weeks ago. She answered her phone to me, which was a miracle, and we started to talk – sort of – but then Jordan came into the room and she broke off the call. I've emailed her again saying she can contact me any time, that I'm always here for her. I keep hoping she'll get in touch when he's not around.'

'You think this git is controlling her?'

'I don't know if he's physically controlling her, or using emotional pressure.' Chloe shuddered. 'Either way, it's very hard not to jump in the car and confront him.'

He nodded sympathetically. 'I must admit, I have sympathy. I'd want to do the same, but Connor's only a child and Hannah's an adult. Do you think that pride won't let her leave Jordan or that she's genuinely scared?'

'I don't know. She's in a difficult situation, even if she wants to get out. Leaving will prove us right – though God knows I'd never ever say "I told you so". I only want her and Ruby to be safe and happy.'

'I'm very sorry to hear it. I can't imagine – I daren't imagine – what it would be like to lose complete touch with Connor, or be stopped from seeing him. Do you think there's any chance Hannah might come to your birthday? After all, it is a special occasion.' He smiled. 'It'll be my turn soon enough and I reckon you're only forty once so enjoy it.'

'I doubt it,' Chloe muttered and knocked back the rest of her whisky. It burned her throat and she coughed.

'You never know. It might be just the excuse she needs to get in touch.' Drew held up the bottle. 'Top-up?'

'I didn't realise I'd drunk the last glass so fast.'

'Nor me.'

The empty glass in her hand surprised her. Maybe a drink in the pub and a whisky weren't the best ways of rehydrating after a Zumba class. She'd had no dinner either. If she stayed for another, she might end up answering more awkward questions. Drew must already be wondering that she was a very young granny, but be too polite to say so.

'I should be going.' She stood up and felt decidedly wobbly. It really *was* time to go. 'Thanks for listening.'

Drew got to his feet. 'You too. I don't often talk about Connor. Or my love life.'

He hadn't really talked about his love life at all. Neither of them had. They'd talked about relationships and family but not love in the romantic sense. Which was both a relief and a shame, because even though she'd been scarred by her

194

experience with Fraser, it hadn't totally put her off men. Gabe was gorgeous but out of bounds. Drew had a girlfriend and an ex-wife. If she'd moved here for a simple life, she would be disappointed. Porthmellow was just as complicated as Surrey, only with big waves.

'You can talk to me about this – or anything – any time. Just call me Uncle Drew, the agony uncle.'

'You don't really want to hear all my woes.'

'I hear everyone's woes on the *Marisco*. When these city types are hauled out of their cocooned worlds, and suddenly all their tech and strategies aren't worth a flying fart, excuse me. It's them and the elements and you see them in the raw. It makes my day.'

'I bet.' Chloe laughed. How had she known Drew for the best part of nine months and not seen what a great guy he was? A little rough around the edges, but that was part of the attraction.

Drew softened his tone. 'Most of them have far less to worry about than you do. Pick up the phone or call round whenever you want.'

'Thanks. Bye.'

Chloe reached up and kissed him impulsively, aiming for his cheek but he moved at the last moment and the kiss ended up on his lips. He kissed her back – or she thought he was kissing her back, and she threw her arms around him before suddenly coming to her senses.

She wanted the floor to open up and swallow her when she realised she'd smacked him full on the lips with a definitely-not-platonic kiss.

'My God. Fuck. I'm sorry. Sorry for saying fuck and sorry for that . . . it . . . the thing happening.'

He was gracious enough to smile. 'Don't be. It . . . the thing was lovely but this really isn't the greatest idea. I like you, Chloe. I *really* like you, but now's not the best time for either of us, is it? From any point of view.'

'No, don't go any further. I've made such a fool of myself. I have to go.' It *was* terrible. Not the kiss, but the fact he might have a girlfriend, not to mention the fact that he was over a decade younger than she was . . . both of which somehow had conveniently escaped her notice while she'd been kissing him. Damn, she'd have been at college and partying when Drew hadn't even left Porthmellow Primary School. How would he feel if he knew that?

Well, she certainly wasn't going to tell him *now*. There'd been enough confessions for one night.

'You don't have to run off now. Why don't I make you a coffee?' he said.

'I'm not drunk,' she blurted out.

'I didn't say you *were*, I only meant, don't leave like this. Please.'

'I *do* really need to get home. Look at the time.' She pointed at the clock in the hall. and reached for the door lock.

'What? Half past nine?' Drew said.

'Late enough,' Chloe muttered, fumbling with the top lock and wrenching the handle. It rattled loudly. Shit, why were other people's doors always so difficult to open? Especially when you were desperate to get away.

Drew reached in front of her and twisted the knob. 'You have to turn the Yale at the same time.'

He had a half-smile on his face but her cheeks burned. 'Thanks.'

'You're welcome.'

'Right.'

Chloe burbled something as she exited the house but it definitely wasn't 'bye'. She didn't actually run away; she had the presence of mind to realise that hurtling out of Drew Yelland's house, with tears running down her face, at nine thirty on a Tuesday evening might possibly arouse suspicion – especially with the town band emerging from the Dame Doris Thurlow Memorial Centre and the ladies' rowing gig returning from practice on the corner of the road.

She gathered her dignity, what was left of it, and held her head high, walking briskly through the village and up towards her house. When she got back she gave her dignity a massive slap round the chops and threw her keys on the counter top. They'd probably leave a lovely dent.

She caught sight of herself in the polished steel of the cooker. So that's why they called them 'eye-level ovens'. She wished she hadn't cleaned it so well because in the mirror-like surface, she could see every shameful detail. Her mascara had smudged, in fact it now looked like two spiders had done a painting under each eye. What a day. She'd poured out her heart about Fraser and Hannah. She'd made a pass at a much younger man who was in a relationship and who'd tried to let her down gently because he was a lovely guy. She felt needy and a hopeless mess. Well, she had to pull herself together.

She would henceforth return to her previous status: not getting involved with anyone, however charming, sympathetic or sexy. She'd reached rock bottom and rebuilding her relationship with Hannah and the festival were the only things she would focus on from now on. Before then, deep joy, she had her 'special' birthday coming up, but even that was soured by the fact that her friends had no idea quite how 'special' it was.

Chapter Nineteen

Porthmellow Festival Facebook page

Faye P: is the festival programme out yet? When's Gabe Mathias going live?
Joe Bloggs: Never I hope. Sick of this bloody festival. The people running it are only out to line their own pockets. Bet bloody Gabe Mathias is making a fortune out of it
Faye P: Shut up, hater!!!!!

Sam swore softly after seeing the latest comments on the festival Facebook page. She'd been taking a quick look at the social media while she waited for the kettle to boil at the Institute and now she wished she hadn't. With just three weeks to go to the festival, most of the comments were positive and excited, asking about the bands and when Gabe would be in the Chef's Theatre, but there were always a few moaners. Bryony was obviously one of the Twitter brigade but 'Joe Bloggs' could have been anyone, including Bryony. Sam had grown a thick skin over the years but the implication she was out to make money and the slur against Gabe got her back up.

Troy appeared in the doorway with his arm in a sling. Hastily shoving her phone in her pocket, Sam broke into a broad smile. It was great to see him back.

'Evening, my maid.'

'How are you?' she asked, seeing how gingerly he moved around.

'A mite sore but I don't complain. I've always had a high pain threshold. Anything to get out of tea duties. I hope you're going to leave that to brew properly. I can't stand any of that wishy washy stuff.'

'I wouldn't dare,' Sam said.

A few minutes later, she carried the tea tray into the meeting room where Drew was asking Troy how he was managing with his sling. Sam exchanged a quick smile with Drew. She'd seen Evie at the post office the day before and she'd confessed that Troy had been 'driving her up the wall' asking for drinks, food and generally enjoying being fussed over and waited on, long after he really needed it. She'd told Sam she was thinking of buying him a bell that he could ring whenever he wanted service.

Chloe arrived, looking immaculate but not as bouncy as Sam had expected given her birthday party was the hot topic while the tea was made. Troy made a few jokes about 'life beginning . . .' and 'bus passes' and Drew joined in with the banter. Chloe smiled and threw a few comments back, but Sam thought she seemed on edge.

'Much as I'd love to talk about my party all day, should we get down to business?' Chloe asked with a smile that only partly softened the tension in her voice.

'Good idea,' Sam said. 'But before we start, I just wanted to tell you we've had a few negative comments on the Facebook page.'

Zennor rolled her eyes. 'I just saw the latest from Joe Bloggs. He's pathetic,' she said.

'Don't folk have better things to do?' Troy grumbled.

'Clearly not,' Chloe said.

'There's nothing we can do about the Twitter comments except ignore them or block people,' Zennor said. 'Ben deletes the Facebook messages as soon as he sees them and I've just removed the latest. Anyone know who Joe Bloggs could be?'

Everyone shook their heads apart from Troy who suggested the new Methodist minister from Porthmellow Chapel, a timid young man who happened to be called Rupert Hartley-Bloggs. This resulted in peals of laughter before Sam suggested that he was an unlikely culprit and called the meeting to order so they could get on with the scarily long agenda.

With the festival now just over three weeks away, there was a sense of urgency and seriousness that hadn't been there before, especially as this was set to be their biggest event ever. It never ceased to amaze Sam how the festival had grown from one day of local food stalls around the harbour to the massive undertaking it now was. She had no idea how she'd ever managed without Chloe.

Zennor and Ben gave their report on the latest publicity,

which had now ramped up with ads and features appearing in the Cornish lifestyle magazines.

Everyone in the village had to be informed and reminded of road and harbour closures and alternative arrangements, most of which Troy dealt with in his own unique way. His sore shoulder hadn't stopped him from issuing orders.

Each year there were new health and safety regulations to be followed and risk assessments to be done, which thankfully was Drew's area of expertise, as was dealing with the marquee people. The marquee itself was due to be pitched two days before the event and then the fixtures and fittings put in place the following morning: a stage, power and lighting and a bar.

After the reports, she handed out copies of the final list of exhibitors and performers. Seeing the scale of the festival printed across several sheets of paper led to gasps from Zennor and even a 'bugger me' from Troy. This year, the food market would spread into the streets and onto the football pitch behind the harbour, with producers from all over Cornwall and further afield. You name it, if it was grub or grub related, it was there, from jams and oils, to cookery books, pots and pans and novelty aprons. Ethnic and local producers using local food in creative ways or fusions of Cornish and 'foreign' recipes, as Troy called them.

The festival marquee was pitched on a farmer's field above one side of the harbour, which also provided one of the car parks. It provided an all-weather venue for artists ranging from bands and comedy acts to spoken word performers that kept punters around until late in the evening.

The final item on the agenda related to the real heart of

the festival, the Chef's Theatre, where Gabe and local restaurateurs would work their magic with Cornish produce in front of a live audience.

Chloe had already held a meeting with the three chefs who had been invited to cook at the festival and reported back on their requirements. Gabe had to be in London for a couple of days and couldn't make the main meeting so Chloe emailed him and arranged to meet him at the pub the following evening. However, Chloe had a small bombshell of her own to drop.

'I'm really sorry but I'm not going to be able to make the meeting with Gabe tomorrow night. I double booked and promised to go to a Zumba friend's birthday party,' she said. 'I know you're busy but do you mind doing it?'

Sam hesitated a moment too long.

'Of course, if it's difficult, I could rearrange a date with him although I'm not sure what his schedule's like.'

'No, it's fine,' Sam said with a smile that went no further than her mouth. 'It shouldn't take too long.'

'Best to get it over with,' Chloe said. 'I mean, best to have the meeting while you both have time,' she added hastily.

'Look, are we going to the pub before closing time or not?' Troy chipped in, saving Sam from replying.

She still hadn't decided how she felt about meeting Gabe on her own by the time she left the pub – or how he would feel about meeting her.

For a Thursday evening at eight p.m. it was relatively quiet inside their chosen pub. Nonetheless, heads turned when she and Gabe walked in. Sam took out her iPad and notebook, carrying it so that anyone who might think otherwise would know she was here on festival business.

'I'd like to run through the Chef's Theatre programme,' she said loudly to Gabe as they paid for a G&T and a pint at the bar.

The landlady handed the drinks over, an amused smile on her lips that could have meant anything.

There were two men nursing pints standing a few feet away, making no effort to keep their conversation quiet. 'Nice of him to come back when he turned her own brother in to the police,' the younger of them muttered, wiping foam from his mouth. 'Ruined his life.'

The landlady shot the pair a withering glance. 'Button it, Robbo,' she snapped, causing more eyes to turn in their direction. The guy called Robbo smirked then moved away from the bar, glass in hand.

Sam cringed but Gabe had a tight smile on his lips. They chose a booth in the far corner of the lounge that hopefully gave them a bit of privacy. 'I knew this was a bad idea,' she murmured as she slid behind the table.

Gabe chose the stool opposite her. 'What, meeting me or coming in here?'

'Both.' She toyed with her pen, clicking the top anxiously.

'Don't let a couple of prats upset you. That's not the Sam I knew.'

'That's just it, Gabe. I'm not the Sam you knew,' she said quietly.

'That goes for both of us.'

Sam took a breath and treated Robbo to her best death stare. He immediately took an interest in his pint.

She pulled out a file and handed Gabe a piece of paper. 'OK. Moving on to the – um – business in hand. Here's the schedule of demonstrations for the day. I've emailed you a copy as well, but I thought it would be easier if we could see the whole plan in one go.'

As he took it, the hairs on his arm brushed her wrist. 'I haven't had a chance to look at it yet, so thanks.'

He studied the piece of paper she'd given him while Sam sipped her G&T and tried not to inhale his gorgeous smell, which was headier than any botanical in the gin. Goosebumps kept popping up whenever his skin made the slightest contact with hers and the delicious tingly sensation had started to infuse her from the middle outwards. Sitting next to Gabe was like being surrounded by a mouthwatering feast. If she touched even the tiniest morsel, she knew she'd want to wolf down the lot.

'Is there enough time for you to – you know – do your thing?' she asked, trying to unscramble her brain.

'I think so . . . But if there's time in the schedule, I could do with another fifteen minutes afterwards?' He gave her a questioning look. 'I usually invite a couple of people on stage to taste the dish. It goes down well with the audience if they feel part of the action.'

He slid the paper a little closer to her.

Sam made a note on the sheet. 'Sounds like a good plan. Yes – I think we can accommodate that.'

He flashed her the kind of smile that would turn a slab of

chocolate to liquid in a heartbeat. 'Great. Can I run a few of my plans for the cookery demo by you while we're here? Get your feedback.'

'You want *my* feedback on your demo?' She was genuinely surprised.

'I'd like to get an idea of the kind of people who will be there. Get a feel for the temperature of the crowd.'

Sam wanted to fan herself. She knew what her temperature was right now: the mercury was ready to explode.

'I'd be interested in what you think would go down well with your audience,' Gabe added, then smiled. 'I can always ignore it, naturally.'

'Naturally.'

She forced herself to concentrate on his ideas for the dish he planned to prepare and she told him what she thought the audiences had enjoyed in the past. Judging by the way she'd seen him work the audience on his TV show, however, she was confident he'd have everyone eating out of his hand.

She'd no intention of telling him that, of course, and tried to keep the conversation brisk and practical. It was difficult, because he kept making her laugh with anecdotes about previous demos and some of the celebrities he'd worked with. Without her even realising it, another round of drinks were being consumed and Sam was smiling more and more often as the pub filled up and noise levels increased. She relaxed and almost missed the ringing of her phone in the bag by her feet.

'Sorry, I ought to see who this is.'

She reached down to scoop it out of her bag, but her fingers fumbled and it dropped onto the slate floor and slithered under Gabe's feet.

'Shit.'

The phone stopped ringing.

'It's OK. I'll get it,' said Gabe, leaning down.

She made a grab for the phone at the same time as he did and their fingers collided under the table. Not only brushed against each other but lingered. It might have only been seconds, but Sam felt Gabe link his fingers with hers, so lightly . . . Sam didn't let go for a few seconds either and slowly, they straightened up together.

She shivered. The contact had been electric. Gabe was smiling as he held out the mobile. 'Here you are. No damage done.'

'M-maybe not. I don't know . . .' She was out of breath.

'Sam. I think it'll be *fine*.'

'I – I need to check it out.' Flustered, she examined the screen. It was unscathed but there was a missed call from Stefan.

Sam called him back. 'Hi. Stefan,' she said. As she listened to his breathless news, her heart sank. '*What*? Oh God, no. Have you rung the police yet?'

Gabe waited until she'd finished her brief conversation. 'Trouble?' he asked as she shoved her phone in her bag.

'Someone's chucked paint over the mobile unit. It's a mess.'

Gabe swore under his breath. 'What? Who would do that?'

'No idea but I have to go. Sorry.' She shoved her tablet and notebook in her bag. That was all she needed with a string of events coming up. Maybe it wouldn't be as bad as Stefan was making out.

Gabe was on his feet. 'Hang on. I'm coming with you.'

Sam decided in a second that she didn't mind some extra moral support and from experience knew Gabe would have followed her anyway. 'OK,' she said, and they dashed to the unit together, too intent on reaching Stefan to say more than a few words. Sam rounded the corner and her skin turned cold. Stefan was standing outside with two police officers. As soon as he saw her, he waved at her and the police turned with grim expressions.

She recognised the police officers. They were occasional customers of Stargazey. 'What's happened?'

Stefan spat the words out but looked close to tears. 'Someone's trashed the fecking van. Look.'

They all moved to the rear of the unit. 'Oh God.'

The van had been covered in crimson paint, obliterating the Stargazey logo and spattering the sides. Sam felt slightly sick: her pride and joy and livelihood looked like it had been at the centre of a gory movie.

Sam covered her face in her hands in disbelief. 'Oh no . . .'

Gabe was at her side. 'What a mess. Who the hell would do something like this?'

'Clearly, someone who hates us,' said Sam, catching Stefan's eye. He folded his arms and looked at the sky. He was on the verge of tears.

'I'm afraid all the tyres have been slashed too,' said the policeman, an older guy who'd been around in Ryan's day. 'It's not roadworthy.'

'Shit. We're meant to be at a music festival in St Just tomorrow night,' she said.

'Not unless we can get the tyres replaced at short notice. I've already phoned the garage and they've said they'll come out and tow us on the trailer ASAP. The van looks like it's been in the *Texas Chain Saw Massacre*. Would you buy an artisan pie from that?' said Stefan.

'Not unless I was Sweeney Todd,' said the policeman then looked sheepish. 'Sorry.'

'No, you're right. It's a bloody mess but there's no way we can get the paint job redone by tomorrow evening,' said Sam. 'We'll have to get the tyres fixed and turn up and make the best of it.'

Stefan's eyes were bright. 'I might not even have seen the van at all if I hadn't had to come back to the unit to collect my tablet. I left it here earlier so I thought I'd pop down for it. Then, I saw this mess. Maybe if I'd been here sooner, I could have scared them off.'

'There are some real bastards around,' Gabe said, shaking his head at the trashed van.

Sam felt like crying herself, but held it back for Stefan's sake. It must have been a shock to find the van in that state. She hugged her colleague tightly. 'It's crap, but we'll get it sorted. The van can be fixed and repainted. I'm glad you didn't disturb them in case they turned on you, Stef.'

After taking more details, the police left, promising to do their best to find the culprit. Porthmellow was a small world but there was no CCTV at the rear of the unit, and in the initial enquiries by the police, Sam and Stefan revealed that no one had seen anyone acting suspiciously. Trashing the van must have made a hell of a mess of someone's clothes, judging

209

by the red paint spattered on the parking area, so Sam hoped more news might come to light.

She sent Stefan home to calm down. Gabe hung around while she made some calls to the garage and re-spray centre, and, being honest, Sam was grateful not to be alone. When she'd finally finished her calls, she put her phone away with a sigh. After the initial adrenaline had worn off, she was shaky with shock.

'I'm so sorry. This is a shitty thing to happen,' Gabe said. 'The police said it could have been anyone because there's been a football tournament on the rec ground this evening. They're going to make some enquiries, but it could have been any one of hundreds.'

Sam glanced over the recreation ground on the far side of the units. You could see the floodlights from here and yes, people from all over the area would have been milling around in the general vicinity but she still wasn't convinced by the police's theory. 'I don't think it's a random attack, I think it's someone with a grudge.'

'Against the festival?' Gabe said.

'Probably.' Reality was dawning on her, it wasn't only the loss of income, it was the state of her beloved van with its gorgeous paint job destroyed. First the poster-ripper and the social media trolling and now this . . . it was on the tip of her tongue to tell Gabe about the trolls but she didn't want to add fuel to the fire. He'd be bound to kick off, thinking she needed protecting, and she could look after herself.

'Is there anything I can do to help in the short term? Pay for it to be re-sprayed?' he offered.

'No,' she snapped. She didn't need a hand-out.

Gabe held up his hands. 'OK.'

She cursed her reaction. He was only trying to help. 'Gah. I'm sorry for snapping. Thanks for the offer, but we're well insured and you wouldn't be able to get it done any faster. Luckily I've got hold of Karim from the re-spray centre and he says he'll do his best but it's going to take a couple of days to fit it in.'

'Will you lose out on any business?'

'We'll probably miss the St Just gig and a night on the harbour side, but it'll hopefully be ready for the folk music evening in Helston next weekend and the festival, of course. The garage is coming out to tow it now and replace the tyres first thing tomorrow. They said they'd check it over for any other damage too. Stefan couldn't see anything wrong when he checked out the equipment inside but who knows what else they could have done to the engine or brakes.'

'Best to be on the safe side.' Gabe shook his head again, swearing under his breath.

Sam felt devastated, staring at the ruined van, holding her arms around her body. Online trolling and a few damaged posters were one thing, but this nasty act of vandalism had shaken her up. To think someone hated the festival enough to make such an obvious statement. *If* the trolling and the vandalism were linked, she reminded herself. She needed to get a grip, they could be completely unconnected.

He touched her shoulder briefly. '*Are* you OK?' he murmured.

'Yes. Yeah . . . I will be. It's just . . .' She let out a massive sigh. 'Who would be cruel enough to do this?'

211

'Far too many people,' said Gabe, moving by her side. 'And I know you can manage on your own but if there's anything I *can* do to help, you only have to say.'

She glanced up at him. He meant it, but instinct told her she didn't want to owe Gabe anything, no matter how tempting it was.

'Sacha! Hee-eel!'

Bryony's bellow cut through the air. Sacha bounded up, racing around the van, snuffling around the burst tyres.

'Sorry, there'll be no pies to sniff for a while,' she said to the dog, before noticing that Bryony was carrying a large supermarket bag. It looked heavy.

Bryony's attention was caught by the van. She snapped to a halt, and for once Sacha fled to her side. 'Who did that to your van?'

'I don't know,' said Sam. 'Have you seen anyone hanging around?' she said. She tried to sneak a look at what was in Bryony's bag, although if it was a large tin of bright red gloss, Sam realised, Bryony would be unlikely to be carting it around with her now. She thought of asking Bryony directly if she'd done it. She probably had an alibi, out on her broomstick with Sacha on the back.

That was uncharitable: moaning all the time was one thing but chucking paint over the van was a big escalation.

'Sam's van has been attacked,' said Gabe, eyeing Sacha warily as he inspected his Timberland boots. A sliver of drool coated one of the toes and under other circumstances, Sam might have laughed at it. 'We only wondered if you'd seen anything suspicious while you've been walking your dog,' he added.

'No, I haven't. I went to the Co-op to get some washing powder,' said Bryony haughtily, as if buying washing powder was an act of civic duty. She opened her bag. 'I saw you looking at it and no, it's not a can of paint.'

'I didn't think it was,' Sam said pulling her foot out of Sacha's way.

'Really?' said Bryony sarcastically. Sacha lay down at her feet.

'No one's accusing you, Bryony. We only want to find who did this,' said Sam. 'Because it's not the first thing. Someone's been tearing down festival posters up on Stippy Stappy.'

'Oh?' Bryony looked at her dog.

'You haven't seen or heard anything, have you? While you and Sacha have been walking?'

Bryony held onto Sacha and pursed her lips. She'd gone a shade of red to rival the paint. She puffed herself up and folded her arms. 'OK. So I pulled down a few stupid posters. So what?'

Sam was dumbstruck. She hadn't expected Bryony to confess. Bryony lifted her chin defiantly.

'That's so petty,' Sam said. 'What *is* your problem with the festival?'

Bryony's colour deepened. 'I've told you. I hate the crowds and the music and the way it turns our lives upside down for months, but don't try to pin *that* mess on me,' she said, nodding at the van, 'because I had nothing to do with *that*. Call me petty if you want but I'm not a lawbreaker.' She turned her attention on Gabe: 'And *you* should never have come back here, either, swanning into the village acting like its saviour.'

Astonished at the outburst, Sam managed to slot in a word.

'Have you been posting comments on the festival Facebook page?'

'Facebook? I'm not even on it. I've better things to do. Come on, Sacha.' And with that, she stomped off, jerking Sacha's lead sharply so he had to trot behind her to catch her up.

Too amazed to speak for a few seconds, Sam flopped down on the step of the van. 'Oh God. That woman makes me want to do something I'd get arrested for. What is wrong with her?' And why was she so angry with Gabe, Sam wondered.

Gabe crouched next to her. 'I don't know. Do you believe her about not trashing the van? And what's this about online messages?'

'Oh, we get those every so often. Messages on the Facebook page and Twitter feed . . . I must admit the van isn't Bryony's style.'

Gabe allowed himself a smile but his eyes were full of concern. 'Even so, being trolled is no fun.'

'Least of my worries. I don't think Bryony posted them or damaged the van. She seemed proud enough to admit to ripping down the posters so maybe she'd have told us if she'd done the other stuff.'

'Or perhaps she was terrified of getting into trouble with the police?' Gabe said. 'The posters are hardly crime of the century, even if it was a spiteful thing to do, but criminal damage is something else'.

Sam glanced up. 'I don't know. People do strange things when they're desperate. I'm sorry you've been dragged into it. I don't know why she had a go at you just now.'

Gabe shrugged. 'People have a go at me all the time, and

214

being in the public eye, let's be honest, I ask for it, but you don't, Sam.'

He held her eye and she shivered. She thought for a second he was going to reach for her. If he did, she might not push him away. To be held by him, even for comfort, for a moment or two, would be so tempting. His arms around her, the warmth of his skin against hers . . .

'Hey, look, the tow truck's here,' he said. 'Let's get the van sorted and try and forget Bryony. She's always angry with someone or something, even back in the day.'

He left Sam seething with conflicting emotions. The shock of finding the mobile unit vandalised, the effect of her row with Bryony, and Gabe's support . . . he was there again in her time of crisis, even if only in a small way. Could she have been wrong about what happened with Ryan? Was he right to turn her brother in? She thought about that middle ground again: her seesawing between love and anger. This evening, feeling vulnerable and upset, she didn't know what she would have done if he'd pulled her into his arms to comfort her. The seesaw was tipping lower on the side of love again, and that was the most frightening thing of all.

Chapter Twenty

Reluctantly, Gabe left Sam at the door of Wavecrest Cottage and headed the short distance towards Clifftop House. He'd tried to leave her on a happier note by saying he was looking forward to Chloe's party. She'd nodded and said 'me too', but obviously, her mind was still on her van.

Maybe her mind was on other things too. For a while back in the pub he'd thought they were making progress. He'd made her laugh and he could almost kid himself that nothing bad had ever happened between them.

What exactly had he expected her to be like? She might have been in a relationship for all he knew. She might still be, and he simply didn't know about it.

Gabe was too restless to go home yet so he headed for the coastal path and made his way towards the sea. The coconut scent of the gorse filled the air as he traced the little 'rabbit run' through the prickly plant, the yellow flowers catching the final rays of light. When he was a youngster, on a summer night like this, he'd sometimes come up to the cliff after the chip shop had closed to catch the final tinge of sunlight on the horizon as it changed to the blue of night. He'd imagine what lay beyond the horizon, the people waking up in other parts of the world, and dream of travelling there.

He'd been lucky and seen quite a bit of that world now, from New Zealand to Sri Lanka, the States. Whereas Sam . . . she'd stayed here and devoted herself to her family.

A melancholy settled on his shoulders and suddenly the evening night felt cold. Earlier in the pub, he'd felt the old spark between them was back, but even more intense. He thought that peace had broken out for a while when they were talking about the festival, right up until she'd received that call. He had immediately regretted offering to pay for the van damage.

Big mistake, Sam seemed to have taken his offer the wrong way and assumed he was trying to undermine her independence. She guarded that fiercely, and he didn't blame her, having succeeded on her own for so long. She didn't need some guy charging in and playing Lord Bountiful – especially when that guy was him. The man who'd let her down and hurt her.

She'd had a shit night, though. Stargazey was her livelihood and the vandalism was petty and vicious. Then bonkers Bryony had added to her woes by admitting to ripping the posters down and bringing up Ryan again. Ryan had upset and hurt a lot of people in Porthmellow and from what Gabe could see since he'd been back, the wounds were still raw.

Sam had said she was a different person now and she was right.

'Fuck!' Lost in his throughs, Gabe hadn't been looking where he was going. He stopped just in time, then took a step backwards, his heart was beating like mad.

The turf a few inches ahead fell away sharply in a broad V shape to a narrow ledge a few feet below him. Below that was fresh air, then the stony beach fifty feet down, the pebbles silver in the twilight and a frothy line of foam breaking. The crevice might cut yards back into the cliff for all he knew.

He hadn't seen the cliff fall because it had been hidden by the brambles and gorse. He'd ignored the warning sign at the top, thinking he was on safe ground, ground he'd trodden a thousand times before, but he didn't know this territory as well as he thought he did. It had changed, was continually changing, and he needed to recognise that.

Like Sam. He wasn't sure Sam was the woman he fell in love with. She hadn't been since the moment she'd discovered he'd reported Ryan to the police. He'd never forget the look in her eyes as she'd crumpled onto the sofa. She'd been crushed by his news, but then, she'd been angry. He'd known in that instant that there was no coming back.

The worst part of it was he could change her perspective if he wanted to.

Was she worth his ruining another one of her relationships? She still loved Ryan but if she knew the truth, would she even thank Gabe?

He'd kept quiet too long – she'd hate him for delivering the news too late, or delivering it at all.

What good would it do?

So why did he decide to return to Porthmellow and invest

here? Was it purely out of a wish to put something back into the community? Sam's comments about her passion for her own food had set him thinking harder about re-opening the Net Loft. She'd reminded him that there was a wonderful array of ingredients right here on his doorstep, and reminded him of his deeper connections to his Cornish roots.

She'd also made him start to reassess whether he belonged in London or back here in the south west. He hadn't questioned that since he'd left Porthmellow, swearing to put its small town mentality behind him.

Perhaps, a small voice whispered, coming home was actually because he longed to be close to Sam again and the festival invitation has been the catalyst for desires he'd suppressed for a long time? Maybe he needed to put his hand into the fire again and test out how that felt. Even if Sam wasn't quite the same as the young woman he'd left behind all those years ago.

Or was it because he still loved her, pure and simple?

Gabe looked heavenwards at the stars that were pricking the darkening sky. If that was true, after what he'd done, how could he ever convince her to love him back?

Maybe he'd have a chance to find out at the party.

Chapter Twenty-One

Delicious smells filled the Crow's Nest as Chloe added plates and cutlery wrapped in paper napkins to the dining table she'd set up in the sitting area. After getting back from a two-day trip to Surrey for business and to celebrate with old friends and colleagues, she'd taken yesterday off to get ready for her Saturday night party. Everyone in Surrey knew her real age, of course, and for a couple of days she'd been able to relax and enjoy the celebrations.

Two weeks today the festival would be in full swing, but for now it was time to celebrate her birthday. To say she had mixed emotions about the event was putting it mildly. She should have confessed the first time her age came up, or at Drew's, or at the previous meeting, but the longer she put off her revelation, the harder it had become. Excuses came easily: she hadn't wanted to embarrass herself in front of Drew; then she hadn't wanted to make her revelation distract the committee from an important meeting.

Well, she was going to have to come clean tonight. Chloe pulled a bottle from the fridge and poured herself a generous glass while she got on with something she did feel happy with: playing hostess came naturally to her, even without it being her 'day job'. She'd always loved feeding her family and friends. Her mother and father had been brought up in the Chinese and Welsh traditions of making guests feel welcome with food, so any occasion at home had been marked by cooking frenzies.

She'd already prepared Welsh cakes as a nod to her Welsh heritage, and was now putting the finishing touches to the table and room. The open-plan living room and kitchen area was a light and airy space, but with eight people in there, it would soon feel very cosy so it was a good thing that the evening was fine so that people could spill out onto the terrace. Clouds scudded past, causing the temperature to drop sharply every time a shadow came over. She added cushions to the patio armchair for Evie, and draped a couple of fleece blankets over the arm. Everyone else would probably want to stand outside with their drinks.

Glasses were waiting on the table and a couple of bottles of Cornish 'champagne' were chilling in the ice buckets. There was plenty of beer in the fridge for Troy and anyone else, alongside some very nice New Zealand Pinot Gris. She had more champagne ready for midnight to ease the pain of the moment when she would actually hit the big five-oh.

Chloe let out a squeak, realising that everyone was going to think she'd been hoodwinking them. 'Oh God, what have I done?'

She swept up a couple of cards she'd opened and left on the coffee table and shoved them in a drawer. The big metal badges saying 'Oh No, Five-Oh' and 'Nifty Fifty' were a bit of a giveaway. Fraser had sent one, she recognised his handwriting, but there didn't appear to be anything from Hannah.

Telling herself to brace up, she put on some music – Kylie Minogue and why the hell not – and the intercom buzzed. Her stomach did a somersault. It was D day. Arghh.

'Hello! It's us!' Evie's voice was cheery as ever.

Chloe's guilt ramped up another notch at the thought of lying to this lovely woman. 'Coming down now!' she said and went downstairs to open the door.

Evie stood at the door holding a shimmery balloon with a huge smiley face and 'You're 40!' on it.

'Happy birthday!' Evie declared.

Chloe's jaw hurt from forcing herself to grin. She took the balloon and kissed Evie, feeling a bit like Judas. 'Thank you. You shouldn't have.'

Troy held up a coolbag with his good hand. 'Grub's in here,' he said.

Evie had brought all the ingredients for a dish she said was a surprise, and that she had to cook from fresh so Chloe wedged the various components into her already overloaded fridge.

'Are you going to celebrate with Hannah?' asked Evie. 'Will we get to meet her?'

'Oh, she's so busy. I expect we'll get together sometime.'

'I'm sure she'd want to celebrate with her mum. You wait, I bet she surprises you with some flowers.'

Chloe smiled. 'Maybe she will. Can I top up your drink?'

Chloe moved into the kitchen, busying herself with pouring fizz into Evie's glass when the door buzzed again.

She opened it to find Drew smiling at her and holding a white polystyrene box. Inside there were two dozen scallops nestling on a bed of ice, garnished with lemon chunks.

'I thought it was a special occasion. You do like scallops?' he said.

'Yes, I do. Wow. Thank you.'

'I bought them from Helford not more than an hour ago. I'll open them if you like.'

'Definitely,' Chloe said, taken aback by the sight of him in a white shirt and trendy waistcoat that brought out the deep blue of his eyes. She had butterflies in her stomach like a teenager as he removed the shellfish from the box, accidentally brushing against her in the small kitchen area.

'I just need a tea towel and a board, and when we're ready, I'll give them a quick pan fry with some lemon and wine. They don't take long.'

'Thanks.' Chloe's heart sank further. No matter how gorgeous he was, and even if he didn't have a girlfriend, she'd have no chance with him once he found out her real age.

'Hello! We're here!' Zennor called cheerily from the door.

'We've made vegan pizzas,' said Ben, following Zennor into the flat. 'They just need warming up in the oven.'

'Wow. What a feast,' Chloe said, pleased to have a distraction from Drew and her deception.

'Is Gabe here yet?' Zennor asked.

'No,' said Chloe, sensing that the question was loaded.

223

Zennor gave a small hmmph and Chloe suddenly realised that her party might be the first time Zennor had seen him. If there had been tension between the Lovells and Gabe, it could make for an awkward 'reunion'. It was going to be an interesting night all round, she thought, steeling herself.

'Shall I put the pizzas in the fridge for now?' she asked cheerfully. 'They smell delicious.'

Sam arrived not long after, with a tin of miniature Cornish berry tarts and two pots of clotted cream. 'I made these. Hope everyone likes berries.'

Evie squealed in delight. 'We'll none of us get out of the door.'

Not only were her friends laden with food, but they'd also brought cards – oh God – and gifts, which Chloe put on the sideboard, laughing off hints to open them immediately. She needed more than one glass of wine before she faced that moment. Come to think of it, when was the right moment?

The balloon danced in the gentle breeze from the French windows, taunting her. Chloe felt like stabbing it with a fork . . .

Soon the Crow's Nest was filled with laughter, the pop of corks, chink of glasses and continual 'sorrys' and 'whoops' as everyone started to unload their food on the table, put it in the fridge or give instructions as to how it had to be heated up or served. The expression 'too many cooks' had never been more appropriate so Chloe put Troy in charge of serving drinks just to keep him out of the way. Ben was on his motor-bike so he was on soft drinks.

Gabe was last to arrive. When he walked into the room

with a large plastic tub of food, Chloe spotted Zennor exchange a look with Sam. Sam greeted Gabe pleasantly enough but Zennor didn't join in with the chorus of hellos, but Gabe probably hadn't noticed because everyone else was making so much noise.

Troy steepled his hands together. 'Oh, here's the professional. This had better be good – or is it cod and chips?'

Everyone laughed and Gabe rolled his eyes good humouredly. 'I've kept it simple and brought mezze so hopefully everyone can find something they like.' He opened the coolbag and brought out some plastic tubs. Homemade hummus and tsatziki. 'The taramasalata was made to my grandma's own recipe. It's just roe, onion, bread and parsley. None of that pink gloop.' Gabe grinned. 'There are some giant beans from my mum and olives too. Ben – the hummus, beans and olives are vegan-friendly, as you probably know.'

Ben smiled. 'I love giant beans. So does Zen, don't you?'

Zennor shrugged. 'They're OK.'

Troy pulled a face. 'They make me windy too.'

Evie poked him with her stick. 'Troy! Don't put people off their dinner!'

'No chance of that,' said Drew, pointing to the array of tubs, tins and Tupperware on the table. 'Look at this lot. It's a feast.'

'It's fantastic. Thanks, everyone, you've spoiled me. Now, shall we start with some champagne and Drew's scallops?'

Zennor went pale. 'They're not compulsory, especially not for veggies,' said Chloe, laughing at her horrified expression.

Gabe and Sam decanted the mezze into bowls while Drew brought plates of scallops in from the kitchen, served in their shells with a splash of wine and lemon. Gabe, Troy and Evie proved the biggest fans, downing the shellfish with gusto. Chloe found she enjoyed them a lot more than she'd expected.

Sam had several. 'They're so much nicer than oysters. I can't stand them, slimy things,' she said.

'You might prefer them cooked,' said Gabe. 'They're delicious served with a herby butter sauce. Then you top them with breadcrumbs and pop them under the grill.'

'I'll admit that does sound good,' said Sam, sipping her wine again.

'Maybe I can cook them for you sometime . . .'

'If Drew can get hold of some.'

Drew winked. 'Definitely. Just say the word though it will be September before they're in season again.'

'There you go,' said Gabe.

'Maybe . . .' She downed the rest of her fizz. 'This is delicious too. Any chance of some more, Chloe?'

'Of course. I'll bring it out with the mezze if you all want to move onto the balcony.'

'I'll get rid of the shells and clean up the mess,' said Drew.

As Chloe went to the fridge, she exchanged a glance with Drew who was disposing of the shells in the bin. She followed his gaze to Sam and Gabe who were standing in the doors to the balcony chatting to Troy and Evie. They were angled towards each other, as close as they could be. Sam's laughter was rich and relaxed and she kept touching Gabe very briefly on the arm, very naturally, almost as if she wasn't even conscious of it. He whispered something in her ear and she stifled a giggle. Zennor didn't seem so impressed but after the first half an hour when she'd given Gabe some pretty scathing looks, she seemed to have decided to relax and enjoy the party.

Even so, Chloe was convinced that Sam and Gabe had no idea of the signals they were giving off. She'd done a course on body language as part of her training as an events planner. She was no expert, but she was sure that while there was tension between Sam and Gabe, it was the romantic kind. There was no mistaking the electric attraction between them, no matter how much Sam insisted otherwise.

During the conversation, Gabe had effectively invited Sam over to his house for a meal and Sam hadn't said no. They certainly seemed to be getting on better than at the pub a few weeks ago. Sam had mentioned that Gabe had stayed with her when she'd found out about her trashed van, so perhaps that awful experience had had a small silver lining. Then again, they might have simply been putting on a show of civility for Chloe's big night.

Oh God. That thought snapped Chloe back to the reality of the situation and her deception.

Drew removed the full bag from the bin. 'I ought to put the shells straight out in the bin, if you don't want the house to smell like a fishmonger's.'

Chloe threw him a smile that hid the turmoil inside her. 'Good thinking. The dustbins are in the store behind the building. Thanks for helping out with such a dirty job.'

'I've done a lot worse than this.' He grinned and held up the bag, showing off his muscular, tanned arms without even realising it. Drew did so many things that showed what a lovely, sexy guy he was without him ever having a clue. He

227

was so different to Fraser who was handsome, yes, but carried his attractiveness around like a Rolex, keen for everyone to notice.

Chloe delved into the pot on the counter top. 'Hold on. You'll need the keys to the bin store,' she said.

She handed him a key on a wooden penguin fob. Hannah had given it to her. Drew let the bag rest on the floor and pushed the key in his jeans pocket.

'I'll be back in a minute,' he said.

His blue eyes twinkled. Chloe felt a twinge of lust, which was most inconvenient when a man was holding up a bin bag and you'd resolved not to fancy him anymore. She also reminded herself that he probably had a girlfriend and that, in a way, she would be two decades older than him in a few hours' time, but even this unhappy thought didn't dampen down the fire.

'I'll take the mezze onto the balcony,' she said.

After Gabe's dishes had been hoovered up, it was time to re-heat and serve the hot food. The smells were divine, with an array of aromas competing with each other.

Chloe had pre made the *jiaozi*. The horn-shaped dumplings were filled with pork and chopped leek, spring onion and celery. They were a little misshapen, and not consistent, as always, but then Chloe didn't get much practice these days. Hannah had loved making them when she'd been younger and had been surprisingly good, calling them 'mini stegosaurus'. Her daughter had been proud of her Chinese and Welsh heritage, still was . . . Perhaps, one day, Ruby would be too.

She put the dumplings on to boil. The flat would get a

little steamy, but she couldn't help that. They needed to be served hot. She lifted them out of the pan with Sam's help and fried them before serving them up on a large platter to 'ohs' and 'ahs' and squeals of delight.

Evie's dish was a shrimp creole recipe that had been handed down from her father. It had to be made from fresh, so Gabe offered to help, with Evie standing over him. He fried off onions, peppers and celery before adding tomatoes, bay leaves, spicy sauces and creole seasoning to the mix, under Evie's watchful eye. 'I can't believe I'm here cracking the whip over a TV chef,' she said as Gabe added juicy local prawns to the pan. 'But I remember when he was only the cheeky little monkey from the chip shop.'

The aroma of sizzling onions and spicy tomato sauce now filled the flat. Chloe's own mouth watered. The dish was poured into a large bowl and added to the table with some rice and the other dishes.

Troy hung over the table, with his fork poised. He pointed it at Gabe, who stood back with his arm around Evie. 'My Evie makes the best shrimp creole in the world so you've a lot to live up to, lad.'

'No pressure, Troy,' said Gabe, handing him a plate of steaming rice and sauce.

Troy tucked in, tasting a forkful of prawn dripping with tomato sauce. He chewed then dipped in again while Gabe served everyone else.

Troy smacked his lips. 'Not bad. Not bad at all for an apprentice, I suppose.'

'Not bad? Get on with you, Troy Carman,' Evie said. 'It's

bloody fantastic, even if I do say so myself. You can help out in my kitchen any time, Gabe. You'd be more use than Troy.'

'I got the prawns!' Troy protested.

Everyone laughed and crowded round the table, helping themselves to the different dishes, many going back for seconds. There was a lot of talk about the foods and promises to exchange recipes. Evie related some stories about her father, who'd been born in South Louisiana and spoke French as well as English.

'My dad didn't go home to America after the war like most black GIs. He didn't leave my mum, he married her. You can imagine how that went down with my gran and grandad. In the forties and fifties, there were hardly any mixed-race or black kids so I was different.'

'Wow,' said Zennor, her eyes wide. Even Ben was transfixed.

'He used to call my mum and me *cher* but he pronounced it "char",' Evie said, her fork poised over the plate. 'I wish you could all have known him. He was a lovely man, very brave to have fought in the war and then stayed here. So was my mum, marrying a man of colour back then. That's what they called my dad in his hometown, a *gens de couleur*.'

Troy beamed proudly and gave his wife a squeeze. Chloe felt a little misty-eyed. Some partnerships did last a lifetime.

The pizzas were also brought from the oven and polished off, with even Troy having two slices and declaring how much he'd enjoyed them. There wasn't much left on the table so Chloe asked:

'Anyone for seconds?'

Zennor shook her head. 'I'm so full.'

230

'It was all delicious,' Gabe chipped in.

'So, no one has room for pudding?' asked Sam. 'As well as the tarts, I made a vegan choc cherry fudge cake for anyone who doesn't do dairy.'

Ben's eyes lit up. 'Choc cherry fudge? I'll take it home if no one else wants it!'

Zennor stared at him and even Chloe did a quiet double take. It was possibly the most emphatic statement she'd ever heard from him.

Gabe rubbed his hands together. 'No chance of that, mate.'

Evie patted her stomach and groaned. 'Can we have a bit of a break first?'

'Good idea,' said Chloe. 'I need to make room.'

'Of course,' said Sam. 'And anyway, I wanted to say a few words. Now seems the perfect time.'

Six pairs of eyes lasered in on Chloe. Everyone had a butter-wouldn't-melt expression on their faces, which meant they were all up to something. She braced herself for a cake – a cake with forty on it – oh God, they might have clubbed together to get one and spent their hard-earned cash on a lie. She was going to have to come clean.

Ben had sidled off while Sam had been talking, but he now emerged back into the room with a large rectangular parcel covered in giftwrap and a frothy bow. It wasn't cake-shaped but even so, Chloe wanted to sink through the floor with guilt. She gulped down the remaining fizz in her glass.

'I know you said no presents, but we couldn't let the occasion go by without getting you something to mark it.'

'What have you done? You shouldn't have.'

231

'Ah but we have!' Everyone laughed and Sam grinned. 'Wait until you open it.'

'Oh, I hope she loves it,' Evie murmured and Chloe died a tiny bit more.

'I'm sure I will.' She rested her hands on the paper. It had been so carefully and lovingly wrapped . . .

'Don't keep us in suspenders, maid,' Troy grumbled.

Unable to delay any longer, Chloe pulled off the paper with trembling fingers. Underneath, she found a bubble-wrapped package.

'Oh! Thank goodness. It's a picture!' Her relief that it was clearly not something with 'Chloe is 40' splashed all over it was intoxicating. She sounded like Hannah used to on Christmas morning.

Troy let out a cackle. 'Did you think it was a voucher for Botox in a great big box?'

Evie batted him on the arm. 'Shut up, Troy! You don't need it, Chloe my love. You're only a spring chicken.'

The bubble wrap was heavily taped so Sam handed over some scissors so Chloe could slit it open. Everyone stared at her like puppies around a food bowl at feeding time. Now the initial tension was over, Chloe was desperate to make her delight seem genuine, even if it turned out she hated the picture. Which she was sure she wouldn't . . . She picked off the final piece of tape, opened the layers of bubble wrap and – her gasp was audible.

'Oh my God, that's just incredible.'

She lifted the print up, speechless.

It was a canvas photograph showing the harbour in the

grip of a tremendous winter storm. It had been taken from the opposite side of the cove to the Crow's Nest, and a wave of monstrous proportions was breaking over the clock tower and the far sea wall. It was a horrifying scene in one way, but also it summed up what made Porthmellow such a unique and exhilarating place.

'Do you like it?' Zennor's voice was high and hopeful. 'Ben's cousin Carla took the photograph. It's been on the telly.'

'It's amazing. I've seen small images like this but blown up to this size, it's breathtaking.'

Everyone moved in to get a better look at the picture. Ben started to explain where his photographer relative had taken the shot from during a famous winter storm a few years before.

'Oh! There's the Crow's Nest,' said Chloe, spotting her rooftop flat in the middle of the picture. The angle of the shot made it seem as if the crest of the wave would surely thunder down and flood the flat.

'The water wouldn't have reached up here, would it?' she asked.

'No. That's only an illusion created by the angle it's taken from. Clifftop House took a battering from some of the other waves that night. They had to close the coastal path and shore up the sea defences beneath the house. Even Wavecrest had a few stones against the windows.'

'Bryony Cronk had her front window broken by debris,' said Evie.

Chloe let out a breath. 'Wow. I missed that, but I saw it on TV,' she said

Gabe nodded. 'I came to see how Mum and Dad were and

they told me all about it. I was glad they'd moved out of the harbour. I hear half the businesses were flooded out and the Smuggler's had to board up the windows.'

'You missed a treat,' said Troy, as if the storm had been a gigantic party.

'I've missed a lot,' said Gabe. 'I remember the storm of 2003 – but Mum and Dad told me 2014 was a lot worse that that.'

'Worst I've ever known,' Troy declared. 'Mind you there was that blow the winter our Aaron was born. Boats tossed up on the football pitch.'

Chloe stared at the picture in horror. 'On the *football* pitch?'

'You'll know it's bad when the fishing fleet ends up berthed in front of the post office,' said Drew.

'Or the bin lorry gets washed out to sea,' added Sam.

'Now you're having me on!' said Chloe.

'Nope,' said Drew, Sam and Gabe altogether.

Gabe nodded. 'The bin lorry thing happened when I was at school. There's some footage on YouTube. Take a look if you don't believe us.'

'Yes,' said Drew. 'And worse.'

Chloe burst out laughing. 'You're all so funny,' she said, pointing a finger at Drew.

She looked up to find everyone looking at her. No, they really weren't joking. 'Well, even if the Crow's Nest is one day swept away by a giant wave, I still absolutely love the picture. It's magnificent. And . . . I wasn't going to make a speech . . .' she began. She took another breath, knowing that, finally, *this* was the moment.

Chapter Twenty-Two

Her friends had shown her so much kindness and honesty, they deserved to know the truth about her. Chloe only hoped they'd be as generous after they'd heard as they had been before.

She cleared her throat and made the mistake of catching Drew's eye. He looked at her expectantly, perhaps a little puzzled. This was so hard. She felt light-headed.

'There's something I have to say. When I moved to Porthmellow last autumn, I was not in a good place. You all know I came here to make new memories somewhere I'd been happy, but it was a hope. I had no idea if it would work out and I don't mind admitting that behind the Chloe you might see, I was pretty terrified.'

'Of us? Why, maid?' Troy murmured.

'Shh.' Evie poked him.

'Because I was the stranger, the incomer. That woman from Surrey with the hoity toity accent who looks a bit different.'

Evie nodded. Drew gave her an encouraging smile.

'I don't mind admitting that there's been the odd person in Porthmellow who hasn't welcomed me with open arms.'

'Funny buggers,' Troy muttered.

His comment made Chloe smile and gave her courage. 'But you – the committee – have made me feel like a friend, not a stranger. I know I'll never be Cornish like the rest of you –' Everyone laughed, and looked at her expectantly, boosting her confidence further '– but I *do* feel like part of Porthmellow. You made me feel like part of the community and part of your lives. And that is why I want to share something – a few things – with you that you don't know about me.'

Her stomach twisted as the words came out. She hadn't known until a few moments ago what she was going to do.

She saw people exchange glances. Zennor's mouth opened. Evie straightened in her chair.

'It's about my daughter, Hannah, and . . .' She paused for breath. 'My granddaughter, Ruby.'

'*Granddaughter?*' Zennor's eyes widened. 'I didn't know you were a *granny*.'

Zennor's response was almost comical. Anyone would think she'd announced she was an alien who'd landed from Mars – but there was now no going back.

'No one knows about Ruby, apart from Drew, and he only found out recently,' Chloe went on, willing herself to get the story out and over with while she had the nerve. 'You see, I've been economical with the truth and I hope you'll forgive me. Hannah isn't a student now. She's twenty-two and she has a little girl, Ruby, who's not quite one. I've never seen Ruby, only in a photograph that a friend found online and shared with me. Hannah and I aren't in contact at the moment. I won't go into why but . . .' She paused for a breath, trying not to think too much about the expressions on her friends' faces.

No one spoke, waiting for her to continue. 'So, I haven't been able to tell anyone before, because basically, it's far too painful to talk about and I miss her and my granddaughter so much, it's like a stone in my stomach that I'm carrying around all the time. I don't want to make people miserable with my tales of woe because everyone has problems of their own. Right now, I don't know how to fix my family, I've hit a brick wall, but because you are my friends, and I trust you and know you'll be kind and discreet, I wanted to share this with you . . . it's the least I can do to thank you for being amazing friends. For being like a family.'

Chloe stopped. She felt as if she'd finally unleashed a tightly coiled spring of emotions she'd held in for so long.

'And finally, there's something else I need to get off my chest. Something that even Drew doesn't know. I got so used to keeping my problems with Hannah inside that I stopped telling the truth at all. I forgot that the thing I owed you most was honesty.'

Every eye was trained on her.

'The thing is, I'm not actually forty.'

'I knew it! I knew you were younger. Didn't I tell you, Evie? But why are you having the party?'

'Shh!' Evie hissed at him.

'Oh Troy, I love you to bits sometimes,' Chloe said. 'The party isn't for my fortieth, it's my fiftieth.'

'What?' said Sam. 'No way!'

'Yes, it's true.'

'Wow.' Gabe whistled.

Zennor let out a squeak, then said, 'I hope I look that good when I'm that old.'

'Zen!' Sam cried, but Chloe laughed. 'I kept trying to say, but when you all assumed I was forty . . . well, the moment never seemed right to tell you and to be honest, forgive me, Troy and Evie, but fifty does seem old. With all the other stuff going on in my life, I don't really think I wanted to own up to it . . . it is half a century after all . . .' She finally had the courage to meet Drew's eye. She smiled at him. 'I'm sorry I wasn't honest. I truly am. I hope you can forgive me.'

Drew's mouth twitched briefly. 'I guess this really does call for a drink,' he said and walked into the kitchen.

Chloe's heart sank a little. Of all the people she should have been honest with, Drew probably deserved it the most and now she'd well and truly lost his respect.

'Oh shit. This was meant to be a party not a wake. Cheer up, everyone!' she said.

Her joke unleashed a torrent of relieved laughter. Chloe's eyes were moist, but she also felt as if a burden had been lifted from her shoulders. No more having to pretend that everything in her life was rosy, no more putting on a show . . . but there would be questions, she knew that, lots of questions, some of which she couldn't or wouldn't want to answer.

'I don't know about you lot, but I think we all need another drink after that,' said Evie. 'And Chloe most of all.'

'Thanks, Evie. And I know that being the lovely people you are, you'll want to help me and ask me more. That's fine, I need all the help I can get, but for this evening, can we forget about my problems and focus on enjoying ourselves? It's not every day I'm going to reach my half-century so, please, everyone, let's get the party started.'

Zennor and Ben opened the bottles and started refilling glasses, while Sam and Gabe plated the tarts and vegan fudge cake.

Drew handed Chloe a fresh glass. 'Well done. Do you feel any better?' he said quietly.

'Maybe. A problem shared is a problem doubled, or octupled in this case. Or something. But I feel I've let you down. I wanted to say something when we were at your house.'

'Why didn't you?' Drew asked.

'I thought I'd shocked you enough for one evening.'

'The kiss didn't shock me. Nor your news about Hannah and neither would I have been bothered to know your real age.'

But he was bothered by her deception? Chloe didn't blame him. 'I'm sorry for that. I wasn't thinking straight. That's no excuse.'

'We all make mistakes,' he said.

'Thanks,' she said, but she was by no means sure that he'd forgiven her. 'Where's these puddings, then?' Troy called from the balcony.

Drew smiled. 'Better get our priorities right,' he said.

239

'True.' She kept her voice light but her heart was heavy. She fancied Drew more than ever now he was even further from her reach. But she had to remind herself he'd been within it. Caitlin was a lucky woman.

While everyone tucked into the desserts, Evie asked about Ruby, and Chloe told her as much as she knew, which was very little.

Sam discreetly mentioned she was always available if Chloe ever needed to talk. Sam was the first close friend she'd made in Porthmellow and, after Drew, it was to Sam that Chloe felt she owed an apology for not telling her more sooner.

'I should have been brave enough to tell you earlier. I almost did a few times but never found the right way.'

Sam gave her a hug. 'I'm not offended. We all have parts of our lives we want to keep private until – if – we're ever ready to share.'

Beyond that, no one pushed her to reveal any more, and the evening passed with banter, stories about old festivals, gossip and wine. *Lots* of wine. Chloe had drunk way more than she had for years, and was pleasantly sozzled while dimly aware that alcohol suppressed your inhibitions. Judging by the feelings that stirred every time she watched Drew pouring drinks, clearing tables, laughing, drinking or breathing, it was all she could do not to launch herself on him in front of everyone else. Instead, she tried to avoid him, sitting as far from him as possible – which wasn't easy in a one-room space – and trying not to get into any deep private conversations.

Just before eleven, Zennor and Ben left, stating they were knackered, which the 'oldies' remarked was hilarious, considering they were meant to be young and energetic. Sam had told Chloe that her sister and Ben were just good friends, but it was hard to believe there wasn't more between them as they seemed pretty inseparable. Whether they were going back to Wavecrest Cottage or Ben's chalet on Porthmellow Park, Chloe had no idea.

Troy and Evie went home a quarter of an hour after 'the young ones', and after Chloe had seen them off, she hauled herself upstairs, feeling a little light-headed, wincing at empties in the recycling bin which told their own story. Gabe, Sam and Drew had dragged chairs onto the terrace and were sitting under the fleece blankets looking out over the lights of the harbour.

'Coffee, anyone?' she said.

There were groans.

'I've got a very nice bottle of Armagnac to go with it.'

Cheers followed.

'I'll lend you a hand,' said Drew, finding mugs while Chloe spooned the coffee into the cafetière. She still preferred hers made that way rather than in an automatic machine. 'Are you OK?' he asked her.

'OK. No, *more* than OK. I've had a fantastic evening.'

'Good. This was a really great idea.'

'I hoped so. I went to a friend's bring-your-own-supper party and that went down a storm. It was a lot easier for me as host and people seem to enjoy bringing one dish that means something special to them. Those scallops were fabulous, by the way, even if not everyone was keen.'

'Thanks . . . Have you heard from Hannah since we spoke?'

Chloe's fingers tightened around the handle of the cafetière. 'No.'

'Have you thought of actually going to see her in person?'

'I've thought about it, but if I'm honest, I'm afraid of the reception I'll get. I'm scared of the look on her face and of being thrown out. I'm worried that it would only make things worse.'

'Chloe . . .' Drew's voice was soft. 'Enjoy this evening and tomorrow, when you've had the chance to think, then why not think about visiting her? I think if you could just speak to her, even if she's angry at first – and she may well be – you might at least start a conversation again.'

'Maybe. I just don't know.'

'It could be a fresh start.' Drew brushed her fingers with his. 'In more ways than one.'

Chloe was taken aback but decided that she should be up front with him. 'I'm not sure I know what you mean?'

'That tonight could be the moment for a new start with me. If you're interested, of course.' He hesitated, doubt clouding his eyes. 'I'm sorry if I'm way off the mark.'

Chloe opened her mouth as the reality of his words dawned. 'What about Caitlin? I don't want to be the other woman in any relationship, even if it's new, or break a couple apart.'

Drew smiled. 'Caitlin won't mind.'

Her estimation of Drew plummeted. She should have known he was too good to be true. He was another cheater, like Fraser. 'Drew. How can you know that?' she asked.

'Because . . . Caitlin is over a hundred years old.'

'What?'

'She's a *boat*, not a girlfriend. The sailing trust – with me as chief – have been thinking of buying another historic vessel for a few months so we can preserve her and take out more groups on trips. It's been a big decision to spend that much money, but I finally signed off the contract to buy her yesterday.' He grimaced. 'You're not the only one who's been a bit economical with the truth.'

Chloe let out a squeak. 'You . . . you . . . but why didn't you tell us all she was a boat?'

'Well, like you, I started with a tiny fib and then it grew . . . At first, buying the boat was confidential business information, but I'd had some ribbing from a few of the guys on the quayside about my "love life" and one day a few months ago when I let slip that I was interested in a Caitlin from Falmouth, they assumed it was a woman and I decided to go along with the joke. I like to keep my private life private, which isn't an easy thing to achieve in a place like Porthmellow. As you know.'

Chloe struggled to reply but then the bubbles got the better of her and she burst out giggling. 'You're outrageous, Drew, and very very wicked for tormenting us all like this – does Sam even know?'

'Not yet. You're the first. I'll tell her later. I promise.' He bit his lip.

'You *should* and she'd have every right to be pissed off.' Chloe shook her head again, still not sure whether to be annoyed at his fibs or delighted that Caitlin was no real rival. Although, being a boat, she might well be.

'So . . . our white lies have cancelled themselves out and

243

there's no reason why we shouldn't get to know each other better and, possibly, if you want to, as more than friends.' He screwed up his nose. 'Mind you, after winding you up about my other woman, maybe you've changed your mind about *me*? Whatever you decide, I'm not going to rush anything. You're in control.' He sighed. 'After what happened at my house, when I pushed you away, well, I wouldn't blame you for being angry with me. You see, a little white lie about your real age is nothing compared to the way I've behaved.'

'I was annoyed, I'll admit it, but mostly with myself for jumping on you.'

He smiled. 'You didn't exactly jump on me. It was only a kiss, but a very very nice kiss. In fact, it was too nice. I realised then how much I'd love to have kissed you back – properly – and what it might have led to. But how could I have done that after you'd just told me about your problems with Hannah? What kind of a bloke takes advantage of a woman who'd finally decided to trust someone? Who wants him to listen to her not use the opportunity to drag her into bed?'

Chloe took a gulp of her wine before replying. She hadn't expected him to be so up front, even though it was refreshing. Drew was no Fraser, willing to use his charm to get what he wanted, no matter who he hurt. She touched his cheek, looking into his gorgeous eyes and shivered deliciously.

It was possible for a kind and gentle man to be sexy. And *how* . . . 'You're a lovely man, Drew, and I can forgive you for fibbing about Caitlin and for ending things at your place when you did. It's true, I wasn't in the right frame of mind and I'm not sure it would have ended well.' She paused for breath. 'But – what about the age gap between us? That's a fact that we can't ignore.'

He shrugged. 'So what?'

'Because – because . . .'

The clock tower struck twelve. The chimes tolled out her answer.

She abandoned her glass to clamp her hands over her ears. 'Oh my God, I've hit my half-century.'

Drew pecked her on the cheek and Chloe stared at him. He grinned and her stomach did the kind of flip that she hadn't felt since she was about twenty, let alone fifty.

The last chimes rang out from the tower. 'That's it. I'm officially old,' she said.

'Well,' said Drew. 'Consider this. It's not so bad so far, is it? And I did wonder all along if you'd been holding something back. You seemed on edge around me lately and I thought you might still have feelings for your ex. Now I know it was nothing but a number and if that doesn't bother you, it certainly doesn't bother me.' He brushed her lips with his, before moving away so the rest of the guests could hug her and offer their congratulations. As she was engulfed by her friends, and more corks popped, Drew stood on the sidelines, watching. He'd made his feelings clear, now all she had to do was decide if she had the courage to respond.

Chapter Twenty-Three

'Whoa.'

Gabe steadied Sam as she walked down the stairs from the Crow's Nest.

They emerged into the street that led up to Stippy Stappy Lane. The sky was clear with a few ragged clouds drifting past, playing hide and seek with the moon. It was a perfect summer evening, with the kind of velvet twilight that sometimes lasted all night at this time of year. It brought back memories of kissing Gabe on the beach as the waves gently lapped the shingle.

She stumbled on the cobbles and Gabe steadied her with a hand at her elbow. His fingers were warm on her bare skin. He let go and slowed his pace to match hers as she tottered up the lane. Fresh air hitting her lungs made her a little light-headed but it had been a wonderful evening.

'Good party,' said Gabe, echoing her thoughts.

'Oh, it was. Much more fun than I'd expected, to be honest,

but I wish I'd known about Chloe's family sooner – and her age. My card has forty splashed all over it.' Sam groaned then giggled. 'Too late now.'

'She definitely looks a lot younger,' said Gabe. 'But I guess being fifty isn't her real problem.'

'I feel so sorry for her to be kept away from her daughter and her baby granddaughter. I know what it's like to be separated from someone you love. With Ryan, I mean,' she added hastily, in case Gabe thought she meant him, although she probably did mean him too, by accident.

'You still miss him a lot,' Gabe said.

It was a statement as much as a question.

Sam sobered instantly. 'Of course, I do. Even when I hated him for what he'd done, I missed him. At least I know he's alive. Or he was a few months ago. I had a birthday card from him, saying not to worry. No contact details though.'

'I thought Chloe seemed to enjoy herself,' he said, moving the subject onto safer ground. 'It seemed to help that she'd told us about her family.'

'Yeah. I knew there was something not quite right, but she's good at putting on a front.'

'So are you.'

'I've had no choice. Zennor needed me. Ryan too in the early days.'

'I know. Zennor gave me a few looks but I expected that. It can't have been easy for her to meet me again tonight and I don't blame her for being pissed off with me for my part in what's happened to your family.'

Sam had also been worried about Zennor's reaction at

meeting Gabe again but considered things had gone as well as she could expect. 'It was difficult for her but I asked her to be civil for Chloe's sake. She worries about me – she needn't – and she probably hasn't realised what you and your parents did for us after Mum died, bringing us food and keeping an eye out for her while I worked late. You were a big help until . . . until it all went wrong with Ryan.' She stopped talking, realising that she was getting too close to dangerous ground in terms of the past. It had been a lovely evening and she didn't want to ruin it.

'I'm—' Gabe began.

'Don't say you're sorry again.'

'I was going to say I'm cold,' said Gabe.

After the warmth of the flat, Sam also shivered. Gabe put his arm around her back but didn't pull her too close. Sam flinched in surprise, but she didn't move away. Instead, she left it there, testing herself to see how she might react . . . was she playing a dangerous game? Did she care? That was the booze talking, she thought dimly, but still didn't pull away from him.

'Sam, I wish so much that we could move on from the past,' he said. 'At first I thought coming back here was a mistake but lately . . . We've been civil too.' He smiled and her heart beat faster. 'More than civil . . . are we at least on the path to something beyond that?'

His face in the streetlight. Lips parted, eyes intent on her. He held her round the waist.

She nodded. 'I don't know but . . . us continuing to argue, me continuing to blame you. Well, that's never going to bring Ryan home, is it? Only he can decide he wants to do that.'

Gabe dropped his hands from her waist. The warmth where they'd been evaporated. What had she said to make him let her go? She'd thought it was a major step forward. Crashing disappointment, or was that the booze wearing off?

'Gabe?'

'You're right. Only Ryan can decide.'

'Wherever he is,' said Sam, looking out to sea, as if her brother might suddenly materialise from the waves, before refocusing on Gabe's face, a few inches above hers. 'I wanted to apologise for snapping at you after you offered to help with the van repairs. I've managed my own business for years now and I didn't – don't – want you to think for a moment that I'm after you for your money.'

Gabe burst out laughing. 'After me for my *money*?'

'Well, yeah. You know, now you're kind of – well a bit famous.'

'*Famous?*'

'Yeah. You are and stop laughing at me, you git. It's true. Lots of people have heard of you and you're on the telly.'

He wiped tears from his eyes but Sam wasn't amused. She gave him a little push. 'It's not funny!'

He brushed a hand over his face and turned down his mouth in a serious expression that lasted all of a second. 'I'm sorry, but it feels weird to hear you say that. Or anyone. OK, I have done well, but I'd never think you were after me for my money.' A cheeky smirk spread over his face and his eyes gleamed wickedly. 'But you *are* "after me . . ."'

Sam groaned. 'I *never* said that. I mean, I didn't mean "after you", literally.'

He made a little fishing reel motion.

Sam squeaked in indignation. 'Gabriel Mathias, you are a horrible wind-up merchant and you'll never change!'

'Ah but I have changed. That's the point, but not when it comes to how I feel about you.' He reached for her hand and pulled her closer. His expression changed into something far from amusement. She'd seen that look before: intense, sexy, full of desire. Desire for *her*. An electric thrill shot through her from top to toe.

He leaned forward to kiss her. Sam allowed him to support her back with his hand and slide the other under the hair at the nape of her neck. In the moonlight, a shiver of pure lust ran through her and every pore was alive with delicious sensation.

How had this happened? How had she let him get so close? She wasn't *that* drunk, she was letting him do this; inviting him . . . not resisting, wanting the kiss. He moved his hand to her chin and tilted her face upwards. His fingers were warm and every inch of her skin felt as if it was glowing. Every part of her was alive again. She met his mouth with hers. She kissed him and tasted smoky Armagnac.

They weren't far from the cottage now, and a light popped on in the porch. The door opened and voices cut through the quiet. *'Nightttt!'*

'Bye!'

It was Ben and Zennor saying goodnight. Ben hadn't gone home then . . .

Gabe shook his head and leaned in again, but the moment had passed. The bubble had burst and that was probably just as well. Joking with him, relaxing in his presence, kissing him had felt so enjoyable and natural, she'd forgotten the reasons that had and still kept them apart. The unanswered questions about his betrayal of Ryan: why did he choose to do the 'right thing' over his love for Sam?

'Too soon,' she murmured, stepping back a little. Gabe said something but it was drowned out by the throaty rev of Ben's motorbike starting up.

'OK.' Gabe caught her hand, raising his voice as Ben roared off down the winding lane. They paused, waiting for the din to fade. 'Does that mean there will come a time?'

Her pulse skittered. She'd taken a leap forward – or perhaps back – in the past few minutes. She simply couldn't bring herself to say no. 'Let's take it slowly. Get to know each other again first?' It was a huge cop-out but Gabe's eyes gleamed with happiness.

'Take all the time you want,' he said.

She smiled. 'I will. Goodnight, Gabe,' she said as she moved towards the cottage.

'But hurry up!' he called after her.

She saw the light in the porch like a beacon of safety. She might be soaring on possibility, but what happened if she came crashing down to earth again? If that happened again, she didn't think even the festival would save her.

Chapter Twenty-Four

After her party, Chloe had woken with a dry mouth and made a vow never to consume alcohol again, which she knew would pass far more quickly than she deserved. The burden of her 'secret' had been lifted, but now she had a new load to deal with. Whether to act on Drew's suggestion of making an unscheduled visit to Hannah. One moment she would decide to call Drew and go; the next she'd realise it was the worst idea in the world.

She had no time to dwell on her hangover or anything else over the following week, which flew by as the preparations continued. Bunting had appeared all over town, strung between the buildings and lampposts, adding a party atmosphere overnight. Shopkeepers had put festival-themed displays in their windows and banners had gone up outside the pubs and cafés advertising their special festival menus and events. A hundred emails had gone out to all the stallholders, allocating their pitches and detailing all the hygiene and health and safety regulations they had to comply with. Those forms would come back and all had to be checked, a job which fell to Evie and a friend from her bingo club.

In a flash, the week leading up to the event itself was upon them. It was Chloe's first festival as a 'local' and it amazed her to see how its tentacles spread from the main venue on the harbour through the side streets and up to the marquee field. Overnight, yellow signs warning people about road closures and directing them to festival car parks had gone up. Shouts and clangs drifted across the harbour from the Smuggler's as the staff erected a party tent over the beer garden, while the Tinners' was advertising an all-day hog roast.

On the Thursday before the big event Chloe was up early and on her way to a morning meeting in the harbour office with Troy. Two large vans passed her, one of which pulled up on the grassy area next to the inner harbour while the other ground up the hill towards the marquee field. Chloe realised they were the chef's tent and the festival marquee. It felt as if the Festival Beast was now unstoppable and it made Chloe tingle with excitement and nervous energy.

At the harbour office, steaming mugs of sailor's tea were handed round while the harbourmaster delivered the weather forecast, saying that things were looking a bit 'lively' for the couple of days running up to the festival. No one had told the weather it was meant to be flaming June, then, Chloe thought. Over the weekend itself, it was supposed to be mostly fine, but with some showers – 'that could land anywhere across the South West' the Met Office had said helpfully. Troy didn't seem concerned, pointing out that as long as the rain wasn't too heavy, people would turn out. In fact, if it wasn't blazing hot, that was a good thing because they were more likely to choose the festival than the beach.

Chloe took notes on the meeting while they discussed the provisions for emergencies, evacuations in the event of fire, rogue waves or, heaven forbid, a terrorist attack. Troy rolled his eyes but Chloe, having been involved in organising events in central London, knew that however remote, this was a threat they needed to be prepared for, just in case.

They ran through a host of dull but essential safety items before a heated discussion about obscure aspects of harbour operation between Troy, the harbourmaster and a woman from the council.

Chloe tried to follow it, but soon zoned out. She'd had half an eye on her phone for messages about the festival and she was still holding out hope Hannah would wish her a happy birthday. When she slid a discreet look at the screen, there were two missed calls. Not from Hannah but from Fraser.

Chloe frowned, but decided to pick up the call. The meeting had almost finished anyway. She made her apologies and went outside, finding a spot by a pile of lobster pots.

'Hi. Chloe. I've been trying to get you for hours. I'm in Austria and supposed to be in a conference seminar,' Fraser said. He sounded terse but that wasn't unusual. Chloe struggled to hear him above the sound of chatter and tannoy announcements on his end of the phone and gulls squabbling over the scraps from a recent catch.

'I've had the phone on silent while I tried to get on with some work for Porthmellow Festival.'

'The Mellow *what*?' he shouted,

'Porthmellow Festival. I'm one of the volunteers who organises it.'

'You, a volunteer? You mean you're working for nothing?'

Chloe wanted to scream. 'Yes, Fraser. What's the matter?' She turned cold. 'It's not Hannah, is it?'

'Yes and no. Don't worry. I've no bad news. Could be very good news actually. I bumped into Antonia Craddock at a breakfast meeting. She works for one of our competitors now but more importantly, she's an old friend of bloody Jordan's parents.'

Chloe gripped her mobile, willing Fraser to get to the point.

'Antonia told me that Jordan had gone home.'

'What? As in home to his parents in London? With Hannah and Ruby?'

'No, on his own.'

Chloe tried to process this news. 'So has he left them? For good?'

'Possibly. Antonia didn't have any more details apart from that Jordan had moved into the granny annexe and was driving his mother mad expecting to be waited on hand and foot. The little toe rag won't say too much more, but apparently Jacob is furious with him.'

'What about Hannah and Ruby?'

'Still in Bristol as far as I know.' Fraser swore. 'I feel like going round to the Reeses' as soon as I'm back in England from this conference and teaching that bastard a bloody lesson.'

'Don't even think about it, Fraser! This isn't about you or Jordan. It's about Hannah. If he has left her on her own with the baby, imagine how she must be feeling. Unless she kicked him out. I do hope so!' Chloe was ready to rush out herself, but not to thump Jordan.

'I know how I'm feeling,' Fraser continued. 'Relieved and bloody furious. If I . . .'

She listened to Fraser ranting for a while, itching to get him off the phone so she could decide what to do next. Eventually, she managed to convince him to let her deal with things and promised to phone him the moment she knew any more.

It took all her composure to walk back into the harbour office to say she had to leave, but the meeting had finished so she practically ran back to the Crow's Nest. She needed space and time to work out her next move – if any.

She went out to the balcony where the *Marisco* was motoring back into the harbour under a warm morning sun. Drew had taken a group to Brixham and while in port he'd said he would visit Katya and Connor. Hannah wondered how he must feel, with the possibility of his son moving so far away.

An idea lodged in her mind, as unstoppable as the festival itself . . . Drew was back home now . . . If she was going to see Hannah, now or tomorrow were the only times she could get away, especially if she wanted to take Drew with her, as he'd offered.

Immediately, she thought of Fraser. He'd go mad and probably rightly so if Chloe went off to Hannah behind his back with a stranger. Then again, the very fact that Drew was neutral might be the best thing. Fraser would be bound to kick off, and Hannah might feel ganged up on with both parents there. Drew didn't even need to enter the house, he'd just be in the background for moral support, and perhaps, Chloe admitted, to offer an impartial perspective. He said he'd share the driving with her to Bristol. They could be there and back in a day and if her plan worked, she might be reunited with her daughter and granddaughter within a few hours.

The prospect was so wonderful, so enticing, that her stomach clenched in excitement, followed by dread at the alternative outcome: Hannah vowing to break off contact forever because of Chloe's interference. She would have to tread very carefully.

Moments later, Fraser sent a WhatsApp saying that he'd heard more from Antonia and that Jordan had let slip that Hannah was still in the Bristol flat 'as far as he knew'. Fraser added a few choice expletives and that he'd a mind to fly back to Bristol and bring Hannah home whether she liked it or not.

Chloe could have screamed in frustration. Hannah was twenty-two not thirteen; she made her own decisions. She messaged him back, warning him she'd never speak to him again if he did anything like that and, eventually, he agreed to leave things with her for a couple of days.

She threw the phone down

She had to do something *now*, before Fraser rushed in like a bull in a china shop or Jordan decided to go back to Hannah. She couldn't bear the thought of Hannah being on her own, dumped by that little sod, not knowing where to turn or wanting to come home and not knowing how.

Drew was right. She needed to meet Hannah face to face and have one last try at getting through to her. But how could she possibly leave the festival with only two days to go?

Chapter Twenty-Five

That morning Sam had been in early at Stargazey Pie with Stefan, baking extra stock for the festival weekend. Stefan was manning the van with a part-time assistant as Sam would be completely taken up with her festival duties. At lunchtime, she nipped out to make some calls and check out the Chef's Theatre, which was taking shape by the harbour. Dings and clatters filled the air, and Pirate FM blared out of a ghetto blaster. The seating was already in place, and the contractors were installing the stage, some of them bare-chested under their hi-vis waistcoats. Although it was only half past nine, the sun was beating down, leaving the builders with a sheen of sweat as they worked. Sam had heard the weather report and found it hard to believe that strong winds were forecast to blow in that evening.

After its re-spray, the Stargazey van was looking better than new in its slightly upgraded livery. The insurance had agreed to pay and the re-sprayers had done a cracking job so that was one thing off her mind. Sam had been worried that the Phantom Paint Flinger might try again but there was nowhere else to park the van other than outside the unit, so she'd had no choice but to cross her fingers and pray there was no further damage. The police had drawn a blank in their investigations and obviously, with more serious things to deal with, Sam had resigned herself to never finding the culprit.

As for Gabe . . . since the party she hadn't seen that much of him as he'd had to return to London for most of the week. She hated to admit she'd missed him, or think about the way her stomach did a flip when he waved at her from outside the Tinners'. Even if they resolved their differences over Ryan, another worry had taken root. Gabe had hinted he wanted them to get back together, but how would that work? Practically, she supposed he could spend part of the time in Porthmellow, though the physical distance didn't bother her as much as the way their lives had diverged. Gabe was used to the pace and glamour of London, and he might enjoy the attention of his fans far more than he let on. Sam lived a quiet life in the company of her friends in a town that would probably never have been big enough for Gabe, even if they hadn't split up over Ryan.

She turned away from the Chef's Theatre, planning to go back to the unit and get on with another batch of pies when she spotted Gabe walking away from the Net Loft. It wasn't clear whether he'd been in the premises or not and she didn't want to ask him what his plans for it were. She was still in a dilemma over whether she wanted him to hang around Porthmellow or not. Her heart said one thing – her head another. One thing that wasn't in doubt was the impact he had on her physically. With shorts that showed off his tanned legs and a sexy linen shirt, Gabe looked hot enough to burn up the quayside.

He waved and strode over to join her and gazed at the half-finished theatre with admiration. 'Wow. It's a thing,' he said.

Sam smiled to herself. 'Yes, it's definitely a thing.'

'I've cooked at festivals before but to see this in Porthmellow is really something. It must feel good to watch it finally coming together.'

She laughed. 'More like terrifying. No matter how many times I do this, I always get the same feeling of horror about what I've unleashed on the town. There's a weather front moving in and there are so many things that could go wrong . . .'

'I'm sure that Sam Lovell can handle anything.' His words were innocent but sent a shiver down her spine. Unlike the party evening, she was now stone cold sober but the same hopes and fears were still there. In fact, they'd only intensified while he'd been gone.

'I always dread that there might be something I haven't thought of or something that comes completely out of the blue and is too big to manage. That's scary.'

'What could possibly ever go wrong in sleepy little Porthmellow?' he said, with a look and a tone that were unmistakably bittersweet.

Sam drank in the deep brown eyes under dark lashes. She could lose herself in those again so very easily. Perhaps she already had. 'I can't imagine,' she said, guessing he was refer-ring to their past history.

260

Gabe returned his attention to the theatre site. 'I've been thinking about after the festival,' he said, too casually.

'Oh yes,' her heart pitter pattered.

'My meeting in London was to finalise details of the Net Loft. In fact, I've just met the agent for another look at the place. I've signed on the dotted line for the property and found a head chef.'

She searched his face. 'So it's definitely going ahead . . . but you're not staying as chef yourself?'

'Sadly, I'm too committed with other parts of the business, but of course, I'll be very hands-on, especially at the start.'

So, he wasn't moving to Porthmellow. Sam cursed herself. Just a month before, she'd longed for him to leave, now she was disappointed he wasn't staying. 'OK. You must be very busy. I should have realised you wouldn't be able to run it yourself.'

'I didn't say I wouldn't be closely involved. I just haven't decided quite how hands-on to be yet. I'm going to see how it goes, you know . . .' His voice petered out and he turned to her. 'Sam?'

She nodded. She couldn't think of any words that wouldn't reveal how she felt. How torn she was between wanting to be with him and wanting him three hundred miles away. She still had a lot of forgiving to do – so did he – and she couldn't shake the feeling that some of her questions about Gabe and Ryan still hadn't been answered.

A workman dropped a sledgehammer with a *clang* and they both jumped.

'I must get back to Stargazey. I still have to make a ton of pies for the festival. We've sold half the stock from the unit to all the festival workers, so we're nowhere near having enough to keep us going over the festival. Stefan and a local teen from the village are running the van over the weekend, but I can't expect him to make the stock on his own.'

Before Gabe could reply, Sam's phone rang. 'Sorry, have to get this. It's Chloe. Hi, Chloe. How's it going?' she said.

As Sam listened, Gabe scrolled through his phone, but she saw he started to pay attention as she tried to soothe a clearly frantic Chloe. 'OK. OK. Well, you *have* to go. Family comes first . . . stop worrying about us. The festival will be fine . . . Oh, OK . . . right. See you when you can. Good luck, I hope everything works out for you.'

She put her phone in her pocket again and heaved a big breath. Her life had just become a little more complicated.

'That didn't sound good. What's happened?' asked Gabe.

'That was Chloe. Apparently, her daughter's shitty partner has left her on her own with the baby. Chloe's worried, naturally, and wants to go to see her in Bristol.'

'Sounds like a tricky situation. Not the best timing either.'

'Nothing ever is. Chloe's ex is away on business so Chloe's desperate to check that Hannah and Ruby are OK. She's decided to turn up on the doorstep unannounced and see what happens.'

Gabe sucked in a breath. 'That's risky, but I can understand why. When is she going?'

'Right now,' said Sam, already running through a list of Chloe's jobs in her mind. 'And Drew's going with her.'

Gabe winced. 'I'm guessing that leaves you without two of your key team?'

'Team?' Sam managed a smile. 'They're volunteers . . . but yes, they are both big shoes to fill.' And Sam herself would probably have to fill them, even though Chloe and Drew had asked some of the volunteers to help with their duties. People couldn't be expected to step in at such short notice, not when they already had their other roles.

'Can I help?'

'You?' Sam didn't mean to be so abrupt but her mind had just reached Peak Festival. She was blindsided by Chloe's news, and overwhelmed by the prospect of filling in for Drew and Chloe *and* getting her stock ready for the weekend. Finally, she'd bitten off more than she could chew. And for the first time, panic set in. This was too much . . .

'I might not be able to do any of the specialist stuff, but I'm willing to try anything,' Gabe continued. 'I know more about the festival now and if there's any dirty work – little tasks – anything I can do so you can handle the big stuff, then let me.'

'Thanks for the offer, but I don't know what you can do . . .' Sam racked her brains. 'You're the headline name, after all. There's some fetching and carrying you could do and I guess you could liaise with the chefs . . . if you don't mind?'

Gabe touched her arm and his voice was soft, seductive. 'I don't mind fetching and carrying or liaising with my fellow chefs . . . I'm a Porthmellower first and foremost, but I've got another idea.'

'I'm glad someone has because right now, my brain has fried. Fire away.'

'You know all those pies you have to make for the weekend?

263

Well, have I ever mentioned that I enjoy a bit of cooking? In my spare time, of course. I'm no professional but if you need a kitchen hand, I'm here.'

Sam's jaw fell open. 'You are joking?'

'About being a professional?' He grinned.

Sam was too overwhelmed to joke. 'No, about offering to work in Stargazey . . . I mean . . . Aren't you busy?'

'Always, and my PA is going nuts already, but I've cleared my diary until next week. While I'm in your kitchen making pies, you can concentrate on the festival.'

'I – do you think you can cope with doing all the prep? Would you mind being supervised by Stefan?'

'That's fine. I'm willing to learn; I've got all my hygiene certificates.'

Sam burst out laughing. 'That's a relief but . . . Oh, my God, Stefan will have *kittens* when you rock up at Stargazey as his apprentice.'

He rubbed his hands. 'That sounds like fun.'

'It'll be something, that's for sure.' Sam folded her arms and gave him a hard stare. 'Thank you. This is probably the maddest festival decision I've ever made but beggars can't be choosers so let's get you into an apron, Mathias, and start licking you into shape.'

Chapter Twenty-Six

It had been with a heavy heart that Chloe had phoned Sam to break the news that she wanted to leave the festival at such a crucial time. She felt awful for bailing out with less than forty-eight hours to go but Sam had been amazing about it. 'Family comes first,' she'd said, with genuine feeling.

Chloe was sure Sam was putting on a brave face but she'd made her decision now. While she collected some stuff and waited for Drew to bring his car round to the flat, she tried to delegate some of her jobs for the day to other volunteers but it had been hard to find anyone at such short notice. She'd promised to stay contactable by phone and the journey up to Bristol had given her the chance to make and take a few essential calls. It had also helped divert her mind from what she might face once she reached Hannah's flat.

It was lunchtime before they drove into Clifton, a chic suburb of the city, and managed to find a parking space almost opposite Hannah's flat.

Drew turned to Chloe who was sitting in the passenger seat of his Land Rover. 'Are you sure you don't want me to come up to Hannah's flat with you?'

'No. Thanks. You stay here. I'm sure you need to get on with some work calls,' she said to Drew. 'I feel bad enough for bunking off myself, let alone dragging you with me at such a crucial time.'

Now she was here, all thoughts of work had evaporated. There was no denying she was about as nervous as she'd ever been in her life. Sunlight shining through the trees dappled the pavements and added a mellow glow to the brick and stone facades of the Georgian houses, but Chloe was in turmoil. Her heart pounded. Her throat was dry. She'd had second, third and twenty-third thoughts about the trip from the moment they'd driven out of Porthmellow earlier that morning. Even with Jordan gone, would Hannah still reject her?

The flat was situated at the top of a row of once-grand townhouses. It was on the very edge of the trendy area, but hadn't seen as much of the gentrification as the streets they'd driven through, which reminded Chloe of fashionable suburbs of London, with their pavement cafés and boutique shops.

The paint on the main door was peeling and some buildings were in decay, while others had skips parked in the gardens, but Chloe could see that the area was on the up – you only needed to see the artisan coffee house on the corner, and the hipster barber and health food store.

She clutched her straw tote bag tighter, cradling the gift it contained for Ruby, and peered up to the top of the block, wondering if the dormer window was Hannah's flat. Her daughter could be looking out right this moment and down at the street.

'Which is Hannah's place?' said Drew, as if reading her mind.

'I think it's the very top. Not ideal for lugging a pushchair up, but it could be a lot worse.'

'Much worse. This area looks pretty expensive to me.'

'Hmm. Jordan must have been paying the rent. Hannah can't afford this, even when she does go back to work, with nursery fees on top.'

'Is it what you expected?' he asked.

She sighed. 'No. It's much nicer. In one way I'm hugely relieved but . . .'

'Disappointed it's not some hell hole?'

'Not exactly, but I do know what you mean. I've asked myself that question many times. How would I have felt if Hannah had been genuinely happy, yet still cut off all contact with us? I've tried to convince myself that I would accept whatever she decided, and whoever she was with, if only she was happy. No parent can realistically expect more than that.'

'You're not a saint, Chloe. None of us are.' Drew's wry smile made Chloe smile too. She was glad he was here. He'd tried to distract her on the way, and helped her keep things in perspective. It was a great gift to be able to see the world as it truly was, a talent that few people had. She was in danger of falling for more than his rugged good looks and twinkly blue eyes. Much more.

'I'm definitely not a saint,' she said. 'You know that . . .'

She gazed up at the building again. 'I think it's time to face the music.'

'OK. I'll wait here for you, but please call or text me if you plan on staying and I'll make myself scarce for a while.'

'Thanks. I can't help thinking this is eating into your time. We should both be at the festival. I felt bad telling Sam I needed to come down here, but she told me to forget the festival and look after my family. She's amazing.'

Drew laughed. 'She is, and you needn't worry about me. I wouldn't have come if I was worried. This is important. I'll hang about and answer some emails until I know you don't need me and if you do want to stay longer, I'll go down to look at the SS *Great Britain*. You won't be worrying about me messing around on a boat, will you?'

He'd made her smile again. The tension eased a fraction. 'No, I won't. Although I might never see you again.'

'You will. Now off you go and good luck,' he said.

Chloe closed the door of the car softly, as if anything more might somehow, impossibly, alert Hannah to her presence. Taking calming breaths, she crossed the street and made her way up the steps to the front door. There was a row of buttons with names next to them, but the top two flats had no names at all. That meant nothing, as maybe Hannah and Jordan hadn't bothered to add theirs. Even so it would have been reassuring to confirm she'd got the right flat. Chloe went to buzz the top button, bracing herself for a conversation that could end any way: with shouting, crying or – if a miracle happened – being let in. She could be moments from being reunited with her daughter and finally meeting her little granddaughter.

The competing emotions of dread and anticipation were almost too much. She had to breathe deeply and force herself to calm down. She had to damp down all her excitement and pent-up feelings. She had to tread so carefully. This was about Hannah and Ruby.

On an impulse or because of some sixth sense, she decided to try the front door instead of ringing the buzzer. She gave it a little push and it moved. Someone had left it slightly open or unlocked.

She walked into the hallway. It must have been very grand once, with its high ceilings and staircase curving upwards, complete with ornate balustrade. The door to the ground floor flat had been freshly painted in a smart blue, but the one opposite was scuffed and mucky around the handle. There were leaflets for yoga classes and takeaways on the hall floor, and a child's trike propped up under a shelf. Too old for Ruby, of course. The gift wrap rustled around the presents in her tote bag. Were the stacking cups and cuddly hippo OK? She'd asked around friends and decided on something for Ruby to play with now and something she could cuddle and keep. She hadn't wanted to get anything too ostentatious and didn't want to be seen to be trying too hard . . .

She started to climb the stairs, feeling a bit like an intruder, which, actually, she was, having gained entrance to the place by stealth. Voices drifted out of one of the flats on the first floor, and rap music from another. Someone had the telly on very loud on the second floor and there was an Amazon delivery box left outside another flat. That was trusting of them . . . or lazy of the driver.

269

At the foot of the final flight of stairs, she stopped. She was breathing way more heavily than she ever did when she climbed from the harbour to the Crow's Nest. She tried to calm down again, listening for the sounds of a baby crying or Hannah singing . . . but there was silence.

It was now or never.

She climbed the final flight and walked up to the top flat door. There was no name outside, no buggy or any other clue that the most precious things in Chloe's world were closeted behind that discoloured gloss door.

She knocked.

Silence.

She listened and heard a faint movement. Footsteps approaching from the inside. Her heart rate took off.

'Hannah, it's Mum,' she said as the door opened. 'I'm sorry I just turned up—'

'Hello?'

The woman who answered was about forty, dressed in a navy trouser suit and heels.

'Oh. I'm sorry. I thought Hannah was living here.'

'Hannah?' the woman frowned. 'May I ask who you are?'

'I'm her mother,' said Chloe. 'Ruby's grandmother. I was . . . in the area and I thought I'd drop in on them.'

'Oh.' The woman frowned. 'Well, didn't you call them first?' The woman spoke coldly, obviously not quite believing Chloe.

'Er . . . no,' Chloe squirmed. 'This was meant to be a surprise.' She held up the gift. 'I bought Ruby a present . . . It's a hippo.'

The woman looked at the tissue-wrapped lump in the bag,

270

then at Chloe and recognition – of a sort – flickered in her eyes. 'Oh, right. OK. Yes, you must be her mother. I see that now.'

Chloe realised that this strange woman had processed the fact that she had Chinese heritage with the fact that Hannah and Ruby had too. She'd made the assumption, rightly but for the wrong reasons, that Chloe must be telling the truth. But I could be anyone, thought Chloe . . .

'So, is Hannah in?' she asked, too desperate not to offend or question this woman too sharply.

'I'm afraid not . . . but . . .' The woman frowned again. 'Hannah moved out yesterday.' Her tone cooled again. 'Didn't she tell you?'

Chloe just managed not to put a hand on the door frame for support. 'No. I mean, she might have emailed me or texted . . . my phone, you see. I left it behind and—'

She was so ashamed, so poleaxed with disappointment that she lied, rather than let this cold stranger know that her own daughter had moved without even telling her.

'I'll go and call her. My friend, he's waiting in the car. I'll borrow his phone . . . You – I expect she's sent her new address but you don't happen to know it, do you?' she asked.

'No idea, I'm afraid. Good luck with finding out. I'm sorry but I have to get on with the assessment for the next tenant.'

Then she closed the door, almost in Chloe's face.

Chloe stood there for what felt like an age before the instinct to get away from this crushing situation kicked in. She scooted down the stairs, past the smells and sounds of other families' lives. The disappointment weighed on her like a rock. Hurrying, she opened the door and stumbled down the steps.

271

Drew was out of the car and on his phone when he saw her, but she rushed past him, the bag banging against her legs.

'Wait!' he shouted after her.

No. She could not let him see her pour out this grief, which summed up all the loss and disappointment of the past few years. No one should see it.

But he followed her. Once he'd caught up with her, she forced herself to calm down. 'She wasn't there. She's gone. I've no idea where and neither had the letting agent. I'm back to square one. Worse than that. I don't even know where she is now.' She was shaking. 'And we should be in Porthmellow, sorting out the festival not here on a wild goose chase.'

Drew grabbed her by the arms, gently holding her. 'For God's sake. Stop trying to be brave. Scream if you want. Shout. Hit something, as long as it's not me.' He looked her straight in the eyes. 'Just have a bloody good wail and then, when you have, we are going to start again and we are going to find her, festival or no festival.'

Chloe sat in the car for a while and composed herself, before Drew persuaded her to have a quick walk around Clifton and even force down some tea and a scone in one of the pavement cafés. She hadn't eaten in hours, it was a long drive back to Porthmellow and they both needed a break.

Once the initial shock was over, it was very rapidly replaced by concern. If Hannah wasn't living at the flat with Ruby, where were they living?

'I hope she hasn't gone back to Jordan. Although perhaps that would be better than nothing.'

'They might be in a hotel nearby,' he suggested, adding a large spoon of sugar to his tea.

'I don't know how much money she has. Her dad and I would willingly help her out at the drop of a hat. She only has to ask, but I expect she's too proud. I hate to think of her alone in some hotel room, wondering what to do. I suppose we could call around the hotels, but they won't tell us anyway.'

'That letting woman, she said that Hannah had left, not that she'd been thrown out because the rent hadn't been paid, didn't she? That means Hannah made an active choice to leave.'

She replaced the cup carefully in the saucer. She felt as fragile as the delicate china. 'You're right. That is a good thing. It means she must have plans. I'm going to have to call Fraser, even though I don't want him knowing I've come over here. I suppose he has a right to know.' She checked her watch. It was the middle of the afternoon and for Drew's sake she thought they should go home – he'd already had to delegate his festival jobs too, and it was totally unfair to keep two of the committee away from Porthmellow because of her family problems. 'I think we'd better set off soon. It's no use staying here, Hannah could be absolutely anywhere.'

'You could call her . . .'

'Yes. I will.' It seemed the obvious thing to do, but Chloe had been too bowled over by the disappointment of finding Hannah had moved to think straight. She called Hannah's number, holding her breath. But within a couple of rings, the call went straight to voicemail. The silence only added to her worry, but Chloe left a message, saying she'd tried to visit her at the flat and asking Hannah to call her.

'Do you think it's worth asking around the flats to see if anyone knows where she is?' Drew suggested.

'You mean knock on a few doors?'

'Exactly.'

She glanced back at the building. Banging on doors to see if anyone knew her own daughter's address would seem very odd. Was she desperate enough for that? She decided she was.

Steeling herself, they went back into the building and got an answer from a couple of flats. One was a new tenant who didn't even know who Hannah was, and the other said he'd seen her move out but hadn't known her well enough to ask where she was going.

They trooped back to the car. 'I refuse to contact Jordan,' she said. 'I don't trust myself. I hate to say it, but I think we're going to have to go home and keep trying her phone. I'll try to get hold of Fraser too, though he's at a conference in Austria. I can't think of anything else.'

'It's a plan,' said Drew, laying his hand on her arm. 'I won't say try not to worry, but if Hannah's left Jordan, it can only be a good thing.'

'I know . . . but until I know she's safe, I won't rest for a moment.'

Chapter Twenty-Seven

Gabe stretched his arms above his head and groaned as various parts of his body clicked and protested. He'd finally taken off his Stargazey apron in the unit staffroom as the afternoon drew to a close.

He was knackered. How many pies had he made? He'd lost count. He knew what hard work was, having spent many hours in top kitchens and the fish and chip shop, but man, mass producing artisan pies to a tight deadline had been a *lot* harder than he'd expected. Hundreds of the buggers were now prepped, filled, cooked and chilling in the fridges. Personally, he never wanted to see another pie as long as he lived, let alone eat one.

Stefan had thought Sam and Gabe were having him on when they turned up at the unit. Later in the day, she'd called to check that all was going well . . . to which he and Stefan said it was, of course. So what if it was a little white lie? So what if his first batch had been rejected by Stefan as 'looking

275

like cow pats'? Who could have guessed that Stefan would turn into Gordon Ramsay's evil twin once he was put in charge of a kitchen? Gabe did get the hang of it eventually, but Stefan was merciless, speeding up as soon as Gabe had mastered the process.

Stefan left for the day with a pat on the back for Gabe, leaving him alone in the unit to wait for Sam.

'Hello!' she called from the staffroom. 'Everything OK?'

'Fine,' said Gabe, pasting on a smile as she walked through the door. 'How were your meetings?'

'Don't ask. Council officials, emergency services, harbour authorities, more council people . . .' She ticked them off on her fingers. 'Thank God I didn't have to work here as well.' She frowned at him. 'You look knackered . . . and there's flour in your hair . . . or you're going grey.'

'Both probably, Stefan is a tyrant.'

Sam laughed. 'He's a sweetie, really. He probably felt in awe of you and over-compensated.'

'That's one way of putting it.' Gabe smiled. 'On the upside, we finished all the pies.'

'Thanks. That's a load off my mind.'

'I'll send my invoice, shall I?'

'You volunteered, remember?' She stepped forward and peered at him. 'There's flour on your nose too.'

She rubbed the tip of her finger against his nose. Gabe held his breath. She had no idea what she was doing to him. She was dressed casually as ever, in a vest and denim skirt that showed off her slim figure and shapely legs. Her cheeks were glowing from a day spent outdoors and the sun had bleached natural highlights in her hair. Gabe's brain scrambled. He was in trouble here. Deep trouble.

'Sam.'

The syllable was all he got out before his arms were around her waist and he was kissing her. Wow. The feel of her. The taste of her . . . after more than eleven years . . .

She pulled away moments after he touched her.

'Gabe. I can't handle this right now.'

'I'm sorry. I shouldn't have—'

'No. I – Thanks for doing this. Stepping in, today . . . the committee are really grateful for your help.'

'You're welcome . . . I'm not only doing it for the festival, but you must know that. I want to repair some of the damage I've done.'

'In my experience, some things aren't worth repair. It's better to start all over again.'

'And could you – start all over again?'

'I don't know . . . Ask me after this is over. If you plan on sticking around,' she said. 'But now I *have* to concentrate on the festival.' Her voice was a plea.

Gabe nodded. He knew when to back off, even when every cell of his body was screaming at him to kiss her again. It was obvious that gaining Sam's trust would be a long hard road and he had to tread carefully if he was ever to have a chance of winning her back.

Chapter Twenty-Eight

Chloe took more than a few calming breaths as Drew drove away from the flat and out of Bristol. Soon after they were heading far away from the suburbs and onto the M5. After rehearsing what she was going to say to Fraser, Chloe called him, but his mobile went straight to answerphone. She tried Hannah again, got her answerphone, so followed it up with a text and a WhatsApp, which was delivered but not marked as being read. She was past caring about harassing Hannah. This was an emergency.

She leaned back against the headrest and stared out at the flat Somerset fields. The green grass flew by but all she could think of was a variety of scenarios involving Hannah and Ruby, none of them particularly pleasant. She could be back with Jordan or in a hotel or a grim B&B. Chloe had no idea if Hannah had any money to spend on a safe, clean place to stay with Ruby. Why had she left at all if Jordan had paid the rent or she had the means?

Fraser called as they'd crossed the border from Devon north of Launceston. Predictably he was worried and it all came out in an angry rant against Jordan.

'What's he done to her? I'll kill him if he's done anything. God, why has this happened while I'm in bloody Austria!'

'Calm down,' Chloe pleaded. 'You shouting won't get us anywhere and it isn't helping.'

'Are you driving?' he asked out of the blue.

'No, I'm with a friend.'

'Who?'

'Does it matter?' Chloe snapped back, annoyed – she wanted to focus on Hannah.

'I suppose not . . . I suppose everyone knows our private business now.'

'Oh, Fraser, don't be ridiculous. Everyone back in Surrey knows about Hannah and Jordan – including bloody Antonia. If I want to talk to my friends about my family, I will do.'

Fraser didn't reply immediately. 'I'm sorry, I'm worried. I want to know where my daughter and granddaughter are. I can phone Jordan's father and see if he knows.'

'If you think it will help but for God's sake, keep calm.'

'Yeah.' The phone clicked off.

Chloe sank back against the headrest. 'Arghh.'

Drew let her simmer down for a few seconds. 'Try not to worry,' he said. 'Hannah sounds like someone who can take care of herself. If she's anything like her mother, she'll be fine. She probably just needs a bit of time to work out how to approach you before she contacts you or her dad.'

'I hope so . . . but where on earth can she have gone?'

279

'Grandparents?' he asked.

'My mum and dad live in Wales. I doubt she's gone there, but I'll call them . . . though it will only make them worry too and my dad's health isn't great. Fraser's parents are dead, unfortunately.'

She toyed with her phone, uncertain whether to alarm her elderly parents. 'I think I'll give it more time. Mum would have let me know anyway if Hannah had turned up . . .' That was one avenue closed, Chloe decided. 'There are a couple of her friends from uni and school who I could Facebook message. I don't want to resort to it, but I'm getting desperate.'

Chloe was still dallying with the idea while hoping and praying for a call from Hannah herself, when they were a few miles from home. She was ever aware that tomorrow was the day before the festival. Hannah and Ruby were her number one priority, and she'd hoped that she would at least know they were OK, so she could help out with the preparations. Poor Sam having to manage without her deputy at such a crucial moment.

Porthmellow appeared on the road signs when her phone went again and Sam's name flashed up on the screen.

'Hi Chloe.'

'Sam. Is everything OK?'

'Fine, but I have some news for you about Hannah.'

'What?' Chloe cried out, causing Drew to glance at her in alarm.

'Don't worry. She's absolutely fine.'

'How do you know? Where is she?'

'Here in Porthmellow,' Sam said as if it was the most natural thing in the world. 'I just met her and Ruby in the Harbour Café. She's been trying to call you.'

A few minutes later, Chloe phoned the Harbour Café number and the owner answered and passed her on to Hannah.

'Hannah?'

'*Mum*? I've been trying to get you. I had no signal and then my battery ran out so I came to this café. You know that place that used to have the chocolate eclairs that you and Dad used to like, but it looks a lot different.' Hannah lowered her voice. 'It's gone all trendy with artisan coffee and vegan brownies . . .' She giggled nervously. 'Who'd have thought Porthmellow would turn hipster-ish?'

Chloe didn't know whether to laugh or to weep with relief. This was the Hannah she used to know. The one she'd known until a couple of years previously when she'd met Jordan.

'I've been to Bristol to the flat,' Chloe said.

'I know. Sam told me . . . and I've been here. We've been going in opposite directions. I should have called, but I didn't know what to say after everything that's gone on between us. In the end I thought it would just be better to see you face to face so I drove down here and found the Crow's Nest, but you weren't in and your neighbour wasn't sure when you'd be back . . . I was petrified you'd gone on holiday or something then I realised you wouldn't because you've been organising this festival.'

She listened, astonished that Hannah had known about the Crow's Nest and the festival. Her emails and messages hadn't fallen on deaf ears. Hannah *had* been interested . . .

'But why are you in the café?'

'Ruby needed feeding and changing and I asked if I could charge my phone. Then your friend Sam walked in and I heard them mention your name . . . and I said who I was. They were so nice. Sam offered me her phone, but the woman who owns the café let me use the landline. That was when Sam mentioned you'd gone to Bristol to find me. She seems really nice.'

'She is.' Chloe thanked her lucky stars for her friends and that she'd finally told them the truth about her situation. 'Hannah, I'm almost in Porthmellow now. Will you be OK to wait at the café? It closes at five.'

'Not tonight. They're open until nine because they're having a music event, but they said I can stay until that starts at seven. The harbour is heaving with workmen setting everything up for the food festival. Mum, it's *huge*. I can't believe you're involved.'

'Yes. I'm involved.' Or *should* be, thought Chloe, reminding herself to text Sam after she'd spoken to Hannah. 'Is Ruby OK? Do you have everything you need for her?' she asked.

'My car's rammed with stuff but your marshals wouldn't let me onto the harbour car park so I'm ages away on some field. I've got everything I need for Ruby for the night but I had to leave loads of stuff with a friend in Bristol.' There was a pause. 'Mum, I couldn't stand it any longer with him and I threw him out. I'm so sorry. I know I can't expect to just come running home after what's happened but I didn't know who else to turn to and anyway . . .' There was a telltale break in her daughter's voice. 'I wanted to see you.'

Chloe's heart almost stopped. She was so relieved to hear her daughter say those words, yet angry and upset at the hurt she'd gone through. 'I want to see you too. I said I'd always be here for you and Ruby and I meant it. I'll be there in forty minutes or so.' She heard a faint wail. 'Is *that* Ruby?' she asked, her skin tingling with excitement at hearing her.

'Yes. She's hungry and tired. It's been a long day. I need to take her out of the buggy. Mum, I have to go and change her. I'll stay here. I'll see you soon.' Hannah's voice wobbled. 'I can't wait.'

The phone clicked off. And that was it. Hannah speaking almost as if nothing had happened. After all the days, weeks and months – years – of worrying and longing and waiting, in less than an hour, Chloe would see her daughter and meet her baby granddaughter.

The car stopped at some traffic lights. Drew glanced at her. 'That was Hannah in Porthmellow? Is she OK?'

'I don't know . . . tired . . . stressed but very Hannah. She remembered that we used to go in the Harbour Café for chocolate eclairs. She said it had gone hipster-ish. You'd almost think the past two years had never happened.'

'Maybe for now she wants to pretend they haven't. It'll all come out soon enough, I expect.'

'Yes . . , plus there's Jordan to deal with. I don't know whether he'll try to get back with her. I need to let Fraser know. He's bound to want to come to see her. Oh God, I hope he doesn't turn up like a bull at a gate. I'm glad I can spend some time with Hannah first, before he weighs in. He does love her, but he's never been one for subtlety.'

Drew touched her hand. 'I'm sure Hannah knows that. We'll be there soon and you can calm the situation down and prepare her.'

'Yes. You're right.' She was grateful for his sense of perspective.

'And hold little Ruby, of course,' he added, before putting the car into gear and pulling away.

Chloe had to blink hard to make sure she wasn't dreaming. 'I can't believe it. I almost can't handle being this happy after all the tension and worry, even if it's a result of Hannah splitting up with Jordan. I'm happy, but I'm hurt and sad for Hannah. None of it seems right or fair.'

'Who said life is fair? You know it's not, so bloody well make the most of the good bits. I'm sure it won't be plain sailing over the next few months, but for today, I'd take what's been handed to you.'

Chloe texted Sam and thanked her for her call. Although every mile felt like ten, eventually they were driving down the hairpin bend into Porthmellow and the harbour came into view. The tide was in and water glinted in the early evening sun with tiny wavelets rippling the surface. Out to sea, white horses romped over the ocean, and the swell was bigger than she'd expected. The quaysides were a hive of activity with dozens of people fixing up generators and services.

The quayside was already closed to non-festival traffic and Drew had to stop at a barrier, but he was eventually waved through by a woman in a hi-vis vest as soon as she recognised his car.

He stopped on the harbour car park, which was full of

vans and trucks, and turned to Chloe, a gentle smile on his face. 'Will you be OK?' he asked.

'Yes.' She held out her hand and smiled ruefully. 'I'm shaking. Even though I'm going to meet my own daughter.'

'That's understandable.' He squeezed her hand. 'I'm going back home now, and then down the harbour to make sure things are going OK, but you know where I am if you need me. You only have to call.'

'Thanks, Drew. You've done so much already.'

'I'm glad it's worked out, even in a way you didn't expect.'

She leaned over and kissed him. She meant to kiss his cheek but somehow, their mouths met. It was a light and gentle kiss, somewhere between friends and lovers.

'That wasn't meant to happen,' she said.

'The best things never are. Go, now. If you want me, I'm here for you.'

She collected her bags and the presents and walked towards the café. Hammering and the bursts of drilling rang out from all sides as workers put the finishing touches to the Chef's Theatre marquee and larger stalls. The smaller gazebo type stalls and mobile vans wouldn't move in until very early on Saturday morning. Chloe thought that was a good thing, judging by the way the wind was gusting. She assumed the construction teams knew what they were doing. There were shouts and laughter as tradesmen worked, music blaring out from their radios.

It was strange and unfamiliar and added to her sense of disorientation. She tried not to hurry, or break into a run, even though suddenly, it seemed incredibly urgent to get to the café.

What if Hannah had changed her mind? What if they weren't there after all?

She stopped. A group of workmen had moved away and revealed Hannah standing outside the café with the buggy. She was holding Ruby's arms as Ruby made an attempt to toddle towards a seagull.

Ruby tottered on the cobbles, yelling loudly and straining to get to the gull.

'No. You can't stroke it. They're not furry!'

Ruby's wails as she tried to reach the gull cut through the building work and thumping radios. Ruby had on a pair of little red dungarees. Chloe recognised them. They were once Hannah's. Hannah had kept them, then . . .

Chloe held her hand to her mouth, trying not to laugh.

'Mum!'

Hannah had spotted her and was waving her over. Chloe hurried forward and Hannah burst into tears. Chloe joined her, ignoring the workmen who must have been staring at them.

'Ruby kept trying to get down off my lap and move between the tables. She's almost ready to take a few steps on her own so I brought her outside . . . Oh God, I'm so sorry about everything, Mum.'

'Me too,' said Chloe, fighting back a sob.

Hannah picked up Ruby who squirmed in her arms. 'There's so much to say. So much I want to tell you.'

'We both have, but not now. It can wait, my love.'

'I want to hug you but I can't . . .' Tears ran down Hannah's face. 'Shit. I must be all snotty.'

Chloe was laughing and crying at the same time. 'Here you are.' She pulled a tissue from a packet in her bag.

'Th-thanks. Can you hold Ruby, please, while I sort myself out?'

'Try stopping me.'

Hannah passed the wriggling Ruby to Chloe who almost burst with joy and relief. Ruby stared at her, taken aback by being passed to someone new. She reached out and tugged Chloe's hair.

'Ow. She's not happy, being bundled off to a strange woman.'

Hannah's tearful face turned to a smile. 'She'll get used to it.'

'You're staying for a while, then?' Chloe asked, holding Ruby's chubby fingers in her hand. Ruby was transfixed by her, brown eyes wide and hands clutching at Chloe's hair.

'Yes,' said Hannah. 'If you'll have us.'

Chloe wondered if it was possible to faint from happiness. Nothing could ever match the joy of having her family back with her. Not all the riches on earth. 'Oh, I think I might be able to find room for you.' She kissed Hannah's cheek and Ruby's forehead. 'Come on, you must be knackered. I know I am. Let's go home.'

Chapter Twenty-Nine

That evening, the Crow's Nest rang with unfamiliar sounds. Squeals of laughter pierced the normal quiet as Ruby splashed in the bath. Chloe had resisted the urge to go in and see if Hannah needed help. Of course Hannah didn't need help: she'd managed for a year now.

Once Ruby had been bathed and put to bed in the cot next to the bed in the spare room, Hannah and Chloe shared a takeout pizza and a bottle of wine. They'd spent the evening talking until they were hoarse, and there had been more than a few tears.

Once he'd heard Hannah was with her, Fraser had said he'd come straight down to Cornwall as soon as he landed back in the UK. He was relieved and delighted, naturally, but she was secretly glad he was stuck in Austria until Saturday. She needed this time alone with Hannah and Ruby. If that was selfish, she didn't really care. Hannah needed some space herself, and dealing with one parent after so much time apart was probably more than enough.

After dinner, they finished the wine in the sitting room.

'Did Jordan stop you from visiting us?' Chloe asked, feeling a little more confident about asking difficult questions. She had to get to know her daughter all over again and vice versa.

'Not physically . . . but he made it clear he'd rather I didn't come home. At first I thought he was different from the other guys I'd met at uni. Cheeky, anarchic, funny . . . and even when I found out that he was loaded, I believed him when he said he wasn't interested in the money or any of the "Surrey mafia" as he called them.' Hannah screwed up her nose, as she often did when she felt awkward or embarrassed. 'Sorry.'

'You know what, Hannah? When I first married your father and moved to Surrey, that's how I felt myself. It's not easy being different. Welsh, I mean . . .'

Hannah giggled. Chloe hadn't heard her do that in a very long time.

'Anyway, it took a lot of fitting in,' Chloe continued. 'Not that I ever really did. I felt far more at home in London, and curiously, more at home here. I might be different, with my heritage and city ways, but Porthmellow is a quirky place that draws in an eclectic bunch from all over. It's not perfect, but by and large, people are accepting of difference in others. Or they'll come right out and say what they think, rather than smiling on the surface while they're planning how to ignore you.'

Hannah groaned. 'I know it was hard for you. I hadn't realised how hard.'

'I could say the same about you and Jordan.'

'Yeah . . . I can't believe how controlling he became. He wanted me to cut off ties with my old friends and family, and somehow I got sucked in to that, especially when Ruby came along. She demanded most of my time and I hadn't realised how much of it I was spending in the flat, looking after her – while he was off drinking in trendy bars or making trips back home, saying he wanted to sort out his trust fund so he could be "properly independent". I was so stupid . . .' She firmed up her voice. 'But I don't want to play a victim, Mum. I could have made the decision to come and see you and to leave him.'

'But you *did* leave him.'

'I was going to, I swear, but it took me a long while to screw up the courage. I planned to get away for weeks before I actually did but I didn't know how to do it. I felt I'd gone so far down a road away from you and Dad that I didn't know how to get back. I've hurt you so much.'

'We've all done things we shouldn't. Your father and I didn't handle the divorce well and we're both sorry for spying on you. That was wrong.'

'I was angry that you didn't trust me to make my own choices. Looks like you were right,' she said, closing her eyes.

'No, you have to make your own choices. Don't let anyone persuade you otherwise. Not Jordan. Not your father – or me.'

Hannah gave Chloe a hug. 'Oh, Mum.'

'I won't lie. I was hurt,' said Chloe. 'It's been horrible, but you're here now. You did find your way home – or to

Porthmellow at least. Time to look to the future, when you're ready.'

Hannah nodded. 'Right now, I don't know what to do next. I need a job. A home.'

'Well, you can stay here as long as you like until you're back on your feet.'

'Thanks, Mum.' Hannah looked brighter.

'But let's cross that bridge another time. Your dad will be here the day after tomorrow.'

Hannah wrinkled her nose. Chloe could tell she was in two minds about seeing Fraser. 'I want to see him, I *do* love him, but I'm nervous about his reaction.'

'Don't be. To be honest, I feel the same . . . we'll deal with him ourselves. He's been terrified too. He . . . we made mistakes that made things worse between us.'

'We've all made a lot of those . . .' Hannah seemed to be distracted by something. Chloe stayed quiet, wondering if she needed time to compose herself, but then Hannah got up and walked to the mantelpiece.

She picked up one of her birthday cards.

Chloe laughed nervously, realising Hannah might be in for a surprise when she examined them more closely.

Hannah opened a card with a painting of the *Marisco* on the front. It had been given pride of place in the centre of the mantelpiece.

To Chloe, have a fantastic birthday. Hope the next year brings all you've been dreaming of. Lots of love, Drew xxxxxx

'*Lots* of love? And *five* kisses.' Hannah blew out a breath. 'Wow.'

'Drew and I are very good friends,' Chloe burst out.

'He's the guy who drove you to Bristol?' Hannah still had a cheeky smirk on her face.

'Yes. He's a good man.'

'You're definitely not getting back with Dad, then.'

'Did you expect me to?' said Chloe, unsure of what Hannah was wanting her to say. A few months ago, Chloe might have admitted that she'd consider giving things another go with Fraser, if he left his girlfriend, but she felt very differently now.

Hannah carefully placed Drew's card back in its slot on the mantelpiece. 'I hoped so once. I lay awake dreaming of it, but now . . . not now I've seen you here. This is you, Mum, your new life. I hope we'll all always be together, as family, and watch Ruby grow up. You're Mum and Dad, but I don't expect you to be wife and husband. I want you to be happy.'

Chloe had to fight back tears.

Hannah picked up another card. 'Mum, why do some of these cards have happy fortieth on them?'

Chloe bit her lip. 'Um . . . that's a long story . . .'

'You haven't been lying about your age, have you?' Hannah said with a smirk.

'Well, maybe, just a little bit.'

'Mum!'

'When I mentioned a special birthday, people kind of assumed I was forty and they kept joking and somehow I didn't have the heart to tell them the truth and then it became harder and harder to confess.'

'Would this have anything to do with Drew?' Hannah eyed her shrewdly. 'Because I think he must like you a lot to have left Porthmellow with this festival happening, just to drive you to Bristol.'

Chloe had no answer.

'You didn't want him to know you were older than him, did you?'

'No. I didn't. I kept meaning to tell him but I had so many other things on my mind, I couldn't face disappointing him.'

Hannah tucked her arm through Chloe's. 'You are silly. You look amazing for your age.'

'For my age. That's the point. I'm twelve years older than Drew.'

'Does it matter?'

'He says not but it does matter to me. I'm still not sure it's a good idea for us to get more closely involved.' She sighed. 'Even though I do really like him.'

'Wow. He must be special. Is he anything like Dad?'

Chloe burst out laughing. 'No. Not in any way. He has a ponytail and an earring and he's the skipper of a vintage sailing trawler.'

'An earring? Oh my God. He sounds like Captain Jack Sparrow!'

'Jack Sparrow? I'll have to tell him that,' Chloe said.

'Don't you dare. Oh Mum, if he likes you that much to drop everything and drive you to find me and he doesn't care how old you are, you should go for it. What are you waiting for?'

To be sure I was over Fraser, thought Chloe. To make sure there was no hope of us ever getting back together . . . But before she'd been sure of that, she'd actually moved on herself.

'We'll see. I've other things on my mind at the moment.'

Hannah kissed her. '"We'll see". You always said that to me when you wanted to give me what I asked for, but weren't sure you could.'

'There you are, then,' said Chloe, hesitating. 'I'd appreciate it if you didn't mention Drew to your father.'

'Of course. And talking of cards, I've got something for you.' Hannah went into the room Chloe had made up for her and came back with a card. 'It's very late and not much. I'll get you a present. I promise.'

'You don't have to.' Chloe took the card. The envelope was a bit the worse for wear, creased and with a red mark on it.

Hannah wrinkled her nose. 'That's jam. Ruby got some on her fingers and grabbed the envelope.'

Choked up, Chloe opened the envelope and slid out a card, which had a simple picture of a hippopotamus on it, wallowing in mud. It simply said: Hippo Birthday, Mum.

'Don't you remember you always used to sing that silly old song that Grandad Farrow likes? *Mud, glorious, mud* . . . It's a silly card and I never plucked up the courage to send it, but there you are.'

'It's wonderful. It's . . . perfect. Wait.' Chloe hurried off, not daring to look at Hannah. She went into the hallway and found the gift bag from the cloak cupboard.

'I meant to give you this earlier in Bristol, or when we met at the café, but there was so much happening. It's for Ruby. Maybe I should wait until she wakes up?'

Hannah took the gift bag. 'I don't think I can.'

'OK. We were always desperate to open presents and I'm

sure Ruby won't mind. If you leave the box-shaped parcel for her and just have the tissue-wrapped thing in the gift bag.'

Hannah pulled out the box and put it aside on the sofa. She unwrapped the tissue paper and her eyes misted with tears. 'Oh God. It's a hippo. A hippo like I had. I still have him, Mum.'

'I thought you might.'

'It's probably more for you – and me – than Ruby. Very indulgent. A granny present.'

Hannah flung her arms around Chloe, squashing the hippo between them. 'Thanks, Mum. Thanks for everything. Shit, I've made you cry now,' she said, spotting Chloe's tears. Her own eyes glistened. 'So that makes both of us.'

'It's f-fine,' Chloe stammered. 'Sh-shall we both have a bloody massive blub and get it over with so we can start again tomorrow?'

A short while and a fresh box of tissues later, Chloe and Hannah sat down with the last of their wine. Hannah finished her glass and yawned. 'I've been so wound up I thought I'd never sleep again, but I feel knackered.'

'No wonder. It's been a very big day. Go to bed and I'll clear up.'

'OK. Thanks,' Hannah said, but her voice was almost drowned out by the wind rattling the flat. 'God, if we make it until morning.'

'This is nothing, according to Troy. He's lived here for over eighty years and he knows what he's talking about.'

Hannah laughed. 'Troy, Drew, the festival . . . I knew you'd get into village life. Organising has always been your thing.'

Apart from organising my own life, thought Chloe.

'You love living here, don't you?' said Hannah,

'I wasn't sure at first but I've made some friends I'd never have got to know otherwise.' Chloe looked again at the photograph she'd received for her birthday, with all its dramatic energy. 'Now, I can't ever imagine living anywhere else.'

Chapter Thirty

On Friday morning, Sam had been to a pre-festival briefing at the harbourmaster's office when she received a call from Chloe to say that her first night back together with her daughter had been a positive one. She stopped on the quayside to have a quick chat. Chloe insisted on resuming some of her duties later in the day, which was a big relief to Sam who felt overwhelmed with responsibility. She kept telling herself that she always felt like this on Festival Eve, but she hadn't liked the sound of the forecast that the harbourmaster had passed on.

Grey clouds mustered on the horizon like an army waiting to strike. Heavy rain would put a huge dent in the festival attendance, but more importantly they had to make it to festival morning with an intact marquee and Chef's Theatre. The wind had freshened significantly while they'd been inside for the briefing, thought Sam, holding her hair off her face. The harbour office was an exposed spot anyway, so that was nothing unusual. Seagulls fought the breeze, hovering over a trawler chugging into the harbour to land its catch. Others gathered on the harbour wall, their raucous cries filling the air.

She saw Gabe waving from outside the Net Loft and then start jogging to meet her. He was in a T-shirt and shorts, his strong calves tanned by the sun. The air was humid as if it was storing up an epic downpour. Sam felt hot and shivery.

'How's it going?' he asked.

'Manic as ever. Niggling little problems, but that's normal. It's the forecast that bothers me more.'

'I saw on the news.'

'Troy was full of doom. "The last time I saw clouds like that was over Treverrow in 'fifty-seven. They were mopping up for weeks and roads were closed till Christmas."' Sam imitated Troy's gloomy voice.

Gabe laughed out loud. 'Gotta love Troy. Don't worry. I think the worst of the rain and wind will miss us.'

'I hope so. The Met Office said they couldn't predict exactly when and where it will land,' Sam said, determined to be optimistic. 'Though I'm worried about the marquee.'

'It'll be fine, I'm sure.' He rested his hand on her bare arm. Her lips tingled with the memory of their other skin on skin contact: the kiss after Chloe's party and the look in his eye in the kitchen at Stargazey. He took his hand away. 'And hey, if it does end up in Mount's Bay or knocking the roof off a house, I guess you're well insured.'

Sam rolled her eyes. 'Thanks. I'll sleep easy knowing that. I have to go . . .' She didn't want to leave him but she didn't trust herself to linger or let herself wonder about her future – their future – on the eve of the festival. 'There's a row over some of the stalls. Two fudge makers have been accidentally allocated spots side by side and they're *not* happy.'

Gabe whistled. 'Oh, Fudgegate. Sounds nasty. Call me if the confectionery starts flying. In fact, call me for anything. I mean that. I'm going to a rehearsal in the Chef's Theatre later, but I'll be around the Net Loft for a while, talking to the architect and making sure it's ready for tomorrow,' he said. He'd kindly offered to let the volunteers and emergency services use the Net Loft and its facilities as an extra rest area during the festival.

'OK. Thanks again, and for the pie making.'

'You're welcome . . . but maybe you should see what the customers think first.'

She laughed.

'Seriously, if there's anything else I can do for you, I'm here whenever you need me.' Sam could think of a lot of things, none of which she dared say out loud.

'I will,' she said, a little croakily. 'See you tomorrow morning then?'

He gave a salute. 'Bright and early.'

She hurried away, pulling out her phone pretending to look at it but simply desperate to put space between them before she said or did something she might regret.

Despite what Sam had told Gabe, sleeping easy was the last thing she did that night. Lying in her bed late on Friday evening, listening to the wind howling around Wavecrest

299

Cottage, all she could think of was the marquee flapping wildly like a giant bird, before it took flight and cut a swathe through the cottages next to the harbour. She could hear waves battering the beach below the cottage.

It didn't help that she'd taken a call from the professional security firm earlier in the evening, saying they weren't prepared to leave anyone up on the field 'in the current conditions'. Sam was still a little concerned about the possibility of sabotage but she had to agree and hope for the best; there was no way she'd ask any volunteer to spend the night in that marquee.

It was unlikely, but all the same, she knew she wouldn't sleep until she'd gone to check that everything was OK. She crept downstairs, pulled on wellies, a fleece and a waterproof, grabbed a head torch from the porch and headed out. The rain started when Sam reached the field, like fine needles against her skin. There was a tang on the air, as if it was laced with salt and ozone from the sea. Torchlight swept the field as Sam circled the marquee. She froze momentarily before Gabe's voice cut through the night.

'Sam? Is that you?'

A beam flickered and Sam blinked in the light. 'Yes. What are you doing here?'

Gabe lowered the torch and jogged to her side. 'Same as you, I'm guessing. Checking the marquee's still standing. What a night!'

She was more relieved to see him than she'd ever admit. 'Just what we needed.' She had to raise her voice to compete with the wind and rain, the flapping of canvas and clanking of ropes and metal.

'What's that noise?'

He pointed to the tent. 'There's someone inside.'

'Oh God. There's no security. It might be someone trying to sabotage the tent. Maybe the same people who vandalised the van. I'll catch them red-handed!'

She darted towards the tent flap, but Gabe pulled her back. 'No, you won't. You're not tackling some stranger in the dark. I'll go.'

'I'm fine.'

'You don't know who it is. Stay here.'

Gabe moved towards the opening. She followed behind, but before they'd reached the entrance, the marquee flap lifted and a tall man with a mobile phone emerged. For a fraction of a second, Sam was startled at the pale, angular face until she recognised Ben. A Ben without his Goth make-up on, but wearing his biker leathers.

He lowered his mobile. 'I was checking the inside of the marquee. I couldn't sleep a wink,' he muttered as if he'd been caught committing a crime.

'Us too.' Sam joined him at the entrance. 'How's it looking?'

'One of the external guy ropes had worked loose but I've fixed it. Inside, it's looking fine and everything seems to have held so far. I don't think there's any more we can do.'

'I was worried it might have been sabotaged,' said Sam.

'I don't think it was deliberate,' said Ben. 'If someone really wanted to destroy the marquee, they'd have done a lot more than loosen one guy rope.'

'Ben's right,' said Gabe. 'But we can have a quick look ourselves if you want to set your mind at rest.'

'No. No . . .' She glanced at Ben. 'I trust Ben's judgement. Thanks for coming up here.'

He shrugged. 'No problem,' he muttered. Sam smiled to herself. He might be a man of few words but he was trustworthy and kind. He only needed a bit of confidence . . . although Zennor seemed to like him 'just as he was'. Not everyone was an extrovert or the life and soul of the party.

There was a shout from behind and more wavering torchlight. 'Sam! Ben!'

Zennor galloped over the sodden grass in wellies and a Puffa coat. 'I heard you go out and I phoned Ben but he was already up here. I came to help.'

Sam flashed the light at her. Spangles shimmered at the top of her wellies. Zennor must have come straight from bed in her sparkly unicorn onesie.

'Panic over. We've checked out the marquee and it's OK. Thanks for getting up.'

'No probs.'

Secretly, Sam was crossing her fingers. She was still anxious about the marquee but there was a kind of strange comfort in knowing that everyone else had had the same fears and had turned up too. 'We'll have to hope that it stays that way,' she said.

Zennor pinched the furry hood together to stop it blowing off her head.

Ben lifted his phone. 'Thing is, I've already phoned the marquee contractor. They were called to another marquee on the cliffs above St Agnes because the storm is even worse up

302

there, but they're coming here straight afterwards to double check everything,' said Ben.

'Great idea, Ben. Thanks!' said Sam, amazed that he'd taken the initiative.

He looked down at the grass. 'I thought you had enough to do.'

Zennor linked arms with him. 'Aww, that's lovely of you, Ben.'

It was too dark to see if Ben blushed, but he muttered something inaudible in reply.

Sam wiped rain from her eyes. 'It is, and now, I think we should all go home to bed,' said Sam. 'Come on.'

They all trooped off together, but they hadn't even reached the edge of the field when torchlight flickered in the gloom.

'Ho there!'

Sam squeezed her eyes shut to avoid a beam to rival Wembley's floodlights. She peered through her lashes, wincing at the shadowy figure behind the glare. 'What are you silly buggers doing out here?'

The beam dropped. It was Troy, clutching an industrial-sized torch in one hand while he held onto his hat with the other.

'Same as you,' said Gabe. 'Checking the marquee's still standing. You can go back to bed. It is.'

Troy cackled as he reached them. 'We're a daft lot. Bit of rain and a breeze never hurt nobody. I'd never have bothered turning out myself but Evie was giving me earache until I did. Me with my shoulder still recovering too. She'd never have shut up unless I came out and put her mind at rest.'

303

Zennor laughed and Sam heard Ben chuckle softly.

'Yeah. We'll believe you,' said Gabe. 'There's no need for Evie – or you – to worry. We've all given the marquee the once over and the contractors will be here at dawn to make sure it's OK so you can go home to your bed.'

Troy swept the torchlight over the marquee as if he still wasn't convinced, then huffed. 'S'pose it'll be all right. For *now*,' he added ominously.

'It'll be fine,' said Sam. 'C'mon, let's get out of this rain.'

Zennor touched Troy's arm. 'Shall we keep you company on the way home?'

'May as well,' said Troy.

Sam made to move, but Gabe caught her arm lightly with his hand. 'We'll be along in a minute,' he said. 'Sam wants to have a quick look at the generators.'

'They won't have blown away. They weigh a ton,' said Troy, flickering his torch over Gabe and Sam like a border guard catching escapees.

Gabe's hand tapped the small of her back. What was he up to? 'Even so, better safe than sorry, eh?'

Sam stared at him but didn't say anything. What was this 'we' about?

'Can we please get back to bed?' Zennor sounded desperate and cold. 'See you in the morning. Oh wait, it already *is* the morning. Don't stay out too late, you two.' Her voice was laden with irony. Sam cringed. People were jumping to conclusions.

'Let's go,' Zennor said to Troy. Ben led the way, his head torch nodding ahead of the unlikely trio before vanishing through the gate to the field.

'You and I could always take a short cut down the coast path,' Gabe said.

Sam wiped rain out of her eyes. 'You're joking, aren't you? We can't go that way. It was dodgy enough on my way up and the wind's worse now, not to mention the waves.'

'You're probably right. We should play it safe.' His eyes glinted. Sam knew he was challenging her, just the way he'd done when they used to tombstone into the harbour.

'We're not teenagers now. I've too many people relying on me to stay alive. We both know this is a bit hairy for a summer storm.'

He laughed. 'You're probably right. We should take the road.' Gabe peered into the darkness as a wave thundered onto the cliff. 'I'd forgotten how brutal a Porthmellow storm can be. And how bloody magnificent.'

She laughed at him, high on adrenaline and sheer relief. He was soaked, and his dark hair was plastered to his head. Water ran down his face yet he'd never looked happier. Sam felt buoyant.

'I've missed it here.' He looked around him and back down at Sam. 'Missed you too.'

Her heart skipped a beat and a few more to boot. She'd missed him so much herself. Just how much she dare not tell him. She wanted to but she didn't trust herself. It would mean taking a step she'd vowed she never would. A step towards forgiving him and betraying Ryan.

'Come back to the house with me,' Gabe said.

She shook her head. 'I can't.'

'I'm only offering you a hot cocoa. Nothing else.'

Did she really believe that? She wasn't sure. 'I can get cocoa at home. It's two o'clock in the morning and I should be going to bed.'

'Is there any point now?'

'Maybe not but that doesn't mean I should come to your place.'

'You keep saying "should", Sam, as if you're afraid of something. If it's me, you needn't be . . . I won't push you into anything you might regret.'

'I'm not afraid of you,' Sam declared. Only of myself, she could have added.

'Look, let's at least walk that way together and then you can decide once we're up there. There's no harm in that, is there?'

She shook her head and they walked off into the night towards both their homes. All the way, Sam thought of Zennor and her loaded comment about not staying out too late. If she did decide to go back to Gabe's, Sam should text her in case she woke and worried where she was, unless Zennor really *had* guessed what might happen between them. And, man, she wanted to go into his house, even though she knew, somehow, that she'd probably be taking a leap into the unknown, in so many ways.

'So, are you coming in?'

Gabe stopped opposite Wavecrest. In the streetlight, raindrops glistened on his face and the hopeful look in his eyes was too much for Sam. She wanted to go with him – but what would Zennor think?

'A nightcap?' he asked. 'Whatever you decide, can you make

it quick before we both get washed away?' He smiled and a jot of desire shot through her. She hadn't felt anything like it in such a long time and it was impossible to resist even though there were still so many questions she wanted answers to. Even though she might not find them, no matter what happened next.

She decided. 'Just a quick one, then.'

They ran the short distance towards the house, Gabe unlocked the gate and they crunched over gravel. The moon peeked out, lighting up the gothic tower.

'Dracula's castle . . .' she murmured, recognising the tingle of foreboding and excitement she felt at having decided to go back with him.

'What?' Gabe turned from unlocking the studded wooden front door.

'Nothing.'

He pushed it open and stood back so she could go ahead of him. She had a wobble, momentarily, crossing that threshold. Walking into Clifftop House was walking into the unknown, but she was doing it anyway.

Chapter Thirty-One

Sam gawped at the entrance hall of Clifftop House. A statement staircase with a polished banister led up to the first floor. The walls were oak panelled with elaborate cornices and even a stained glass window at one end. The room had obviously been meant to impress when it was built in Victorian times, and by the current owner, who'd spared no expense in restoring it.

'Wow.'

'Yeah. That's what I thought when the agent showed me in. I never dreamed I might live here one day. Even for a little while.' Gabe pointed to her wellies. 'Are you going to take your coat off or stand there making a puddle on that nice carpet?'

She glanced down at the water soaking into the exotic rug, but Gabe was smiling.

'Drat. I'm sorry.' She shed her dripping mac and Gabe collected it. 'I'll leave my wellies here.'

She took them off while he hung up her coat in a room

off to the side. When he returned, he was wearing a thin grey jumper that showed off his torso beneath. She didn't think he had anything else under it and guessed he must have thrown it on after jumping out of bed, just as she had. She suddenly remembered her own outfit and groaned. She was wearing silky sweat pant bottoms and a matching top.

'You'll have to excuse my pyjamas. I didn't have time to change.' And hadn't thought she'd need to, of course . . .

She couldn't miss his glance at her outfit. 'None of us did. Um . . . you are a bit damp. Would you . . . um . . . like a dry top?'

She caught sight of her reflection in the window. Oh God, that cami left almost nothing to the imagination, and the sweatpants weren't much better. 'Yes, please,' she muttered.

'OK. I'll be back in a sec.'

He jogged up the staircase, leaving her marvelling at the period grandeur of the house and becoming even more amazed that she was standing in it, wearing not a lot.

He was back within a few minutes with a navy long-sleeved T-shirt in one hand.

'Hope this is OK. I don't have much that's clean.'

Sam took it. It was soft and warm. 'Thanks.'

'No problem. I'll make us a drink if you want to change. There's a washroom off the kitchen. I'll show you the way.'

The kitchen was a surprise, all granite surfaces and white foiled units. Sam didn't think its stark modernity went with the rest of the house, but she was in no mood to give it a proper assessment, only keen to get out of Gabe's sight and into something more decent. She took the T-shirt into the cloakroom and swapped it for her damp cami. It was obviously straight from his drawer, freshly laundered with the scent of Lenor.

She had to roll the cuffs up but the top had the advantage of hanging low and hiding the clinginess of the silky fabric over her bottom. She grabbed a comb from the shelf above the washbasin and tamed some of the tangles in her hair while pots clanged outside the door. It was nearly three in the morning – what on earth was Gabe doing? What on earth was *she* doing?

She emerged to a scent that made her toes curl in delight, even if they were encased in the fluffy purple socks that Zennor had given her for Christmas.

Gabe was leaning over a copper pan on the Aga, stirring something.

'Mmm. What's that?' Sam stood beside him, peering into the pot, which was half full of a dark and gooey liquid.

'My version of cocoa. A grown-up version.'

As he poured rich dark liquid into two glass mugs, Sam's tastebuds went wild. 'That looks and smells amazing,' she sighed.

'It's the best dark chocolate, but this is the really grown-up bit.' He reached for a small bottle and poured a generous measure of a pale liquid into it.

'What is it?'

'Something I picked up on my travels. Wait and see. I've no cream, I'm afraid.'

He dusted the top of the chocolate with some cocoa powder and picked up the mugs. 'Come on.'

In the sitting room, Sam sat on the sofa next to him, almost sinking into the squidgy leather. Gabe handed her the chocolate. 'Careful, it's very hot.'

You can say that again, thought Sam, but she took refuge from her wicked thoughts in the steam curling off the chocolate. The alcohol fumes and heady scent made her gasp in delight. Wow. It reminded her of a Bakewell tart . . . or was it something else, richer? She took a sip. Sweetness combined with the kick of booze. A warmth spread instantly from her lips and mouth, down her throat and through to her toes. This was both dangerous and delicious at the same time.

'Well?' Gabe asked.

'It's like a liquid Black Forest gateau. It's amazing.' She sipped again, letting the flavours and alcohol sink into every cell of her body.

'That's because it's made with black cherry bourbon. I picked it up when I was last in the States. One of the better things to come out of there.'

Sam sipped and sighed. 'The best, I think. It's gorgeous.' Like the man who made it, lounging next to her with his dark hair tousled and damp, and no idea of the sinful thoughts in her mind or the feelings he'd aroused in her body.

'Glad you like it.'

As they sipped in silence, she became aware of the sensuousness of her surroundings: the sofa, the warm wooden furniture and thick brocade curtains drawn either side of a curved bank of windows facing the sea. The moon had retreated behind the clouds again so outside the night was dark, though rain spattered the windows and the roar of the waves was still loud. Sam heard the clock tower strike the quarter hour. In a very short time, the first slivers of dawn would creep into the sky. The festival was hours away . . . but it might as well have been years.

'This is a spectacular house, Gabe. I'm impressed.'

Gabe shook his head. 'Don't be. None of the furniture's mine.'

'What was in the removal van, then?'

'You mean you didn't have a look?'

Sam rolled her eyes. 'No.'

'Cooking stuff and gadgets, mainly. Office equipment like a desk and chair. A few home comforts – sound system, computer stuff, TV.' He smiled. 'And my own mattress. The one in the master bedroom must have seen some action so I'm glad I brought my own.'

Her cheeks warmed up. She wished she hadn't asked.

Her sense of the surreal was also taking over. Had she dreamt all the years of loss and struggle, rebuilding her life? And here he was smiling at her, all damp, tousled hair and firm body beneath the thin sweater. She was as much in danger of falling in love with him as she had ever been, and her initial anger that he was back had cooled.

He'd said the hot chocolate was grown-up, and so were they. Perhaps it was time they talked properly. After all, they might never have the chance again.

'That night after the trip to the hospital, I really thought it was Ryan at the crossing in Marazion. That was silly, of course, he's probably at the other end of the country.'

Gabe sipped his drink before answering. 'It could easily have been him . . . it was dark.'

'No. It was my wishful thinking.'

'There's nothing wrong with wishful thinking. Nothing wrong with hope.'

'Really? After Mum died and Ryan was put away, I lost my hope.' And we split up, she wanted to say but didn't dare.

'For all I know he might have a family,' she continued. 'He might be on the breadline or ill or depressed. Knowing he's alive isn't enough. I want to know he has a life, despite what he's done.'

'I wish you wouldn't blame me,' he said quietly.

'I know you thought you were doing the right thing, but I can't forget that you let me down. No matter what the reasons, I can't forget.'

'Or forgive?'

'I don't know. I think I can *understand* and accept what you did but forgiveness . . . means I have to forget. I . . . I felt too much for you. I cared too much, which meant that the crash to earth was so much worse, and now I'm worried that too much time has gone by between us to pick up where we left off.'

Gabe took her hand. 'I don't want to pick up where we left off. That's impossible, but we could start again at a whole new place.' His voice was passionate. 'I was angry too, for all kinds of reasons, and I didn't come back here to re-ignite something that's long been dead. I came because the town needed me. Because I thought I was helping Porthmellow – and yes, helping *you*. Which was more important to me, I can't decide, but one thing is certain: I never once wanted to cause you any more pain than I have already.'

'You did cause me pain but it's eased. I don't blame you anymore. I blame Ryan. I've accepted he was wrong. I blame myself for not seeing sooner the way he was going. For not noticing that my own brother was so desperate. Maybe I put that on you when you thought turning him in was for the best.'

Gabe's jaw dropped. Sam had surprised herself. Maybe she could forgive him after all.

'Earlier you said you'd lost hope but you hadn't. You carried on, you built the business up and cared for Zennor. You didn't lose hope. You made it.'

'Made it is a relative term.' She smiled.

'You said I'd made it too but you're wrong.'

She frowned. 'What do you mean? Look at this place. The money you've made, the empire. You're our headline draw for the festival.'

He shook his head. 'Granted, I've had some success with the business but the money means nothing to me. I lost the thing that really mattered to me. You.'

Sam was so astonished she laughed out loud. 'Me? A stressed-out girl from Porthmellow who runs a pie van? Oh, come on, I've seen you with other women on the news sites. Glamorous women. Wasn't one of them a Lady?'

'None of them could hold a candle to you.'

Sam forced another laugh but her hands were shaky. A lump formed in her throat. Oh shit. The exhaustion, the stress of the festival, the emotions and the booze at three in the morning on an empty stomach – they'd all got to her. 'It's this grown-up hot chocolate making us talk like this. I wish I

314

hadn't drunk it, perhaps I should have left.' Perhaps she still should go, she thought.

'It's true and being grown-up is vastly overrated, but I'm glad you stayed.'

This was all going too fast, much too fast. 'You've had too much of the grown-up hot chocolate, too, Gabe.'

'Maybe, but I've never seen more clearly in my life. Please can we try again?' Gabe moved away slightly. 'I'll let it go if you don't want to . . . but why not?'

His dark eyes were intense. Serious, longing . . . All the youthful feelings of lust and love flooded back. She might only have this one chance. They'd moved so far since he'd arrived back in Porthmellow. She glimpsed a moment beyond tonight when they might move even closer, but how could she build a new life with someone who had once destroyed the life they had together?

She tried to stand up, wobbled a little. 'I really ought to go.'

'Why?' Gabe got up and steadied her.

'Because I don't trust myself.'

'To do what?'

She was terrified she might forgive him and restart her life. Their lives. Imperfect. Far from even approaching perfect, but finally moving in the right direction: towards each other not further away.

'This.' She reached up, put her arms around his neck and kissed him. What the hell was she doing? Even as Gabe kissed her back, she was still asking the question and answering it with: 'I don't care.'

315

How long had it been? Rewind to the moment before Gabe had walked into the cottage that night to tell her about Ryan. Rewind all of that and wipe the tape. Focus on now. On this very instant. Take it a second at a time. Gabe's mouth on hers. That feathery way he kissed, little light kisses that she knew would lead to so much more. The delight in his eyes when he realised that she was staying. The taste of him; sweet cherry and smoky bourbon. The kiss ended and she licked her lips and giggled.

'What?'

'Wow. A guy who tastes of cherry and chocolate. Must be a dream combination.'

He laughed. 'I aim to please.' His tone softened. 'Sometimes. Except when I hurt someone. I'm sorry. If I could turn back the clock—'

'Don't carry on. You'd do the same again. I wouldn't expect any different. Don't spoil the now.'

His eyes widened a little. She still had the power to surprise him. She was in control. 'So, there *is* a now,' he murmured.

Oh yes. She wanted the now so much. Her body told her how much, that was obvious, but she wanted to be with him again, hold him and be held by him. Skin on skin, the way they had way back. And yes, Gabe coming back had made her life harder. Falling in love with him again had made it ten times more difficult, but right now, she didn't care. Like the festival, regrets could wait until tomorrow. Except it already was tomorrow and already too late to go back.

She stood up and lifted his hand in hers. 'If you want there to be.' Then she kissed him again.

Taking her cue, he took her hand and led her out of the lounge and upstairs. Her legs were like jelly, and she was trembling but wildly excited. 'Please don't say you've chosen the bedroom in that turret?' she asked when they reached the landing.

'Is it a deal breaker?'

'Might be.'

'Shit.' Gabe grimaced and pointed to the door in the curved stone wall at the end of the landing. They both laughed at their youthful fantasies but with every step, Sam knew that this was real and serious grown-up stuff, only she didn't want to grow up.

Sam rolled her eyes. 'Remember when we used to joke about who lived here and that once you entered, you could never leave.'

They reached the bedroom door. 'I think you're confusing it with Hotel California,' said Gabe.

'Don't tell me you have a four-poster in there?' she asked.

Gabe pushed open the door, and let her go inside first.

Sam groaned. 'You do have a four-poster, and with tapestries too. Oh Gabe, that's so cheesy.'

'Like I said. It's not mine.' He sat on the bed and pulled her between his legs. Still giggling at the outrageous cheesiness of the bed and the outrageousness that she was even here at all. 'So, *is* it a deal breaker?' he asked.

Sam sighed. She could hold out no longer. She pushed him back onto the cover and gave him her answer.

Chapter Thirty-Two

At six a.m. on the morning of the festival, Gabe blinked awake and turned over, expecting to feel Sam's warmth next to him but the sheets were cold and the bed empty.

He threw off the duvet. 'Sam?'

The door to the en suite was wide open. She couldn't be in there. Maybe downstairs making breakfast? He pulled on some boxer shorts and jogged down to the entrance hall, calling as he went: 'Hey there, you haven't asked me how I like my eggs . . .'

But the house was silent as the grave inside, and the only sounds were the wind rattling the windows and the cries of gulls wheeling around the house.

The kitchen was empty, the copper pan still on the worktop, the scent of chocolate thick and sweet on the air. Gabe strode through the sitting room and the hallway, then threw open the front door.

She'd gone.

Shit.

He found the note in the kitchen by the coffee maker. It had been written on the back of an envelope from the letting agent, with a gel pen.

Sorry I left without waking you. Last night was . . . you know what it was.

She'd drawn a wobbly smiley.

This will sound like a cop-out, and it is in a way, but I need time to think about it . . . this . . . us, I suppose, and it's the festival too. See you later. S.

'Damn.'

Gabe leaned back against the worktop and combed his fingers through his hair in despair. The cold light of day had shone its unforgiving rays on the reality of the situation. A reality that had been all too easy to ignore last night, making love with Sam. Being in her arms again, sharing the warmth of her body, had been all he'd cared about.

He walked through to the sitting room, the envelope dropping from his fingers, and stared out at the sea, willing it to give him some answers. Grey clouds rolled across a sky that was a washed-out colour that couldn't seem to decide whether to be blue or white. Foam-topped waves broke on the swell. He opened the window and smelt the morning air, imagining he felt the cooling spray against his face and chest.

Sam only knew part of the reason he'd reported Ryan. If they were ever to move closer, he had to tell her the real reason. No matter what the consequences, and who he hurt – and it would hurt many of the people he cared for – there had to be no more secrets between them. Without that, he couldn't even begin to glimpse a future for them both. And there was the most terrifying part. He had glimpsed a future – one that only a few weeks ago he'd thought was dead and buried forever.

When the festival was over, he resolved he would tell her the whole truth.

The bed would never be a deal breaker, but the secret he'd been keeping for the past ten years might be.

Chapter Thirty-Three

'Sam? Is that you?'

Oh crap. Sam had hoped to creep upstairs and change without waking Zennor, but her sister called from her room before she'd even reached the landing. She'd already given up any hope of sleep. After she and Gabe had had sex the first streaks of light were already showing in the sky.

She leaned on the door frame of Zennor's room. 'I got your message about Gabe. We had hot chocolate and a long talk and er . . .'

Zennor pulled up the hood on her unicorn onesie. The padded horn bobbled. She slapped her hands over her ears. 'Stop. I don't need to know any more . . . I don't suppose you want breakfast if you've already had it at *Gabe's*,' she said, loading the words.

'I didn't say I'd had any breakfast,' Sam said warily. 'I'll put the kettle on.'

Zennor joined her in the kitchen. Gareth and Harry were

up, wheeking around their palace, exploring it like they'd not seen it a thousand times before.

While the kettle boiled, Zennor lifted Gareth out and nuzzled him.

'Are you angry with me for staying with Gabe?' said Sam.

'Do you care if I am?' Zennor kissed Gareth.

'You know I care, but I didn't plan on him coming back to Porthmellow or taking part in the festival. I didn't plan last night or ask for it all to start over again.'

'Start over again? You were in bits the last time. I was young but I could see the pain you were in. I was hurt too, worried about Ryan, still missing Mum. I still miss her now. No, Samphire, I'm not angry but I am worried. I hope you know what you're doing. I don't want to see you hurt like that again.'

Sam flinched. Zennor's eyes burned with a fierce fire. Backlit by the rising sun, in front of the sink unit, their mother was brought back to life for a few seconds. How could she not have noticed Zennor growing so like her? Sam squashed down the lump that clogged her throat and the voice that came out was scratchy with emotion. 'That's what Mum would have said.'

'Yeah, and she would have been right. Does this mean you've forgiven him, then? Just because you have, doesn't mean I have to.'

'I don't expect you to. I won't try to persuade you to. I don't know how I feel about him – him and Ryan – myself. It's more complicated than that . . .' She'd managed to separate the Gabe she'd loved and was still drawn to physically and emotionally from the harm he'd done her family. She'd found a key and started to turn it, and seen into his reasoning, his point of view. Last night it had seemed a grown-up thing to do, a mature way to proceed, but now she wasn't so sure. Had 'mature' simply been an excuse for sleeping with him and giving in to her own selfish desires?

'Samphire?' Zennor used her name. Such a hesitant, fragile word. Sam knew that her sister wanted comfort, reassurance that Sam hadn't changed and wasn't going to leave her, like their mother had done, like Ryan had done. That she wouldn't abandon her for Gabe. Zennor was grown-up but she was also, still, the kid sister who'd relied on Sam for guidance and support. They'd ended up parenting each other, Sam realised. Love flowed both ways.

'There comes a time when you have to move on,' she said. 'Life is never going to be perfect . . . Stop looking at me like I just served Harry and Gareth up for dinner.'

Zennor gasped. 'Cover your ears, Gareth,' she said to the pig and put him back in his palace where he shot into his shelter to hide. Two eyes peered out at Sam from the shelter. 'That's not funny. It's horrible. I care about you, sis. I love you. We were doing OK. You were doing well and you'd worked hard to build your life, and I don't want Gabe Mathias to ruin that.'

'The business was doing well but as for the rest of my life . . . I know I talk a good talk but I *have* been lonely, Zen. I'm ashamed to admit it. I've missed the buzz of being in love.'

Zennor flew on her and hugged her. 'Don't say that.'

'It's true. I tried to hide it. I tried to convince you, Gabe, me most of all, that I didn't miss him and I didn't care. I was lying because I had to hold this family and myself together.'

323

'We knew you were putting on a face. Even Ben did.' She paused. 'So you and Gabe. You're A Thing again? Will you be going public?'

'No! We're not a "thing" and we're not going public. We're not ready for that. Hell, I don't know about any of the other stuff myself yet. I don't know if last night changed the way he feels. Hell, I don't even know how I feel. Last night might be a one-off.'

Zennor snorted. 'We both know it won't be. Look at you.'

Sam laughed. 'Knackered, like I've been dragged through a hedge. I haven't even changed yet.'

'I was going to say happy. Happy like a lantern with a candle flickering inside it.'

Sam shook her head, embarrassed at her happiness being so transparent. 'Don't be silly.'

'I'm being honest,' said Zennor, a mutinous look on her face.

Sam's phone beeped. Was it Gabe? She read the message in the festival WhatsApp group. It was from Chloe.

Is the marquee still standing? Got up in the night with Ruby and saw lights on top of the cliff and hoped everything was OK.

All OK, she sent back. *Speak later.*

Sam gave Zennor a quick hug. 'All I know is that I need a shower, fresh clothes, some breakfast and to somehow find the energy to go straight out of here and into town on an hour's sleep. You too. For the next forty-eight hours, my love life and our problems don't matter. We have a festival to put on.'

Chapter Thirty-Four

Sam always loved festival morning. The moment before it all began, when the town was on the edge of waking up. Excitement was high and the mayhem hadn't started. This moment, and it would only last for the time it took her to walk from Wavecrest to Festival HQ, was hers alone. She didn't have to share it, or have it marred. Sam had showered while Zennor rustled up veggie sausage and egg sandwiches and then she was out.

The marquee was indeed still in place on this breezy but fine Saturday morning that promised to rapidly warm up now the clouds had blown away. That electric undercurrent running through the town as the sun rose higher over the cliff. That was her doing, hers and her team's, and this morning it all had a fresh dimension.

The stallholders were setting up as she walked to the Institute. The ones who had arrived at the crack of dawn already had their goods on display, others were connecting up generators and gas bottles. Some were wheeling trollies full of stuff from the exhibitors' car parks, or manoeuvring their mobile vans into place – Stargazey was already in its spot and she'd had a quick word with Stefan to check he was OK. There were always latecomers, still struggling to put up their gazebos and be ready for when the festival opened at nine thirty . . . shouting at each other to hurry up, while other stallholders exchanged banter and anecdotes before the masses arrived and they were flat out serving customers. It was all part of the buzz, the excitement, the joy of seeing months of hard work springing into life.

She ought to be exhausted but adrenaline, and perhaps hope, had given her a fizzing energy. She'd felt the jumpiness before, but this time it was different. Her night with Gabe had added a new and dangerous edge to her high spirits. Bring it on, she thought, bring anything on: I can deal with it all this morning.

She was bound to hit a wall, of course, probably sometime around three p.m., and be found dead to the world on a pile of reeking lobster pots behind the Institute, but she'd cross that bridge when she came to it.

At one minute past seven, her mobile started ringing. She whipped it from her pocket, expecting it to be Gabe, demanding to know why she'd slunk off without waking him. She had no real answer beyond needing time and space to take in what had happened. Wow, what a night. The intensity of her feelings, physical and emotional, had scared her, even while she'd allowed herself to be swept along. The things they'd done – slow, tender, hot . . . – in Gabe's ridiculous bed.

She caught herself smiling until her jaw ached, her cheeks flushing. Wow. She closed her eyes. She wanted to do it all again right now.

She looked at the screen and saw it was Troy. 'Hi there, my lover . . .' she said cheerfully.

'Sam. There's a drain overflowing outside the Smuggler's. We're erecting a barrier and moving the hot sausage van away from the scene. Sam? Are you there.'

'Thank you, Troy. Are you sure it's, um . . . sanitary?'

'Will be. Drains people are already on scene. Me too, while some were still in their beds.'

Or someone else's, thought Sam, then wondered if Troy had spotted her creeping out of Clifftop House. She sincerely hoped not. She wasn't ready to go public yet and if Troy knew, she may as well broadcast that she'd slept with Gabe over the festival tannoy. Even the idea of that sent her into a momentary spin of remembered pleasure and misgivings.

'Thanks, Troy. We all appreciate all your hard work, and getting up at dawn to deal with crap – well, that's going above and beyond the call of duty.'

'No need to thank me,' he said.

'I know there's no need,' she laughed. 'But I mean it all the same. Thanks for everything you and Evie have done.'

'My, you're in a good mood. What have you had for breakfast, maid?'

'Veggie sausage and egg butty,' she tossed back, knowing it was the treat she'd had before the sandwich that had made her feel she could take on the world. 'See you later. I'm off to Festival HQ to open up.'

Sam didn't have to open the Institute because there were already a dozen people in there. Representatives from all those organisations who had come together to make the festival happen. The St John Ambulance, police, the chief steward, local Sea Scouts, WI, technical specialists and the official announcer, a retired local Radio DJ who lived in the town.

Sam thought of Chloe, meeting her granddaughter for the first time. She would sorely miss her second-in-command today, but hadn't the heart to be annoyed. Moments like that, as Sam knew, were precious . . . and there were plenty of people to help.

Drew was there, of course, making the tea for all the people at the pre-event meeting. Zennor and Ben arrived not long after Sam. Once everyone had a drink and biscuit in their hand, Sam listened to each person give a very brief report on any issues to look out for during the day. While they spoke, she took a few discreet calming breaths before she said her own words. Finally, it was her turn.

She stepped out in front of the assembled volunteers and had to swallow a lump in her throat. They were an eclectic and faintly comical bunch in their hi-vis waistcoats, freshly pressed uniforms, shorts and woggles. Almost twenty faces, some lined and world weary, others eager and rosy cheeked. Maybe it was the lack of sleep, or the significance of the night that had just passed, but Sam felt momentarily choked with emotion. Ben was at the back, peering at her. Zennor popped her head up by his side and mouthed: *You can do this*.

Sam gave a thought to Gabe. Where was he? Had he found the note? He might be preparing for his stint on stage but she was bound to see him sooner or later. Would he regret what they'd done or be as full of hope as she was?

Sam took another short breath in, then out, tried to look positive and excited and launched into her battle speech.

'Wow. It's happening. First of all, thanks for even being here. I'm glad everyone could make it and hasn't been blown away. This is the biggest festival we've ever put on, and I know you've all had to work harder than ever to make it happen. All I can do is thank each and every one of you and your teams. Without your contributions, Porthmellow Food Festival would still be a mad idea scrawled on the back of a menu in the Smuggler's. At this moment –' she smiled and blew out a breath '– I wouldn't blame you for wishing it had stayed that way.'

Soft laughter and nods.

'But it *is* happening so . . . good luck to you all. I'll be on the radio all day if you need me for anything and I'll do my very best to help – or hinder you.

'All that remains is for me to say good luck, stay safe and try to enjoy yourselves. I hope you all have a wonderful festival weekend.'

Chapter Thirty-Five

By ten a.m. visitors were pouring into the streets and flowing around the harbour from the car park, from buses, on foot, by bike, on mobility scooters, pushing buggies and wheelchairs and laden with empty bags for their purchases.

Sam was making her customary tour of the stalls, taking everything in before the inevitable firefighting of minor niggles. It was another moment to savour: when miraculously and against all the odds, the festival was Actually Happening.

Blindfold her and she could have found her way around the town by smell alone. The pungent spices of Indian cuisine, of spicy Mexican food, earthy lemony tagines, tangy citrus at the juice bar, hoppy ales, the juniper of gin, sweet honey, candy floss . . . and comforting aromas of fish and chips, pulled pork and briny seafood. She could have found her way round by sound too; the pop of corks from the champagne bar, the chink of glasses, tannoys crackling, generators humming, laughter, babies crying, a buzz of conversation from the craft beer tent that would grow in volume as the day wore on (she was praying that it didn't turn from banter and cheering to fisticuffs). The first strains of music started up from street performers: a local choir singing breezy songs of summer and young love to suit the morning mood of excitement.

Then the crackle of the announcer telling people that the Chef's Theatre would soon be hosting its first cookery demo.

Gabe was on after lunch, following a popular local chef from the Spindrift Café. Sam needed to find him in the melee. She hadn't spoken to him yet, just answered his text: *Why did you run away?* with: *I needed some time and space. Festival to put on! Don't worry. Xxx*

She made her way towards the Chef's Theatre. Gabe was putting on a headset and chatting to one of the technical staff. He spotted her and raised a hand, before saying a few words to the techie and coming to meet her.

'Before you say anything about the note, I'm sorry I scooted off but I needed some time to get myself together before the festival.' Her words came out in a torrent, and she was almost breathless after saying them.

'That's OK. I mean, it would have been nice if you'd told me, but I understand. This is new territory for both of us.'

'I don't know what's going to happen next . . . last night was . . .' She felt herself blush as she remembered just how amazing the night had been. 'Nice.'

Gabe raised an eyebrow. 'Do you regret it?'

'Of course not.'

331

He lowered his voice to a murmur. 'I'd love to take you back to Clifftop right now if you weren't busy and I wasn't on stage soon.'

A jolt of lust shot through her. 'Well, I *am*, and even if I wasn't, we can't bunk off, even though it would be very very nice.' She sighed. 'Very nice indeed.'

He raised an eyebrow. 'That good, eh?'

She wagged her finger at him, but she was laughing. 'Gabriel Mathias, I'm not going to boost your ego any more, but it was pretty special. Today, I'm Sam, Festival Director and I can't afford to let anything get in the way of that. You do understand?'

His eyes glinted. 'Yes. One step at a time. Sam, I want to talk to you.'

'Talk?' About the future. About them. 'I can't now. Or tomorrow.'

'It has to be soon.'

She waved her hand at the crowds milling around the theatre. 'When this is all over.'

'OK, tomorrow night, then. At Clifftop House.'

She could tell from the firm tone of his voice that he was serious. She nodded, though her stomach swirled at the prospect. The future, even one so near as the following evening, scared and excited her in equal measure. Butterflies danced in her stomach.

'I'd better let you get ready for your performance.' She grinned. 'Troy told me that a group of your biggest fans have been camped out since nine o'clock to get a front row seat.'

Gabe rolled his eyes. 'Troy's winding you up.'

332

'I don't think so.' She pointed out a dozen women and a few men in the front row, some clutching recipe books. Imagine if they knew what their idol had been up to the previous evening, thought Sam, then reminded herself that they didn't know the real Gabe; the skinny, bolshie daredevil from the chip shop.

'I'd better get ready, as you say. Will you—'

'Can visitors please stop throwing rubbish in the harbour.'

Gabe's next words were cut off by a loud boom from the tannoy, which seemed to have been turned up to maximum volume. People ducked as if a bomb had gone off.

'People with pets. If anyone is caught leaving their dog in a car, I will find them and I will deal with them.'

Sam's hand flew to her mouth. 'It's Bryony! How did she get on the tannoy?' Static crackled followed by an ear-piercing whine from the speaker next to the stage.

'Jeez.' Gabe put his hands over his ears.

Sam spotted Troy walking past the stage towards the Institute. She dashed over and took him aside.

'Troy. Do you know why Bryony's doing the announcements?'

'The announcer's been stung by a wasp and had a reaction. The first aiders are with him.'

'Can't someone else step in?'

'No. There's an urgent harbour issue. I was desperate and Bryony was passing so I let her in.'

Suddenly a blast of heavy bass blared out. People stared.

'My God, is that Metallica?' said Sam.

The music stopped abruptly. *'I've been asked to let you know that the folk band, The Wildflowers, is about to play a set in the festival marquee.'*

'Oh God,' said Sam.

'It starts at twelve.' Bryony paused. *'If you're the kind of sad person that enjoys that sort of thing. I did email the committee to book Halestorm but no one listened, as usual.'*

Troy rubbed his chin. 'Hmm. I think I need to find someone else to take over.'

'Thanks,' said Sam.

Troy scuttled off towards the Institute but Bryony was only getting into her stride.

'I can see a few people feeding scraps from the stalls to their dogs. Human food is really bad for them. Bryony's Grooming Parlour near the post office has a wide range of healthy foods for your pets and is open throughout the festival for responsible owners.'

Sam threw up her hands in horror, but Gabe was killing himself.

'Stop laughing.'

'I can't, it's the *Vicar of Dibley* and *Doc Martin* meets Royston Vasey.'

'Woman with the Labradoodle behind the ice cream van. You have not picked up your dog's waste. How would you like it if I came and crapped in your garden?'

Sam squealed. 'No! I have to get her off the tannoy before there's a fight or we're sued.'

There was a high-pitched whine that made everyone flinch followed by clunks and raised voices and sharp barks.

'I have to do something!' Sam was about to dash to the

Institute when a new voice came over the tannoy. A warm female voice with a local accent as thick as clotted cream.

'Thank you, Bryony, for the animal welfare advice. I'm sure all the canine festival goers appreciate it.'

'What?' mouthed Gabe.

Sam's jaw dropped as the voice continued, like honey running off a hot spoon. 'Now, my lovers, can I draw your attention to some lush sounds from the St Piran's fishermen's choir? They've travelled all the way from the Isles of Scilly especially for the festival so you don't want to miss them, now do you? They're about to do a set on the harbour stage so if you want to make your way over. Meanwhile in the craft beer tent on the headland, you can enjoy the sounds of DJ Stormy Pete spinning the decks.'

Sam and Gabe exchanged glances. 'Spinning the decks?' Gabe mouthed, 'WTF?'

'It's Evie Carman,' said Sam.

People all around had paused to listen. They were breaking into grins, smiling and shushing their kids as they listened to Evie.

'So, my lovers. Sun's out in time for one of the upcoming highlights of the festival. Our very own celebrity chef, Gabe Mathias, is going to cook up a storm in the Chef's Theatre. Who needs Love Island when you can watch Gabe in action with a courgette? Get in early for a front row seat because what that man can't do with a vegetable isn't worth knowing. If I was thirty years younger, I'd certainly be offering to slice his aubergines.'

Sam gasped. 'What is this, the Victoria Wood show?'

Gabe spluttered. 'The punters love it.'

'It's also X-rated. I'll have to ask Evie to tone it down. There are kids around.'

Gabe grabbed her. 'Don't. It's hilarious and look . . .' People were already starting to move towards the Chef's Theatre in droves.

'I'd better get down there and start to do my prep. Mind you, how can I possibly live up to that billing, now?'

With a lightning-fast peck on the cheek, Gabe scurried off. Sam headed in the opposite direction and found Troy walking out of the Institute. Evie was exhorting people to fill their bags with local produce from the festival market and not to miss the gigantic cucumbers on the organic fruit and veg stall. People were tittering and smirking but it seemed to be working.

'Hey. Troy. Did you know Evie was such a star?'

Troy chuckled. 'She does the bingo calling at the memorial hall every Friday and her mum loved am dram. Evie used to be in Porthmellow Musical Theatre back in the day but they can't get enough people under seventy to play the parts now. No one wants to be Yum Yum or Thoroughly Modern Millie these days.'

'I'd no idea she was an entertainer,' said Sam.

'She'd have stepped in straightaway but she can't move so fast, as you know, and I thought Bryony couldn't do too much damage for five minutes. Evie had to wrestle the mic from her, but fortunately Sacha took a liking to a Labrador and Bryony had to prise them apart before they did the business on the steps of the Institute.'

Sam burst out laughing, then felt her phone vibrate in her pocket.

'Are you going to make time to watch Gabe do his turn in the theatre?' asked Troy.

'I um . . . I want to but . . . damn.' Her heart sank as she read a message from one of the stewards. 'Those two confectionery stallholders are kicking off again about being side by side. I genuinely thought we'd separated them but now it looks like we've got Fudgegate on our hands. I'd better go and keep the peace.'

'I'll sort the buggers out,' said Troy. 'You should go and watch his Highness.' He peered at her. 'You look done in already, my girl. You need a break. Have you had anything to eat?'

'Actually, no,' said Sam, feeling her stomach rumble, which was ironic considering she was running a food festival. She reminded herself that she'd been up almost all night, engaged in some pretty strenuous activity. That breakfast butty seemed a very long time ago.

She made her way to the Stargazey van on the way to check all was well and to grab a spinach and ricotta pie. Stefan was red-faced and slightly flustered but declared everything was in hand and business was rocking. He'd already restocked once from the chiller at the unit.

Feeling guilty for abandoning her team, Sam made sure they were coping while she ate her pie. She moved on again, dealing with a couple of queries from stewards en route to the theatre. By the time she finally arrived, there wasn't a seat in the house but the volunteers in charge found her a space at the technical desk. She had a prime view of the stage. She found she was holding her breath; her heart beating faster. Was this real? Gabe, commanding this kind of crowd? A hush descended and the MC asked everyone to give 'Gabriel Mathias, TV chef, and Porthmellow lad made good' a warm welcome. Music blared out – 'The Boys are Back in Town' by Thin Lizzy – and there were cheers and applause as Gabe strode onto the centre of the stage.

Chapter Thirty-Six

'Good morning, Porthmellowww!'

Gabe strode onto the stage with a flourish, and began walking up and down the set, making sure he caught the eye of the entire audience. The smile was fixed on his face, but he felt weird. He'd done this before, many times at other festivals and on live TV, but this was Porthmellow, with all its memories.

He caught Sam's eye, didn't dare linger and took his place behind the kitchen counter. He had a small team of tech guys and a stage crew waiting behind the scenes, but for the next hour he was on his own.

'It's great to be back in my hometown.'

'You took your bloody time about it!'

The shout came from a guy about Gabe's own age whose face was vaguely familiar. However, the rest of him wasn't. He had a huge beer gut and long greasy hair. Then it dawned on Gabe that the guy was one of the 'lads' who used to wind him up mercilessly in the chip shop. The heckler's partner grabbed his arm and shh-ed him.

Deciding to ignore his critic, Gabe carried on with his spiel, joking and laughing as he warmed the audience up, talking about being back 'home', about the dishes he was going to create and mentioning jokily that they were featured in his new cookbook.

This part was always the hardest. You had to get a feel for the temperature of the audience and the mood they were in. At least he was on after noon, when a few beers and the odd glass of wine had been consumed.

But there was a definite buzz. The dry weather helped and there were a few familiar faces throwing out the odd comment that he could banter with.

'Right. Let's get cooking,' he said and slipped behind the counter. Immediately he was into his stride, working with the ingredients, making the fresh hake dish he was preparing seem so easy that anyone could try it. Which was what he wanted the audience to think. No point making something they couldn't relate to and didn't want to eat.

He dropped butter in a frying pan and it sizzled instantly. Two fillets of hake dusted in herby flour went in next, fresh off a boat that morning. While they were browning, Gabe took a knife and started to chop fresh spring onion and carrot into tiny matchsticks. The buttery hake smelled glorious and he could imagine mouths watering in front of him. He kept up the banter as he chopped at lightning speed to laughter from the audience.

He glanced up, took another spring onion, laid it on the

chopping board and raised his knife when he spotted Ryan at the back of the crowd.

'Shit!'

His heart pounded. The audience let out a collective gasp. Gabe glanced down. Red liquid oozed onto the plastic board around the scallion. Cuts happened from time to time and usually looked worse than they were, but here in public, with blood oozing from his thumb over the food, it must seem like a horror movie.

Gabe was aware of a pulse of pain in his hand and put the knife down. 'Sorry for the language. My top tip for this dish, be careful not to chop your fingers off,' he said, trying to laugh off the mishap while he scanned the crowd for Ryan again, expecting Sam to see him too.

As people murmured and muttered 'yeughh', Gabe grabbed some paper towels and pressed them to his injured thumb. It was probably a shallow cut but he couldn't continue without getting it cleaned. There was no sign of Ryan but that didn't mean he wasn't there. Gabe was one hundred per cent certain he'd seen him at the back, smiling.

Gabe spotted the St John Ambulance team at the side of the stage, already poised to come on and help him.

He forced a smile to his face, even though he was all over the place. 'Occupational hazard. Sorry, guys, I'll have to get a plaster on it and restart the recipe as soon as I can. Back soon. If anyone wants to clean up and restock with fresh ingredients, I'd be grateful.'

Seconds later, Sam walked onto the stage, smiling. She obviously hadn't seen Ryan – but how long would it be before she did notice him? He couldn't be far away. 'Hey. Knew you couldn't be trusted. Why don't you let a professional step in?' she asked him.

Laughter and a few cheers rang out as Gabe pulled his headset off.

'Are you OK?' she murmured as they walked to the small backstage area. The audience were talking, and the buzz of voices grew louder.

Gabe's heart was in his mouth, still fearing Ryan would appear again at any moment. 'I'm fine, just caught my thumb. Like I say, occupational hazard.'

Sam pulled a face. 'Tell me about it. Why don't you get yourself sorted out while I help clean up and lay out fresh ingredients.'

'You must be busy. There's no need—'

She smiled at him, shaking her head in mock frustration yet her eyes told a different story. 'Shut up and get your hand seen to, Mathias. That's an order from your festival director.'

Gabe saluted with his good hand and had no choice but to submit to the medics' attentions while Sam cleared away the prep area with the help of one of the volunteers. The medics cleaned his thumb and the blood eventually stopped flowing. The buzz of chatter rose from the audience, some of whom were standing up and stretching. A couple of gaps had appeared but there was no sign of Ryan, at least from what Gabe could see. Why had the idiot decided to turn up at the festival right at this moment?

'Hmm. I don't think it needs stitching.' The medic prodded his hand with a gloved finger.

Gabe squashed down a wince. 'I don't have time for that anyway.'

The medic tutted. 'You'd have no choice if it was any deeper. I'll patch you up for now but you'll have to be careful it doesn't get infected.'

She put a dressing on and taped it up. Finally, Gabe was allowed to go. It seemed a ridiculously large bandage for a small nick, but it was in the crease of a knuckle and hard to stem. It was going to be difficult to continue the demonstration.

Sam came over. 'How is it?'

'The cut will heal, but they've bandaged me up like a mummy.' He waggled his hand.

Sam screwed up her nose. 'Does it hurt?'

'Nah. I've had far worse, but it's going to be tricky to prep and cook now. Plus, who wants to watch a chef with a bandage preparing food?'

Sam frowned. 'Um . . .Why don't you let me help?'

Gabe hesitated. Under any other circumstances he'd love to have Sam by his side but not with Ryan lurking, having her in front of the audience, facing them, staring into the faces. He was scared that she'd find out why Ryan was there while they were in the middle of the demonstration. Gabe needed to get to him first so he could find out why he'd turned up at all.

She obviously took his hesitation for lack of confidence in her. 'It's not my thing. I've no experience. I can't do the banter and I won't do it how you do, but people have come to see you and I know the recipe after you talked to me about it, and so why not?'

343

Gabe's heart thumped. She was right, it *was* the perfect solution and how could he say no?

'Are you sure?'

'I wouldn't have suggested it if not. Can you park your massive cheffy ego and get out there on stage?'

'Well, as you've put it so nicely.' He flashed her a smile. 'Come on, let's rock the house.'

A few minutes later, after the fastest briefing ever, they both walked back on stage together to loud applause. Gabe scanned the faces, but there was no sign of Ryan.

'So, ladies and gentlemen. Thank you for your patience. The fantastic St John Ambulance volunteers have patched me up and I still have all my fingers.'

There were groans of horror and laughter from the audience.

'However, it's going to tricky to do the prep with a bandaged hand so a brilliant chef who some of you know from Stargazey Pie has generously offered to help me out. Ladies and gentlemen, please give a big hand – no pun intended – to my impromptu assistant for the session, Porthmellow's own, Samphire Lovell!'

The cheers were way louder than they had been when he'd been introduced on his own. There were a few calls from locals, but everyone seemed to relax, ready to enjoy the double act.

Sam took a little bow and held up a veg parer. 'Thanks, Gabe, but let's get one thing straight.' She brandished the knife. 'As you can't be trusted with sharp objects, I think it's better if you're *my* assistant.'

The audience laughed.

'I'm in no position to argue with that.' He gave a little bow. 'So what do you want me to do, chef?'

Gabe forced himself to smile as he fetched some herbs from the end of the counter. It wasn't easy with his gammy hand. At least the audience was happy but he was bricking it. At any moment he expected Sam to freeze midway through chopping veg, and run from the stage in pursuit of her brother.

Damn you, Ryan. Damn himself for not coming clean years ago, for being persuaded that protecting Sam and helping Ryan was the right thing to do. Possibly forgivable when he was young, but not over the years when maturity and experience should have made him know better.

Considering the circumstances, Sam was making a fantastic job of the dish and even seemed to be enjoying herself. She was a natural in front of the audience, and their banter with each other drew laughter. In fact, he was far more entertaining with her than on his own, and it was much more fun.

Or, at least, it should have been.

They finished the dish and invited a couple of audience members up on stage to taste it with them. The delighted duo, who Gabe recognised as a couple of 'super fans', sat around the counter, shyly tucking into the dishes. The MC asked everyone to thank Gabe and especially Sam, and the applause and cheers rang out.

That was it. Over. Smiling and chattering, some of the audience picked up their bags and left the theatre for a break, while others waited for the next chef to come on. Gabe had a moment of panic when he thought he saw Ryan sitting on the bench seats, but it turned out to be a lookalike scrolling through his phone. He was getting paranoid now. Maybe it hadn't even been Ryan earlier . . . he *had* promised to keep away. No, it was clutching at straws to think it hadn't been him.

Gabe and Sam went into the area behind the stage that acted as a green room for the performers. One of the tech guys handed them a glass bottle of water each. Sam unscrewed the cap for Gabe before opening her own.

'Thanks for stepping in.' He grimaced at his bandage. 'I'm due at a book signing in twenty minutes.' He waggled his hand. 'Lucky I'm left handed, eh?'

Sam jigged around, grinning. Gabe knew the feeling: she was high on the adrenaline, and the relief it was over and had gone well.

'I can't believe I'm saying this but I actually enjoyed it. I was terrified but once we got started, I have to admit it was fun.'

'You were great,' Gabe told her.

'Aww. You don't have to be kind. I know I stammered a bit and my hands were shaking so much at the start. I was terrified I'd drop a pan, set fire to the set, or the dish would be a disaster.'

'No, it was much more fun with you, and anyway,' he grinned, 'I never pick stuff that can turn out to be a disaster.'

She sipped her water and then became serious. 'I was a little bit worried about you before you hurt your hand. You seemed to have a . . . moment when you weren't with us?'

That moment came back to him now and he swallowed

hard. 'Yeah. Stage fright. I always have a few nerves and you've no business being on stage if you don't, but it's not normally an issue. Today was . . . a bigger thing than I'd anticipated. I was suddenly looking out over all those people, some of them I'd known for years. Being back here after all this time is strange and it hit me.'

'I thought that's what might have happened. It's only natural.' She smirked. 'I liked your moment. It shows the great Gabe Mathias is only human like the rest of us.'

'Oh, I'm human all right,' he said bitterly. 'But you already knew that.'

'We all are.' She squeezed his good hand. 'It's OK. You *are* back and no one threw a brick at you. You survived. So cheer up. You've still got your fingers.' She glanced at her watch. 'Eeek. I should be in the Institute to check on the announcer. See you later this afternoon for the next session?'

Gabe groaned. 'Argh. I'd forgotten there's another one to do this afternoon.'

'There's tomorrow too, if your hand hasn't recovered.'

'You won't have time to help with all of them.'

She beamed. 'What? After my taste of fame, you try to stop me.'

'Now my lovers, get yourselves over to the festival marquee where the lovely Gabe Mathias will be signing copies of his new book, Gabe's Mediterranean Odyssey.' *Evie's voice purred over the tannoy. 'You don't want to miss the chance to be up close and personal with the Greek god of cooking, do you? The gorgeous Gabe has hurt his hand and deserves a great big hug. And if I wasn't stuck on duty at Festival HQ, I'd give him one myself.'*

347

Sam groaned. 'Oh no. Now she's gone too far!'

Sam scurried off to the Institute while Gabe was escorted to the marquee by one of the stewards. He'd have to pray that Ryan had made himself scarce until he could call him and tell him to keep out of the way.

It was growing dark when Gabe got home, though the festival was still going on. He'd left after watching one of the bands with Sam, Zennor and Ben and he could still hear the music from the marquee at Clifftop House.

What a day. He was totally knackered. Since their double act at the Chef's Theatre, he hadn't been able to talk to Sam properly again. In the end she'd been too busy to help him for his second afternoon session so one of the local chefs had stepped in. Their paths had crossed on and off during the day, but Gabe was naturally not her priority. He'd been a cat on a hot tin roof, expecting Ryan to materialise at any moment, like the creature from the black lagoon, right in front of Sam.

Gabe had stuck close to her at the festival concert, but thankfully, Ryan had kept clear. Her brother's nerve in turning up at the Chef's Theatre still amazed him. What was he playing at? The situation couldn't continue.

Which was why Gabe had called him and why he was wearing out the expensive rug right now, waiting for Ryan to arrive up at Clifftop House. With Sam now back at her cottage, Gabe was pretty sure they could meet undisturbed. Even so, he'd asked Ryan to use the cliff path to avoid passing the Wavecrest.

348

Just as Gabe was beginning to think Ryan wouldn't turn up, the intercom buzzed and Gabe answered it via his phone. 'Hello, mate,' a voice said through the speaker. 'It's me. Ryan.'

Gabe hesitated a moment before replying. 'You'd better come in.'

Seconds later, he opened the door to a man who had changed the lives of so many people in Porthmellow all those years ago.

He hadn't seen Ryan close up in the flesh for nearly a year. Since then, he'd cultivated a beard any Shoreditch hipster would be proud of, but Gabe didn't hold it against him. He looked fitter and healthier than Gabe had seen him for a long time. He had Sam's hazel eyes and slight build. Gabe vowed to keep a lid on his anger with Ryan, whatever the provocation.

'Thanks for seeing me.' Ryan looked around him wide-eyed. 'Wow. I always wondered what this old pile was like inside. Impressive. You've fallen on your feet.'

'I'm only renting it. The owner did it up.' He led the way into the sitting room. Ryan crossed immediately to the window and looked outside. Gabe had left the balcony door open now the weather had improved.

Gabe stood behind him, arms folded. 'Why did you come back to Porthmellow without warning me?'

Ryan scuffed the rug with his trainer and took his time before answering. 'Probably because I knew you wouldn't like it.'

'Did you come back *because* I was here?'

'Yeah. Partly. Bit of a coincidence in some ways though.'

'I don't believe in coincidences.'

Ryan nodded. 'I should have warned you. I'd heard you were at the festival.'

'Ryan. *Everyone* heard I was at the festival.'

'Yeah and I – me and my girlfriend – had been thinking of making a move down here anyway. You know that addiction rehab charity I work for? Well, they're opening a new centre near Truro and need a counsellor so I applied and got the job. Tilly's managed to get a post as a teaching assistant down here, starting in September.'

Gabe fought the temptation to swear. Ryan seemed to have everything worked out. 'Does this mean you're moving back permanently?'

'Might do. We've found a cottage to rent in Roche while we decide. Tilly loves it, and her kids love it. They're great lads. I've missed Cornwall.'

'But Sam doesn't know,' said Gabe, anger with Ryan bubbling beneath the relief that he was still keeping his life on track. 'Unless you've managed to tell her in the past hour.'

'I haven't told her. I was testing out the water.'

'By hanging around the festival. Jesus, Ryan, why did you take a big risk like that? She might have seen you.'

'I've been careful. I'd no idea she'd walk on stage with you and we've been through it before, Gabe. I was in a mess for years when I got out. I'd caused enough trouble and seeing her and Zennor again would have meant coming clean about everything. For both of us. But . . .' He paused and sat down on the leather sofa. 'I think it's time. I can't do it unless you agree. I presume you and her – well, it's all on again?' He grinned. 'Despite me.'

Gabe swallowed an expletive. 'Whatever you think is on again, you're wrong. Sam still hasn't forgiven me for turning you in, let alone for the other stuff you had planned. She's come to terms with it to a degree and she and I – well, let's say it's early days between us. Very early days and I don't want that jeopardised in any way.'

'So you *don't* want me to tell her I'm back in Cornwall?'

Gabe groaned. 'Yes, I do.' He walked to the window, unable to look at Ryan. 'I do want you to, but not today or tomorrow. Not yet. Shit. She's coming round tomorrow night after the festival ends.'

'Shall we tell her then?'

'I don't know. Maybe. Hell. Yes, I suppose so.'

'There's never gonna be a good time, mate, if you don't mind me saying. I have to be back for a meeting at the new centre on Monday so, you know, if we're going to do it, then we should just get it over with and take the fallout.'

Gabe put his head in his hands. 'Remind me again why I ever agreed to keep your secret from Sam? Why I carried on doing this and helping you?'

Ryan hesitated, shrugged and then said, 'I dunno, mate, but probably because you love her . . .' He hesitated. 'How do you think she'll react?'

'I don't know,' said Gabe, his stomach stirring unpleasantly. 'But it's not going to be pretty.'

Chapter Thirty-Seven

@**Porthmellowchick** Best festival ever?
@**CornishMaid** Deffo. See you at the gig tonight, hun. X

A nd – *breathe*.
       The evening sun warmed Sam's face, bathing
Porthmellow in its gentle rays as Drew and his band set up on
the harbour stage. With the musicians tuning their instruments,
she felt she could finally enjoy herself – hopefully with Gabe.
The daytime bustle had mellowed, giving way to a relaxed
evening vibe. Sam loved this time of the festival too, the joyous,
chilled-out gentle conclusion, which meant stewards and volunteers could finally relax at last.

It would soon be all over for another year – barring the
clear-up operation, of course.

The lack of sleep and excitement had caught up with her,
and she'd collapsed into bed – her own – late on Saturday

night and slept like a stone until Zennor had woken her at seven this morning. They'd both been far too busy to spend more than a few minutes together since Friday night.

Throughout Sunday, Sam had taken a few calls to deal with minor incidents but as festivals went, it had been a big success. She hadn't seen the figures yet, but it looked like a record attendance. They should have enough in the bank to look forward to next year's festival, although someone had already suggested holding a Christmas event. She'd parked that idea until she was less knackered.

She looked around at the smiling faces, chatting over their drinks and food. Chloe and her family had come down to watch the early evening music acts. A man Sam assumed to be Chloe's ex Fraser looked nervy in his smart chinos and shirt, with a wriggling Ruby in his arms. Chloe, in contrast, radiated happiness now her family were reunited, and Hannah was smiling, taking the yelling Ruby from her grandad's arms.

Gabe had gone to fetch some drinks and Sam glanced behind her, looking for him. She spotted him queuing at the bar – or what she thought was him, because he was a long way off and she was looking directly at the setting sun. He was a fair way down the queue so he'd be a while yet. Drew and his band members started their set. Her friend was playing guitar while the lead singer started to power out a popular folk song. The band would be performing a mixture of folk and their versions of modern ballads. Some of the music was a bit middle of the road for Sam's tastes, but they also put a fresh spin on old favourites that had her tapping her feet and singing along. Zennor and Ben were somewhere in the crowd with their mates. She wasn't sure where Chloe was now, but guessed they'd gone home again to put little Ruby to bed.

As the applause rang out for the second song, Sam peered behind her to try and see how far Gabe had got. He was at the front of the queue and a man was talking to him. Sam squinted into the sun. She shaded her eyes. The man with Gabe – it looked like Ryan. OK, she couldn't see the detail, but there was something in the way he held himself.

The band started a new song. Someone accidentally jostled Sam and apologised. When she glanced behind her again, Gabe was giving his order at the bar and the Ryan lookalike had gone.

She shook her head, telling herself it couldn't possibly have been her brother and to forget her worries and just enjoy the music.

Moments later, Gabe had found her in the audience. 'Hello, my luvver,' he said, greeting her with his version of the local accent.

She leaned close to his ear. 'You don't sound like that anymore.'

'I'm still the same inside though. You can take the boy out of Porthmellow, etcetera.' It was true. He'd supported her through the festival, and the scars of their past were healing slowly. Tonight, they would talk. He'd reminded her again earlier, and had seemed on edge and nervous. She'd never let on to him but she liked the wariness and lack of confidence. She didn't want him to be too sure of her even though she knew in her own heart that she'd made the decision to start a fresh journey with Gabe and see where it led.

She'd spent far too long allowing bitterness and regret to dominate her life and perhaps this was the time to start to forgive Gabe. She'd also decided to try and contact Ryan again. Her recent 'imagined' sightings of him had encouraged her to make a renewed effort to search for him. Even the thought of healing old wounds had given her a sense of peace and hope that had been missing from her life for years. So, maybe she and Gabe *would* 'talk' tonight, but she also had other plans in mind that didn't need any words. Tomorrow or the next day would be soon enough to start building the emotional bridges.

They moved along to the beat of the music, accidentally on purpose bumping shoulders with each other. To be in such close proximity was a kind of delicious agony that she was glad to suffer. They kept exchanging glances, safe in the knowledge that amid the swaying, singing, clapping crowd, no one would notice their looks and secret touches. A hand on the small of her back; a brief brush of his forearm. Gabe was in jeans and a faded blue linen shirt with the sleeves rolled up. He'd been able to ditch the bandage.

With the harbour and slowly sinking sun as a backdrop, the smell of delicious food in the air and the sounds of lively people and music, Sam gave herself up to happiness. For the first time since she'd heard Gabe was coming back to Porthmellow, she felt she could truly relax and look forward with optimism to a new future.

Drew and the band launched into a cover of 'I Will Wait' by Mumford and Sons with a young woman who worked in a local florist playing the banjo furiously. Everyone was already standing up, stamping and singing along. Some people were dancing. She caught hold of Gabe's good hand.

'Come on, let's dance!' she shouted.

Gabe hesitated. 'I'm hopeless at dancing.'

'Rubbish! No one will care. No one's looking at us.'

He nodded and took her hand and they swayed along and jigged as the banjo played faster and faster.

Suddenly, Sam felt someone jostle her. 'Sam!' She turned, but it was only Troy. He put a hand on her arm. 'Oy!'

Gabe let go of her, pulling a face because they'd had to separate. People around them carried on dancing and waving their arms in the air, knocking into them.

'Whoops, sorry, Troy!' She laughed then saw his face. 'What's the matter?'

'You'd better come over to the harbour office.'

'*Now*? Can it wait?' She had to shout above the music. She knew from the look on Troy's face that she had to go, but she'd hoped that for a little while at least, she could relax and enjoy the close of the festival – and some time with Gabe.

'No. It can't.'

'What's up?' Gabe asked.

Troy's grim expression made Sam's skin prickle. The high of the music and atmosphere ebbed away. 'OK, I'll come, but can you tell me what's happened?'

'Some money's gone missing. A collection the Fishermen's Mission made from their seafood barbecue. They'd put it in the harbour office, but someone left the door unlocked. And it's gone.'

Sam relaxed again. It was a bad thing to happen, but not

356

the serious incident she'd expected. 'OK, I'll come, but aren't the police dealing with it?'

'The harbourmaster wanted to call them, but I stopped him.'

'Well, I think we need to do that.' Sam reached for her phone. Gabe was still by her side.

Troy put his hand on her arm. 'No, maid.'

'Why not?'

'Because . . . come away from this noise.'

'I'll come with you,' said Gabe.

'OK . . .'

With a sense of unease, Sam followed Troy out of the marquee where they could have a proper chat without shouting down each other's ears.

'What's going on, Troy? Why haven't the police been called?'

'Harbourmaster wanted to call but I don't want to get them involved yet. Sam, there's no easy way of saying this, but just before the money was reported as missing, I saw your Ryan hanging around the office.'

'*Ryan?*' Sam burst out laughing, sure that Troy had been mistaken or had one too many ciders. 'You can't have.'

'Maid, my eyesight might not be what it once was, but it's not *that* bad. It was your Ryan and if you don't believe me, you ask Evie. She saw him too.'

She stopped laughing and fought back a rising tide of annoyance. How could Troy assume that any theft in Porthmellow was down to her brother when he wasn't even in Cornwall? 'No. It can't be,' she said firmly. She turned to Gabe for support. 'It's impossible that Ryan had anything to do with it. Isn't it, Gabe?'

357

He hesitated, just long enough to make the hairs on Sam's neck stand on end. Eventually, he said, 'We don't know it was Ryan for sure . . .'

'I saw him!' Troy protested.

Gabe patted Troy's back. 'I'm sure you did, mate. No one's saying you're wrong.'

'What? That Ryan stole the money or that he's here in Porthmellow?' Sam demanded.

'Before we jump to any conclusions, let's go to the office and find out more,' Gabe said soothingly.

'That's what I've been trying to tell you,' said Troy.

Sam started walking towards the harbour. 'Come on. Let's get this sorted out so we can enjoy the rest of the evening.'

Sam's stomach clenched with unease. Troy was mistaken, he had to be, and Evie too. They weren't young, no matter what they said. There must be a Ryan doppelganger around – probably the same guy she'd spotted in Marazion that night and earlier at the bar. Thousands of people from miles around had been at the festival.

They reached the harbour office, where the harbourmaster was talking to a man from the fishermen's charity. Understandably, they looked serious.

'Hi guys,' said Sam. 'Troy says that some money has gone missing.'

'It's true. We put the cash box from the barbecue in here and thought it was safely under lock and key, but it turns out that one of the stewards popped in to use the toilet and forgot to re-lock the door. When I came back half an hour ago, the cash box had gone.'

'I'm sorry to hear that. Is there any chance there's a mistake and someone's taken it home?'

'I've spoken to the only other person who knew it was in here and they don't have it.'

'Dozens of festival goers were around when Trevor brought the box in,' said Troy. 'Any of them could have been watching and taken their chance when the steward left.'

'And yet you think it was Ryan?' said Sam.

'I don't know it's him,' said Troy, clearly hurt.

Sam kicked herself. She was fighting a losing battle to stay calm. 'He's not even in Cornwall.'

'Do you know where he is?' said Troy. 'Maid, you've told me often enough he rarely makes contact.'

'Yes, but—'

'Ryan wouldn't steal a charity cash box,' said Gabe firmly.

'He's taken stuff before,' said the harbourmaster. 'As you know better than anyone, Gabe.' He looked at Sam. 'I'm sorry, Sam, but you know he's stolen from local people in the past.'

'That was years ago. You're right, I don't know where he is now, but he did tell me he was trying to mend his ways. He said he'd changed.' She sounded desperate because she *was* desperate. 'And you're all accusing him just because you think you saw him in the vicinity? You can't do that.'

'I can see you want to help, Sam, but how do you know?' said Troy.

'You were the one who went to the police in the first place,' the fisherman said to Gabe.

'I'm sorry, Sam, but we have to get the police involved.'

359

'No!' Gabe almost shouted. 'No, don't do that. Don't accuse Ryan. I know he wouldn't do it.'

'How? Because you know he wasn't here?' said the fisherman. 'If that's true, it would be easy for him to defend himself and no harm in mentioning it to the police, then.'

'No. No . . . he was here.'

Sam gawped. 'What?'

'Ryan was here. Or at least, he's around Porthmellow. He was going to come and meet me tonight at Clifftop House – and you, Sam. We arranged for him to come to talk to you after the concert. So, he might well be around the harbour.'

'I bloody knew it!' said Troy.

'I'm calling the police,' the harbourmaster declared.

'No, wait. Ryan's not the same anymore. He's changed. He changed a long time ago and he'd never go back to the way he was.'

Sam held onto the back of a chair. Her legs felt wobbly. The debate flew around her head, whirling and making her feel sick. Gabe was certain Ryan was in Porthmellow, which meant he'd lied to her *again*.

'Stop it! This is my brother you're all talking about and accusing. What do you mean, he's here? Gabe?' She clutched his arm. '*Gabe!*'

'I'm sorry. I should have told you earlier . . . yesterday. Way back. But I couldn't.'

Everyone stared at him. Sam dropped his arm.

Sam turned and walked out. She didn't care what anyone thought. But if Ryan was in town, she had to find him and get the truth out of him.

Chapter Thirty-Eight

S am paced the quayside, scanning the people walking past.
The food and drink stalls had packed up from this loca-
tion, so there were only a few people around. Most were down
at the concert. The music was frantic and joyous, cheers and
applause filling the air, but Sam felt as if she was being
crushed.

As she turned for another loop of the area, Gabe ran up
to her, stopping by her side, out of breath. He slipped his arm
around her back. 'You're shivering,' he said.

But she moved away from him. 'Gabe . . . what am I missing
here? How did you know my brother was here in Porthmellow?
When?' She stopped, her eyes focusing on his hand with its
tiny red scar. It was all making sense now. The man chatting
to Gabe at the concert bar. Gabe stopping midway through
the cookery demo, the shock on his face . . .

'You saw him at the Chef's Theatre. That's why you lost
concentration and cut yourself.'

'Sam.'

She shrank away from him. Answering her own questions because he was too ridden with guilt to be honest.

'You lied to me.'

'I didn't *lie*.'

'You may as well have. Oh my God. That evening when we were driving back from the hospital through Marazion when I thought I saw Ryan crossing the road to the pub. It was him! You put me off, you said it was dark.'

'I didn't say it *wasn't* him. I offered to drive back so we could check. I wasn't sure myself at the time.'

'But you were sure yesterday.' Sam was staggered. 'How long has he been hanging around down here? We were at the hospital weeks ago. What's been going on?'

'I didn't know Ryan was here until yesterday. I swear to that.'

'To that. There you go again. Swearing to half the truth. There's more, isn't there? A lot more I don't know and it must involve Ryan or you would have told me. The reason you won't tell me is that it must be something I won't like. I want to know *everything right now*. I deserve that much and so does Zennor. But first I have to find Ryan.' She broke away but Gabe stopped her with a hand on her arm.

'There's no need. I'll call him.'

'*Call* him? You have his number? I tried it a few months ago, but it was dead.'

'He's changed his phone recently.'

She shoved her hands through her hair. 'Jesus, Gabe. What else have you been keeping from me?'

362

'Sam!'

She snapped round as a voice from the doorway drew her attention. She hadn't heard it for so long or seen its owner.

He looked different. Leaner and yet more muscular, with corded muscles in his arms and breadth to his chest. His once boyish features had been sculpted . . . sharper cheekbones, a hard edge to his mouth and yet it was still her brother.

'Ryan?' Her voice came out as a croak.

Ryan walked forward. She was shaking. She hated him, she loved him.

Sam flung her arms around him and burst into tears. She began to cry, big racking sobs she couldn't stop and she didn't care who saw her. Ryan held her until she managed to get a grip of herself and remember how angry she was and the trouble he was in – again.

'People are l-looking for y-you,' she said.

'I heard. One of the fishermen I knew from way back called me over. I was on my way to the harbour office to sort it out when I saw you.'

'Why are you here? What's going on?' she begged.

'Sam. I'm sorry you had to find out I was back like this. I meant to tell you. I promised Gabe I would.'

She let go of him. The questions pecked at her again. So many questions. 'You promised *Gabe*?'

'Yeah. Please don't blame him. It's not his fault.'

Ryan exchanged a glance with Gabe. The knot in Sam's stomach tightened. 'We were going to tell you this evening. I will tell you but I have to sort this out first. Don't blame Gabe. He's been looking out for me. I'm so fucking sorry I haven't been in touch. I've been too ashamed, but now I've finally got my act together, now I'm finally not so much of a disgrace to my family, I want to come home. I can never make it up to you and Zen but I want to start to try.'

'Better deal with this mess first,' said Gabe.

'But you haven't taken the cash, have you?' Sam burst out. 'Tell them you didn't do it.'

Oh God, where had she heard those words before? They were almost identical to the ones she kept saying at the police station after the arcade robbery. Ryan's guilty face that night should have told her everything, but she hadn't wanted to believe the truth. History surely couldn't repeat itself.

'Of course I haven't. This time you can believe me,' he said firmly.

The fisherman and harbourmaster watched them like hawks, listening to the exchange. They seemed amazed that Ryan had turned up, but no one could have been any more gobsmacked than Sam.

'I told you it was Ryan.' Troy approached them and folded his arms.

'Why would I come back here if I had taken this money?' Ryan said. 'I heard people were looking for me and I came to sort it. Does that seem like the act of a guilty person?'

'I suppose you have a point,' said Troy grudgingly.

'That's all you need to know,' said Sam.

'What time did this cash go missing?' asked Gabe.

'Between around eight and twenty past,' said the fisherman, glaring at Ryan.

'Were you around, then?' the harbourmaster asked Ryan.

'Yes. I was plucking up the courage to face Sam later. I don't deny I passed this way but I went to the gents', I didn't take any money.'

'Troy?'

'There you are. If he says he didn't take it, he didn't,' declared Gabe. 'How could he possibly know the money was left in here?'

'Stop! Stop this,' Sam said. 'Ryan has nothing to do with this. You're clutching at straws.' Even as she spoke, she was transported back in time. Even now, against the evidence, she was still willing to believe and defend him, no matter what . . . She might have had suspicions, yet this time, Gabe was on Ryan's side too. Gabe was adamant Ryan was innocent. There was so much she needed to know but right now, her priority was protecting Ryan. 'I want to speak to my brother. I'm taking him home.'

'Sam, I'm not sure you can,' said the harbourmaster. 'Not until we've looked into this properly and Ryan can prove he wasn't involved. He does have history.'

'I don't care. We're leaving.'

'Sam . . .' Gabe touched her arm. 'Hang on. Let me help.'

'Looks like you've helped enough already. I want you both to come home and tell me what the hell's been going on.'

Sam was sure she would have dragged her brother out of the office kicking and screaming had Bryony not walked in. Sacha was with her, but more subdued than usual. Oh God, thought Sam, that's all we need.

Bryony stared at Ryan. For once she was momentarily speechless.

'Hi Bryony,' Ryan said as jauntily as if he'd bumped into Bryony in the post office. Sam could have hit him.

'Bryony, this isn't the time, maid,' Troy began.

Finding her voice at last, Bryony ignored him. 'I heard you were looking for a thief and that you'd been after Ryan Lovell. Well, Ryan didn't take the money. I did.'

Ryan folded his arms. 'Told you.'

'What?' asked Sam, Gabe and Troy together.

'Harry Seddon asked me to take it home for safekeeping. It's in the safe at the grooming parlour.'

'Harry? The bugger never told me!' said the fisherman. 'Why you?'

Bryony lifted her chin. 'Because he's a good friend of mine.'

The fisherman blew out a whistle. 'A good friend. You mean, you and Harry are . . . you know?' He winked.

'That's none of your business,' said Bryony, and for once Sam agreed with her. 'Anyway, now that's all sorted, Sacha needs his dinner so we're going home,' she added and marched off with her dog as if nothing had happened.

'That's OK then.' Sam glared at the other men in the room. 'Come on, we can go home too now it's all been cleared up,' she said to Ryan and Gabe.

'All's well that ends well,' said Troy.

Sam felt a wave of guilt for refusing to believe Troy and Evie when they said they'd seen Ryan. She turned to him. 'I'm sorry, to you and to Evie for doubting you'd seen Ryan. Thanks for not getting the police involved.'

Troy patted her arm. 'No matter, my maid. You should go. I reckon you all have a lot to talk about.'

Sam hugged Troy and murmured, 'Thank you,' in his ear before following Ryan and Gabe out of the office. However, she spotted Bryony a little way along the harbour, pouring Sacha a drink of water from a bottle into his bowl.

'I won't be a minute,' she told Gabe and Ryan, then added, 'Don't go anywhere without me.'

Gabe nodded and Sam hurried over to Bryony outside the office. 'Bryony! Can I have a word, please?'

Bryony glanced up, with the bottle in her hand. Sacha drank his water, spray flying from his jowls but turned to look at Sam as she grew near. He suddenly flopped down on the cobbles and Sam stroked his ears warily as he licked her hand gently. Sam had to smile, even though she had a drooly hand. He really was a lovely dog . . . when he wasn't near her van.

'Sacha looks as exhausted as I feel,' she said, wary of Bryony's reaction.

'Yes, well . . . it's been a long, hot day and he's a big dog. I need to take him home for his dinner and a rest.' She gazed adoringly at Sacha who seemed to feel the same way about Bryony.

Sam smiled. 'I don't blame Sacha. We all want to go home, but I couldn't let you go without thanking you for coming into the harbour office so quickly and vouching for Ryan.'

Bryony hmphed. 'Soon as I heard people were looking for him, I came over. I told you before I like to say what's on my mind.' She eyed Sam. 'Did you find out who wrecked your van?'

'No. I doubt I ever will.'

'Hmm,' said Bryony. Sacha let out a sigh and rested his

jowls on the cobbles. 'We'll be off, then. I expect you've got a lot to talk about, with those two.' She flipped a thumb at Gabe and Ryan, deep in conversation a little way away.

'You could say that.'

Bryony seemed about to leave then spoke up. 'Ryan wasn't all bad, you know. Not when he was at school. We were in the same year together. People used to bully me because I liked metal and Mum and Dad had the grooming parlour. They said I smelled and that I looked like a dog.'

'That's vile. No one should have to put up with that kind of comment.'

'Ryan overheard them shouting at me one day and pushed one of them in the harbour.' Bryony allowed herself a satisfied smile. 'I've never forgotten that. I'm sorry he turned bad.'

Sam winced. Ryan's past would always follow him.

'But that's what gambling does to you,' Bryony went on. 'My grandad used to back the horses. He spent every penny and left my nan and mum destitute. Grandad jumped off the cliffs at Hell's Mouth, but that was before I was born.'

Sam was horrified. 'I'm so sorry, I had no idea.'

'Yes, well, you don't know a lot about me . . .' She paused before going on gruffly. 'No one does and I don't let them see how I really feel. I'd rather have my dog than people any day. People can be cruel, but Sacha will always love me.' She ruffled his ears. 'I'm a young fogey and I don't care, do I, baby?'

Reluctantly, Sacha got to his feet. 'You'd better get back to your brother,' said Bryony. 'And your boyfriend.'

'Gabe isn't my boyfriend.'

Bryony snorted. 'You used to say that at school. Even when

everyone knew you were both nuts about each other. You think you know everything that's going on in Porthmellow, running the festival – the one everyone relies on – but there's some things right under your nose that you must be blind to.'

'What do you mean?'

'Ask your brother.'

Chapter Thirty-Nine

A short time later Gabe led Sam into the sitting room of Clifftop House. Ryan was already there, standing with his back to the window. Twilight had fallen over the sea, but being the end of June, the light was deepest blue, with a paler glow over to the west. The initial shock of seeing Ryan, alongside the worry over the missing cash, had shaken Sam badly.

'Drink, anyone?' said Gabe. 'I need one after that.'

'No, thanks,' said Sam.

Ryan shook his head. 'Water's fine for me. I need to drive home afterwards.'

'*Home*? Where's that, then?' Sam asked.

'Roche. I'm – me and my partner – are renting a cottage in the village.'

Sam let out a breath. 'How long have you been back in Cornwall?'

'A few weeks.'

'My God,' said Sam, needing time to take in Ryan's reply.

A minute later, Gabe brought water and a glass of whisky from the kitchen. 'Here you go.'

'Thanks,' Ryan said, taking a sip of the iced water Gabe had handed him, then sitting down on the sofa.

Gabe sat next to him. Sam felt they were ganging up on her, or more likely, that they needed each other's support to face her. She looked at each of them, searching their expressions. Ryan looking down at his feet, Gabe holding her gaze, his expression sombre. Her stomach fluttered.

'OK,' she said. 'Who's going to start?'

Ryan took a sip of his water before he spoke. 'It had better be me . . . I need to go back to before the robbery. Just after Mum died, when I first started working at the arcade, you probably know I was getting into debt. I was playing the arcade machines and poker, borrowing on my wages, and from "friends".' He bracketed the word and snorted. 'One of them decided to call in my debts and said I could pay up by doing some jobs with them.' Ryan looked down at his hands. 'I'm not proud of it. I wish I could change it.'

'*Jobs?*' Sam steeled herself. She dreaded hearing the rest but she had to. Suddenly, she was very glad Zennor wasn't there. 'You mean, the arcade wasn't a one-off?'

Ryan coughed then took a large gulp of water and looked to Gabe as if he needed helping out, which only ratcheted up Sam's apprehension.

Gabe looked back at Ryan who cleared his throat again and said, 'I think you'd better take this up, mate, for now.'

'You know what happened next – part of it,' Gabe said. 'You guessed at the time, or Ryan told you, that it was while

I was working in the chip shop as well as part-time as a chef and at catering college. *Everyone* used to pass through the shop and I overheard all sorts of gossip. Ninety-nine per cent of it was bollocks, people mouthing off, bragging what they'd *like* to do . . . but occasionally, some of it had a kernel of truth. Some people – sorry, Ryan – can be pretty stupid.'

'No need to apologise. I've been a total twat.' Ryan sounded quite chipper about the insult. He hadn't changed a bit in that respect: still the same old Ryan, never taking anything too seriously.

Gabe, however, was far from chirpy. She hadn't seen him so uncomfortable for a long time, which made her even more twitchy about what was to come. 'Over the years, I learned to shut my ears to all of the talk. It was none of my business. Until I heard something that *was* my business. Very much my business. Because it related to you, Sam, and to Zennor.'

Sam's stomach clenched hard. *Her and Zennor?* She felt cold. Ryan fixed his eyes on the rug but Gabe's voice was steady, stronger as if he'd gained courage now he'd started.

'I knew something was kicking off and I was emptying the trade waste behind the shop. I heard Ryan and his so-called mates mention a snatch of the plan to rob the arcade and I didn't know what to do. I didn't want Ryan to get into trouble, I suspected that he was in deep trouble with debts but, for your sake, I did nothing, hoping that a solution might present itself.'

Sam had no words. Her throat was too dry.

'Don't blame Gabe,' said Ryan. 'He found me in the pub one night. Took me round the back, gave me the mother of all bollockings and warned me not to take part in anything dodgy. I said I wouldn't, but I was lying. He thought he'd shock me out of getting involved in the job but I was in too deep. Too addicted to get out. It was far worse than you knew, Sam. I owed them over fifty grand with the interest they charged.'

Sam let out a wail. 'Fifty *grand*? Oh God, how did I miss what was happening in my own family?'

'You were grieving for Mum . . .' said Ryan. 'I guess we all were but that's no excuse. You were trying to get Stargazey off the ground, look after us and keep a roof over our heads. That should have been my job, as the eldest, and I'm ashamed I shirked my share of the responsibilities. I didn't want to worry you even more and I genuinely thought I could get myself out of the shit. You're not Superwoman, Sam, even though you like to pretend you are.'

'Me? Superwoman? I was just trying to survive from minute to minute back then. I'm— I didn't realise how bad it was for you.'

'You need to know the whole of it.' Gabe was grim faced. 'I hoped Ryan would bail out and I took his word, but I still kept an eye on him. One evening, he left the shop with his chips and left his Nokia phone on the counter. I picked it up and saw a message that could only mean something was happening that evening.'

'At the arcade?' said Sam.

'Not only the arcade,' said Gabe.

Ryan cut in. 'I was desperate and in deep trouble. You knew that.'

Gabe exchanged a look with Ryan.

'I met up with Ryan and I told him I knew and I said I wouldn't shop him if he promised to leave Porthmellow and start again somewhere else. He swore he would and I believed him, but he wasn't telling the truth again. Were you, mate?'

Ryan rubbed his face. Sam knew that nervous gesture all too well. '*Ryan?*'

'I promised Gabe something I never should have. He didn't know that my mates were planning other raids. I said I wanted out of it all, but they were having none of it. They said I was a danger and they wanted me to prove I wasn't going to go to the police. They wanted me to do some more robberies to prove it. They showed me a list. Places closer to home. The Cronks' shop in Porthmellow and . . .' He put his head in his hands. 'I'm sorry, Sam.'

'What? What was on the list?'

'The chip shop and . . . and Stargazey.'

'But – but – there wasn't much money in Stargazey. I never left more than a small float in the unit.'

'I knew you used to leave the takings inside the filing cabinet at the unit on a Saturday night so you could bank them on Monday morning. I also knew you kept the key to the unit and the cabinet in your room and that you were going out with some friends to the pub.'

'Oh Ryan! Don't tell me you were actually going to creep into my bedroom and take my keys?'

He nodded his head miserably. 'Yes, but I thought I could get in there and take the cash, then replace the keys without you ever even realising it.'

She felt physically ill. 'But I would have known on Monday morning when I'd lost the Saturday takings! Oh, Ryan. I can't believe you could even have thought about doing it.'

'I was in a bad place. I was desperate. They said I had to tell them and it was a test. After that, they said they might leave me alone. They said, if I didn't do it, they would come round to the unit and take the money themselves. They said they might even go in when you were there one evening and that they couldn't guarantee you wouldn't get hurt, you being a feisty sort . . . So I thought I'd better steal the money myself, only I didn't get far, did I, because Gabe found out.'

With a cry of shock, Sam rushed into the kitchen and locked herself in the cloakroom. She had to hold onto the basin because she was actually shaking. She might even be sick. A tearful, pale face stared at her from the mirror, mascara smudged under her eyes.

'Sam!' Gabe called through the door.

She splashed cold water on her face and opened the door to find his expression full of concern. 'Are you OK?'

She laughed at him. 'Of course I'm not bloody OK. I've just heard my own brother planned on robbing me.'

'It's terrible, I know, but Ryan didn't actually go through with taking your money. He was trying to protect you, in his own deluded way,' said Gabe.

'Only because you went to the police.'

'I had to. How could I not?'

'I know why you did it now but . . .' She pushed him away. 'Why have you helped him since? How could you?'

'Because everyone deserves a second chance. Because I knew

you loved him really. Because, as Ryan pointed out to me the other night, I love you.'

Ryan appeared in the kitchen doorway. 'Don't blame Gabe for anything. I begged Gabe not to tell you and Zennor what might have happened and he didn't. We were arrested while we were robbing the arcade and no one ever knew what else we were planning.'

She wiped her eyes with a wad of tissues.

'How many times can I say I'm sorry?' said Ryan. 'It'll never be enough. I'm glad Gabe went to the police. I hated him for a while afterwards, but nowhere near as much as I hated myself. After I came out of prison, I slept rough for a couple of years and lived hand to mouth.'

'You could have come back to us,' she said. 'I offered to help. You cutting yourself off from us made things worse.' But that was before she'd known the full story, she thought. Would she have felt differently if she had known he was going to steal from his own family?

'I was too ashamed to come back to you for help and too afraid you'd find out what I'd really been planning. I was at rock bottom again until Gabe turned up. He tracked me down and became my sponsor and supported my rehab.'

She stared at Gabe. '*You* paid for Ryan's rehab?'

'I was doing well and I could help, so I did.' Gabe spoke quietly.

Sam was torn between anger at Gabe's deception and gratitude for his help. It could have been so much worse for her brother if Gabe had stayed silent in the first place or not helped him back on his feet.

376

'Look, Sam. You can't blame Gabe, it was all my fault. I begged him not to tell you or Zennor what might have happened. I promised things would be different when I came out. I swore I'd make a fresh start. I did – eventually. It was harder than I'd thought. Much harder, but with Gabe's support, I got there and turned my life around.

'I've been working as a counsellor for a gambling rehab charity for a while now. They're opening a new centre in Truro and when I saw the chance, I applied. I took it as a sign that I should take the next step. Making amends to the people you've hurt is part of the rehab process . . . but I wanted the festival to be over before I dropped a bombshell like this. I'm sorry I couldn't keep away over the weekend. I tried but I wanted to see you and Zennor – everyone here – again, before I came out with all this.'

Gabe put his hand on Sam's shoulder as Ryan continued. 'There's plenty of time for us all to say whatever we want to. I'm not expecting to be forgiven. Understood, maybe, but not welcomed back with open arms. I just wanted you to know. I knew Gabe was back here and I was offered this opportunity. The stars – fate, any of that stuff – seemed to be telling me to come home.'

Sam sat down on the kitchen stool. 'I don't know how I'm ever going to explain this to Zennor. I don't know if I even should. Oh, Ryan, I don't know what I feel.'

'It's not your job to explain to her, it's mine, and I'm going to see Zennor now. Zennor can handle it. She's grown up. We all are.' He gave a sad smile. 'Even me.'

After that, Ryan left her and Gabe alone. For a short while, they sat in silence. She was out of words. The things she'd just heard were overwhelming, terrible things, lies, deception taking place over many years, but for good reasons. Could she ever begin to forgive Ryan for what he'd contemplated? Would he ever *really* have allowed her to be scared, robbed and hurt by his mates?

She hoped not. He'd certainly looked close to tears when he'd finally told her the horrible truth. Was it genuine? He said he was a new person. A new version of the same person . . . Could she trust him? Perhaps it would take a lifetime, perhaps she'd never be able to entirely. People could say sorry all they wanted but only actions would prove it, and even then . . .

And Gabe had kept it all secret, all these years.

She had no idea how she could ever forgive them, no matter how much she wanted to – or how much she loved them both.

She grabbed some more tissues and wiped her eyes.

Finally, Gabe spoke. 'After we split up, I was torn. I'd done what I thought was right. Some people in the village hated me for it. Did you know some guy spat in my face outside the court?'

'No, I didn't. I was angry with you, but I never wanted you to suffer that kind of abuse.'

'Now you know why I didn't tell you. After the trial, I left and got a job in a London hotel and I worked every hour while I tried to bury Porthmellow, Ryan – and you. Yes, I got on in my career, but the bitterness and hurt lingered. At Ryan, at you – and at myself for being torn. All this time, I longed to come home and tell you everything, but I didn't want you to know the truth about Ryan, and the longer I kept his secret, the harder it was. I never meant us to start up again, but now I know that was hopeless from the moment I saw you at the pub.'

'So you contacted Ryan to say you were back?'

'No. I had no idea that Ryan was back in the area. I was as shocked as you when we saw him after the hospital.'

'I knew it was him!'

'I wasn't quite sure, but after that I called him. And when I saw him at the festival, I told him it was time to come clean with you, and he agreed.'

'I – I'm glad Ryan's turned things around and I'm grateful for your help but I need to ask this,' she said, emotion almost choking her words. 'How will I know you're not keeping things from me again? How will I know you're not lying because you think it's best for me?'

'I won't ever do that again. I love you.'

And she loved him, but was that enough to overcome everything else? And even if it was, would Gabe really want to stay in Porthmellow after the festival was over? Come back to the humdrum everyday rhythm of life there? The adulation he'd received at the festival had shown her how far he'd moved on in his life.

'I can't handle this now. I need to go to Zennor and Ryan. Give me some time to take it all in. Please.'

She walked out and across the road. The last light streaked the sky. The music had stopped below in the harbour. She gazed up at the sky, searching every star for a brighter one.

Any sign that she wasn't alone in her decision-making. 'Mum, I've no idea if you can hear me, but if you can, please tell me what to do. Forgive? Forget? Neither? Both?'

Then she hurried over to Wavecrest Cottage, let herself in and closed the door behind her. A cacophony of sobs, squeals and pig-wheeking greeted her. The Lovells were finally back together again, but she still had no answer to her questions.

Chapter Forty

Chloe finished putting her hair up and went into the sitting room where Hannah was zipping up Ruby's day bag. What a load of paraphernalia a little one came with. She'd forgotten how much. Ruby was making her wobbly way between the furniture in her dungarees and T-shirt. The sunshade was on the buggy.

It was now Tuesday afternoon and Hannah was going to the beach with Ruby. Fraser had left on Monday evening, driving home to Surrey. The marquee and stage had gone, the streets were being cleared up and Porthmellow was a lot more . . . mellow. It would not be as easy to clear up things between Jordan and Hannah. Hannah had already called him. He was Ruby's father, after all. He did want to see his daughter and he'd have to be responsible for supporting her, alongside Hannah. Hannah wanted him to be a part of Ruby's life if it was possible.

After she'd helped Ruby and Hannah down to the ground

floor, she went back upstairs. The Crow's Nest was unnaturally quiet, and, briefly, Chloe had a reminder of what life had been like just a few days ago. Hannah and Ruby would stay with her while they got themselves sorted out, but Hannah planned to get a job. Chloe was going to help with the child-care, but Hannah had insisted she had her own career and Ruby would need some extra nursery care. That was all in the future. All up in the air.

Chloe had to start preparing for her next event soon – but first, she had a more important job to do. It was a hot July morning so she pulled on a sundress she hadn't worn for a couple of years and casual pumps, and went out onto the balcony.

A strange vessel was motoring into the harbour. On Monday morning, Drew and his crew had driven up to Brixham to collect *Caitlin* and sail her home to Porthmellow.

Enjoying the sun on her shoulders, she wandered down to the quay where the crew was busy tying up alongside the quay. The harbourmaster, Troy, Evie and several of the local fishermen were admiring her so Chloe bought an iced coffee and sat at a café nearby. She didn't want to disturb Drew while he was busy, but like the other tourists around her, she was fascinated as the crew carried their kit off the boat and loaded provisions back on.

Eventually, he caught sight of her and beckoned her towards him.

Leaving her empty cup she walked to the quayside, looking down at him.

'Welcome home,' she called.

He grinned. 'Thanks. Would you like to come aboard?'

Chloe realised she'd never been on board any boat remotely like *Caitlin*. It meant a lot to Chloe that Drew had invited her on board for a special tour. 'OK. Yes, I'd love to.'

She walked across the gangplank and stood on the deck with him. 'She's fantastic.'

'I think so too,' said Drew proudly. 'I hope she behaves as well as the *Marisco*. We can double our trips now. We have to, to pay for her.' It was funny the way he spoke about *Caitlin* as if she was an actual person.

She took in the scrubbed decks, gleaming wood and rigging. *Caitlin* was truly beautiful.

Drew stood by her shoulder. 'I wanted you to be the first person from Porthmellow to meet her.'

'Wow. That's an honour.'

'Will you come for a sail on her sometime?' He was like a dog with two tails.

Chloe was no sailor, but now seemed to be the time for new beginnings. 'I'll try anything once as long as I don't have to climb the rigging.'

'Don't worry, we don't make newbies do that. Not on their first time, anyway.' He winked.

She looked up at the sky, blue through the rigging. Was it possible to be happier than you deserved?

'I saw Katya and Connor while I was in Brixham,' said Drew.

Chloe returned her attention to his face, wondering what was coming next. 'Oh?'

'They're not moving to Poland.' His face lit up with joy. 'Katya's been offered a promotion and anyway she said she

383

didn't think she could uproot him or take him so far from me. So I won't lose Connor.'

'Oh, Drew, I'm so pleased for you.' She threw her arms around him and they hugged. Then she became aware of Troy and Evie and their harbour mates watching from above. She let him go. 'Oh dear. We've been rumbled.'

Drew gave the Carmans a nod and a grin. 'I'm not bothered if you're not,' he said as he took her hand and walked to the other side of the boat, away from their audience.

'I don't give a toss about the age difference. I like you. You're brave and clever, and beautiful and for God's sake, I fancy you.'

'Stop. I'm embarrassed now,' she said. He was over ten years younger than her. She was a granny. 'You know I fancy you too.' God, how teenage that sounded, but *I find you sexy and attractive and you make my toes curl in pleasure and bits of me tingle that I thought were dead,* sounded *much* worse.

Drew shook his head. 'We could have slept together that evening after you told me about Hannah. Believe me. I wanted to. It really did take me everything not to kiss you back – properly – and drag you upstairs to bed.'

She squeaked in amazement. '*Drag* me upstairs to bed?'

He winced. 'Well, you know me. It's not really my style, but you get the idea.'

She laughed in delight. 'I'm glad you didn't do it then – but only just! I *wasn't* drunk. Dying of embarrassment but not drunk.' She winced. 'Perhaps a little bit the worse for wear . . .'

'Only a little, but I held back because after you'd poured your heart out, I thought I'd only be a comfort shag.'

Her gasp turned into laughter. 'Drew!'

'Sorry to be blunt. You know I've no way with words. I thought you had too much to deal with and if we'd done it then, you'd have regretted it and backed away for good.'

'Maybe. Who knows? What's important is that we're here now and I do really like you, and yes, I want us to get to know each other better. Much better . . .' Argh. Even at fifty, it was possible to blush.

He quirked an eyebrow. 'I sense a "but" and I think I know what kind of "but". Would it involve family?'

'I need time to get to know Hannah and Ruby first. I need time to rediscover who I am and be with them. Time to sort my shit out, as they say. It might not take long . . . but I can't ask you to hang around.'

'I can wait.'

'Not long, I hope, just until I find my feet. I want you to get to know my family too. Not Fraser, obviously.' She laughed.

'Perhaps not a good idea.'

'One day soon though. I couldn't care less what Fraser thinks. Um. I did wonder, as a start, if you might like to ask Connor to come for a picnic with us the next time he's in Porthmellow, if he can stand being with a toddler?'

'He'd like that. He doesn't mind little ones and I might have already mentioned you to him – and to Katya.'

'Oh.'

He grinned. 'She's not bothered what I do with my life. All I care is that she's staying. For now, while we're taking time to get to know each other – as *very* good friends, of course – how about I show you around *Caitlin* properly? The skipper's quarters included.'

385

'Down there?' She pointed at the hatchway in the deck.

''Fraid so. Mind the ladder, though. You go down backwards, by the way.'

Drew was down the ladder-like stairs in seconds, while Chloe took them at a slightly more sedate pace. They emerged into the saloon where the crew and guest sailors hung out. The wood-lined space was cosy and basic but spotlessly clean.

You really couldn't swing a cat in the minuscule cabin and it smelt of lemon, as if someone had just cleaned it. Tangy but not unpleasant. There was a photo of Drew and Connor on a small shelf and a drybag, probably with his clothes in it, in the corner. The cabin had all the essentials, nothing frivolous, but still, to her eyes, it managed to be romantic and full of character.

Very much like her owner, thought Chloe, looking at her handsome skipper, leaning in the doorway, anxious to know what she thought of his second home.

Hmm. That single bunk, spread with a thin mattress and a sleeping bag wasn't much more than a large shelf. Chloe sat on it. Any kind of bouncing was out of the question but it was very firm.

Drew seemed anxious, sensing she might be having second thoughts. 'It *is* very basic. All these vintage vessels are,' he said.

'It is a little bit spartan . . .' She bit her lip. Suddenly all thoughts of only being friends fled out of her mind. 'But I still love it and you know what I said a few minutes ago about taking things slowly? Well, I'm not sure I can wait that long.'

'I see.' His voice took on a serious tone as he closed the cabin door. 'You do realise that there's going to be a hell of a stir if we don't come up from here for a while? Troy probably

386

has a stopwatch on us and the gossip'll be halfway round Porthmellow by sunset.'

'The whole of the town by teatime, I'd say, but I don't mind.' She held out her hand to him. 'If you don't.'

'I couldn't give a flying . . . whatever.' They both laughed and then he kissed her and pulled her hair from its updo so that it fell onto her bare shoulders. The sun shone through the tiny high porthole. The boat rocked gently on the harbour waters. If anyone had a mind to sail past and peer inside, then they were well and truly scuppered. Bloody hell, what on earth would Fraser – or anyone back in Surrey – think if they knew she was shagging a sexy younger Cornishman in the cabin of a trawler with half the town watching?

And frankly, thought Chloe, giving herself up to the most delicious sensations she'd experienced in a very long time – who cared?

Chapter Forty-One

Since Sunday night, after tears, raised voices, hugs and talking into the night, Sam and Zennor had made some kind of peace with Ryan. Sam believed he was genuinely sorry and desperate to build a bridge with his family again. The next morning, at Ryan's request, they had gone to visit their mum's grave on the hill above Porthmellow and lay some flowers. Sam had fought back tears even now at the memory of the three of them at their mother's funeral, holding onto to each other like they were drowning, sobbing.

'Mum wouldn't have wanted us to blame each other; she'd want us to stick together,' Zennor said. 'Now we're all here, we should start again.'

Still too full of emotion to speak, Sam nodded and, for a change, let her siblings take the lead.

She and Ryan stood a little way off while Zennor arranged the flowers in an urn at the grave.

'I can't help feeling I didn't look hard enough for you,' she told Ryan.

'I didn't want to be found. I couldn't see any way out of the mess. I don't know what I'd have done without Gabe offering a helping hand. He contacted me not long after I got out, but I was too angry and raw then. I told him to get lost – though they weren't the words I used.'

'I would have helped you – at any time, all you had to do was ask. All I knew was that you were alive somewhere, but I was always on edge for a call from the police to say something had happened.'

Ryan winced. 'I'm sorry. I felt I'd taken enough from you and Zen. And coming home to Porthmellow . . . even if I could have faced the town, I could never have faced you both again, knowing what I'd planned. I'd have had to tell you everything and that was a step too far so it was easier for me to stay away. I thought a clean break would be less painful for all of us.'

'Clean breaks are never painless and I've learned that the hard way . . . It took a lot of courage for you to accept Gabe's help,' Sam said.

'Not as much as it took him to offer it again – and again – until I finally realised he was handing me a lifeline. If he hadn't paid for my rehab, God knows where I'd be now. It's still tough to walk by the bookies, or keep off the online sites, but I'm dealing with it.' He hugged Sam. 'I can't believe what I put you all through.'

'There's only one way now. Forwards,' said Sam, hugging him again.

'It's not for me to interfere in your love life, but if Gabe keeping my secret is stopping you guys from being happy, then I'll never forgive myself. I might not be here at all if he hadn't helped me.'

'I know. I'm only just coming to terms with finding you and the truth.'

'I'm the last person to offer advice, but I don't buy that. You're scared of asking him to stay here, aren't you? Scared it won't be enough for him and he'll disappear and you'll be hurt again.'

Another truth hit her smack in the chest. She opened her mouth to deny it but couldn't. 'He'll leave. I know he will. I've not heard from him since Sunday night.'

'Really?'

'I asked him to give me space and time.'

Ryan swore. 'Then what do you expect? He's a bloke doing as he's told for once and you're still not happy?'

Sam batted him gently. 'Cheek!' Her brief smile faded.

'I'm joking but . . . he's opening the restaurant, isn't he?' Ryan said.

'That doesn't mean he'll stay. How can he be happy here in Porthmellow after the life he has in London? I'm not starting anything knowing he could leave again.'

'Look, Sam. When Gabe makes a decision, you know he sticks to it. If he says he's staying around, you should give him a chance. If you can give me another chance, you can surely give Gabe one.'

That was just it. Gabe had hinted he'd stay but because of *her*. What if he realised that she wasn't enough? Ordinary Sam, living an ordinary life in a little Cornish village that had

had its five minutes of fame for the year. Then again, she supposed she could go to London with him . . .

'And,' said Ryan softly, 'Mum would want you to forgive Gabe. She'd want you to smile and dance and be happy with someone you care about.'

Sam turned to him, fresh tears in her eyes. 'You're right about that.'

But one glance at Zennor standing by the grave, wiping her eyes, and at Ryan by her side, had decided Sam. Now she had her family around her again, no matter how much she loved Gabe, she could never leave them or her home.

That Tuesday night, she lay awake turning over Ryan's words about Gabe and their mother. He left very early, to see his family before a meeting at the new rehab centre but not before they'd all arranged to meet his partner, Tilly, and her children the following weekend. She realised that she might soon have a new family to welcome to Wavecrest. It was a time of new beginnings – for some.

Zennor kissed him at the door, but Sam walked to his car with him. 'Ryan, before you go, there's something else that's been bothering me. Something Bryony said after the festival.'

'Bryony?'

'Yes. She said that you were kind to her at school and that you pushed some guy who'd been hassling her in the harbour.' Sam decided not to mention the part involving Bryony's grandfather jumping off a cliff.

Ryan laughed. 'Yeah, I remember that. He was a tosser and he deserved it. Is that what you wanted to ask me about?'

Sam smiled. 'Not totally. Bryony was trying, in her own unique way, to explain why she'd raced over to the office to get you off the hook. I get that she had a tough time at school from the bullies. I didn't realise how much, her being a few years older, but she also said something about Gabe. She said I'd no idea about him . . . and after my van was vandalised, she really went for him as if she hated him. I think she ripped down the posters because they had Gabe's name on them.'

'She had a massive crush on Gabe. Didn't you know?'

'What? Oh God, no. I'd no idea.'

'She told me after I pushed that bastard in the harbour. She ranted about how miserable she was and how she hated everyone in Porthmellow and Gabe didn't even know she existed. I think Bryony carried a torch for him for years after, even when he'd left town.'

'I wish I'd known. You haven't mentioned it to him, have you?'

'No way. What's the point if she's over it now and she's obviously found someone else, even if it is Harry Seddon,' said Ryan, pulling a face.

'None, I suppose, and you don't think Gabe has any inkling she was in love with him?'

He laughed. 'Not a clue. I'm not sure anyone else ever knew. It was Bryony's secret.'

Sam sighed. 'OK. I'll leave it alone. Some secrets are best left buried.'

He kissed her on the cheek. 'Forget Bryony and start living your own life. I'll see you next weekend. I'm sorry for all the trouble I've caused you. I love you, Sam.'

Sam gave him a little push. 'Go on. Get to work.' She called after him, 'Love you too!'

He climbed in the car and tooted his horn, before driving off, leaving Sam alone, wondering what else she didn't know and how to solve her biggest dilemma of all: Gabe.

The next day, Wednesday, the harbour was eerily quiet. Everyone was partied out and Stargazey was closed too, but it had been a bumper weekend of business so they all deserved a break. Sam had spent the time after Ryan had left helping to clear up and soon almost every trace of the festival had been removed during the mammoth clear-up. Now, basically, it was all over for another year.

Sam had heard nothing from Gabe since Sunday evening. No questions, or apologies. No pressure on her. That in itself was unsettling . . . but if she contacted him again, she needed to be absolutely sure of what she wanted and in her present state of mind, that wasn't easy to work out.

It was late afternoon when she climbed down from the stepladder after removing the last of the posters from around the harbour. She folded up the ladder and lugged it towards Festival HQ, or the Institute, as it was now back to being. Without its bunting and banners, or risqué announcements – it had changed back from fairy-tale coach to pumpkin again.

In fact, there was virtually no sign of the momentous events that had taken place over the weekend at all. Apart from the ache in her heart and the constant turning over of thoughts about Gabe. They came over and over like the waves rolling up the beach.

The ladder was heavy and she had to rest in front of the Net Loft. Its windows were empty and the original sign was still up. There was no evidence of work starting . . . as if Gabe were waiting for something.

He might be in as much agony as she was, she thought.

Ryan was right. She had to start trusting someone and there was no one more rock solid than Gabe. No one had ever remotely made her feel the way he did.

'Hello, my maid!' Evie emerged from the travel agents, closely followed by Troy, whose arm was out of its sling now.

'How are you?' Evie asked. 'You must be worn out, I know Troy is; he slept until ten o'clock this morning.'

'I've been working hard!' Troy protested.

'You both have,' Sam said. 'Thanks for everything you've done.' She noted the stack of brochures Evie had in the pocket of her roller. 'Planning a trip?'

'We're going to Crete in the autumn,' said Evie. 'The agent has arranged special assistance at the airport so I won't have to worry.'

'VIP treatment,' said Troy and planted a kiss on Evie's cheek.

'That sounds amazing.' Sam smiled. 'You deserve it.'

'You should get away from Porthmellow too,' Evie said.

'Maybe to London . . .' Troy had a glint in his eye. 'I heard Gabe was packing up again. We passed the removals van when I drove her down here.'

'Removals van?' Sam blurted out.

Evie smiled. 'Yes. We had to reverse back to let the driver through. He said he was on his way to Clifftop House and asked us if we thought he'd get the vehicle past the overhanging window.'

Troy chuckled. 'I could see he'd be OK but I put the wind up him anyway and warned him not to take a chunk out of the cottage.'

'Did you not know Gabe was packing up?' Evie asked Sam.

Shock had robbed Sam of a reply. Gabe was going to leave without telling her? Had he given up on her or changed his mind about them making a fresh start? Suddenly she felt as if the sky was weighing down on her, rather than only the ladder, but she was also seized by a sense of urgency. A sixth sense told her that she had to make her decision now.

'I – I expect he was going to,' she said. 'Thanks for letting me know . . . I – I'm sorry but I have to go. Erm, do you mind getting someone to return this for me?'

Abandoning the ladder on the harbour, she left the stunned Carmans behind and started to jog towards the coastal path, a feeling of dread impelling her on. By the time she reached Clifftop House, she was gasping for breath.

Sure enough, the removal van was on the drive.

'Stop!' She darted up to the cab.

The driver paled. It was the same man as before. 'Not you again! You're not having the keys this time. Look, I brought a smaller van.'

'I don't care. You aren't going anywhere,' said Sam.

'What?' he called, but Sam had already scooted through the open doorway of the house.

Now she knew Gabe was going, she had to speak to him. How could she let him go? The prospect of losing him – this time for good – had brought everything into the sharpest focus. Even though he'd kept her in the dark and caused her pain, it had been for all the right reasons and because he cared for her – he loved her. He'd helped her brother and saved her and him from far worse. She knew he'd done it for her as much as Ryan.

Ryan was right. Their mother would have told her to grab that kind of love with both hands. Now, it looked as if she'd let it slip away again.

'Gabe!' she called from the entrance hall. There was no answer, then she heard footsteps up above her. She ran upstairs towards his room, her heart pounding.

She could not un-love Gabe, just as she couldn't un-love Ryan.

They both deserved second chances. Would Gabe give her another chance too?

Chapter Forty-Two

Gabe stared at the wild woman in his bedroom. Her face was scarlet, and she was out of breath, but she looked gorgeous to him.

She seemed transfixed by the shirts he was holding. 'W-what are you d-doing? Don't say you were leaving without telling me.'

He held onto the pile. 'Well . . . I don't know if it's worth me staying here.'

'What do you mean?'

'I've given you time and space. I want to stay, but not without you,' he said, finding his heart pounding too, and all he'd done was fold a few clothes.

She stepped into the room. 'I *want* you to stay. I want it more than anything else in the world. I love you, for God's sake, but I don't know how you can be happy here.'

Love. He didn't dare dwell on that word in case he lost it completely. 'Simple. Because you're here,' he said, laying the clothes on the bed as if they were thistledown, ready to fly away into the air if he moved too quickly or suddenly. 'Do you need another reason?'

'But . . . the removal van—'

'Has brought more of my stuff from London. Sam, I'm *unpacking*, not leaving. I'm here to stay.'

She looked around her then at him, her eyes full of the fire he'd always loved. 'Oh my God, you devil, Gabe Mathias. I saw the van and I thought . . . and you let me think you were *going*.'

'I didn't actually *lie*.' He smiled, hoping he hadn't made a huge mistake with his tiny deception. She met him by the bed and he almost lost it again. He reached up to touch her cheek, feeling the softness – the fragility under the strength – and noticing the dark circles under her eyes. She'd had a rough few days, a rough eleven years, a rough life that she'd faced and weathered like a Porthmellow storm. 'You asked me not to keep anything from you again. Then here's the truth. I love you and I always have loved you.'

'Me too.'

'Sam.' He gathered her to him and rested his hands lightly on her waist, half afraid she might change her mind and take flight. 'You're here.' He was every bit as astonished as he sounded.

'Looks like it.' Her tawny eyes searched his. 'I'm sorry. I was bitter and angry after Ryan went away. I've wronged you too. I didn't try to see your point of view and even when I did finally see it, a few years after you left Porthmellow, I'd never have admitted it to you.'

'What good will it do now? It's time we buried the past, or at least put it into cold storage.'

Sam nodded. 'After we'd all finished screaming and crying, we came to a sort of truce, for Mum's sake as much as ours. She'd have wanted us to put the past behind us so we've arranged to meet Ryan's new partner, Tilly, and her kids. They're coming to Porthmellow to see me and Zennor next weekend.'

'That's great. I'm glad for you all.'

He touched his forehead to hers. 'Sam. Stay here. This place is way too big for me on my own.'

She raised her eyebrows. 'You're not scared that the ghosts will get you?'

'Not now you're here.'

'My home's with Zennor for now, I couldn't leave her, but if you were only a minute away, I'm sure I could spend some time – a lot of time – here.' She kissed him and he closed his eyes, relishing he firm, hot press of her mouth on his. Nothing more was said. Nothing more needed to be said. They lay down on the bed and gradually, inch by inch, as the deep evening blue stole into the sky, Gabe finally believed that he was home and it was where he belonged.

Epilogue

A Few Weeks Later

Sam opened another window in the Institute. Although it was evening, the sun was still bright and the air was stuffy. Late July had brought a heatwave to Porthmellow and the harbour and beach had been rammed with families enjoying the first week of school holidays.

Everyone, apart from Troy, had swapped the usual tea for Evie's homemade lemonade, which Sam thought was a vast improvement. Drinks in hand, they took their places around the table.

'So, here we all are again. I'd like to welcome the newest member of our committee. I think you know him so I won't waste time introducing him. Welcome, Gabe.'

There was laughter and a groan from Troy. Gabe gave a little bow. Evie smiled and wafted herself with a Japanese fan.

'I also have good news,' she began, slightly unsure of the

reaction. 'I'm delighted to announce that if we all agree, next year our main festival sponsor will be the Net Loft.'

'Wow!' said Chloe, positively radiating happiness.

'Nice one, mate,' said Drew, getting up to shake hands with Gabe.

'He can afford it,' said Troy. 'Or did you have to twist his arm?' he asked Sam.

'Troy!' Evie rapped him with her fan.

'It's a pleasure,' said Gabe. 'And there was no arm twisting or coercion of any kind necessary.' He mouthed 'sadly' to Sam and she had to glance away from him to avoid blushing. She'd spent most of her nights over the past few weeks at Clifftop House.

After everyone had voted unanimously to accept Gabe's offer, she finally called the meeting to order.

'I also have some news that's not *strictly* related to the festival but you might be relieved to hear. The police have found out who trashed my Stargazey van.'

'Oh my God. Who?' said Chloe.

'It was some guy with a mobile pasty van. We had a row once at a festival when he accused me of taking his custom, which I hadn't. I hadn't realised that he'd also been threatening the festival organisers and stewards so they booted him off his pitch and wouldn't have him back this year. He saw an interview I did for a magazine about our festival and was so pissed off, he decided to take it out on me by wrecking my van.'

'What a scumbag,' said Drew. 'I'm glad he was caught.'

'Nasty little bugger,' said Evie. 'I wish I could get hold of him.'

Troy cackled. 'His life wouldn't be worth living if she did!'

'How did they find the idiot?' asked Drew.

'Well, it turns out he's also been behind some of the posts on our social media pages. I have to thank Ben and Zennor for tracing his IP address and doing a bit of cyber detective work that led us to him. We mentioned his name to the police and can you believe the idiot hadn't been able to resist boasting about it on his own Facebook page? They even found a photo of my trashed van on his phone!'

'Ben's a genius,' said Zennor proudly.

Ben looked at his hands. 'It wasn't that hard once I had the time to hunt for him properly after the festival.'

'There will always be people who don't love the festival, but it's good to know that, thanks to Ben, there's now one less person to cause us trouble.'

Zennor smiled. 'And we also have some news,' she said, sharing a glance with him. 'Don't we, Ben?'

She took his hand and held it on the table top. Sam noticed looks were exchanged between her fellow committee members and that everyone's eyes were drawn to the silver ring with its sea glass stone sparkling in the evening light on Zennor's finger.

'We're engaged,' said Ben, barely audibly.

'Eh?' said Troy.

'We're getting married!' said Ben loudly.

Troy snorted his tea. 'I heard that.'

Evie patted him on the back as he spluttered. 'Oh, you dark horses. You kept that quiet. Congratulations, my loves – to both of you.'

402

'You took your time about it, but I'm that happy for you,' said Troy, recovering at last. 'Will it be one of those vegan weddings?'

Ben smiled but the attention was clearly too much for a young man with social anxiety/chronic shyness. 'Probably,' he mumbled, his knuckles whitening as he gripped Zennor's hand tighter.

Zennor's eyes were dancing with delight. 'You're all invited, of course, when we eventually get around to it. We need to find somewhere to live first. Ben's chalet isn't big enough for two.'

Sam felt she might burst too. She'd been the first to know about Zennor and Ben, and had had to keep it a secret. It hadn't come as such a huge surprise as it once might, seeing as Ben had spent most of his nights at Wavecrest while Sam had been with Gabe. It seemed that Ben had been keen for a while but Zennor hadn't wanted to leave Sam on her own.

'Let's raise a toast,' said Chloe. Sam couldn't help but notice she and Drew had arrived at the meeting together and seemed very close.

Drew laughed but raised his glass. 'With lemonade, but the sentiment's there. To Zennor and Ben. Congratulations!'

Troy lifted his mug. 'Well, I bloody hope we're going to celebrate with a real drink when we're finished here.'

'Definitely,' said Gabe. 'I might even get the first round.'

Sam felt his hand on the small of her back, a soft firm touch through her T-shirt. She had the strangest feeling that from now on, he would always be there by her side. She cleared her throat and began.

'OK. Before we can all go and party, we need to discuss the main item on the agenda. The inaugural Porthmellow Winter Solstice Festival in December. We don't have long, so does anyone have any bright ideas?'

THE END

Acknowledgements

Whand part of your job requires eating, drinking and visiting food events, I think you can safely say you're living the dream. This book was originally inspired by a visit to a food festival in a Cornish harbour town, although I stress that everyone in it is completely fictional and I have made up all the incidents!

Huge thanks go to some great people in Porthleven including Julia Schofield, the co-founder of fabulous Porthleven Food Festival, and Chris, chef and owner of Sea Drift restaurant, for their insight and help with the logistical aspects of organising a festival. Also thanks to the renowned Cornish photographer Carla Regler, whose famous photographs of the town in a storm provided inspiration for this story, and to the Albatross Gallery for their help.

The pie-making information was provided by the chef and staff of Buzzards Valley Vineyard restaurant near Tamworth and I can vouch for the fact that their handmade pies are delicious. Nikki, who I met at Lichfield Food Festival and who runs Marvellous Mixes, www.marvellousmixes.co.uk, gave me some great insight into attending a food festival as an exhibitor. My Cornish friend and reader Elisa Leah also helped with some vital local touches.

The ideas for Evie's creole party dish came from US friends Leah Larson and Shyra Latiolais, while my daughter's friend Wis suggested the Chinese food that Chloe makes for the party. Thanks also go to my writing friends Liz Hanbury, Nell Dixon and bookseller Janice Hume.

Rachel Faulkner-Willcocks has again worked her special brand of editorial magic, helping me to turn my first draft into the finished book you see and have hopefully enjoyed. I'm so grateful to the entire Avon team including Jo Gledhill, Sabah, Elke, Katie, Molly and Dom, who are always friendly, approachable and brimming with ideas. I'm also lucky enough to have the best agent in the business, Broo Doherty, who has helped guide my career and supported my work for fourteen years now.

Finally, thank you to my amazing family, who have cheered and commiserated with me since I started writing. Lately, it's been wonderful to share far more highs and lows. I will love you forever, John, Charlotte, James, Mum, Dad and Charles.

Escape to the the stunning Cornish Isles of Scilly,
with Phillipa Ashley

 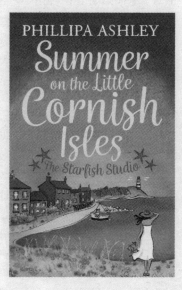

Available now!

Join Phillipa Ashley and the gorgeous cast of
her bestselling Cornish Cafe series.

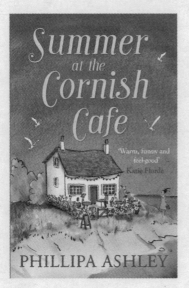
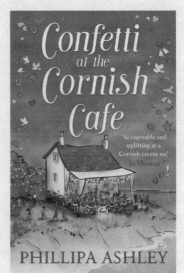

Available now!